Former restaurant reviewer Sarah-Kate Lynch lives in Queenstown, New Zealand. She has a full-time job explaining how travelling to places like Venice and New York to research food and wine is work, not fun. Her next book is set in Champagne, France. You can find out more about her at www.sarah-katelynch.com.

Eating with the Angels

Sarah-Kate Lynch

BLACK
SWAN

ALSO BY SARAH-KATE LYNCH

By Bread Alone
Blessed Are
Finding Tom Connor
The Modern Girl's Guide to Life
Stuff It! A Wicked Approach to Dieting

National Library of New Zealand Cataloguing-in-Publication Data
Lynch, Sarah-Kate.
Eating with the angels / Sarah-Kate Lynch.
ISBN 1-86941-624-4
NZ823.3—dc 22

A BLACK SWAN BOOK
published by
Random House New Zealand
18 Poland Road, Glenfield, Auckland, New Zealand
www.randomhouse.co.nz

First published 2004
© 2004 Sarah-Kate Lynch
The moral rights of the author have been asserted
ISBN 1 86941 624 4

Cover photograph: Brendan O'Hagan; styled by Mark Robins
Cover design: Sciascia Brothers Advertising
Text design: Katy Yiakmis
Author photograph: Monty Adams
Printed in Australia by Griffin Press

For Anna and Ken

Prologue

If I'd ever thought to draw up a list of the people most likely to turn my life upside down, I seriously doubt Woody Allen would have made the top 10 let alone occupied the number one slot.

Sure, I never much cared for his movies post *Hannah hnd her Sisters* and I guess I was moderately vocal on the whole icky marrying-his-girlfriend's-adopted-daughter thing, but that was no reason to take away my livelihood, was it? To destroy everything I had once held dear? To make me question, and I mean really *question*, my entire reason for being?

Yeez, the guy almost put me off pretzels for life. What a sentence! In fact I still can't see one without wondering how things might have turned out that day had he brought an apple from home. And while we're on the subject of home, what is it with Woody and Central Park? I mean, hell-o-o, there are other locations in New York City. It's just that had he not been filming on the Bow Bridge that day or had Soon-Yi baked Woody a cookie, my life would have remained right side up — not been blown into smithereens and splattered all around Manhattan and beyond like some booby-trapped multi-coloured layer cake, heavy on the frosting. But hey, this is probably not making much sense to you. Not yet anyway and believe me I know how that feels. Big time. So let me give you a word of advice right off the bat before you get any more confused, before you go any further, and that word of advice is this: relax.

Don't try to make sense of it too soon.

It'll come to you the way it came to me, seemingly clear until you get to the end when it will become *really* clear — making you realise how fuzzy it was at the beginning.

I'm not explaining myself so well, am I? Okay. Have you ever seen one of those magnified pictures in a kids' magazine? Something totally run-of-the-mill that they've zoomed in on times a thousand and you win a pen if you guess what it is? Well, a person can go pretty nuts looking at one of those pictures: there's something about it, something you can't quite put your finger on, it's on the tip of your tongue, but you never get it and it bugs the heck out of you. Then when the magazine publishes the zoomed-out picture it turns out to be something so simple, so familiar, so perfectly everyday — a blade of grass, a speck of sand — that you can't believe you didn't see it right from the beginning.

What I'm trying to say is that you'll discover little pieces of the story the same way I did, bit by bit, right up close, but it won't be till you stand back at the end that you'll recognise the whole enchilada.

Talking of enchiladas I've just realised that I could eat a horse (something I'm ashamed to say I have done in the past and quite enjoyed). Today, though, I think I'll leave Black Beauty in the barn and maybe . . . maybe what? Once upon a time I would have jumped on the subway down to Joe's for a slice of pizza. Just the thought of that piping-hot fresh mozzarella bubbling across the perfect crispy base has my taste buds quivering in anticipation. In fact, my mouth is watering so hard my jaw hurts and I hate it when that happens. But then my mouth is on hyper-drive these days.

Right now, believe it or not, while my mind is definitely on a slice of pizza from Joe's, I am also subconsciously trying not to count each fat golden grain of organic unrefined sugar that I've stirred into my Big Cup take-out latte — because I swear I can taste every one of them. My buds are on standby full-time, poor battered things, and if you think that sounds whacko, get a load of this: from here I can smell, with just one sniff, that the Sailor's Delight washed-rind cheese in my refrigerator has less than 19 hours to go before it reaches its prime; that the loaf of Rock Hill Bakehouse sourdough I bought this morning is missing one 20th of a teaspoon of salt. But those Sycamore Farms New York strawberries? Perfectly ripe and ready for eating.

I know what you're thinking. You're thinking lay off of that caffeine, Connie, because you're talking like a high-wired crazy person — but honestly, by the time you get to the end of my story, when you stand back and see the whole thing in context, you will understand why being able to savour every little morsel gives me such a thrill.

Of course, before you get to the end you will probably go through quite a stretch of thinking that I am a complete nut job and you would not be alone on this one, so don't go feeling bad about it. Hey, even I thought I had lost the plot and was never going to get it back for a while: not helped by the big stack of medical evidence to just that effect, I might add.

But I have emerged from these past few months of hell — and heaven — not only relatively unscathed but with a new insatiable hunger for life that I never ever had before. Or if I did, I was standing too darn close to see it.

They say that things happen for a reason, that bad things happen to good people, that what doesn't kill you makes you stronger ... and yes, for most my life I thought that was baloney too. But now, I'm not so sure. (Hey, there you go! Only 18 hours till my Sailor's Delight hits its peak.) Anyway, all I know is that because of what happened to me, because of Woody Allen and that freakin' pretzel, I am now the person I was supposed to be, not the person I was turning into, and for that I believe we can all be truly thankful. And while it may seem weird that I've chosen to tell my story the way I saw it, which as you will learn is not necessarily the way it was, it was my own particular take on events that led me to reach the monumental life-changing conclusion that 50 bucks might buy you a hamburger with short ribs and foie gras — but there's no price too high for the perfect tomato.

Kind of a turning point for a restaurant critic, you might say. Especially in New York City, a town where people don't eat their young, they sell them so they can pay for that hamburger.

It's a matter of taste.

One

I'd be lying if I said my husband failing to show up for our second honeymoon didn't rattle me. It did. It seemed rude. And not the slightest bit romantic.

But there I found myself, sitting up in Business Class on the tarmac at Kennedy Airport, my luggage snuggled below in the hold bulging with little(-ish) black dresses and negligées, the plane pointed hopefully toward Venice, Italy, and a great gaping hole where my husband should be just to my immediate right.

'Your friend is cutting it kinda fine,' the flight attendant, Ashlee, smiled as she poured me a glass of champagne. My initial reaction was to ask why her parents hadn't spelled her name the correct way, why they had found it necessary to add her to the Tiffinis and Taylas that littered the aisles of large aircraft, but I didn't. I'm too polite. Too polite to show that my life was quite possibly unravelling before Ashlee's very eyes thus forcing me to turn on her over the spelling of her name.

'Oh, he'll be here,' I said smoothly instead. 'He was late for our wedding, no reason why he'd be on time for our honeymoon.'

Ashlee, who sported an engagement ring the size of a baseball — you would have to be blind to miss it — got a goofy look on her face and clutched the champagne bottle close to her chest, biting her ripe bottom lip.

'You're just married?' she cooed, her youthful brow crumpling in delight.

'Just 10 years ago,' I answered with an enthusiastic nod. 'It's a honeymoon of the second variety.' I took a slurp of champagne and watched the blissful look slide off her face as she looked again at the empty seat beside me and moved to the next row. I guessed second honeymoons didn't hold much sway any more. I guessed most people had their second honeymoon with a second husband and that made it more exciting. More exciting than having a honeymoon without any husband at all, anyway.

It was true, by the way, about Tom being late for our wedding. Traditionally it is the bride who keeps everyone waiting but I have been spot-on-time since the minute I was born (as my mother is fond of telling me and anyone else within a five-mile radius). My arrival into the world wrecked a perfectly good game of gin rummy, so she says, when everyone knows first babies are supposed to be late. And Myrna Linkloft's favourite sitting-room chair was ruined, I tell you, completely ruined. You'd be surprised how often this comes up in conversation, given the fact that the waters heralding my arrival ruined, I tell you, completely ruined Myrna Linkloft's favourite sitting-room chair more than 30 years ago. And it's not even as though my mother sits on the chair these days. Something about the jack of spades and a cardigan sleeve. Please, you don't want to know the details.

Anyway, Tom and I were high-school sweethearts. We'd actually known each other since kindergarten when I bashed him on the nose with a dump truck after he pulled my braid for trying to eat his pink and yellow Play-Doh cake. Not surprisingly, this took quite a lot of getting over but by 10th grade we were dating and, I guess, in love. We were married on October 21, 1991; not just because we were crazy about each other but because my mother had been wearing black and spitting tacks ever since we'd moved in together three years earlier.

By the time we got married I was a fledgling freelance

newspaper reporter while Tom was working just off Bleecker Street in the West Village at Il Secondo, the Italian restaurant where he had washed dishes, bussed plates, peeled carrots, chopped onions, handmade pasta, plucked chickens and cured hares before finally becoming a sous chef (if that's what it's called when there are only two of you and the other one's the boss). Reaching these dizzying heights had taken eight years and cemented Tom's place in the bosom of the Marzano family who owned the joint. This suited Tom down to the ground because he never much cared for his own family. Despite being pale of skin, ruddy of cheeks and in many ways as Irish as Paddy Delaney's goat he wanted, more than anything, to be Italian. At first, I found this cute. Who among us didn't at some stage want to escape the bondage of our familial ties? Didn't pray to God that they were adopted? Didn't beg to be kidnapped by aliens? But while most of us moved on and grouchily accepted our families for the fatheads and dimwits they are, Tom never could and as he grew older he got more and more Italian.

Now, this is not a very nice thing to do but I am going to break a big confidence here. I swore I would never tell anyone but I guess I've changed my mind: Tom is a natural brown mouse. Yes, that thatch of jet-black hair of which he has long been so overtly proud actually comes courtesy of a little plastic bottle from the drugstore. He has been seeking refuge in the dye bottle since he was 19 — he wouldn't recognise himself au naturel any more. Nobody would. His hair suited his skin a darker colour, he told me. And in the poor lighting of Il Secondo that jet hair and those ice blue eyes did take on a Mediterranean sort of a hue, not hugely unlike that of portly Pippo, Il Secondo's owner, who treated Tom like the son he so longed to be.

It was no surprise to find, then, that Pippo would be our best man and the wedding reception would be at Il Secondo. The only surprise was that when it came time to take our vows at Our Lady of Perpetual Suffering, my husband-to-be was reported missing in action, last seen at the restaurant arguing with the poor sap who'd delivered a bunch of slightly wilted zucchini blossoms flown up from Florida. I loved that he cared so much about the smallest detail of the tiniest mouthful of the first meal we would be served as husband and wife. But I hated that he was more concerned about that than anything else, including actually turning up for the wedding ceremony.

'What have you done to him?' my mother (the *other* Lady of Perpetual Suffering) hissed at me through the window of my cousin Kevin's limousine as we pulled up outside the church for the fifth time in a row. She'd never really liked Tom: she thought being a chef was on par with being a janitor — it all went down the same drain, according to her — but she still liked him more than me. Or so it seemed.

'You just had to go and ruin my special day, didn't you? Of all days. A Wednesday! Who gets married on a Wednesday?' She looked at me accusingly through the open limo window and dabbed dramatically at her eyes with a silk handkerchief that exactly matched her canary-yellow suit. She'd bought it five years before, convinced we were going to marry then, and it had dated pretty badly. It had a peplum jacket and matching frilled skirt and made her look like an angry chick. She has real skinny little legs and was wearing a hat with a yellow feather plus her eyes were pink with rage or embarrassment or whatever it is an extremely hard-to-please woman feels when her only daughter seems to be getting dumped on her wedding day.

'Typical, Mary-Constance. Typical! But why should I be surprised? My own daughter ruining everything for me? It's not like it hasn't happened before. Hah!' She allowed a small hiccup of grief. 'If only.' She stepped back from the limo, slapped her hands on her little yellow thighs and looked around as if there might be a better daughter planning a weekend wedding standing behind her. There wasn't but there was the next best thing: an audience. A scraggly group of people I didn't even recognise was soon sucked into her

14

vortex of disappointment and began lavishing her with sympathetic looks and words of encouragement. If I wasn't mistaken, one of them, a dowdily dressed middle-aged woman, actually curled her lip at me — the bride — and at this, Mom put one hand over her eyes and flapped her silk handkerchief in my direction as if to say, 'Get rid of her. Take her away.'

'Once more around the block, Kevin,' my best friend Fleur instructed, leaning across me to close the window, and we lurched off in a cloud of exhaust.

'Her special day?' I was stunned, tears pricking my eyes, threatening the painstaking make-up job Fleur had spent one hour and half a bottle of champagne applying. 'What about my special day? My boyfriend hasn't shown up for our wedding and I'm ruining everything? Where does she get this stuff?'

No matter what the crisis (real or imagined), my mother seemed to have a knack for finding a way to blame me. When the kitchen in the apartment three doors down from us caught fire when I was in seventh grade, for example, it was my fault because I had given Mindy Brokawski, who lived there, my favourite recipe for butter cookies. The poor inexperienced girl had tried to bake them unsupervised, in so doing, according to my mom, burning her kitchen and almost the apartment, the entire building, the rest of the block, the Upper East Side, the whole of Manhattan to a crisp.

Everybody else seemed to accept the Fire Department theory that the extractor fan was faulty, but not Mom. If I had to apologise to Mrs Brokawski once, I had to do it a thousand times. After a while, she started avoiding me in the elevator and the hallway and eventually, in fact not that long after the fire, they moved to Jersey. In the end, it may have been me who drove them away but in the beginning the disaster could not truthfully be pinned on me despite my mom's insistence otherwise.

And that's just a mild example. It all went downhill from there, which you will understand later on when I tell you about the kidney.

But getting back to my wedding day: I twisted around as we drove away to see my mother through the rear window of the limousine, accepting soothing pats from her gang of sympathetic admirers, and I marvelled at my satin-gloved hands, which remained clenched and still in my lap when they should rightfully have been tight and getting tighter around her throat.

'You think someone might have told her yellow is not her colour,' Fleur said helpfully. 'He'll show up, Connie, don't let her get to you.' But it was too late. Perhaps I had done something to Tom. Perhaps I had ruined everything.

'He has been eyeing up that pert little Angelina, you know, the new waitress,' I said, fear clutching at my heart, which was already under quite a bit of pressure thanks to the restrictive corset of my powder-puff dress. Tom was late for everything so it hadn't really occurred to me up until that point that he might actually be declining his invitation to our own wedding. 'And I did yell at him for asking Pippo's next-door neighbour's next-door neighbours. Jesus, Fleur, you don't think he is actually jilting me, do you?'

Fleur tossed her expertly styled honey-blonde-highlighted hair over her shoulder and laughed. 'Connie,' she said, 'if there is one thing in this world of which I am absolutely sure it is that Tom Farrell loves you and only you with all his heart and soul. He will be there at that altar to have and to hold you from this day forward till death do you part and blah blah blah so please stop worrying. And don't cry, I got those eyelashes cheap. They're past their use-by date.'

By the time Kevin got around the block again, Tom was indeed standing outside the church looking impossibly handsome, his black (!) hair shining, blue eyes twinkling, beaming from ear to ear, while my mother fluffed and pecked beside him. The thing was I was so darn thrilled to be saved the humiliation of not getting married in front of 120 of our closest friends and family and their neighbours (and *their* neighbours) that I wasn't even angry about the zucchini blossoms. I suppose it was a sign, though, when I look back.

'I'm sorry, Mrs Farrell,' Ashlee the flight attendant said, trying not to let me see her eyeballing Tom's empty seat again. 'We're about to take off. You're going to have to do up your seat belt now.'

'Can't we wait a few more minutes?' I asked brightly. 'He must be on his way. I'm sure he won't be long. He'd be late for his own funeral, you know.'

I tried to make my voice sound bubbly and confident but the words got stuck in my throat and sounded kind of phlegmy.

Ashlee blushed as she leaned in to pick up my champagne glass. 'I'm real sorry,' she said, twisting her engagement ring subconsciously on her finger so the enormous rock moved around to the inside of her hand. 'I've just spoken to the ground crew. There are no further passengers to board so we will be departing on schedule. Your seat belt, please, Mrs Farrell. And up with your tray table.'

There are no further passengers to board? We will be departing on schedule? Well, that was putting a positive spin on it, I thought. Shouldn't someone be acknowledging that one of the passengers who had failed to board was in fact putting quite a hole in the schedule of my anticipated honeymoon, my future, my whole entire goddamn life? If the captain had time to switch the seat belt sign on and off, I fumed silently, you would think he could have spared a few moments to apologise for sacrificing my marriage just to keep the air-traffic controllers happy. 'There are no further passengers to board, especially no Tom Farrells,' he could have said, 'so according to our calculations that makes Connie Farrell, yes, she's the one in 6A, a sad, lonely — let me just check with the co-pilot here — yes, pathetic party of one on her way to the world's most romantic city all by herself. Okay. On the plus side, we have a tail wind so should have you on the ground outside the terminal slightly ahead of time. Oh, and try the fish, it tastes like chicken!'

Actually, it wasn't until I felt the wheels of the aircraft leave the ground that it really sank in that Tom wasn't coming. For a moment I panicked, just the way I did on our first honeymoon, which was also supposed to be in Venice but which turned out to be on the West Coast. I'd had a long-distance love affair with Venice ever since I could remember and just assumed we would spend our first nights as a married couple there. We'd talked about it when we were teenagers even, but it had been Tom's job to book the trip and instead he'd bought tickets to San Francisco and taken me to Chez Panisse. Venice wasn't really Italy, he said. The food wasn't special. It wasn't even Italian, just some hybrid slop invented to please lazy tourists who didn't know their tortellini from their tiramisu. At Chez Panisse, he promised me, we would have one of the most memorable meals of our lives. And he was right. I can still taste that grilled Paine Farm squab with its star anise sauce on my tongue and feel the glow emanating from Tom at having Alice Waters emerge from the kitchen, her spiky red hair lit from behind like a henna halo, to ask him if he was the young Italian chef from New York.

It was an experience that opened my eyes to the true potential of food; that showed me we had all the ingredients, the skill, the talent of the French and Italians right here in America but just needed a personality of our own to pull it off — and you could argue that this set me on the road to my illustrious career. Chez Panisse does that. But still, it wasn't Venice. And as my Italy-bound plane took off from Kennedy Airport all those years later, I felt my stomach attempting to stay on the ground, just like it did on my first honeymoon. 'Stop!' I had fought the urge to shout to the cockpit on my first honeymoon. 'I forgot something!' Of course, then I'd had Tom beside me to hold my hand and whisper comforting thoughts in my ear. This time, he was the something I forgot.

Perhaps there had been a terrible accident, I hear you cry. Perhaps he was on his way to his own funeral. Perhaps he was lying in a ditch or collapsed over his steering wheel; or his private parts had got caught in his suitcase zipper and he was crumpled on the bedroom floor bleeding profusely from his nether regions. Perhaps my mother had finally found the real Connie, the one she was clearly convinced the nurses had swapped me for at the hospital, and had talked Tom into flying away on honeymoon somewhere else with her.

Yes, perhaps. But in my heart I suspected he was alive and well, just doing it someplace else. We'd had a fight on the phone earlier in the day, although when I tried to remember the details they were jumbled up in my head. Was there a single thing I'd said that could have led him to believe I didn't want him to come on our second honeymoon? Not that I could remember, but then we'd had so many fights in recent months that I couldn't nail down this particular one as being anything out of the ordinary.

That in itself was a depressing realisation. I guess you don't need an analyst to tell you that if all your arguments are blurring into one then your marriage is probably in trouble. According to my mother, I have all the intuition of a desert rock but even I could see that lurching from one disagreement to another with little to distinguish them spelled danger. I loved Tom, I had always loved Tom, I couldn't imagine ever not loving him, but sitting there in that over-sized seat on that Italy-bound airplane, an uneasiness sloshed around inside me like badly made borscht, something I'd had the bad luck to sample on at least three separate occasions.

Our second honeymoon had been engineered to patch the holes in the life raft of our marriage. But what could possibly save us now? That was what I was left wondering as I stared out through the clouds and watched the towers of Manhattan growing smaller and smaller beneath me.

As soon as Ashlee was back on her heels, I summoned her and asked for more champagne. I knew drinking alcohol at high altitude was bad for you but there are times in a girl's life when only French champagne will do and this was definitely one of them.

I sipped the Moët and let the bubbles dance around on the back of my tongue and top of my throat. It tasted drier up in the air, but still did the job, buoying me up, lightening my mood. Moët is my favourite even though most arbiters of taste prefer its fancy close relation Dom Perignon: every now and then I can actually afford the poor cousin, which goes a long way in my book.

Of course Tom didn't like champagne, preferring (no surprises here) the dry red Italian wines that Pippo brought over from the old country or a decent pinot grigio if he could find it. If I had champagne I had it on my own or with Fleur, who drank anything that came in a bottle and, more than once, things that came in chipped old cups and greasy old jars. Tom didn't care for anything French. He wrote off the entire nation as a bunch of arrogant know-nothings, in doing so often managing to sound much like one of those himself. I thought I knew why, especially as he had gotten so angry when I suggested this. New York is a food town, a restaurant town, THE restaurant town, everyone knows that (apart from all the inhabitants of San Francisco and most, apparently, of Vancouver). Anyway, forget about them, mere pretenders to the throne; New York rightfully wears the crown and there are levels at which all loyal subjects worship. At the bottom, there are your pushcart pretzels (more about them later, a curse on you Woody!) and hot dogs, then there's the pizza-by-the-slice joints, Chinatown's noodle bars, your neighbourhood trattoria, the expensive theme restaurant, your fancy bistro and, at the top of the chain, there's the likes of Jean Georges, Le Bernadin or Daniel, the four-star restaurant in which the who's who of Manhattan parade and preen while picking at Monsieur Daniel Boulud's delightful fare. Many of the city's finest chefs have trained under M. Boulud and gone on to shine in their own rights. Tom, of course, was not one of them and perhaps resented his position at the neighbourhood trattoria level.

I took him to Daniel for a romantic night out once and he was utterly scathing from the moment we walked in off East 65th Street and took in the elegant hall stretching to the maitre d's desk, never mind the private dining room and chic bar off to our right. He glared at every captain, bus boy, hapless bystander and fellow diner we passed on the way to our table on the raised outer side of the grand two-tiered dining room. The plush velvet drapes, the vigorously well-heeled clientele, the ornate floral displays, the impeccable service, the hypnotising smells and sights seemed to catapult him into a dark and ferocious mood. Me, I was transfixed by the diamonds glinting, the necks craning, the staff gliding around the room like well-rehearsed ballerinas, part of the ceaseless ebb and flow of restaurant theatre. But Tom failed to be impressed by any of that; instead he snapped at the sommelier, argued with our delightful waiter, ridiculed the entire premise of a tasting menu, hissed at me that I had more money than sense — and then he tasted the food.

Suddenly he went quiet.

The Jerusalem artichoke soup with black trumpet mushrooms and sage oil removed his scowl but the nine-herb tortellini with Parmesan foam shut him up big-time. After one forkful of the guinea hen with porcini and glazed Muscat prunes, the colour drained from his face completely. With each mouthful he looked more despondent and by the time my hand was reaching out to scoop up the last of his fig tart, having long finished my own chocolate upside-down soufflé, I thought he was going to cry. It was that good.

Now some young chefs might have taken this experience and turned it into something to strive for but not Tom. He turned it into something to strive against. He just loved that flawless French food so much he took against it and all other things even slightly ooh-là-là.

'Top-up?' Ashlee smiled, her face a symphony of sympathy as she offered me more Moët. I couldn't decide whether to smile and nod or whether to smash the glass on the armrest and shove it into her neck scarf, but in the end I went with the smiling and nodding.

'Fabulous,' I said as I raised my glass at her then turned to the window to hide my mortification. The ridiculously puffy clouds were doing their best to disguise the distance that grew between me and my husband but with every breath I took I felt the miles stretch further and further.

How did I get here? That's what I kept asking myself as I swatted away the awful peanut-free freeze-dried whatever-they-ares that Ashlee insisted on offering, that great hopeful diamond of hers winking meanly at me. Where did it all go wrong?

We had been growing apart these past few years, I could see that from 35,000 feet. The whole solo honeymoon whoopsie perhaps shouldn't have come as quite such a surprise.

We came at everything from different angles, Tom and I, even food, which we both adored and around which we had developed our jobs, our lives. I loved to eat and he loved to cook — you would think this would be the perfect combination and in some respects it was but in others we were on opposite sides of the soup pot. After the dump-truck incident at kindergarten, for instance, so soon after that he still had snot running into his mouth and tears flowing down his cheeks, I remember being genuinely surprised at his distress. Ignore the whole Play-Doh part of the scenario and what reason was there to make a cake but have people eat it? It looked so good — pink with yellow frosting — what else was he going to do with it?

When we were at high school we compared our homemade sandwiches with great interest; the difference being that even if I didn't like something, I would still eat it whereas Tom simply could not stomach even a simple tomato sandwich on white bread if it was under-salted or over-peppered or slightly soggy. As for peanut butter and jelly — forget about it. That was for the riff-raff and he was certainly not riff-raff. I liked that about him then. I liked that he knew what he wanted and nothing else would do. He couldn't care less about hanging out with other teenagers, shooting hoops or smoking cigarettes or doing whatever else was considered hip. Instead, we spent our afternoons on eating adventures, happily schlepping up to Papaya King for hot dogs or down to Katz's for pastrami or over to 6th Street in the East Village for dhosas.

Tom opened my taste buds, really. He changed my world. Before him, food was something I had to choke down without retching (Play-Doh gâteau, for example) or throw in the garbage without my mother seeing me.

Mom was, and still is, the world's most awful cook. I know that sounds uncharitable but seriously that's just about the nicest way I can put it. Her taste is all in her — actually, I don't know where her taste is but it is not in her mouth. Or her nose. You only have to walk into her apartment and smell the slightly past-its-prime chicken breast marinating in sake and acidophilus yoghurt to get an inkling of this. And unlike other awful cooks, who usually buy their meals ready-made or leave the cooking to someone else, my mother has boundless, truly boundless, enthusiasm in the kitchen and absolutely no idea how unpalatable her heinous concoctions really are. Without a shadow of a doubt she is taste-blind, completely and utterly.

Mind you, I think that my father should shoulder some of the blame. He has an iron constitution. I've never even seen him hesitate, let alone retch, the way my brother Emmet and I used to before our tender juvenile stomach linings hardened up and stopped resisting things that were slightly off, a funny colour, indescribably seasoned, or hopelessly mis-matched with something equally awful. But not only does Pop to this day wolf down her inedible meals, he encourages her. 'Estelle, you've surpassed yourself yet again,' he'll say, rubbing his stomach and leaning back in his chair. 'Aren't I the lucky man?'

Mom will ignore him — that's their marital dynamic — but next thing you know she'll be poring over Julia Child's *Mastering the Art of French Cooking*, changing the ingredients to match whatever's left over in the fridge or suits her mood, until the end result bears no relation whatsoever to the name of the dish nor certainly the picture. I've never worked out why she loves that cookbook so much because Mom has always thought food should be 'thrown together', something that, in my opinion, should only be practised by seriously talented chefs. But the things my mother throws together are not things that should be seen in the same city, let alone the same street nor, heaven forbid, the same plate. They are things that should be thrown in opposite directions at great speed while you head to the nearest diner, quick smart, without so much as a backward glance.

'Cranberry omelette? What's not to like?' she would say, serving up something that looked as though it had been removed in a surgical procedure and called, like most of her inventions, Estelle's Surprise. 'Try it with the aged salami, it's spectacular,' she'd suggest although the word 'aged' was not one you wanted to hear at meal time in our house, trust me. 'Look, your father's eating his.'

When I was young, I used to beg her to follow the recipes just to see what would happen but she always refused. 'They all make such a fuss,' she would say, even of Julia. 'Who wants to make such a fuss? It's only food.'

She's a complicated woman all right, my mother. On the one hand relishing her own 'flair' for cooking but on the other belittling its importance in the great scheme of things. You can imagine how thrilled she was that her daughter became a restaurant critic married to a chef.

Anyway, by the time Tom and I hooked up as 15-year-olds it was no wonder I was ready and willing for him to educate me about food that tasted good and stayed down. By then he had already befriended Pippo and was sweeping floors and polishing glasses and worming his way into the Marzanos' affections. All he ever wanted to do was cook there and while this wasn't much of an ambition, boy did I admire him for having it at such a young age.

Knowing what his home life was like, I could see why he loved Pippo. Tom's dad was a big, brutal beast of a man who successfully bullied his four sons into hating his guts. His mom was a nervous wreck with more than a passing fondness for the sherry bottle and who could blame her? Well, Tom did but anyone else who counted her bruises or watched her limp up and down the stairs to their apartment thanked God that she was finding solace in something.

So, little Tommy, the youngest of the four, got himself out of the Farrell clan and into the Marzano one, pronto. Pippo and his wife 'Cesca, whose two daughters had long flown the coop and had no interest in Il Secondo, could not have been happier. And Tom really was at home in an Italian kitchen, anyone could see that. Like I say, he even looked Italian in certain lights, usually low-wattage ones. I told him that once and he pretended to be annoyed, brushing me off, but secretly he was delighted. I know because he made me fall squash risotto, my favourite, and it wasn't even on the menu that night.

Anyway, a mediocre student in most subjects, I myself managed to get accepted into NYU thanks to good grades in English and the help of my teacher Mr Johansen whom Tom always suspected had the hots for me.

My mother was horrified with my choice of journalism and this was before it even had anything to do with food. Where she came from, reporting on people's activities happened behind closed doors, through a crack in the curtains, one hand clutching the telephone. You sure as hell didn't do it out loud in public with your name attached in capital letters.

My younger brother Emmet got mildly excited when he put together in his pot-addled head that I might one day meet big rock stars with fantastic drug connections, but my dad merely smiled and said, 'Ah, good on you, darling,' like he did when I brought in the newspaper or told him I'd pooped the dog, Frankie the first, second, third — briefly — and fourth. (They'd always had dachshunds and they'd always called them Frankie, which I personally thought was a poor choice of name given the typical dimensions of the breed.)

Even Tom neglected to get wildly enthusiastic about my chosen career path, which was perhaps my fault as I had failed to mention in the decade or so we'd known each other that I wanted to be a journalist.

'But babe,' he said, worriedly, 'do you really think you have the killer instinct for all that?'

'For all what?' I wanted to know. To be honest, I had not thought much further than wearing power suits and going to the Four Seasons to interview important people. Did Leeza Gibbons need killer instinct, for heck's sake?

'For chasing ambulances and fingering crooks and flushing out mafia goons,' Tom answered. 'You do realise that's what journalists do, don't you?'

'Of course,' I answered. When he put it like that, though, I started to wonder if I did have what it took. A crack developed that day in the pitcher of my faith in my professional ability and I'm not sure I ever completely plugged the ensuing leak. Tom sometimes did that, my mom too. Tapped into tiny hidden pockets of doubt that rocked my foundations. 'I'll be fine,' I told him back then, trying to keep the uncertainty out of my voice.

I suppose I was. Fine, I mean. So, I wasn't at the top of the class, or even in the middle, but I got by and even managed to put a little bit of money away pulling shifts at Il Secondo, where my boyfriend continued to impress his employer by being more Italian than the Italians.

Then I got the gig doing restaurant reviews for a giveaway downtown newspaper. The eating-out editor (also the fashion/decorating/automobile editor and advertising sales manager) was an Il Secondo regular and after 'Cesca showed off about me a couple dozen times, he got me to review a slightly unsavoury collection of Thai restaurants in the Village. Next thing you knew, I had a regular job. Of course at $20 a shot, plus expenses, I wasn't exactly about to retire to a Soho loft but the glow of seeing my name on the pages of a tatty little tome other people were going to pick up and read or wrap their potato peelings in, well, that was worth all the tea in India (the world's biggest tea-producing nation, by the way, not China).

'Here she comes, our own Lois Lane,' Pippo would crow when I came into work after that, blowing his basil and oregano breath all over me. 'Whatcha gonna do with her, Thomas. Whatcha gonna do?'

I'd smile, slip on my black apron and start chopping scallions, grating Parmesan, doing whatever was needed, even if it meant helping 'Cesca out front of house or stepping in to assist her special-needs nephew Mikey with the dishes. We had fun, back then, in that hot, noisy kitchen, Pippo and Tom floating around the grill and the pizza oven, glowing with heat and happiness at doing what they both loved best.

Me, I was there because my schoolbooks cost money and other than the guy from the giveaway newspaper, nobody else had offered me a job. And I felt safe with Tom there. And Pippo and 'Cesca watching out for me. College was hard. I felt poorer and dumber and less ambitious than everyone else. I didn't know exactly what it was I wanted to do and it drove my teachers almost as mad as it drove me. After I graduated and put in a few years doing reviews and other rats and mice, though, I found myself enjoying minor notoriety as fill-in and ultimately full-time restaurant critic for the *Village Voice*. Now this made sense of everything about me. Tom and I loved the Village. We had escaped there permanently as soon as we could afford it and loathed the return trips to the Upper East Side. Our new neighbourhood seemed so eclectic in comparison. You never knew who was going to jump out of a cab on Bleecker Street: a starving artist, a supermodel, a bum, a broker. Everyone fitted in down there, no matter how much they failed to do so elsewhere, and I loved being associated with the famous *Village Voice*.

'You know, with your looks, you could end up being a news anchor on a TV station,' Fleur insisted once. 'They love that pretty all-American thing you have going, sweetie. Or you could end up sitting there with Regis, crossing those legs and smiling that smile.'

'Yeah, right,' I laughed and changed the subject, embarrassed. At one level, I knew I was not bad-looking, I really did. But my mother had been onto this pretty early in my life and made it her mission to make sure I never got too big for my boots. Sure enough, I never did. I got too big for pretty much everything else, mind you. While Mom is only just five feet two, I grew to a whopping five nine by age 12, a sin she found hard to forgive.

'Who else is this gigantic?' she would ask, pulling at sweater sleeves that were too short, tugging at the hem on my skirt. 'Who else doesn't know when to stop growing?' She acted like my height was something I had asked for just to spite her and I found myself compensating by curling my shoulders towards my stomach, trying to take up less space.

'She's such a shiksa,' my mother would say to my father's newspaper as she pulled at my hair. You would think this would make her happy but it didn't, nothing I did could make her happy. I could never work out why not looking Jewish didn't thrill her to the core given that she converted from Judaism to Catholicism when she married my dad and has been holier than the Pope ever since. Of course, her main motivation in life has seemed to be pissing off my grandmother. Never mind nose and face, Mom would cut off her entire head to spite her body if given half the chance. It started with marrying the doorman's son, extended into moving into a rent-controlled tenement right next door to the white-glove building where she grew up, continued when she had a daughter and called her Mary-Constance, and progressed further when she sent me to Catholic school in my cute little uniform knowing that my grandmother would look out her window and see this every weekday of her life and presumably wish herself dead so she could spin in her grave.

Although I'd never spoken to her, I knew what my grandmother looked like. My dad had pointed her out to me in a rare moment of not-toeing-the-Estelle line. She was petite and dark and perfectly turned out and had a nose that pointed upwards as if anything below 10 feet was disgusting. She had a dog, a butt-ugly British bulldog, which must have been replaced every few years like Frankie because every now and again it got smaller, and her preferred method of transport was a limousine service. I tried to talk to her once even though I was born knowing this was the only cardinal sin not mentioned in catechism. I must have been six or seven and was walking home from school, skipping along minding my own business, trying not to step on a crack, break my mother's back, when my eyes happened upon a pair of tiny black patent-leather pumps with a delicate set of ankles above them. I lifted my eyes and there she was, my grandmother, staring at me with a look I took to be horror. I started to say something, hello I guess, but one of her hands flew up to shield her eyes and the other shot straight out in front of her. I took it to be a shutting-up gesture and obliged. So much for having no intuition, huh? She was dressed in black and was wearing a beautiful pearl necklace with matching over-sized pearl earrings and a tailored coat like something Audrey Hepburn might have stepped out in. Her dog chose that moment to cough up something disgusting onto the sidewalk and in the absence of knowing what to do next, I sidestepped the two of them and went on my way.

I guess we were dysfunctional before dysfunctional was even invented. That's only on my mom's side of the family though. My father's parents, the Conlans, were pretty normal even though Grandma had more than the usual number of cats. Actually she kind of put me off cats but she baked her own bread and it was something else.

Anyway, as you would imagine of someone who changed her faith just to annoy her mother and moved right next door never to speak to her again, Mom had issues with maternity and these manifested themselves in her giving me the impression that below average was about as high as I should aim. Anything more would be showing off. When I turned 13, though, my face kind of settled into itself and my bosom caught up with my puppy fat and gave me an undeniably girlish shape. Almost overnight every acne-riddled testosterone-fuelled goofball in school started hitting on me. Don't get me wrong, I'm no Cindy Crawford, I'm generally 10 pounds (okay, more like 15) heavier than I should be but I have been blessed with good skin (thanks for that, at least, Mom) and a passable face with turquoise blue eyes (even if, as my half-witted brother Emmet is so fond of saying, I look like I store nuts in my cheeks for the winter). My hair is kind of a boring brown but it's thick and if I torture it with enough electrical equipment it can straighten and look positively Sandra Bullock-ish. Of course, back when I was a goofy teen, I hadn't mastered the art of the blow-dryer and I wasn't quite such a dab hand with the make-up brush either but frankly no boys my own age looked anywhere other than my boobs anyway and the horny little toads liked what they saw. At the time, this new-found attention came as something of a surprise to me. I was used to being a too tall, too heavy, too brunette bit of below-average background scenery so when I ended up being bumped out of that category, it kind of freaked me out. In the circumstances, I was more than happy to start going steady with Tom. He made me feel safe.

I hiccupped into my champagne at this thought, and allowed a tear to slide down my cheek and onto my cocktail napkin. The emptiness in 6B where my husband should have been left me feeling exposed and, I suppose, scared. But that wasn't why I was crying. I no longer felt safe, that was for sure, but even worse, the feeling wasn't new.

Two

Between New York and Venice I had at least four hangovers, all doozies. The flicker of a headache that had started on the tarmac at Kennedy Airport, obviously fuelled by one too many a glass of Moët, grew with a vengeance during the Atlantic crossing, stayed with me when I transferred at Rome, and lightened up only on approach to Marco Polo Airport where the effervescent blue and indigo of Venice opening up beneath me managed to quell if not quash the pain.

Not even having been so recently abandoned by my childhood sweetheart could wipe the smile off my face as the plane circled the city, a tiny glittering jewel set in the shimmering sprawl of vast lagoon. My heart skipped a beat, not with anxiety but with something approaching delight — and a little bit of gas thrown in for good measure. That airline chicken or fish will do it to you every time. Now I know some food writers make a big deal out of taking their own food on an airplane — a sourdough sandwich with prosciutto and arugula from some particular Second Ave deli, maybe, or a fresh goat-cheese salad with blanched asparagus made by a woman in a poncho who comes to town on a donkey every 15th Thursday — but I liked food to be brought to me. Even if it was desiccated fowl or unidentifiable sea creature. And accompanied, thanks to the likes of Ashlee, by enough champagne to give a girl reflux all the way through immigration control.

I pulled my bag full of party dresses into the silvery air outside the terminal and took a deep, long breath, feeling that Venetian oxygen attempting to replenish my oomph. I tried not to fixate on the phalanx of happy couples pushing past me, glowing with the joy of finding themselves there. Where were all the single people, I wondered? Was I the only solitary honeymooner in town? Why did everyone have to look so deliriously in love? These and other questions cluttered my addled mind as I pulled my bag, which chose that moment to develop one wonky wheel, to the water-taxi stand. What was I doing there? Why hadn't I turned around in Rome and gone straight back home to sort out my life? How could I even consider checking into a romantic hotel without Tom? What was the matter with me?

'Hello. Hello. Can you hear me?'

Of course I can hear you, I felt like telling the water-taxi driver on the pier: your face is only two inches away from mine. The sinking sun was behind him and I couldn't make out his features, but his voice sounded loud and slightly supernatural. I stepped back. 'Hotel Gritti Palace,' I instructed him. I would think more clearly when I got there perhaps. He led me to his pristinely kept wooden motorboat. It looked like something in which Grace Kelly would have been at home, posing in a white halter neck and head scarf, head back, eyes closed, mysterious smile tripping across her lips. A mysterious smile was beyond me just at that point, my lips remained un-tripped upon, but I stayed outside the cabin at the back of the boat, my head thrown back, just the same.

The water-taxi driver didn't speak again, just hurled my bag inside the cabin on his way to the bow, then pulled out into a shimmering sea-lane that seemed to stretch forever towards the outline of the magical city I had dreamed of for so long. All I could see was water and sky and the silhouettes of distant spires, blurry domes, swaying towers, precious gems strung along a chain of sterling islands.

It was twilight, the sun was setting spectacularly and in front of my very eyes, my whole world suddenly haemorrhaged pinks and purples and a sparkling sort of silver — the exact hue of which I can still picture to this day if I just half close my eyes and smile a certain way. It was like being in fairyland. It took my breath away and, in the hole in my heart left gaping by my lack of husband, I felt a lurch of unexpected joy — at being alive, at being there in the city of my imaginings. It didn't seem right, yet I could feel the glow of something unbelievably like optimism as we approached the back of the floating collection of enchanted islands, leaving the endless watery blue of the sea, the airport, the rest of Italy, the world, behind us.

As we moved gently into a wide canal Venice sucked me into her bloodstream, took me to her heart. The ancient, crumbling walls of the city rose up on either side of me, crooked and leaning. The buildings had that look of an old woman's baggy pantyhose, still trying to keep up appearances despite inevitable decline. Endearing was not enough of a word.

Once I was there, in the middle of it, I was surprised though — and not unpleasantly — at the suburban nature of my ancient surroundings. Well, not so much suburban, I guess, as residential. I had seen pictures of the basilica, the campanile, the square, of course. Who hadn't? But that particular canal, those particular buildings, that was where people lived; real, normal Venetian people. I could see their laundry. I was passing by their windows as they sat at their kitchen tables sipping coffee and doing crosswords. I was catching a glimpse of their everyday lives. I was marvelling at this in the awe-struck way people do marvel at things when they arrive in Venice, when at one window an extremely fat man picked his nose so violently I half expected his hand to penetrate the top of his head. That was just a little too everyday for my liking.

Then as quickly as she had breathed me into her bosom, Venice thrust me out of the canal at the other end and into the gleaming lagoon. It was like entering the world's most extravagant theatre set through the stage door. My jaw dropped open as we made a right turn in the ocean waters to follow the curve of the city. To my left the milky blue-green ocean stretched to faraway islands, the water bobbing and bejewelled with the lights of different vessels. Up ahead, the sky cascaded down in different shades of violet and mauve into a carpet of pink and orange around the edges of the magnificent church of Santa Maria della Salute, giving the impression that its silhouetted domes and bell towers radiated colour outwards.

On my right, the wide quay of the city was still pulling crowds towards the Piazza di San Marco, their numbers thickening as we approached the Doge's Palace. I craned my neck to see the Bridge of Sighs. The Bridge of Sighs! Just the name left me breathless.

The water taxi sped on past the twin columns at the entrance to the famous piazza, and so we entered the Grand Canal.

Nothing I had ever seen or heard or dreamed about Venice did it justice. It simply smouldered like no other place I had ever been. Of course I had known that it was a collection of hundreds of tiny islands separated by canals and joined by bridges; but it had never really sunk in that there were no cars, no motorbikes, no street noises. Sure there was the thrust and whoosh of the chunky *vaporetto*, Venice's public transport system, as it crashed into stops, spewing out and sucking in crowds of commuters and tourists on either side of the canal. And there was the gentle vroom of the smaller boats delivering people, wine, chairs, even caged birds to my amazement, but other than that there was no aggressive bustle, I suppose you would call it. No honking of horns, no crunching of metal, no squealing of brakes, no changing of gears.

A tiny bashed-up motorboat with two teenage boys chugged past us, a ghetto-blaster modestly pounding out hip-hop: the Venetian equivalent of big-city boy-racers without the bass to shake your bones. A grizzled fisherman put-putted past in his humble vessel, his mongrel dog sitting proudly right up on the bow, eyes straight ahead. A *traghetto*, a commuter gondola, crossed the canal up ahead, its passengers standing up reading the paper, smoking, staring into space. And the sleek black tourist gondolas — curved like modest smiles — swarmed in front, around, behind us, the gondoliers calling to each other, leaning on their oars, raising their hands in salutation, leaning down to listen to their awe-struck passengers. I was transfixed by their grace and camaraderie. They were such a gang. Such a fixture in time and history, with their ancient traditional boats and their matching outfits, shouting Italian shorthand over the uncomprehending heads of blissed-out visitors to their magical city. I would take a gondola ride, I decided then and there, even though it was a sad and lonely thing to do on your own but, hang it, I was damned if Tom's failure to show up was going to stop me from having a romantic break.

My charming taxi driver swerved at that point, yelling what I took to be obscenities and causing me to lose my balance and practise some obscenities of my own. When I straightened up I saw who he was swearing at: a tall, well-built gondolier who had cut right in front of us, his shiny coal-coloured boat gleaming and glinting, temporarily blinding me in the last of the sinking sun.

I heard the gondolier laugh and I shaded my eyes against the glare so I could see him better. He was dark and good-looking, as all gondoliers should be. I watched his biceps, smooth and brown and bulging, as he expertly turned his empty craft in the opposite direction to us. It was almost balletic, the way he travelled gently back and forth on the back of his boat, manoeuvring it this way and that with the single wooden oar. I could not keep my eyes off him and they slid up his body as he passed by — it was that sort of body, a lot of eyes would have slid up it in his time, trust me. But to my embarrassment, when my eyes finished with his hips, his stomach, his shoulders, his neck, his ears, the shape of his head and made it to his eyes, they were there to meet me, ready and waiting. He smiled and raised an eyebrow.

For a moment the world stopped spinning.

Lust, the Jackie Collins sort, completely overpowered me.

It was the most sensual experience I have ever had. And I know what you're thinking: on her honeymoon? But it was only a second honeymoon with the same husband, remember, not very meaningful at all when you think about it. Especially, you know, in the circumstances.

Anyway, so there he was, smiling and raising an eyebrow. It was a moment to die for. My mouth was hanging open in awe though and I hadn't had the presence of mind to shut it, so it was probably not quite so sensual an experience for him. I just kept staring, slack-jawed, as he laughed and slid further away from me. I drank in the breadth of his shoulders as they twisted with his oar, the swivel of his hips as he danced gracefully back and forth on those long, lean legs. Then without so much as a backward glance he turned off the Grand Canal and disappeared into Venice's vast watery network, leaving me panting in a way most inappropriate for an until-very-recently happily (yes, well . . .) married woman. Luckily my water taxi pulled up outside the Hotel Gritti Palace, where a smiling doorman reached for my hand and pulled me onto the pier.

Thoughts of the delectable gondolier evaporated as I took in my home for the next week. The Gritti Palace had none of the Moorish extravagance of some of its neighbours but was one of the best-known hotels in the city. I had chosen it because it was a favourite of Ernest Hemingway and because I'd heard of someone who'd stayed there during the famous Venice *acque alta* when the waiters had worn waders and carried people to their tables through the flooded restaurant. Naturally that kind of dedication to the experience of eating appealed to me.

My room was perfect. Truly. It was painted a perfect green, not a shade I had cared too much for until then. It was the colour of a pistachio, real pistachio (my second favourite nut after the macadamia) not the colour called 'pistachio' that shows up in the windows of chainstore clothing shops dumping end-of-season lime-green pants.

With its smoky gilt mirror, ornate gold-leaf bed-head, glass lanterns and luscious brocade drapes and wall hangings, it was a room made for honeymooners. I looked around, expecting this thought to bring with it a tug of misery, a burr of terror, but none came. I didn't want to be there in that beautiful room without Tom; of course I didn't. It was far from what I had imagined. But on the other hand it wasn't all wretched. This unnerved me. It wasn't right. I stood in the silence of the beautiful room and tried hard not to think of those bronzed arms stretching and bending in the fading sunlight outside. What the hell was the matter with me? I should have been vomiting with grief and crying till my ears bled at the way things had turned out, not feeling vaguely pleased at having immediately found someone new to ogle. The silence grew suffocating so I squared my shoulders and threw open the picture-postcard window, letting Venice in. It was like being hit in the face by the smell of onions caramelising, the promise of things to come, and it distracted me. A peal of laughter floated up from the terrace below, accompanied by the faint clink of glasses and the tinkle of cutlery. I propped myself up on the sill and drank in the view. Across the canal to my left the dazzling dome of the Santa Maria della Salute was now standing in shadow, the pinks and purples of the city and sea dulled to a hundred muted greys. To the right, I could see the sculptures in the canal-side terrace of the Peggy Guggenheim Museum. Below me a vaporetto chugged along the canal, its wake sending water to slap at the sunken hotel walls. Someone shouted, a throaty roar bounced back, more clinks and tinkles, water lap, lap, lapping. I was starting to feel very odd. The city seemed to be disappearing and appearing again in waves of misty pastels like a dream. My eyes were suddenly desperate to close, my mind was calling out for darkness, and it occurred to me I was exhausted. Being left by my husband might not have been what I was expecting but it was hard work all the same. Leaving the window open, I climbed into the great big bed, my eyes lingering on the telephone. I should call Tom, I thought. Of course I should.

Instead, lulled by the sounds of my Venetian fantasy, I slept.

Sometime in the night I woke up, confused by where I was and without whom. I dragged myself out of bed and over to the open window again, my eyes travelling across the terracotta tiles of the hotel roof and down to the Grand Canal. It was almost silent now; the city was asleep. But in the darkness I could sense something out there, something to do with me. It seems crazy, I know, but haven't you ever had the sensation someone was watching you? Weariness clouded my vision as I peered into the blackness. I couldn't see a thing but I could hear something — a watery something, an oar perhaps, moving in the murky waters of the midnight canal? Yes, there was a boat, moving so slowly it was almost stopped. I could almost make out its shape, an inky grin, opposite the hotel entrance on the far side of the canal. I squinted and peered further out the window but it was pitch-black and my eyes didn't seem to be adjusting. All the same, I thought I could identify a figure, and I thought the figure was not altogether unfamiliar. The breadth of those shoulders, the width of those hips. I shook my head. Impossible! What would a man with whom I had only exchanged one look (albeit a humdinger) be doing outside my hotel in the middle of the night? Either I was losing my mind or it was an extraordinary coincidence or a total outrage. I pondered this, my heart hammering, breath held tight in my lungs. My mind did not feel lost, I didn't believe in coincidences and, to my shame, the thought of a total outrage held a certain allure. Enormously. In places separated from my husband for less than two days.

I stepped away from the window — I was giving myself the creeps — and started unwrapping the chocolate from Tom's side of the bed. Well, if he was going to desert me there would be a price to pay. It was dark chocolate, which I love, with little chips of crunchy cocoa bean all through it. Tom was not a chocolate fan. He liked custards and sponges and all things creamy. I looked at the phone. What would he be doing now, whatever time it was in New York? And never mind ringing him, why hadn't he rung me? He knew where I was. On our second honeymoon. In this beautiful room with its big puffy bed and pistachio walls. I lay on the bed and picked up the phone but I couldn't work out what the time difference was, digits bounced around meaninglessly in front of my eyes and I had trouble recalling our home phone number. Well, we never were the sort of couple to ring each other all the time. We never rang each other at all. But you would think I could have concentrated on remembering the number, not found my mind straying, no matter how I tried to steer it in a different direction, toward that black slice of boat and its solitary occupant slowly moving down the canal outside my window. I slipped the phone back into its cradle, shut my eyes tightly and thankfully went back to sleep.

When I awoke again, the sun was just coming up and it was a beautiful day. I was ravenous. I called room service and ordered everything I could think of, groaning with delight when the order was delivered in a heated trolley, its tabletop set as if for visiting royalty. From a huge silver tureen I ladled out a bowlful of the most unbelievably creamy, buttery, salty, silky porridge I have ever had. It smelled divine and tasted heavenly although I thought I could detect a funny aftertaste, a sort of bitter sweetness, a bit like cough syrup. I chased the porridge down with fresh melon and a selection of pastries that I just could not leave alone. The coffee sucked, but then I had high standards on that front — it had to come from Colombia and have two shots with just a suggestion of steamed full-fat milk — but it helped get rid of the medicinal hint of sourness lurking at the back of my throat. I ate so much I had to lie down again. I can pack away a lot of food — it never fails to amaze, and sometimes frighten, people who've not eaten with me before. I think it's because I'm tall with decent hips. There's a lot of me to fill. One of the questions people most often ask about being a restaurant critic is if you ever get sick of food; I think the fact that my answer was always no was why I was not bad at my job. Even then, lying on my bed at the Hotel Gritti, my stomach swollen with carbohydrates and animal fats, I was thinking

39

about lunch and where I might have it and what it might be and what Tom would or wouldn't like about it. But then I decided I would not let myself think about Tom and made a point of lying on his side of the bed, which up until that point had remained smooth and empty.

Trying as I was not to think about him and all, it took me a while to realise that I missed his smell. He always smelled so good, Tom. And it's not like he wore an aftershave: he had no time for that sort of thing. But he had a sort of sweet, base man smell, mixed with a bit of garlic and the faint suggestion of sage, one of his favourite herbs, and that kitchen sweat that most people found disgusting but I found delectable. The thought of it propelled me to reach for the phone again and without thinking about it too much, I dialled our home number.

'Hello,' Tom said, sleepily, when he picked up. 'Hello?'

So, he was there. I opened my mouth to speak but no words came out. He was not dying of a ruptured scrotum or dead in a ditch. He was lying in bed. Alone. In New York.

'Hello?' he said again, sounding more awake, sounding angry. 'Who is it? Jesus Christ, did you hear me? I said who is this?'

Who do you think it is, I silently screamed at him. It's your wife, you freakin' asshole. The one you didn't come on vacation with. I'm lying in bed. Alone. In Venice.

I was so taken aback I hung up. I know! I hate it too when people do that in movies but in that split second I just could not for the life of me think of anything better to do. I lay there, my heart palpitating for a few minutes, wondering if my breakfast had digested. If he didn't give a fat rat's ass about me, then I sure as hell wasn't going to lose another moment worrying about him. Now that I knew he was alive and well, as I had suspected, and not just doing it in some place else, doing it in the same old place, I was going to get on with having the time of my life. I leaped up, pulled on jeans, a tank top and my most sensible shoes, which weren't really that sensible, and headed out into the still empty alleys of Venice.

The nerve! The cheek! The . . . How could he possibly — I mean how *dare* he? Actually, I was at a loss to articulate my anger at what my husband could or couldn't do or had or hadn't done. I know it doesn't make sense, but I'm telling it as I saw it. I was furious with him, of course I was — not to mention hurt and confused and anxious about the future — but the fury felt sort of one dimensional or fake or something. Inside me lurked a suspicion that I knew more than I was letting on but how could I? I couldn't work out what scratched at my innards, so instead, I walked. I would go to the famous Rialto food market, I decided, the pounding of my feet on the cobbled pavements calming my inner turmoil.

Venice is the perfect city for walking, almost as good as New York, and I was a big walker then as I am now. I had learned long ago that if you had breakfast too early in the day you could squeeze an extra meal in somewhere along the line and this must at all costs be avoided. Like I say, I can eat a lot, definitely more than average, but I still can't eat as much as I want to. Not without relying entirely on elasticised waistbands and comfort gussets anyway. When I first hooked up with Tom in high school and we started to eat our way around Manhattan, my butt pretty much ballooned to very non-Cindy Crawford proportions and I found myself veering towards stretch fabrics in dark colours on discount clothing racks.

Those last extra pounds, I eventually admitted, were doing me no favours and I had to lose them, but how? Eating less was out of the question. It was a hobby. So I knew I had to introduce some form of exercise. I had the hand-eye coordination of a snake so that counted out most sports. I sprained my ankle the first time I tried aerobics (and that was just walking up the stairs to the gym) so that wasn't an option. I hated running because, well, only thin pert people with shiny ponytails ran, so that left only the preferred weight-loss method of the day, bulimia. But as someone who had spent most of her mealtimes trying hard not to barf up what had been cooked for her, I just could not contemplate barfing on purpose.

41

I was lamenting this sorry state of affairs to Tom one day as we were about to get on the subway when he stopped me, plucked the token out of my hand, grabbed my arm, and pulled me back up the stairs.

'Walk it off,' he said, and from that day on I walked it off. I far preferred seeing New York from the sidewalk anyway, and most places I've been to since, I start off on foot. That way you get to check out the local faces before the tourist attractions plus you see who is going where to eat and what it looks like in real life, as opposed to just reading the blurb in various (usually hopelessly inaccurate) guidebooks.

That morning — it had just gone eight — Venice took my breath away as I sloughed off all thoughts of my nebulous marital status and negotiated the narrow streets behind the hotel, hitting only a dozen or so dead ends before happening upon an arrow pointing to the Piazza di San Marco. It wasn't, strictly speaking, on the way to the Rialto markets, but then in Venice nothing is, strictly speaking, on the way to anything else so it hardly mattered.

I hit the square from the west side popping out into its huge expanse without realising how far I had come. The basilica rose in front of me, its domes and spires gleaming in the sunlight. It looked like something in which a crazed James Bond villain would live while plotting to take over the universe. The campanile loomed straight-forwardly next to it. The sky seemed too blue, the scene too colourful. I felt wobbly all of a sudden. Alone. Mind you, there was practically nobody in the square, which is not what I was expecting. Everything I'd heard about Venice suggested I prepare for crowds. My friend Roberta, who was a fledgling (that means unpublished) author and trust-fund kid of moderate proportions, had come back from Venice the previous summer determined to dampen my enthusiasm for the place, saying it was packed to the gills with sock-and-sandal-wearing eastern Europeans. It smelled funny, she said. It was falling down. Everything was so old. Enough with that water already. Now I'd been on vacation with Roberta before and knew that what she really liked in a holiday destination was a colourful cocktail bar with lighting so bad that she could still appeal to men 10 years her junior, so I took what she said about Venice with a grain of salt. Tom, however, was delighted to hear her trashing my dream destination. We'd fought about it afterwards I remembered, as I weaved my way through the upmarket stores to the north of San Marco. It was as though Tom resented me having my own private dreams. Had I ever told him this? Had I even realised it? I tried to remember the details of the argument over Venice but they were hazy; I couldn't recall the outcome. Well, actually, I supposed this *was* the outcome.

My attention was grabbed at that moment by some extremely good 'Louis Vuitton' bags set up on the steps right outside the real Louis Vuitton shop.

'You like? You buy?' the treacle-coloured man selling them asked me.

I was tempted. I opened my mouth to start bargaining, something I could only bring myself to do over handbags and shoes, but suddenly I felt ashamed of myself. Hadn't I just been contemplating the breakdown of my marriage? What kind of a woman, a wife, could be so easily distracted? By fake pocketbooks?

I was still beating myself up about this when I arrived at the foot of the Rialto Bridge. I had seen it so many times, in magazines, books, films, on ancient oils and water colours in countless art galleries, and here it was, just the way it had looked hundreds of years ago, steps up and over either side and market stalls in the middle. I felt a lump in my throat, a soupçon of loneliness. I wanted to turn to someone and slap at them and say, 'Wow!' in the way that used to annoy Tom so much but there was no one. Well, there were lots of people but no one I felt I could slap.

But hey, it was a beautiful sunny day and I was in Venice. On the Rialto Bridge no less, within spitting distance of the markets I had been dying to see for so long — so screw having no one to slap, screw being dumped, screw everything but the moment. I threw my hair over my shoulders, held my head high and marched over the bridge, looking up the bustling canal as barges delivered growers' produce to the markets and restaurateurs loaded up for another day of business.

I heard the market before I saw it: raucous voices raised as prices were broadcast in strenuous Italian. '*Radicchio due e cinquanta, cavolo uno cinquanta al kilo, carciofi soltanto un euro al kilo.*'

The only Italian I knew, I'd learned at the hand of Pippo Marzano so I was pretty good on fruit and vegetables, passable on meat and fish, and excellent on modest swearwords. My heart started to beat quicker in my chest as I got closer. I just love a good food market. You could find me at Union Square first thing most market days, picking over the Hudson Valley kale, pouncing on the wild arugula, sniffing at the pineapple sage, fondling the Keith's Farm garlic. Actually, Tom and I usually went there together. He came alive at the market too. This bit of Venice he would have loved.

I stepped off the bridge and headed for the red awnings of the historic market stalls, middle-aged Italian men pushing me out of their way. This was a place of business, I could feel them grumbling, not a circus. '*Maledetti turisti,*' I thought I heard one mumble, which I think means 'bloody tourists' to you and me. Suddenly I regretted my jeans and tank and pale pink Gucci loafers. I looked like a tourist and I didn't want to; I wanted to wrap a scarf around my head and put on sloppy pants and clogs and shop like a chef.

The first thing I saw, of course, was a stack of soft orange zucchini blossoms, poking hopefully out from their crates as though there was any chance in the world they weren't going to be stuffed with something deliriously creamy and deep-fried. 'Five euro a kilo for porcini,' the mushroom-seller barked at me in Italian. I moved closer to the zucchini blossoms. They were a perfect colour, buttery and plump and moist: not at all wilted. But as I contemplated them — the flower of the vegetable that nearly ruined my wedding — the strangest thing, the first in a series of strange things, happened.

I felt it before I saw it, I tell you, it was eerie beyond belief. In one second flat the temperature plummeted; where I had just been feeling the morning sun warming my shoulders, an icy blast brought me out in goose bumps. I looked out to the Grand Canal, only seconds ago a riot of colour; now, nothing. There was nothing. A mist, a great grey wet suffocating mist had rolled in from I-don't-know-where and sucked up every hue on the Venetian palette. It was spectacular. Even the voices of the marketeers seemed suddenly muffled. I looked around, mildly spooked, but nobody else was taking the slightest bit of notice so I stopped lingering over the zucchini blossoms and started to move towards the fish stalls, closer still to the water and its consuming white-grey blanket.

Unlike my local Citarella, however, at the Rialto markets the fish were gutted on site so the cobbles beneath my feet ran thick with a raw gizzard stew that no self-respecting suede would be seen dead in. Unfortunately I missed this detail until a particularly loud squelch drew not only my attention but also the attention of everyone in the immediate vicinity. I had stepped on some kind of discarded seafood cyst, by the looks of things, which had exploded underneath my shoe and sprayed the feet of those around me with a foul-smelling bile that was enough to make you bring up your morning cappuccino. Now, much as I liked a market, I liked shoes, especially my ones, so I was pretty unimpressed — as were those around me. Everyone was inspecting their footwear, shaking a leg, stomping a heel, throwing me dirty looks, which in the muted mistiness was all a bit Cirque du Soleil for my liking. Anyway I myself had borne the brunt of the disaster. Balancing myself with one outstretched arm against an ancient market pillar at the canal's edge, I bent my knee and gingerly lifted one foot up in front of me to inspect the damage. My shoe was dripping with goop. It was gross.

At that moment, as quickly as it had dropped, the mist lifted. Instantly I felt the heat on my chest. I lifted my head and there in the water, right in my line of vision, standing up, his oar keeping him steady, was my gondolier. He was looking straight at me as if he'd known I would be there and when he caught my eye he just smiled.

The spirit of Jackie Collins claimed my loins once again.

My foot squelched back on the ground, red and yellow ooze coating the pretty pink suede. My arms hung limply at my side but at least this time my mouth was shut and I bit my bottom lip to ensure it stayed that way. I hadn't really noticed last time but I saw now he was not wearing traditional gondolier garb, no white sailor top, no be-ribboned straw hat, but rather a black T-shirt that gripped his body, black trousers that rode low on his hips. He had dark hair cut short, spiky on top, and he was taller even than I had thought with big broad shoulders. His face was ridiculously handsome, not too square, not too long, just the right shade of nutty brown. He was in his mid-20s I guessed and as near perfect a specimen as a girl could ever hope to clap eyes on.

He was also sliding away from me, his body still turned in my direction but his gondola about to disappear into the shadows of the bridge's arches. I felt the sort of sorrow you wake up with when you've had to leave an exceptionally good dream. Then the air between us emptied itself of sound.

'I'm not going to let you go,' I heard him say in perfect English. It seemed so loud, so close, so real, that I had no doubt in my mind he had actually said it. He turned, slipped into the blackness of the Rialto's shadows and was gone.

I blew out a lungful of air. I felt dizzy: I was sure I had been holding my breath since the mist rose. The sky was back to being dazzling blue; I felt the heat of the morning sun on my face. The fish gut on my shoe was already beginning to dry and crackle.

What had just happened? The gondolier's words echoed in my ears but the air was filled now with other noises — the market vendors, men loading and unloading crates into their boats, shoppers bargaining over the price of exotic greens. Who was this man who kept sliding in and out of my second honeymoon making me feel breathless and weak at the knees?

I moved distractedly back over to the mushroom lady who was selling all different sorts of fungi and wearing a brown and white swirling Pucci-style print. The whole scene was surreal, the whole morning, actually, my entire life come to mention it. What had he meant, my handsome stranger, when he said he would not let me go? Now he'd brought it up, I'd never felt more let go of in my life.

'È vero — *non ti lascierà scappare*,' the Pucci mushroom lady barked in a way that I took to mean I should buy something or get the hell off her patch. So I shuffled away, stopping to scrape the fish guts from my loafer on the metal rail of an abandoned trolley. I no longer felt like being jostled by bustling strangers and ogling the Veneto's succulent produce. I needed to go somewhere quiet, nurse a latte and get a grip on myself. I was a recently separated single honeymooner suffering improper leanings towards a strange foreigner — a Venetian gondolier! — for God's sake. How much more hackneyed a leaning could a recently separated girl have? It was ridiculous.

For a start, I assured myself, I loved my husband, despite the fact he was lying at home swearing into a telephone while I was in Venice without him. I'd belonged to Tom ever since I was old enough to belong to anyone and that was it, case closed. And anyway, I was just not the sort of person who had flirtations with, let alone, you know, longings for handsome men, whether I knew them or not. I just wasn't like that. On the many occasions I had been out with just my girlfriends and had the chance to play the field or misbehave, even chastely, I hadn't bothered, even though my closest friend Fleur could have flirted for the Olympics. If we were in *Sex and the City*, which is something we discussed a lot, she would be the slutty Samantha, although she looked more like Carrie but with better hair and a bigger butt. I, on the other hand, looked more like Charlotte, only curvier and taller, but acted more like Miranda, only not so brainy and obviously not as well travelled in the sex department having only ever slept with my husband. Actually, now I see that written down I have to say that neither of us are at all like anyone in *Sex and the City*.

47

Anyway, Fleur wasn't the most beautiful woman in the world — she looked a bit like the Mona Lisa — but she had charisma by the bucket-load. Men loved her. All she had to do was walk into a room and pull out a cigarette and the next thing you knew she'd be swatting them off like flies, the sexual innuendo and witty repartee flying left, right and centre. Next to her, I paled into insignificance. Her secret? Confidence. It was in the flick of her hair, the arch of her eyebrow, the clothes that clung to parts of her other women would disguise with baggy sweaters.

She was the second youngest of five daughters and her parents adored the lot of them, even the eldest, Christina, who had scandalised the parish by falling pregnant at 15 to someone whose name she refused to reveal. In any self-respecting soap opera, this would have torn the family apart and started a war that lasted generations but in the McBride household, that baby was just another thing to love. Sounds corny but it's true. Their apartment just hummed with goodwill even though Mr McBride was always broke and Mrs McBride sometimes worked three jobs to keep them in groceries. I loved going there. I loved doing anything with Fleur. She was so self-assured. All the girls were. Their parents had made sure of it.

And with all that confidence coursing through her veins Fleur was one hot tamale on the dating scene. She could juggle slobbering males like a circus clown, and did. I was full of admiration for her in this respect, but I used to worry that what with dating six men at once and all, she would never find anyone (one being the operative word) special, a husband of her own. I knew she wanted children. But after a few years it occurred to me that this girl was having so much fun on the single circuit, why would she swap it for sitting at home in front of *Friends* re-runs sucking on a Bud, no coterie of ardent admirers swooning at her feet, a clutch of snot-nosed brats clawing at her hem? She'd probably die of boredom the first night.

Not that Tom and I sat at home watching *Friends* re-runs sucking on Buds — we both worked nights so that was out of the question — no, we had a much better life than that. But still, without him, I would not have had a tiny little fraction of the fun that Fleur had without a significant other.

I had been crossing back over the Rialto Bridge when this thought hit me and it stopped me in my tracks, whammo. I *was* without Tom. I *had* no significant other. There *would* be no fun. A little bit of the devastation that had been missing hit me right in the stomach then. I was stupid to think I could have avoided it and it hurt, it hurt like hell, in a rock-bottom-here-I-come sort of a way.

I looked up as a well-dressed couple about my own age but more grown up walked up the steps of the bridge towards me. The woman would not be the type to haggle over a rip-off LV handbag; she was wearing a big scarf over her shoulders, the way Italian women can, and everything about her screamed style and money. The man, in blue blazer and impeccable shoes, was appreciatively eyeing a curvy Swedish-looking backpacker in front of me. When she passed him by, his eyes moved on to me and kept moving. They just slid right over me to someone behind. If I hadn't actually stepped out of his way, he would have walked right over me. I was invisible.

On my list of bad moments, this was a biggie. Right up there with Woody's pretzel, although of course I didn't know about Woody's pretzel then.

Here was clearly a ladies' man, a sophisticate with a built-in radar for the feminine, a man who probably couldn't cross a hallway without getting a hard-on for the cleaning woman, and I had not even registered as a blip. This, I thought miserably, was going to be my life without Tom: playing a microbe in the mating game.

I wheeled around, my hand over my mouth, some inexplicable emotion crushing my lungs, and banged, literally, straight into the absurdly fragrant chest of my strapping gondolier.

'*Finalmente*,' he said. 'Finally.'

Three

I know it's ridiculous, trust me, I know. I mean the whole stupid being-on-second-honeymoon-in-Venice-on-my-own thing had crappy romantic comedy written all over it. You think I couldn't see that? And while I knew that some people really have those things happen to them — they meet the love of their lives reaching for the last chocolate-chip cookie in the jar or marry the muscle-bound surfer who saved them from drowning on a Caribbean beach holiday — I was not that sort of person. I was a meet-your-husband-to-be-at-four-years-of-age-and-get-married-because-your-mom-is-pissed-off type of person.

Yet there I was, standing on the Rialto Bridge staring into the amused almond eyes of an exceptionally good-looking gondolier who was holding my elbow and saying, 'Finally,' in that overpowering voice that had sucked the breath clear out of my lungs over by the fish market.

'Finally what, exactly?' I had the gumption to ask eventually, sounding squeaky and small and foreign.

'Finally I've found you,' he said, his voice suddenly seeming quite normal. '*Ti ho cercato dovunque*. I've been looking for you everywhere.'

Up close he was even better-looking than from afar. He had the chiselled looks of a Calvin Klein model, the type of man I would normally consider — if I had ever been in a position to consider such a thing which I hadn't — way, way, way out of my league. Even Fleur would have probably put him in the too-hard basket and gone for his not-quite-so-cute best friend, if he had one. She was always banging on about picking a reasonable target, not aiming too high. Yet here he was, this Adonis, staring at me earnestly, his exquisite eyebrows (already my favourite part of him) raised in some pleasurable secret.

'I have rotten fish on my shoe,' I said.

Plainly, I had never been a hot tamale on the dating scene. Some god-like male creature appears out of nowhere in the city of my dreams saying he has been looking for me, and what do I do? Point out the least endearing aspect du jour; on this particular occasion, a fish tumour splattered all over my loafer. Pathetic.

But to my amazement he laughed as though I had just said the wittiest thing in the entire world and my confused excited heart simply melted, turning the rest of me into mush.

'I'm Marco,' he said and bent down, lifting up the leg of my Lucky Brands and putting his hand around my ankle. His touch felt warm and velvety, like Valrhona hot chocolate would if you drank it on the outside of your body. He had a very nice neck attached to those shoulders and small smooth ears that reminded me of pastry. I wanted to nibble on him. Quite a lot. Of course, instead of thinking such lewd thoughts I should have been wondering what he was doing down there because it wasn't until he tugged at my leg and said, 'Lift,' for the third time that it occurred to me he was trying to take my putrid shoe off.

I followed his instruction and he removed the offending article, then stood again and indicated that I should stay where I was while he leaped nimbly down the steps and over to his gondola. He jumped lithely aboard (another Jackie Collins moment) and moved so smoothly to the back of his boat it barely rocked in the water. He rummaged behind the beautiful blue and gold brocade love seat and emerged with a brush. Then, dipping it in the water of the canal, he sat down, gently dabbed at my Gucci suede, worked his way up to a semi-robust brushing, then looked up at me and smiled.

I wobbled unevenly on one foot as I looked around to see if anyone else was watching but the busy crowd was moving and buzzing, going about its own business, paying no attention to a one-legged tourist and her shoe-cleaning gondolier. It was truly bizarre but I gave a little shrug of my shoulders and went back to feasting my eyes on my Good Samaritan. Behind him, a dozen empty gondolas bobbed up and down in the water, their associated gondoliers gathered in striped shirts and straw hats in different groups on the pier, smoking, chatting to each other or on cell-phones, eyeing up potential customers. They too seemed to take no notice of Marco, whose boat gleamed brighter than any of theirs, I thought, the gold paint on the intricate wooden carving behind the love seat glowing quietly, the little blue and gold flag at the front snapping in the faintest of breezes, while similar flags on the other boats hung limp and tatty.

Marco stood up, admired my shoe, jumped onto the pier and started towards me. Even the way he walked was mesmerising . . .

'There. It's done,' he said.

I nodded, feeling overwhelmed by his attention. I knew I was making a total goof of myself but I couldn't seem to help it.

'Hah!' I said stupidly, looking at the shoe. See what I mean?

The loafer looked almost as good as new and hardly smelled fishy at all. I lifted my foot and he knelt down to slip the shoe on. It was a very Cinderella moment and the silliness of it all kind of gurgled around inside me while I worked out what the next obvious step should be.

'I'm Connie,' I said as Marco stood up straight again, practically dwarfing me with his underwear model physique. 'Constance. Mary-Constance. Farrell.'

'Constanzia Farrelli. Maria-Constanzia Farrelli,' he said, rolling the words around on his tongue as he Italianised the name. How Tom would have loved that, I thought. In fact I was surprised he hadn't thought of it himself. One tiny little letter at the end of his name and he could have been Italian all along.

At the thought of my long-lost husband, of course, I felt a slap of reality, which left me scrabbling in a deep pool of guilty, grubby awkwardness. 'What did you mean before when you said you'd been looking for me?' I asked, mildly belligerent.

'Why, I saw you arrive, yesterday,' Marco answered, surprised. 'We made a connection, remember? On the canal.'

This was a little too forward and frank for my liking. Unless I'm writing a review, in which case I have to cut to the chase or the copy editor will mangle it, I usually prefer an extended period of fluffing around followed by a short stint of prevaricating before meandering hesitatingly towards anything remotely straightforward. His mention of our connection was far too confrontational by half.

'Yes, well I'm just out for a walk,' I said irrelevantly.

He laughed. A deep, sexy laugh that almost made me drool. Seriously, I was all over the place. I didn't know if I was Arthur or Martha as my dad would say. Part of me wanted to jump off the bridge, swim to the airport and fly back into the arms of my husband, another part wanted me to be swept up in a completely different set of arms altogether. A closer set. Much closer.

'Well, walking is a hungry business,' Marco said. 'You must be starved. Let's eat. I know just the place.'

Now, you don't have to know me very well to know that to me these words are like 'abracadabra' to Aladdin. Had Marco been the ugliest guy in the world with a hairy back, little flat butt and a great big beer belly I still would have gone with him. You just don't hear, 'You must be starved. Let's eat. I know just the place,' anywhere often enough in my opinion.

So despite the fact that all I knew about the guy was that he had a strong stomach and a good feel for suede, I reached out and took the arm he was offering. He guided me through the narrow back lanes behind the market, stopping eventually, after a series of twists and turns I had no hope of remembering, at a low doorway under a barely noticeable wooden sign bearing the name Do' Mori. The darkly lit wine bar was slender, another low doorway at the opposite end opening on to the next lane. There were no chairs or stools and along one wall were bottles stacked floor to ceiling in dusty clay pipes; along the other was a bar heaving with bite-sized snacks behind which stood a portly matron, her long grey hair falling out of her bun, her kindly face beaming with a radiance I had rarely seen.

'Marco!' she crowed. 'Saving another one?' Her accent was so thick it took a while for me to work out what she had said and by then my attention was on the bar food. 'It looks fabulous,' I enunciated. '*Squisito*.' My mouth was watering. I licked my lips and looked up at Marco.

'Two glasses of pinot bianco, Signora Marinello,' he instructed the matron. It was not quite 10 in the morning yet at that point I realised the dozen or so older men standing around in little groups chatting on either side of us were all sipping wine.

Marco laughed at my surprise. 'Venetians drink more than any other Italians,' he said. 'And they do it with pride.'

At this, a florid-faced septuagenarian to my right slammed down his empty glass on the counter and nodded his head for another at Signora Marinello.

She raised her eyebrows as she slid our glasses over to us and turned away again to fulfil his request.

'Now,' said Marco, as we clinked glasses, 'I'll tell you about *cichetti*. Venice isn't known for its food, did you know this? Well, not any more. Never mind the fact that the Venetians were once the world's leading traders and the first to invent the humble fork. Actually, the food here is as good if not better than anywhere else in Italy but you have to know where to find it. Any Venetian worth his salt will bring you straight to La Vedova in the Canareggio or here to

Do' Mori for cichetti. It's a favourite tradition of ours, you won't find many other Italians eating like this. It's like tapas, you know, but Venetian-style.'

Marco leaned over the bar and grabbed a couple of round white side plates.

'*Questi?*' he asked Signora Marinello, pointing to a round brown croquette the size of a small orange. She nodded and smiled, putting the croquette on the plate and passing it over to him. '*Tonno,*' said Marco. 'You're going to like it. Trust me.'

He held it up and I opened my mouth, taking a healthy bite out of the soft flesh. It was tuna, light, sweet, mixed with breadcrumbs, parsley and lemon, and gently fried. There was no way it should have tasted so delicate but it did — it made me want to sing. I closed my eyes and groaned, and Marco fed me the rest of it. With every mouthful I salivated at the thought of the next. It was delightful. Signora Marinello clutched her fat hands together in glee in front of her substantial bosom, her rosy cheeks shining.

'*Polpette,*' Marco said next and she plucked a meatball off a tray on the counter, plopped it ever so gently on the tasting plate and Marco again held it to my mouth. It was spicy and dense, pink and fleshy in the middle, crackling with pepper and obscenely moist. In other words, delectable. Before I knew it I had eaten the whole thing and my taste buds were crying out for more.

'Ah,' Marco said, moving closer to me and peering at the plates of vegetables sitting not far from me. '*Peperoni,*' he told Signora Marinello, 'and *melanzane.*' She spooned grilled red peppers and long thin slices of eggplant onto a plate then passed it reverently to Marco who fed me, bit by bit, with a fork. The vegetables were lightly salted and bathed in a nutty olive oil that danced at the back of my throat. I was in heaven.

'She look nice, don't you think?' Signora Marinello asked Marco in a loud voice. 'Like a nice girl.' It should have felt odd, Marco feeding me like that in front of her — I mean it was an extremely personal experience — but it seemed quite natural for her to be there, watching every movement, clocking every groan of pleasure or murmur of delight. Seems creepy when I say it like that but it wasn't. We are just talking about eating, after all, about food.

Next on the menu were thin slices of delectably fresh bread loaded with fried zucchini and fresh shrimp, adorned with nothing but a bit of chopped parsley, a squeeze of lemon, and freshly ground black pepper. I'm a bread freak — the mere thought of the Atkins diet turns my stomach — and that stuff was good. Not ciabatta, closer to a baguette but denser and according to Marco made on the premises every morning by Signora Marinello herself. In my opinion, there is no bread that tastes better than one made just yards and minutes away from where you are sitting. I'm a firm believer in this.

Anyway, while he was feeding me these Venetian treats, Signora Marinello shuffled away only to return shortly afterwards with a plate of squid, tentacles gleaming, flash-fried in garlic, the hot smell still scorching the air. I devoured it. Marco then picked out a bite-sized mouthful of swordfish grilled to perfection; he folded carpaccio, ribbons of rare marinated beef, onto my tongue; and did not take his eyes off me for a second as I savoured *sarde in saor*, plump succulent sardines cooked with wine and a delicate vinegar in such perfect balance that it was simply stunning.

'You are a woman who likes to eat,' Marco said matter-of-factly, wiping a lick of oil from my chin with his thumb. It was true, I was, I knew that about myself. Some restaurant critics loved to cook, others to write, but me, I loved to eat. I didn't care if no one went to the restaurants I wrote about; I didn't care if they thought my writing was too flowery or not flowery enough or lowbrow or high-falutin'. I just wanted them to know what it felt like to taste some heavenly morsel cooked absolutely perfectly by just the right person at the exact moment you couldn't think of anything you would rather be doing than eating it. Because that to me was good as it got. Period.

Snapping to, I realised with a start that Marco was no longer at my side. I hadn't even noticed him go anywhere. What was it with empty spaces where my menfolk should have been? I stood there, looking casually around the bar, then wiped my own chin, oily fingers lighting tracing the path of Marco's long brown ones. His absence made me feel confused and sort of worried, my stomach churning for reasons that had nothing to do with Do' Mori's delectable fare, so I sought refuge in the motherly features of Signora Marinello. She was watching me intently and I couldn't quite pick the look in her eyes — but the gist of it seemed to be concern.

'I'm fine,' I found myself telling her. 'Really, I'm fine.' At this, she leaned over, picked up one of my hands and held it in her own two warm, worn ones. Emotion inexplicably overwhelmed me. I fought the urge to jump across the counter and bury my head in her ample bosom.

'You should try our *spaghetti con le seppie nere*,' she said earnestly, her brown eyes boring into mine, her grip getting firmer. 'It's the best this side of the Rialto.'

I nodded, dumbly, my insides lurching. I was battling the oddest compulsion to tell her my whole life story. It was insane.

'I have a husband,' I could not keep myself from blurting out. 'But he didn't come with me. I mean, he was supposed to . . .' but Signora Marinello was already shaking her head.

'Don't worry about nothing, Constanzia,' she said in her loud, comforting voice. 'Just let Marco take care of you.'

At this, Marco appeared at my side again. 'Have you had enough?' he asked.

Seriously, I could have listened to his voice all day. It purred without trace of an accent, his English faultless, the muscles in his jaw grinding beneath his tanned cheeks. Actually, I hadn't had enough, we'd tasted a lot of things, but they were all snack-sized. There was room for more. Yet that same tinny flavour I'd tasted after my breakfast porridge was batting at my taste buds again, throwing what should have been the aftershocks of Do' Mori's enchanting treats out of kilter. I shrugged in a non-committal fashion and smiled at him.

'Okay,' Marco said briskly. 'Let's go.'

I waved goodbye to Signora Marinello, fending off an absurd desire to take her with me, but she merely waved fondly back and turned to the thirsty septuagenarian again. We retraced our steps through the lanes and alleyways towards the Rialto Bridge and I'm ashamed to say I was afraid to ask Marco where we were going or what we were doing in case he said: 'What do you mean, we?' I liked being a 'we' with Marco. The idea of being just a me for the rest of the day, the week, the month, my life held little or no appeal. But was that really me, alone in a foreign country, trit-trotting around, my tongue hanging out, behind a handsome stranger who for all I knew chopped vulnerable women like me into tiny pieces and spread them on Signora Marinello's bread as a light mid-morning snack? I wasn't sure.

I slowed down, letting the gap between myself and Marco grow. The sun was too hot. Where it once felt warm and comforting it now scalded and suffocated. I could feel the wine that had tasted so crisp at Do' Mori drawing the moisture out of my body, making my temples throb, my mouth dry as sandpaper. I came to a standstill but could feel myself swaying. I was on the steps near the top of the bridge, tourists jostling me, shoving me out of their way. The back of Marco's head disappeared into the crowd.

'Mary-Constance,' a thin voice crackled behind me. It sounded just like my mother and I whirled around, startled, bumping into a little girl on crutches and knocking her into the arms of her father who hissed at me in an unrecognisable language. I was sweating, my heart thumping like a jackhammer. 'Mary-Constance!' I again heard someone say in my mother's irritated tone. I spun around again but there were no small, disappointed American women anywhere to be seen. Instead, an overweight elderly man with three cameras around his neck brushed past me, misjudging the width of his enormous hips and knocking me off balance. I staggered sideways, my legs buckling as my hands flapped blindly in front of me, finding — thank heaven — the warm stone of the bridge's ancient railing. The fat ribbon of sparkling canal water stretching beneath and beyond me suddenly seemed dazzling; the whole scenario blurred into a golden shimmering haze.

'Marco,' I cried weakly, because while most things seemed unfamiliar and out of focus, one thing was clear: I was about to faint. And, being me, I would quite likely land on something recently deceased and foul-smelling. 'Marco,' I whispered as darkness clawed at the sides of my eyes. I needed rescuing, whether he was an axe murderer or not.

The world turned black. I was gone.

When I came back, I was, you have probably guessed it, in his gondola. Well, where else would I have been? Seriously, it hardly surprised me at all, the day was turning out so strange. And you know what, I have since met another woman who fainted in Venice and woke up in a gondola so it's not even really that far-fetched. Of course she was in the gondola before she fainted but still.

Anyway, when I woke up I was lying on that blue and gold brocade-upholstered love seat and the gondola was moving swiftly and silently through the busy canal. It took me a few seconds to work out what was happening. At first I thought the buildings were moving and I was staying still. It was an odd sensation: I felt disconnected from consciousness, as though I were flying in a dream. (Actually, it reminded me of the way I felt the time Fleur talked me into a night of tequila slammers.) My hand ran across the gondola seat's smooth brocade and found a tassel, which I fingered like a blind person reading Braille. I was in Venice, in a gondola, I told myself trying to breathe into the pain in my head. I was with Marco, I reminded myself, as the calming sound of the boat slicing through the city's waterways comforted me. At least I assumed I was with Marco. I felt less comforted. Well, was I with Marco? Or was some other gondolier I knew even less spiriting me away? I twisted around to find that it was indeed Marco standing behind me, steering us down the canal. He smiled at me and my panic leeched away.

'What happened?' I asked him, my voice feeble and odd again.

'Don't worry,' he answered me. 'I'm taking care of you.'

'But where are we going?'

'It's too hot out here,' he said. 'I'm taking you somewhere cool.'

It was okay, he was rescuing me. It occurred to me that had I not drunk wine at 10 in the morning on a hot day in a foreign city without a husband to supervise me, I might not have needed rescuing. But the damage had been done. The wine had been drunk. The husband remained in New York. The gondolier was taking me somewhere cool.

And so I simply rolled back onto my brocade bed and stared straight at the intense Venetian sun so that it obliterated the sight of everything else. I didn't want to think about whether this was a good idea or not, going who-knew-where with Marco, a man I didn't know but somewhere deep inside, down below, wanted to. I knew it was a strange thing to let happen, I mean I was sort of being kidnapped but I didn't seem to mind. It was just like being an ordinary tourist, I figured, only cheaper as I hadn't had to pay for the ride.

We turned off the Grand Canal into a smaller one and after half a dozen twists and turns, each canal darker and narrower than the one before, we came to a wooden grate on the side of a building. Steadying himself against the crumbling concrete, Marco pulled the grate up, sliding the gondola into the darkness inside, his hands shimmying along the stone wall to steer it, his body stretched above me, his T-shirt rising to reveal a line of hair peeking out from his pants leading to — yes, well, never mind.

We were in some sort of Venetian garage, I supposed, the murky basement of someone's palazzo where they parked their boat but to be honest I wasn't really thinking about it too much. I wasn't thinking about anything too much. Apart from Marco. That line of hair. That taut brown skin. Look, I could string this out forever and try to make myself look like something other than an adulterously wanton slut but I think we all know where this is going so let's skip straight to it.

Marco tied the gondola to a post and came to kneel beside me, placing his cool hand on my hot head. I didn't know whether to feel like a five-year-old kid or the happy hooker. I wanted him to look after me, be gentle with me, but I wanted more as well. I wanted him to take me in his arms and make love to me. The word ravish even sprang to mind. I am such a cliché. Who gets ravished these days anyway? By a handsome gondolier? In Venice?

Well, in this instance, me. Yessiree. I have to say. I was ravished. He ravished me. Completely and utterly. Twice.

One moment his hand was on my forehead, my eyes slipping and sliding off his, and the next his lips were on my skin, my back arching to bring my body up to meet his. There was no way we weren't going to have sex and I knew it. I think I knew it when I first saw him, from the back of my water taxi, when he smiled and raised his eyebrow at me. And if I didn't know it then I sure as hell knew it when he cleaned my disgusting shoe. Marco was what every recently separated woman (and a few still married ones as well) dreams of and deserves.

He slid me down onto the floor of the gondola and I lifted my arms so he could slip off my tank top. I wasn't even embarrassed about the doughy squidge of my middle, or the way a soft roll poked out from underneath my too-tight bra. He kissed his way down to my breasts, nibbling at them through my lingerie. It drove me wild. I couldn't get my jeans off quickly enough, kicking them and my g-string (second honeymoon wear; I usually chose underwear with far better restraining properties) down the gondola and pulling him on top of me, then pushing him off again so I could help wrench off his T-shirt, claw at his pants.

Then we were both lying there, naked, staring at each other with such intensity it almost scared me. And without a word, I slithered

61

out from underneath him and moved astride him, so I was on top —
which is most unlike me I can tell you, for reasons of having a pot
belly that looks a heck of a lot flatter when I'm lying down. But there
I was, sitting up straight in that dark watery garage, the gondola
rocking gently in the wake of our movement, our separate parts
sliding into place as though we were made for each other, a fat, heavy
drop of water falling from somewhere into the darkness beyond us
every few seconds in an almost stupefying rhythm.

I'm not going to bore you with details of the sex because, let's
face it, it's nowhere near as interesting reading about sex as it is
having it, especially if it is with Marco. You can trust me on that one.
Just the touch of his skin was electric. Where it merged with mine —
on my thighs, my belly, my breasts — it made me fearful I would
ignite, burn up and disintegrate. Words just cannot do it justice. It
was explosive, completely and utterly intensely explosive. I had never
had sex like that before in my life and I doubted that I ever would
again. It was out of this world.

Afterwards, we lay in the gondola, side by side, holding each
other.

'I've never done that,' I said into the darkness, 'with anyone but
my husband.'

Of course, Marco didn't even know I had a husband but I have
to say it did not seem to bother him in the slightest. He didn't even
flinch. Just held me, my head on his chest, the sturdy thump of his
heart filling me with hope.

But then Tom's face, his dear lovely face, wafted into my mind
and my post-coital happiness completely dissolved, leaving nothing
but guilt and dread and self-loathing in its place. I started to cry, not
little girlie sniffles either, but great big man's howls, my mouth
stretched open as though my grief were too big to get out, my face
swimming with tears, my chest aching with heaving sobs.

How could I do this to Tom? Betray him? Cheat on him? Act so
unlike me I couldn't even recognise myself? Sure we were going

through a rough patch, maybe had been for a while, but weren't couples supposed to cling to each other for support when the going got tough? Not desert each other and turn to total strangers for comfort even if the comfort was extremely good. Better than extremely good. Un-freakin'-believably extremely good?

I stopped crying and felt Marco move next to me. My tears had bothered him as much as my confession that I was married. It was weird to be lying there next to him, skin on skin, having shared so much of our earthly flesh but nothing else. Basically, he was still a total stranger to me. I didn't know the first thing about him, which worried me but perversely, nor did I want to ask him anything. He was just too darn good for me, that was the problem, and I didn't want to do anything to scare him off. He could row out into the world and get 100 lost and lonely wives all a lot better-looking than me with just a snap of his delectable fingers. And I hadn't had my share just yet. Not by half.

To my shame, and I am a good lapsed Catholic girl with hearty Jewish genes so I know when I should feel shame or not, I felt a pang then, fierce and forceful. But not of longing for my lost marriage nor guilt at my betrayal nor even doubt at the sense in my recent decision-making. But of hunger.

I was hungry.

Marco gently extricated himself from my arms, sat up, handed me my bra and looked at me, his eyes frank and uncomplicated.

Please, I thought to myself, please. Let him say the right thing.

'Let's eat,' Marco said, standing up and reaching for my hand. 'You must be starved.'

Four

Well, had I not already been lying down you could have knocked me over with a feather. Marco had just made mad passionate love to me in a way no one ever had before and now he wanted to take me out to eat. Oy. And they say there's no such thing as the perfect man. For a moment I just stared at him in adoration. Then it occurred to me that perhaps he had meant I must be starved of sex. Perhaps the way I had soaked up his touch, his skin, his lips, his whispering in my ear, had made it obvious how seldom Tom and I had made love in recent months. Or was that years? Don't ask me where the passion in my marriage went. I didn't even notice how much we'd had until it was gone. Until it was too late.

We were best friends, Tom and I, we loved each other a lot. But I didn't think Tom found me sexy any more, thought he hadn't for a while. When he looked at me it was quite often with a frown or a kind of wrinkle of disapproval and while I certainly still desired him, that wrinkle could not help but cool my own ardour.

'You will love Bentigodi,' Marco said as he untied the gondola. 'The chef there is positively inspirational. Just wait until you taste her *sarde incinte in agrodolce*. Fantastic.'

He had meant starved of food not sex after all and it looked like I was going to be sated on both counts. This was turning into quite

64

some second honeymoon, I could not help but think. I nestled back in my brocade nest as Marco pulled the gondola out into the canal, closed the grate and we slid away. It was amazingly quiet, just the almost imperceptible groan of the oar against its holder and the occasional pad of Marco's shoes on the rug at the back of the boat.

I watched the laundry fluttering on the clotheslines stretched from building to building across the canal above me. A gorgeous set of sheets, sky blue and adorned with white puffy clouds, flapped against the real thing far beyond; two sets of bright red overalls accompanied an entire row of enormous beige bloomers.

'*Sinistra*,' Marco hollered, and we turned left into a wider canal. I turned my head lazily to one side as another gondolier shouted out something in return. There were so many questions to ask but it didn't feel as though they were in my head. It felt as though they were circling on the outside, like a cartoon character that'd been hit on the head with a frying pan, tweet tweet.

Thoughts of Tom kept trying to invade my thick skull but I just wouldn't let them. I wanted to feel happy for a while, not make too much of anything. I wondered if Marco would marry me and I would move to Venice and have babies with him. Then I realised that didn't really gel with the whole not-making-too-much-of-anything business so I stopped. Then I thought about how I could think about having babies with Marco, a complete (well, almost) stranger yet not with Tom, my husband of 10 years. This made me so unhappy that I stopped thinking about anything and instead just let my eyes slither over the doors and windows that we passed as we sliced through the smooth waters of La Serenissima.

Despite the serenity of the surroundings, the subject of children would not stay far away. I guessed it was at the root of Tom's no-show, or at the root of the problems causing the no-show. Tom wanted babies and I wasn't sure; it was as simple as that. But what wasn't I sure about? If I could contemplate having little Marcos, why not little Toms? I scratched at my nose and fidgeted in my nest. Little

Toms. Why not? But if I knew the answer, it was scurrying around just beyond my comprehension and any attempt to pin it down proved fruitless.

'Just relax,' Marco said behind me, obviously seeing me squirm. He made a delectable little groan as he pushed the gondola back out into the hectic rush of the Grand Canal. 'You are in the most beautiful city in the world and there's no better way to see it than from the water.'

He had a point, so I pushed aside the noisy clatter of dissension going on in my brain and leaned back into that blue and gold brocade, my head turning to take in the lavish hotels, the fine palazzi and their crumbling poor relations on either side of Venice's main street.

'I'm taking you up to the Cannaregio,' Marco said. 'It's the old Jewish quarter. Not so many tourists. A lot of good food.'

The air was full of the sounds of other people going about their business, their vacations, their day-to-day lives, and I let the magic of Venice wash over me, comfort me, keep me from wondering what the hell I was doing. Every now and then I would twist around to smile at Marco, check he was still there, that I hadn't drifted into some parallel universe where lovely things stopped happening to me. But there he was, his eyes — his crow's feet just in their infancy — shining at me.

'How old are you?' I asked him at one point.

'Twenty-nine,' he answered me, his eyes twinkling. 'And you?'

I sank down in my seat, pretending I hadn't heard him. There was only a four-year gap but still, it was in the wrong direction.

Luckily, before I could even wonder why I was thinking about our age difference, we arrived at the Ca' d'Oro pier. Marco came to an arrangement with the gondolier there about leaving his boat and led me through another maze of unmarked lanes and canals, clearly no mystery to him at all, until we arrived at a back-street *osteria*, all white walls and dark wooden furniture and cool, clean tiled floors.

It was less than two hours since we had eaten but I told you, I'm not normal in this regard. I was feeling so many different sorts of hunger by that stage I could barely tell one from the other.

Anyway, no sooner had we sat down than a pink-faced waitress in her 20s came over to us bearing handwritten menus. Marco waved them away.

'Sarde incinte in agrodolce,' he ordered. 'And *fondi di carciofo*. For two.

'Pregnant sardines,' he translated for me. 'The chef here makes the most beautiful stuffed sardines — you'll see how different they are from the sarde in saor that you had at Do' Mori. That's the traditional Venetian way of preparing them but here, everything has a twist. That's what I love about it. And the fondi, the artichoke hearts, they are delicious too. You won't see them much outside Venice either.'

'How do you know so much about food?' I asked him, just wishing he would keep talking.

'I know a lot about everything,' he said. I laughed because I thought he was joking but he remained completely serious. And boy, did he look gorgeous serious. His earnest brown eyes buzzed around the room, checking out the kitchen, the other patrons, the jittery waitress. He drummed his fingers on the table. Actually, even his fingers looked good enough to eat. I was ravenous.

When they arrived the pregnant sardines looked so magnificent I almost didn't want to disturb them. They sat on their plain white plate, fat and succulent and lightly fried, their middles swollen with a blissful stuffing of breadcrumbs, orange juice, raisins, pine nuts, olive oil and parsley. We ate them with our fingers, Marco's glistening with oil as he licked them, looking more delectable than ever. The fondi did not look quite as enticing, sitting greeny-grey and slightly tongue-like in their marinade of oil and lemon, but they tasted divine, almost like a well-aged perfectly cooked slice of beef, believe it or not. And don't you just love it when vegetables taste like meat?

But after the initial burr of deliciousness faded away, again I felt that funny sensation at the back of my throat where I knew a heavenly aftertaste should have been.

'Is everything OK?' the pink-faced waitress asked. I had thought her rude at first but I could see now she was just run off her feet.

'Great,' I beamed at her encouragingly. I always feel sorry for restaurant staff. I had been a kitchen lackey myself so knew that it was true that it was one of the most stressful jobs a person could have. We human beings don't take our food lightly, especially when we are paying through the nose for it.

'You know your brother was here,' the waitress said, quite knocking the stuffing out of me because she wasn't looking at Marco when she spoke but at me.

'*My* brother?' I asked her. 'I don't think so.' Emmet's idea of a trip did not involve international travel, that much I knew. He would never in a million years be in Venice. I didn't even think he had a passport. It was inconceivable that he was there. Of course I had thought I had heard my mother on the Rialto Bridge not so long ago but that was before I fainted from the heat and the effects of a crisp dry white so early in the morning.

'Was there anyone there?' I asked Marco all the same. 'When I fainted?'

He wiped at the fondi oil left on the plate with a chunk of crusty white bread. 'I was there,' he said and bit off the end of the crust, his teeth outlandishly white and efficient.

My ears must have deceived me, I decided. The waitress was mistaken. She had moved away by then and was clearing another table, one hand distractedly trying to push a rogue chunk of strawberry blonde hair behind one ear. Marco was certainly not acting as though anything untoward had happened. Would he not be interested to learn my brother was in Venice? It was ridiculous. I opted to think nothing more of it, leaning back in my chair and resting my hands on my belly. I felt fabulous.

Marco took this in and seemed pleased. 'You know, there is nothing like a little gelato to finish a good meal,' he said. 'Paolin on Campo San Stefano has changed hands but I think the liquorice gelato there is still the best.' He pushed back his chair and stood up.

We meandered back to the gondola, then hit the canal again. It was busier now, our progress slow, the water clogged with gondolas, each one, unlike ours, stuffed full of tourists. It occurred to me that I was keeping Marco from working.

'You must be missing out,' I said, twisting around to talk to him. 'I'm sorry.'

'I'm not missing out on anything,' he said and I felt another lurch of happiness. 'I own 12 other gondolas,' he continued, 'and it has been a good summer.'

'I thought gondoliers could only have one gondola each,' I said. 'That they sort of got passed down from father to son.' I had read this somewhere, along with the fact that gondoliers do not and have never sung to their passengers.

'Sometimes still it goes from father to son,' Marco said, steering us gently through a bottled water delivery boat and two gondolas linked together, holding a dozen glazed-eyed tourists between them, 'but it doesn't have to. And the authorities say that each gondolier must have only one gondola but these boats are expensive and not many of the younger guys can afford to buy in so I loan them the money and they pay me back, with interest.'

I must say I was a little surprised at the lack of romance in this response. 'So how did you get to be a gondolier?' I asked.

'My father is in the business and so was my grandfather before him,' he answered. 'That's the old way.'

I stroked the blue velvet on the cushion I was hugging. Now this was more like it.

'So this is your dad's gondola?' I asked.

'*Destra*,' Marco hollered, indicating a right turn. '*Destra*. No, my old man wouldn't be seen dead in this.'

'But why? It's beautiful.'

'Yes, but it's a new kind of beautiful.' The exertion of rowing lengthened his vowels. It was like listening to music. 'It's made by a friend of mine in Switzerland. It's fibreglass and at 20,000 euro nearly half the price of having a wooden gondola made the old-fashioned way.'

I squeezed the cushion tighter. There was absolutely no reason why this should disappoint me but it did. I shook my head. I was expecting Marco to be perfect but really I had no right to expect anything. Why should it bother me that he was unromantic when it came to tradition? That he had a good eye for commerce? He was overly romantic in other ways after all. Even if he seemed a little, well, closed off, I supposed. And although I hated to admit it, he didn't have much of a sense of humour. But did that matter? When everything else was so right?

'Where is Campo Stefano?' I changed the subject.

'Not far from your hotel,' Marco told me, 'if you would rather go there. The gelato can always wait. It will still be there tomorrow.'

I held my breath, knowing what I wanted to say but afraid to actually say it. And while I'm not known for putting off the opportunity to eat, in this case there was something I wanted much, much more than ice cream.

'The hotel,' I croaked. Bits of me were calling out for the touch of that man's hands in a way I had never even imagined before. I found myself wishing, screw tradition, that the gondola had an outboard motor to move quicker through the canals to the Gritti Palace. My clothes felt hot and restrictive, my breath was short. The only word I could think of to describe the way I felt was desperate. I was desperate for him. I was dripping with desperation for him. It was a foreign feeling and sort of scary because I realised that if he simply dropped me off at the pier and kept going I would probably shrivel up and die.

But he turned into the Santa Maria del Giglio traghetto stop and after a brisk conversation with the gondolier there, who was slothfully sprawled in a chair on the pier, his cigarette burning, newspaper pages spread around him, he tied up his gondola and reached for my hand. Five minutes later we were up in that beautiful pistachio room and I was quivering as Marco's thumbs strummed my collarbone. We stood opposite each other in front of the open picture-postcard window and he slowly removed every last stitch of my clothing until I was standing there naked as a jaybird, shaking with anticipation.

Look, if you think it's easy for me to recount this part it is not. I am not a standing-around-naked-as-a-jaybird-shaking-with-antici-pation type of person. I had worn joke T-shirts to bed with my husband for the past decade of my life and he was the only one apart from my mother to have seen me in the raw since I can't remember when. So for me to be standing there with not one single of my 10 (ahem) extra pounds disguised, exposed in broad daylight to a man about whom I knew nothing, except the satin feel of his smooth brown skin and the way that just looking at him filled the hole inside me, well, I can't explain how out of character it was. And how wonderful. I felt like the old me had flown out that window and was swooping over the Peggy Guggenheim Collection and circling the shiny dome of Santa Maria della Salute light as a feather, leaving a new me standing there throbbing with desire.

Yes, it is fair to say that I was in the clutch of a post-separation lust from which I could not have extricated myself even if I'd wanted to, and so Marco and I went at it like jungle animals. And it was oh-my-God extraordinary. We made love until I thought every square inch of me was rubbed raw with the scratch of his whiskers, the rasp of his tongue, the nip of his teeth, the print of his fingers, the clawing of his nails. I felt things in parts of my body I had forgotten about, craved things I didn't know I could have, offered him parts of myself Sister Thomas Aquinas is probably still churning up soil over.

And then we decided we would go out for dinner. Truly, if every affair were like that, we would all be having them. All the time.

71

There was no room in my head for Tom at all. Not at all.

We showered together, which took a lot longer than any shower I ever took on my own, then I pulled on one of my little black dresses, slipped into my only pair of Jimmy Choos, and let Marco lead me once again through that magical collection of water and stone that was turning me into an entirely different woman.

'You will like it in here,' Marco assured me, as we came upon the doorway of the Trattoria Alla Madonna, an unpretentious older-style restaurant with an enormous vine growing up through a hole in the roof. 'It's where the Venetians eat.'

The place hummed with grumpy old waiters — it was like being in Peter Luger steak house in Williamsburg but without the porterhouse. An ice counter was constantly being re-filled with fresh whole fish, the tables buzzed with chatter. The smell of green beans and garlic filled the air and lifted my heart, already impossibly light. I felt Marco's arm around my shoulder, steering me through the busy room to a table in a side alcove, the waiters acknowledging him grouchily. My feet hardly touched the ground. I floated.

'I'll have a beer,' Marco directed a squat balding man with bushy eyebrows who showed us to our table.

'A man who drinks beer lives a hundred years,' he replied without a trace of humour.

'And I'll have a glass of *soave*,' I chipped in. 'So how long will I live?'

He showed no sign of having heard me, leaping nimbly out of the way to avoid a collision with a tray of *spaghetti alle vongole*, and disappeared into the throng of white-shirted waiting staff.

Actually, my wine arrived within minutes, but not so Marco's beer.

'A man who waits for beer lives two hundred years,' our waiter said and this time I thought I detected a tremor of hilarity in those bushy eyebrows.

We ordered and then we ate, oh how we ate! Tiny little hard-shelled clams that I sucked on till the roof of my mouth stung; thick dark sausages with a white bean stew; spaghetti with fried zucchini and parsley; veal cutlets cooked in lashings of sweet, nutty butter; soft chunks of white bread that drank up spicy olive oil; green beans and fresh peas well-cooked in a salty broth; and, to finish, a chocolate torte so rich and delicious just one mouthful was enough.

Actually, just one mouthful was all I could manage. And by then the waiters had stopped being grumpy and were looking at me with what I can only describe as admiration.

Mr Bushy Eyebrows even pulled back my chair as I got up to leave and Alla Madonna did not strike me as normally being that sort of a joint.

We walked back to the hotel in companionable silence, the streets still alive with giggling tourists and star-struck lovers. It wasn't until I caught our reflection in the window of a shop selling beautiful Italian linen that I saw that was what we looked like too. Or at least, I looked like that: Marco's reflection was harder to catch. He was standing on the other side of me and the reflection of his features was blurred by the sheets and pillowcases and quilt covers draped dramatically on the other side of the glass.

By the time we got back to my room, tiredness was attacking me from all angles. My eyes were having trouble staying open. I could feel sleep washing over me like waves on a pebbly shore, leaving me small windows of alertness before drowning me again in weariness.

Wordlessly, I let Marco take off my clothes and put me to bed. I felt the warmth of his hand on my stomach before drifting away into deep, deep sleep. In my dreams, the blackness swirled like a sinister oil painting with streaks of other colours spurting and spraying in front of my closed eyelids. It was unsettling, angry, confused. Very Jackson Pollock on a bad day. And it went on for far too long, leaving me feeling anxious and out of sorts when I woke up.

'Marco?' I whispered sleepily, turning to face him, seeking solace in his arms. But his side of the bed, of course, was empty. There would be no solace. Marco was gone.

I suppose you would have seen this coming. And had I not been blind to all but Marco's animal magnetism, I suppose I would have seen it too.

As it was, I looked around my gorgeous room, which showed no sign at all of ever having had a handsome gondolier in it, no trace of the man who could make me forget my husband. There was no point in checking the wardrobe or under the bed. I knew in my heart of hearts that he was gone. No doubt about it. Gone. Devastation seeped into every pore, knocking the wind clear out of me.

I mean I knew it was preposterous from the start, someone like me and someone like him, but it had just unfolded so naturally, so perfectly, and felt so right that something inside me must have screamed 'I deserve this!' because I hadn't fought it at all. I hadn't argued with myself that he'd mistaken me for someone else, I hadn't joked my way out of his embrace, I hadn't let the guilt with which I was so heavily endowed overwhelm my instinctive desire. I had seized the day, I had carpe diemed up the wazoo. I had opened myself up to him, despite it all, despite the real me, and I'd had the best goddamn experience of my whole goddamn life.

I sucked back a sob. Whatever Marco had awoken in me I could not bear to put back to sleep. I felt alive for the first time in I couldn't remember how long. I tingled with the memory of him. How could I live without feeling those lips on my skin, those hands on my breasts, those thighs pressed against mine, his breath hot on my neck?

It was morning, the sounds of the city awakening were sifting in through the window, the light casting shadows on my pistachio surroundings. I calmed the panic in my chest. I had found an antidote to my doubts over a future with Tom and I was not going to let it go.

I pulled on my jeans and the cashmere cardigan Fleur had given me for my last birthday and ran out of the hotel. I would find him, I decided. I would bring him back. I would make love to him again and then maybe I would know what to do next. Right then that was all I could come up with; it was as far as I could see — a growl low in my stomach calling out for more of my gorgeous gondolier.

Of course, at Traghetto Santa Maria del Giglio his gondola was gone and the other gondolier there, the same slob who'd been there the night before, claimed to know nothing of Marco but offered to take me for a ride for 100 euros, a snip, he claimed, at that price. He was blowing the smoke of a strong cigarette in my face and eyeing me in a way that made me feel dirty. His gondolier hat was ratty and his white shirt frayed at the collar with a dribble of something red spilled down the front. His teeth were stained brown, his fingers yellow and he smelled of nothing pleasant.

'Marco,' I stressed, realising as I did how little I knew of the man, how few clues I had to help me find him. Not even his surname. 'You must know Marco. He's tall, quite tall, and wears a black T-shirt and trousers. He has 12 gondolas. He was here last night, with me, you must remember.'

A sleazy smile crept over the gondolier's face. 'Oh, so you've been with Marco,' he said. I felt relief for a moment. Perhaps help was at hand. 'Well, let me tell you little Miss Americano — there's nothing Marco can give you that I can't.' He made a lewd gesture with one hand and his crotch, only narrowly missing setting himself on fire as his cigarette end brushed against his acrylic pants.

'Excuse me,' I said prudishly. 'But there is no need to be disgusting.'

The gondolier laughed. 'It is not me who has been disgusting, Signorina,' he said, spitting into the canal as he did so. 'You all think you are so special.'

I tried to tough it out but it was too hard. 'You all? What is that supposed to mean?'

'You think you are the first pretty girl to fall in love with a gondolier like Marco?' This man's face was twisted and mean. I just knew that he was not a gondolier with whom pretty girls fell in love. 'These canal waters overflow with the blood of foolish women's broken hearts. Go home, Signorina. Forget him. Go home.'

I turned and ran, not even bothering to wipe the tears from my cheeks. But running is not my thing, due to not being thin and pert, and no matter how quickly I wanted to get away from the ugly gondolier's lies — or even worse, truths — I just couldn't keep myself jiggling up and down like that. So I slowed to an upset sort of a scurry, then to a walk. I would go to the Rialto where I had seen Marco yesterday, I decided. Of course! Marco had to work! He would be there, or not far away, and I would wait for him. And everything would be all right.

This thought lifted my spirits and I skipped across the Rio di San Moise, the smell of coffee in the air reminding me that I couldn't be too far away from Pasticceria Marchini, which was alleged to have Venice's best pastries. But my heart needed feeding before my stomach and in fact my jeans were feeling a little firm after the feasting that had gone on the day before, despite the high calorific burn factor, so I kept moving towards the Rialto.

Halfway there I caught a glimpse of a tall, dark gondolier disappearing around the corner in his boat, the familiar throaty laugh of a female passenger echoing around the canal. It sounded just like Fleur.

And wouldn't that be just like her, I found myself thinking, to steal my beautiful boyfriend — she who could summon up anyone she wanted and at least five spares. I started to run again then, ignoring the jolt in my knees and the jiggle in my bra, following the direction in which I thought the gondola had gone. But the water is by far the simplest way to get around Venice and trying to follow the gondola on foot I was thwarted at every turn. Within two minutes I had come to a dead end in a dingy little alley and knew I had lost Marco and Fleur forever. But there was no way it could have been Fleur and if it had been Marco, he was probably on his way back to the Rialto.

My heart sank when I got there and saw the clutch of other gondoliers mooching about on the pier, my one not among them.

'Have you seen Marco?' I asked, but the first lot turned their backs on me.

'Marco?' I asked another trio, but they talked amongst themselves and laughed at me, one even jabbing at me with his cell phone, his eyes deep set and dead-looking.

I knew how it looked. I knew what they were thinking. But I just couldn't believe that Marco would do that to me. So I waited. And waited. And waited. But by 11 o'clock I felt that every one of Venice's thousand gondoliers but him had passed me by.

'If he comes,' I told the gondoliers standing beside me, 'if Marco comes tell him I've gone to Do' Mori.'

'*Quello lì, non lo vedrai mai più,*' the tallest one said, shaking his head. While I couldn't be sure exactly what he meant, I could tell that it wasn't good.

It took a while to find Do' Mori. It was not that far from the bridge but the alleys were all narrow and dark and one looked much the same as the other. But eventually I recognised the wooden sign hanging over the hidden doorway.

'Signora Marinello!' I cried with relief when I finally stumbled into the bar. Marco was nowhere to be seen but the sight of her ruby cheeks was most welcome. 'Have you seen him? Seen Marco?'

Signora Marinello poured a glass of wine and slid it over the worn wooden counter-top. 'I've seen Marco, yes,' she said. 'But you don't need Marco no more, Constanzia.'

I pushed the glass back to her. I had thought she was a friend. I felt anger surge through me with near-volcanic heat then shrink away again to a hard little rock, leaving me empty and scared.

'But I do,' I whispered, my eyes sliding desperately over the tuna croquettes, my mouth not even bothering to water. 'I need him more than ever. Why would you say otherwise?'

'Is just the way it is,' Signora Marinello wiped her hands on the dishcloth that was tucked into the apron tied around her substantial middle. 'Is just the way it is, Constanzia. Time for you to move on.'

The concern was still there in her eyes. It killed me. She must have known from the start that Marco was going to drop me like a hot potato. She straightened a tray of polpette, which failed to tickle my taste buds in the slightest. I was really not myself. The tinny taste was growing stronger and stronger in my mouth. The headache that had waxed and waned over the past day or so throbbed violently now in at least three different places.

'You going to be fine,' she said vehemently. 'You going to be better than you was before. You don't need Marco no more. Trust me, my love.'

I started to say something, to argue, to plead, to beg her for any suggestion that might lead me to my gondolier, but at that moment a familiar but most out-of-place face walked into Do' Mori. It belonged to Ty Wheatley, a snooty magazine publisher I knew vaguely from Manhattan — yet he seemed hardly surprised at all to see me.

'There you are,' he said and he leaned in to kiss me, on the mouth.

Now Ty Wheatley was not a man I expected to kiss me on the mouth, nor anywhere else for that matter. He was just about good-looking but not up my alley at all, no way. You may know the type. He'd started if not on the wrong side of the tracks then near them, but came into money thanks to some distant uncle when he was in his 20s. He'd then hot-footed it from Idaho or Iowa or Oklahoma to seek fame and fortune in New York, cleverly buying a property magazine that with the boom turned out to be a brilliant investment. He was squashy around the middle, prone to speaking in a phoney English accent and always dressed in cream linen, something I totally deplored.

He ate at all the nice restaurants, went to all the right parties and was the sort of person so aware of what you should do to fit in that he never quite managed it himself. I'd picked that desperation up in him the first time we met and it rang a nasty little bell inside me too, making me feel like the gawky schoolgirl I had once been and had no interest in being again.

Actually, when I came to think about it, standing there at the bar at Do' Mori, my cheeks flushed, palms sweating and heart thumping so loudly in my chest my temples hummed, I couldn't quite remember how I knew all this. About Ty. I had only met him a couple of times, no more than in passing really. And the last time I had seen him he had wanted to talk to me about something but I had cleverly fobbed him off by going to the bathroom halfway through the conversation.

'Darling,' Ty said, to my horror putting his arms around me. 'You look so pale.'

I looked over at Signora Marinello who had a funny expression on her face, not disappointment — I can recognise that from a hundred paces, I've had a lifetime of that — but not something a million miles away either.

'Try the Giudecca,' she said to me, and with that I wrenched myself out of Ty Wheatley's grasp and fled.

Five

The Giudecca was the long thin island at the south of the lagoon known best, according to the sweating tourist squashed up against me on the vaporetto, for its fading palaces and gardens and the glitzy Hotel Cipriani.

The boat dropped me at Il Redentore, the island's principal monument, and once the crowd dispersed into the church and down the wide quayside facing back to the city I found myself standing on the concrete forecourt not having a clue what to do next.

My headache had gotten worse: it pulsed behind my eyes like an overworked air-conditioning unit. A mild breeze was chilling my body — I was cold despite the warm temperature — yet my face felt flushed and feverish. I didn't know what was wrong with me but I felt completely unglued. It was an ugly sensation made all the more terrifying by the fact that I was sure Marco was the only cure and I didn't know if I would ever see him again. It was clear the Giudecca was not a gondoliers' hangout. The water was rough and choppy between the island and the city, there would be no gondolas out there, and the buildings had a run-down industrial feel about them.

My smelly tourist friend had been vomited off the vaporetto and poured into the church with the rest of the tourist commuters and the only other people still standing outside Il Redentore were two old men, grandfathers I guessed, each with a sleeping toddler in a stroller. They were smoking and enjoying a lively debate, which continued as I approached.

'Excuse me,' I interrupted them. 'Excuse me, do you have a moment?'

They stopped talking.

'I was wondering if you could tell me where I might find any gondoliers?'

Could I have asked a more stupid question if I tried? I doubted it.

'No, no, I don't mean any gondolier,' I continued in a panic as the grandfathers exchanged a look that I was pretty sure meant a finger circling an ear was soon to follow.

'Just one, really,' I carried on idiotically. 'No, definitely! One, definitely! One gondolier.' The grandfathers pushed their strollers around in unison and started to move at a sprightly gait away from me. 'Marco,' I cried. 'Do you know him? It's just that —' but they were gone.

The splodge of wet galoshes on the ground drew my attention to a dark and crinkly skinned fisherman who was walking along the wharf from the opposite direction. He had frazzled grey hair and carried a pail full of twitching fish tails, driving his mutt of a big black dog to distraction.

I approached him more carefully than I had the grandfathers. Calling out before I got too close. 'Excuse me,' I called. 'Do you know where I could find Marco, the gondolier?'

'*Gondolière?*' He at least acknowledged my question. I couldn't even see his eyes; his skin was wrinkled into so many folds it covered them completely. But he threw back his head so he could get a good look at me, slowly checked me out, then pointed towards the other side of the island. '*Squero*,' he said, as I heard a fish tail slap against the side of his pail making his dog whine with longing. 'Boatyard. Boats.'

I walked briskly along until I found an alleyway that went

through to the other side, emerging onto a narrower, shabbier quay that faced out to the wider lagoon.

'Squero?' I asked an ancient, shrivelled woman sitting outside her crumbling apartment, the window box next to her full to overflowing with the crisp brown heads of long-dead flowers. She pointed to my right and off I went, not really knowing what I was looking for until I came upon the wide opening of what looked like an old factory. When I looked in I saw the skeleton of a gondola, pale and naked like the bones of a slender whale, being worked on by a silver-haired man in a red polo shirt.

'Hello?' I called.

He looked up, carefully placed his tools on the workbench next to him and walked over to me. Up close, I saw he was not as old as his hair would have had me believe. Fifty, maybe, I thought, or even late 40s. And his eyes were a shade of pale green so clear they made me shiver. I couldn't stop looking at them. He smiled and his crow's feet winked at me. His skin was sun-darkened and pleasantly wrinkled.

'I'm looking for Marco,' I said. 'Do you know where I can find him?'

'Luca,' he said, holding out his hand. 'Pleased to meet you.'

'Oh, I'm sorry.' I was flustered; that headache was killing me. 'Connie. Connie Farrell. Pleased to meet you too.' I grasped the outstretched hand and it felt warm and strong. I could feel the calluses on his palm and my head was suddenly filled with the faint scent of lemons. He was having a very odd effect on me. I felt floaty and strange. I'd never taken Ecstasy — Emmet had abused enough drugs for both of us — but I wondered if this was what it felt like. My innards felt kind of warm, despite the fact my skin still felt the ache of a chill, and my head was full of puffy clouds.

'Come in, Connie,' he said, and although his voice was sort of muffled, I thought he too spoke perfect English. I could not detect one trace of an Italian accent. Dazed, I followed him into the workshop and over to the skeleton of the half-built gondola.

He picked up his tools — they looked like gynaecological instruments to me — and said: 'Do you mind?'

I nodded dopily, hoping like hell I wasn't agreeing to an internal examination. I had a terrible thirst that raged from the pit of my stomach up through my chest to my throat and my mouth, leaving my tongue stuck to the roof. I wanted desperately to ask for a glass of water but couldn't find the words.

Luca had picked up a chisel and turned back to his boat, gently chipping at it, smoothing the lip of the gondola — although it already looked pretty level to me.

'It's a dying art, you know,' he said, his back to me, as I watched the outline of his ribs under his red shirt, just the faintest patches of sweat under his armpits, the scent of citrus still hanging in the air. 'Gondola-making. There are only three of us left.' He ran his hands over the stretch of wood he'd just been working on, back and forth, back and forth, as though his skin itself might soothe the splinters. 'Nobody cares about the boats any more. It's all about the money.'

The way he leaned over the gondola, his tools in his hands, his arms outstretched reminded me of a pool player, of Paul Newman in *Cool Hand Luke* with that silver hair, nutty skin and those piercing eyes.

'Hard to believe only 50 years ago most people got around this city rowing,' he said, his voice lapping at me like the waters of the Grand Canal against the sunken walls of the Gritti Palace. 'Sure, the tourists go for a spin these days but if you wanted to go from here to Burano in a gondola, the way you might have done back then?' He crouched down so his eye was level with his handiwork. 'Not a chance,' he answered himself, standing up again. 'And you want to know why? Because to be able to do that, the gondolier would have to know how to row properly and how to master and manage his boat. And he would have had to come to me and work with me to create a gondola in the first place that could actually make it to

Burano. In good time. Without killing him in the process. He would have had to be interested from the very beginning. In the gondola.'

It was as though we had picked up the threads of some earlier conversation, the way his voice just kept sailing smoothly along through the peaks and troughs of his words. It was mesmerising, lulling me into some sense of, I don't what, but I was pretty happy just standing there listening. Plus, my tongue was still stuck to the roof of my mouth, which kind of stymied my chances of joining in anyway.

'So there are only three of us left who know how to make boats the old way now — and two of them are nearly past it — and not among us can we find a single apprentice who is interested in learning what we have to teach about the craft. So, the tradition is already lost. It's a tragedy. Simple as that. It's a goddamn tragedy. Don't you think?'

He stopped what he was doing, and turned around to look at me. I nodded as vigorously as I could without falling over. My bones felt like dead weights. I blinked to make sure I still had some sort of control.

'I mean, they're not just any boats, they're gondolas!' He had gone back to work. 'They're the symbol of Venice, for crissakes, our emblem, our logo. You see them in pictures painted a thousand years ago and they are still the same today as they were then. They're what stop us from being a big wet amusement park for fat tourists who for the most part don't spend more than one precious day of their whole miserable lives here. But the gondola's era is over. It's finished. *Finito*. And every now and then someone stands up and asks, 'Why is this tradition dying out?' but nobody does a goddamned thing about it. Our sons are still more interested in making 100 euro an hour paddling around that swimming pool of a canal than they are protecting a tradition that's survived 10 centuries but won't last another two decades. And when it has gone, when it has died out, there will be such a hue and cry, let me tell you, it'll be all "Oh, how could they?" and "If only somebody had done something." And you know what else, once these beautiful boats have gone you may as well sink the whole damn city or drain it dry and stick taxi cabs on every corner because once the gondola has disappeared we're just the same as every other tourist town on the planet.'

He put his tools down again and stood up, stretching his back and lifting his arm to wipe the sweat off his brow, catching sight of me as he did. He wore faded blue jeans and had narrow hips and broad shoulders that were tight with muscle. He wasn't bitter. I could tell that. But there was a sorrow in him, a disenchantment that resonated in me in ways I could not understand.

I thought about Marco and his cheap gondolas from Switzerland. It made sense to me now why talk of them had irked me so much. I believed in tradition too. I just hadn't known it.

'I'm sorry,' Luca said. 'Didn't mean to get on my soap box.'

I swayed slightly on my feet.

'Hey,' he cried, alarmed, leaping forward and grabbing my elbow. 'Are you all right? Connie? Is there anything I can get you?'

'A glass of water,' I croaked. 'Could I have a glass of water?' Not so much as a please or thank you.

'I'm sorry, I should have asked if you wanted anything,' he said. 'You looked kind of parched when you arrived. Here, come outside, get some fresh air. I was just about to take a break anyway.'

He led me back out to the opening of the workshop and pulled two rickety chairs into the shade then disappeared inside again, returning with a bottle of water and two glasses.

I gulped down the first glass of water he poured me like I'd been in the desert for 40 days, then drained a second, a third and a fourth, yet still felt as dry as a chip, that odd taste penetrating my cheeks with an acridness I couldn't place.

'That's quite some thirst you have there,' Luca said, leaning back in his chair. 'So, want to tell me what's happening?'

'I'm on the world's worst second honeymoon,' I found myself saying. My tongue was obviously no longer stuck to the roof of my mouth. The water had loosened it. 'My husband Tom and I have been going through a bit of a down time and so he didn't come with me. He's at home in New York. So, it's just been me here on my own in your big wet amusement park, which believe me is not ideal when you're having a second honeymoon on your own, even with gondolas.'

Luca laughed and my chill started to evaporate.

'He wants to have children, I mean that's basically the problem, I guess, when I think about it, but I'm just not sure.' So, my tongue had not only come unstuck, it was now flapping about in the breeze, blowing any which way it wanted.

'The thing is, I know it's a cliché and I know plenty women like me are probably all lamenting the same stupid thing but I don't know what I want these days. I know what everyone else wants. I know what everyone else wants me to want. Just not me. I have a great job and I love where I live, I really do "heart" New York, but everything else in the equation doesn't seem to add up.'

'What's the job?' Luca asked.

'I write restaurant reviews for the *Village Voice*,' I said, my aching chest swelling with pride the way it always did when I heard myself saying those words. 'I'm a critic.'

Luca raised his eyebrows. 'So you know about food.'

'Uh-huh,' I answered. 'I'm an eating machine.'

He laughed again and I smiled along with him. 'Sounds like you should be the happiest woman on the planet.'

'Well, work's not everything,' I surprised myself by saying, because my job meant the world to me. 'I should be thinking about having a family but I have a lousy mother so I guess I'm scared I'll end up being one myself.'

'Just about every woman I've ever met has survived a lousy mother,' Luca said matter-of-factly, staring out across the lagoon, 'and gone on to be a good one herself. Makes you think maybe all those mothers weren't so lousy in the first place.'

'Puh-leease,' I felt forced to point out. 'My mother told me she was changing the name of her dog to Connie because she wanted to try calling out that name and for once have someone pay her some attention.'

Luca laughed again and filled my glass with water. 'So,' he said. 'Marco.'

'You know him?' I asked. In truth, the fire in my loins for Marco had been doused somewhat by the man sitting next to me and I could not for the life of me tell you why. I mean all I knew about him was that he had a heart full of passion for something that he didn't believe anyone else cared about, which struck a chord with me. But he certainly didn't radiate hot sex like my gondolier.

'Oh, I know Marco all right,' said Luca. 'Where did he take you?'

'Do' Mori,' I said, 'for cichetti.'

'You have the polpette?' he wanted to know.

'Did I heck,' I told him, 'and the tuna and the sardines and Signora Marinello's fresh bread with fried shrimp and zucchini.'

'Ah,' Luca sighed appreciatively. 'Signora Marinello. And then where?'

'We went to Bentigodi in the Cannaregio and I had more sardines with pine nuts and breadcrumbs and fondi, my God, the most exquisite artichoke hearts. Have you been there?'

'Of course. And then?'

Well, I did not want to answer that question. I blushed thinking of what Marco and I had done in that plump cloud of a bed at the Hotel Gritti and skipped straight to the next meal.

'And then we went to Alla Madonna and had hard-shelled clams and sausages with bean stew and green beans cooked with peas and —'

'Chocolate torte,' Luca finished for me. 'The Madonna's chocolate torte. So good just one mouthful is enough, huh?'

I nodded.

'You are a woman who loves to eat,' Luca said softly. Marco had said the same thing but without such tenderness. Tenderness. The word bounced around in my head like a dry bean in an empty can bringing a lump to my throat. Why would the simple words of a kindly stranger make me feel like a dried-up little flower getting its first drop of rain after a long hard drought?

I nodded again and Luca moved his chair over to me, put one taut arm around my shoulders, pulling me closer to him. 'You love to eat but nothing tastes right,' he whispered, leaning into me, his lips so close to my ear I could feel his words as well as hear them. I kept nodding, tears splashing down my face onto hands that lay uselessly in my lap. What was happening to me? How did he know that?

'You love to eat but nothing tastes the way it should. Nothing explodes on your tongue. Nothing dances in your mouth.'

I was sobbing now, big-time, that great big ball of grief I didn't know I had trying to dynamite its way out of me.

'Oh, Connie,' sighed Luca and my name had never sounded so soft, so much like me. 'I know what you need,' I heard him say. 'And you're not going to find it in any trattoria or four-star restaurant or on a fancy white plate with a dozen different flavours. I've got what you want. Trust me. I've got it right here and it is so simple, Connie. So perfect. And when you taste it, everything will be all right again. Trust me. Everything will be all right.'

I turned my body toward him, lifted my face and looked straight into those green eyes, which were so clear and so true I felt I could dive into them. I believed that he knew what I wanted. That he could be trusted. That he could make everything all right. It was truly the weirdest thing. My thirst was gone, the throbbing in my temples had subsided to a distant roll of thunder instead of a deafening roar, I felt a calm the likes of which was totally unfamiliar to me descend around me, wrap me in its arms. Then Luca lifted his hand to my face and stroked my cheek so gently it was like a butterfly kiss, tracing the line of my jaw, running his fingers softly up the other side of my face, then tucking my hair behind my ear. His fingers stopped on my neck, his thumb on my cheek, his eyes on mine. It was a moment of such intimacy words are barely adequate to describe it. In that split second I felt that I knew Luca like I knew no one else in the world and that he knew me, that we were somehow entwined at some deep unconscious level that until then I hadn't known anything about. Yes, I know it sounds all crystal-gazing and kooky and he was old and I didn't feel well but I'm just trying to explain what that moment was like, trying to give you an idea of the wonder of it, the magic, the way I just sank into it, closing my eyes and letting my mind explode with possibilities. None of which included opening them again to find Marco standing there staring at us with a look as sour as vinegar — for which, let's face it, he could really not be blamed.

'Eerggh,' I said, pulling myself away from Luca's touch, nearly falling off my chair in the process. Its legs scraped cruelly along the concrete and my butt caught the edge of the seat, sending a shooting pain up my spine.

'I see you've met someone else, Constanzia,' Marco said. 'Although perhaps "met" isn't quite the right word.'

'Plagh, plagh.' My tongue was stuck to the roof of my mouth again. My head was spinning. I felt so hot I thought I would explode. The magic was gone. My back was killing me.

'So has he been giving you the old sob story about no one wanting to build gondolas any more? About the end of the era?' His voice was snide and cold. He meant to be cruel but I looked at Luca and could see that he was not hurt, not defiant, not embarrassed, just full of that same disenchantment I had seen in him earlier.

'I think I —' I didn't know what I thought. I was dizzy and hot and my back hurt, my chest hurt.

'Marco,' Luca said softly. 'What do you want with her? Leave her alone.'

There was a loud buzzing in my ears. I wasn't hearing properly.

'What do you know?' Marco asked, his voice so full of rage that even in my feverish state it was easy to recognise. 'You don't know anything.'

'I don't need to know anything, Marco. That's the difference between you and me.' Luca's voice was calm and smooth. He shared none of Marco's ire.

'Oh, here we go,' my gondolier spat. 'Let me guess — the love-or-money speech? Well you can fuck off because I have heard it all before and it still sounds like bullshit to me.'

I felt so weak I could barely keep my eyes open, yet my heart was hammering in my chest. What the hell were they talking about?

'Do the right thing, Marco,' Luca said softly. 'Please. Do the right thing.'

'I can't,' I interrupted them, even though the words didn't sound quite right. 'It doesn't.'

'Just look at her,' Luca said with that extraordinary tenderness. 'Have you ever stopped to think about her? Who she is? If she's ever been truly loved? Who out there she might mean the world to?'

His words broke my heart. Just broke it. They really did. Because I didn't know the answers to his questions myself. I didn't know if I had ever been truly loved, if there was anyone out there to whom I meant the world. And it was too tragic to contemplate.

'You don't know shit, Dad,' Marco said.

'I know you like playing God, son,' Luca replied levelly. 'But you're not.'

The realisation descended on me like a Roadrunner one-ton brick. Dad? Son? What the heck was going on? I had slept with Marco, was obsessed with Marco, but had just shared something unbelievably intimate with his *father*? I wasn't sure how bad a sin that added up to but I was certain I would rot in hell for it, my mother would make sure of it. I would burn in the flames of eternity. I would roast, I would cook, I would char. I was already so hot I thought I knew what it felt like.

'You're a stupid old man, stuck in the past, refusing to move forward with the times,' Marco spat.

'I'm 51, you little shit,' Luca replied calmly. 'And I choose to stick with what I believe in, which is what your grandfather and your great-grandfather before you believed in. It took a while for me to work it out, so you should learn from my mistakes. There are two types of people in this town, Marco, in this world. There are the ones who do it for love and the ones who do it for money.'

'Oh,' Marco snarled, 'here we go. And I suppose you're going to tell me you're doing *her* for love?'

Luca jumped to his feet. I could tell that he was not a violent man but that he wanted to give Marco — his son! — a decent pop. I knew I should stand up and get between them, that it was somehow my fault and I should stop whatever was happening. But my bones were so heavy, my body would not obey instruction. Luca stood, the veins bulging in his arms, his fists clenched at his sides, energy radiating from him. He was not as tall as Marco but there were similarities, I should have seen them earlier.

'I say,' I heard a familiar voice. 'What on earth is going on here?' It was Ty Wheatley again. He'd appeared out of nowhere and stood, hands on hips, surveying the scene. The pain in my chest was getting worse, I thought perhaps I was starting to choke, my breath was getting swallowed short of my lungs. It was terrifying.

'You know,' I started to say again, but I felt icy fingers around my throat, that splitting pain in my sternum, pressure from my blood to get more oxygen.

'What's she saying?' I heard a voice that made my starved blood run cold. 'Can't you tell me what she's saying? Did she call for her father? I think she called for her father.'

Darkness was clawing at the edge of my eyes again but I turned out to the lagoon, that big bobbly blue blanket of sea, the brilliant sunshine all but blinding me. There was no mistaking that voice. 'What's she saying?' I heard it again. And unlike the discombobulated voice I had heard earlier, this one had an image to go with it.

'I'm warning you, Mary-Constance,' my mother was looming over me, her eyes dark and unreadable. 'Don't do this to me,

Mary-Constance. Oh, what am I saying? Of course she's going to do it. She always does it.'

I looked around for Luca, I wanted to find his hand, I needed his calm and his strength, but he had disappeared into a vast whiteness that roared around me in a deafening growl.

I turned my head the other way and Signora Marinello appeared behind my mother.

'Give her time,' Signora Marinello said. 'She need time.'

My mind raced, flicking back to that airplane, to Ashlee, the water-taxi driver, the mushroom-seller in the Pucci shirt, cool sexy Marco, the waitress at Bentigodi, Fleur in a gondola, Luca — the man who looked at me the first time and saw all there was to see — and Ty.

Oh my God, I thought, as I tried to breathe but no air could get in. I gasped in terror, thinking this must be what it's like to drown, to suffocate, to die, to leave everyone behind forever.

'Breathe,' I heard Signora Marinello urge. 'For goodness' sake! Breathe, Connie, breathe.'

And with a shudder that jerked every bone in my body, I breathed.

Sound exploded in my ears, my eyes flew open. A vast bright whiteness still surrounded me, a twisted collection of shiny metal reflected painfully in my face, the hisses and whirrs of unfamiliar machines echoed around my head like white noise.

It did not seem possible. Truly. Not possible. But a terrifying comprehension ran through my blood like hot chocolate in the snow.

I was not in Venice on a failed second honeymoon.

I was not sitting in the shadows on the Giudecca being fought over by the handsome Italian I had slept with and his disenchanted father whose fingers I could still feel on my face.

I was nowhere near any of that.

I was in a hospital room. And I was not a visitor.

Six

Well, don't look at me — I was as surprised as you are. I mean, one minute I am having the time of my life in the most romantic city in the world and the next I am lying in a strange single bed — attached to machines, for crying out loud — my mother's angry voice buzzing in my ears and my mind unable to capture anything more than a fragment of a thought.

'I'm not there, am I?' I can remember asking whoever was in the room. But my voice was like a wisp of smoke; as it spread it got thinner and thinner until it just disintegrated into nothingness.

I wasn't alone, I knew that much, and I thought that perhaps Signora Marinello was with me, leastways I had an image — I wasn't sure how current — of her bending over me, that huge bosom bursting out of a nurse's uniform, her hair springing loose from its bun, a light forming a halo behind her head. An angel. But then again how could that be? Signora Marinello was baking bread and frying squid and filling old men's glasses with pinot bianco in a back-street bar in Venice. For a split second I imagined I could smell sizzling garlic and black pepper, drank in the flavour of that nutty olive oil, tasted the dry fruity wine at the back of my throat. But then the overwhelming presence of hospital antiseptic chased away the memory of anything even slightly pleasant, leaving me gagging, choking, gasping for air.

And as for my mother, what was she doing here? What was she doing anywhere? She had been at the squero, I thought hazily, yet I was certain she had also been there in the hospital, sitting on a bed — my bed, I supposed — her lips so pursed they looked ruffled, her eyes dark and accusing.

Well, I say I was certain she had been there but I wasn't really. I wasn't certain of anything. I couldn't remember, truly remember, her presence; rather I had an impression of having seen it, her sitting there, the white lights, the loud noises, everything flashing like a murder scene in *CSI*. It was as though I were watching a video of my own life with some crazy person working the remote control.

I thought fleetingly of Marco then, saw flashes of my naked rump riding him in the parked-up gondola, his hands on my rib cage, his flawless features lost in ecstasy. Then a picture of Tom flashed onto the screen of my mind, him crunching on garlic seeds free for the taking at the Greenmarket, his eyes dancing with delight, my heart bursting with the simplicity of being with him. Even in my clearly incapacitated state I felt a healthy dose of good old-fashioned Catholic guilt. What the hell had gotten into me? How could I have done that to Tom? How would I ever face him? I didn't want to. The shame made me squirm.

Then the crazy person inside my head fast-forwarded to a moving collage of Ty Wheatley and my mom and the grandfathers from the Giudecca sort of swirling around me, all melded into one and chattering at the same time, clamouring for attention. I tried to shake my head to rid myself of them — it was like being kidnapped on the inside by Casper (the friendly ghost) and his best friend Sybil (of the many personalities).

'She need rest,' I heard Signora Marinello say. 'All she need now is rest.'

I clung to the word like a rat to a drainpipe. Rest sounded good. Safe. If it was dark and I was asleep then I knew where I was and what was happening. Just the possibility of that filled me with warmth and something approaching relief. I remembered the feel of Luca's words on my skin and I longed for the sensation that had overwhelmed me as I looked into his eyes. Longed for it. Then I thought of Tom again and my disgrace chased Luca away.

'Ooh, look, she's crying,' I heard an unfamiliar voice say. She sounded sort of freaked out, whoever she was. I tried to open my eyes but realised that they were already open, I just couldn't see properly. I didn't remember the world changing from dark to light but it had, although the whiteness of the room had bleached out all the details. Forms moved around, exaggeratedly tall and grey and thin, like aliens in a science fiction movie.

'Crying?' I repeated, although I'm not sure the words came out as I meant them. I didn't mean to be crying. I didn't feel any tears. I reached up to wipe my cheeks but to my anguish my arms stayed flat on the bed on either side of my body, ignoring my instructions for them to move. Was I awake? My God, was I even alive?

'Her mouth moved!' the same freaked-out voice cried out. 'Nurse! Nurse! Her mouth moved.'

I can't tell you the despair I felt then. If I thought I'd ever felt it before I was wrong. I felt as insignificant as a speck of dust. I had no control over anything. I wasn't in charge of when I slept or woke or what I heard or saw or felt or thought or anything. I just lay there — but I wasn't even sure if I was doing that. Little snatches of sight and sound kept coming and going but I couldn't work out how often they were occurring or how long they lasted. Sometimes I knew I was awake and could identify what was happening, sometimes I knew I was dreaming — Luca was there, talking to me in soft whispers or Tom was sweating over the grill at Il Secondo. Marco's legs were entwined in mine, Ty was showing me his new Prada shoes. I knew that time was passing but I had no idea at what rate; it came and went in surges that seemed like seconds but could have been hours or even days. You would think I might have put two and two together and worked out there was something wrong with me but I didn't. My twos were all in separate rooms not even knowing about addition, let alone making fours. All I knew was that I couldn't think straight and I couldn't move and I didn't seem to be able to communicate with anyone. I didn't know what was happening or what had happened or what was going to happen. I was floating on never-ending clouds, unable to put my feet on the ground, unable to fly, unable to catch anything more than a morsel of comprehension at a time.

And I was tired in a way I had never been tired before. Exhaustion pressed down on me like a slowly descending ceiling, dark and heavy, pushing me through the bed and towards the centre of the earth, deep and suffocating. No longer lured by the safety of such emptiness, I battled to stay awake, to learn more, to understand what was going on. Of course, as soon as I relaxed and let down my guard, unconsciousness seeped into my bones and claimed me; the next thing I knew I was waking up again, angry at having drifted off, desperate to know what might have happened had I been there to see it.

I don't know how long this went on for but when I think about it now I see a sort of Morse code in my mind — smooth dashes of unconsciousness punctuated by staccato dots of being awake. Time didn't mean what it used to: seconds and minutes and hours were like words in a foreign language, I had lost the concept. I was awake or not in no particular order and my dreams seemed more life-like than my reality. But after a while it seemed that the periods of sleep were shortening and emerging from them was less of a struggle. Descending back into sleep again was also more of a smooth transition. My Morse code had turned into a smooth regular wave pattern. Voices came and went in whole sentences. People moved around me acting out sequences I could follow. I felt things on my skin, my scalp, in my heart. I sensed change. Progress, of sorts.

And then, one instant, one point in time that I couldn't quite pin down, that same freaked-out voice I had heard earlier interrupted a dream where I was calling for Tom, begging him to take me home, to make me potato gnocchi.

'She's making a noise!' the voice squawked. 'Nurse! She's making a noise!'

I tested my eyes to see if they were open. They were. This was good. I had meant for them to be open and they had obliged. I had made that happen. I was definitely awake. I felt my stomach muscles unclench slightly, the panic I had grown used to subside. So, the room was still a buzzing white blur, but it was a buzzing white blur that I recognised. My surroundings were familiar. This was where I was now. I knew that. As I looked around the room I realised that the general white blur was in fact separating into different shades of grey; the edges of the darker bits were becoming sharper, the blotches taking on real shapes. I could sense a window, a stout form (Signora Marinello?) shuffling in front of it, and another trim shape, clearly feminine, much closer, unmistakably leaning in towards me.

'Emsie,' the feminine shape said in the freaked-out voice, very close to my ear. 'Emsie, can you hear me?'

Jesus, I thought, whatever had happened had turned me into a whole other person. Emsie? My stomach clenched again, panic returned. How was I going to sort out that mix-up when the power of speech was beyond me? How was I going to get these strangers to know who I really was? Maybe I had amnesia. But then again I knew who I was, I was Connie Farrell, wife albeit disgruntled of Tom, daughter of Estelle and Patrick, sister of space cadet Emmet, restaurant reviewer, friend, New Yorker, human.

Tom. His face snapped into focus, clear as a bell, and for a moment I thought he was in the room with me and my heart swelled with hope. Tom would help straighten out this whole hospital mess, I thought. And then we could just get over our marital hiccup and get on with our lives and I would never go anywhere without him or sleep with drop-dead gorgeous strangers again.

'Emsie?' The voice said.

'Who the hell is Emsie?' I said. I knew I had said it yet no noise came out. I could feel my lips moving, and I was sure they were moving the way I wanted them to, but no air blew past my vocal cords, no sound permeated the room.

The feminine shape's face peered straight into mine and before my eyes it morphed from a fuzzy blur with dark slits for eyes and a gash of pink for a mouth into a collection of crisp lines and muted colours. The face was extremely well made-up but its features were harsh and pointy and would have been ugly on a person without such flair for self-improvement. The hair was a perfectly coiffed blonde bob, razor-sharp.

'Emsie,' the voice said. The face's eyes stretched wide open and its chin got longer, like a witch. 'You've come back. Nurse!' Her head twisted around yet her hair seemed to stay looking straight at me, like a helmet. 'She's back!'

I closed my eyes and drifted away again. I wasn't ready to take up the challenge of not being Emsie. Just thinking about that creature's hair had plum tuckered me out. But at some level I knew there was cause for celebration. I had woken up, opened my eyes, known where I was, and understood what was happening. That was the way things should be. A layer of fear was removed and discarded. It felt good.

When I opened my eyes again, it was Signora Marinello's kind round face — no nasty angles there — peering into mine.

'Constanzia,' she said and I tell you, I was so thrilled not to be Emsie I would have wept had I been able to work out how to.

'Constanzia,' Signora Marinello repeated gently, speaking slowly, watching my eyes follow her lips. 'You are in the hospital. You hurt your head. You been in a coma, Constanzia. Understand?'

I let her words sink right into me. I knew by the look in her eyes they were significant but the meaning of them at that time escaped me, rolled off me like water off an oil patch.

'You hurt your head.'

I rolled this sentence over in my mind. Someone had hurt their head. Okay, I had that. I knew what that meant. It was bad.

'You been in a coma.'

A coma. I thought of Karen Ann Quinlan, the only person I could think of attached to the word. She had died, hadn't she? After years of being curled up and unconscious? So this person with the hurt head had been in a coma. I guessed that was pretty bad too.

'Understand?'

I knew for a fact I did not understand. I couldn't work out how this information she was imparting was connected to me. My eyes remained fixed on her face, searching her benevolent expression for clues.

'You have two surgeries on your brain,' she said. 'You lucky to be alive.'

'You have two surgeries on your brain.'

Something about that notion gripped my heart with an icy cold claw and squeezed it. I could hear it beating in my ears, felt the hot flush of shock in my cheeks. 'You have two surgeries on your brain. You hurt your head. You been in a coma. You have two surgeries on your brain.' Her words were hurling themselves at me like a battering ram.

'You lucky to be alive.'

'You.'

Oh my God. She was talking about *me*.

I had hurt my head? I had been in a coma? I was lucky to be alive?

She saw the panic in my eyes, the horror of comprehension, and her face crumpled like cocoa-coloured satin.

'Is all right,' she hushed me. 'Ssshhhh.'

Of course when I thought about it, it made perfect sense. There was something wrong with my *brain*. That was why I couldn't think straight, why I couldn't tell real from imagined or now from then. But what did it mean? How long would I be like this? How long would it last, this awful cloudy soup in my head? How long would I be trapped inside this foreign personality? Questions jangled inside me, fighting for attention, leaving me struggling to separate one from the other.

'But where are we?' I eventually managed, although again my lips formed only useless soundless words, puffing vacant queries into the room. Signora Marinello placed a cool hand on my cheek and the comfort was such I had to use all my willpower to resist the urge to drift off to never land again. I was hanging on to a thread of understanding, within reach of getting somewhere, of making the missing connection.

'No talking, Constanzia,' Signora Marinello said soothingly. 'We put tracheotomy in your throat, help you breathe. Hook you up to ventilating machine.'

I was suddenly aware of the suck and hiss of a mechanical lung reverberating somewhere behind me. I lifted an arm and, to my great joy, it didn't stay lying flaccidly on the bed at my side, it did what I told it to. I brought my hand to my throat where my fingers clumsily butted into a cold hard plastic pipe sticking out of my skin. My eyes widened. This was serious stuff. I had pipes sticking out of me. I had a machine doing my breathing.

'Okay, Constanzia,' Signora Marinello told me, calming my panic. 'It come out soon. Only helping you a little bit now. You get better. Need rest.' Her fingers stroked my cheek and although my heart was bursting with uncertainty, I just soaked up her touch and slithered off into the murky dark whirlpool my mind had become.

When I woke up again it was daytime and I knew it was daytime so I guessed that was a step in the right direction. It felt good to know something, comforting. I winced, though, when I thought about what else I knew, when I remembered that the poor wretch who had hurt their head and been in a coma was me. I had hurt my head, I accepted that. Deep down I somehow knew it to be true even though I didn't even have as much as a headache, not like the one I'd ended up with on the Giudecca. It certainly explained the mulligatawny in my head. But the coma? Well, I had trouble with that. I mean I believed

Signora Marinello, of course I did; she had no reason to lie to me yet it was a big mental adjustment to take someone's word on something so intangible. I didn't know what a coma meant. I had buffeted the word around so much in my head it had become meaningless. And something else nagged at me constantly, namely, my whereabouts. I still wasn't sure if we were in New York or Venice.

'Did it happen when I fell on the bridge?' I asked.

'How many times do we have to tell you, Emsie?' the blonde bobbed woman asked in a voice decorated with forced brightness. Had she been there all along? I couldn't remember how long I had been awake. 'It was by the Boat House.'

Did she mean Luca's workshop? How could I have hurt my head there, I wondered? I remembered feeling dizzy and faint but I couldn't remember anything dropping on me or banging into me, or anything but Luca and Marco, anger and disillusionment.

'What day is it? What year is it? Do you know where you are?' A different strange voice was suddenly firing questions at me, questions I couldn't answer.

What day was it? I panicked, my mind a blank slate, but I took a deep breath and willed myself to take it slowly, start with the first question, not worry too much that I didn't have a clue about the rest. I could do this, I told myself silently. I could work it out methodically. I had gone to Venice on Sunday, stayed there two nights, or was it two with the time difference? Or did the time difference matter? It would have helped to know which side of the Atlantic I was on but I pushed that aside. Two days, that made it Tuesday, although I had hurt my head and been in a coma. How long did comas last for?

'It's today,' I answered, 'the day after yesterday.' And I heard a snort that could only have come from a nostril belonging to my mother.

'Always, she's got an answer.' My mother, sure enough, was standing at the end of the bed, looking not at all blurry. She had on an orange sweatshirt I'd never seen before and a pair of slim brown pants. She looked small and rumpled and almost unfamiliar. 'She's been like it ever since she could talk. You know, the first time.'

'She need rest,' Signora Marinello said and I heard the clip-clop of my mother's tiny heels across the linoleum of my hospital room floor. 'She no good for your head,' Signora Marinello whispered into my ear. 'She no good for anyone's head.'

Two things, both good, occurred to me very clearly then. One was that it obviously wasn't just me my mother drove bananas, and the other was that I had said something and actually been heard. And with that thought, the fuzzy pieces of the jigsaw puzzle I had been trying to fit together in my mind sharpened up and started gravitating towards their rightful places. I drifted off again, happy in the knowledge that something was coming together, that understanding was close at hand, that things were getting better.

I dreamed of Venice, but I knew it was a dream, everything was sinister and black, not the magical mother-of-pearl colours that the city radiated in real life. I ran through the alleys calling out for Fleur and Marco, Ty Wheatley's spiffy shoes pattering irritatingly on the cobbles behind me, my mother turning into a hideous gargoyle at every turn, old men with strollers coming at me with evil eyes, gondoliers gathering on street corners, their cruel laughter echoing between dripping walls that leaned in too closely for me to get through.

It was a relief to wake up and while I wouldn't go so far as to say I was clear-headed, I definitely had a level of knowledge, of comprehension that I hadn't had the day before, or whenever it was I had last been thinking.

I took stock. I was still lying down in what I thought was the same bed but the room seemed quieter than other times I'd been awake. I thought perhaps there were not as many machines surrounding me. I put my hand to my throat and there was no tracheotomy, just a bandage that, when poked, produced enough pain to make me think there was a hole in my skin underneath it.

Signora Marinello hove into view, her body straining to get out of its uniform, her face beaming with its usual mixture of joy and concern.

'Good morning, my love,' she said, and replaced my pillow. I felt her lift my head, then lay it gently back down again. I heard the crunch of the crisp hospital pillowcase. It all seemed very life-like. Very recognisable.

'Where am I?' I asked her.

'Constanzia, you are in hospital. You have hurt your —'

'Yes,' I interrupted even though it took longer to say than it should have. 'I've hurt my head. I've been in a coma. I know that. But am I —' I lost the thread but picked it up again, 'am I in Venice?' My tongue felt stiff and unfamiliar, my voice was a dull flat monotone.

Signora Marinello stroked my arm, her face full of concern. 'You in St Vincent's Hospital in New York, Constanzia. You been here nearly three weeks. You fall and hit your head, my love, hurt your brain, but she is getting better now.' Her hand moved up to my forehead, which I hadn't realised was burning until the dry coolness of her palm soothed it.

Three weeks? I should have been surprised, horrified, scared witless, but then again I had known that time had not been passing in the usual fashion. Still, three weeks. I would be in deep shit at work. Had I had any reviews up my sleeve before my vacation? I couldn't quite remember.

'I fell?' I asked Signora Marinello. There were so many questions to ask and I couldn't quite sort out the right order. 'After I saw you at Do' Mori? It must have happened on the Giudecca. At the boatyard. I'm not sure. I don't remember.'

My words weren't coming out as crisply as I intended. They were mashed together: bland, with no inflection nor change of tone.

She shushed me and smoothed the sheets over my chest. 'Not to worry, Constanzia. Is normal. Not to worry about nothing. You been full of drugs to help your brain, stop her from swelling. She coming down in size now. Not pressing on your skull no more. Time to wake up but slowly.'

'I've been asleep for three weeks?' I was still trying to grasp the

103

concept but it kept slipping away. I knew things had been weird for a while, but how long was a while? That long?

'Oh, no, you been awake for long time,' she said cheerfully. 'You just don't know it. You in a coma five, six days, then we start to wake you up, every day a little bit more but not every day you remember. Same with everybody. Your brain, she is just working a little bit at a time. Not to worry, Constanzia. Is normal.'

'What day is it today?' I asked her.

'Is Wednesday,' she replied.

'Wednesday,' I repeated, 'Wednesday.' I looked at the clock on the wall opposite my bed. It was 10 minutes past two. It was 10 minutes past two on Wednesday. Signora Marinello took a chart from the end of the bed and started marking things down on it. I looked around me. It was just like *ER* only I had my own room. A machine that gave the impression it'd flat-line as soon as look at me hummed to my left, wires sprouting out of it and going somewhere behind me. I was aware suddenly of a scratchiness between my thighs and up deep inside me, a catheter I supposed. I didn't even want to think about the other business.

I had a horrible tube going up inside my nose and down my throat, a drip attached to my arm and something clipped to one finger. My body felt foreign. I licked my lips, they were dry and chapped. Swallowing felt alien.

'Is it still Wednesday?' I asked. Signora Marinello laughed and I looked at the clock. It was 13 minutes past two.

'Yes,' she said. 'Is still Wednesday. You looking very good today, Constanzia. You got some colour back. I think is all downhill from here.' She followed my gaze to the clock. 'Your best friend come soon, I think. She always come about now.'

'Fleur?' My heart thumped with happiness, but Signora shook her head.

'No, not Fleur,' she said. 'I don't know Fleur. No, this best friend is Paris. You know, fancy manager lady.'

My brain resisted this piece of information, or jumbled it somehow. Mention of Paris threw me off track but before I could ask for clarification, the blonde bobbed woman who'd woken me up with her freaked-out voice strode in the door, her witchy-poo features splitting into a grin as we made eye contact.

'Darling!' she cried and sashayed her way to the bed, leaning in to nearly kiss me on each cheek with perfectly glossed lips. 'Emsie, you look fabulous. Doesn't she look fabulous, Mrs um, I'm sorry, I've forgotten your name.'

'Marinello,' I said but I couldn't tell if the bob had heard me.

'And it's about time, too,' she prattled on. 'You've had us worried half to death, Emsie, with this whole brain-swelling thing. Why, we thought we'd have to turn the machines off for a while there, didn't we, erm, Mrs . . . Anyway not good, darling. Must do better!'

Why was this strange woman here but my husband nowhere to be seen? I was lost. I looked helplessly at Signora Marinello but she was busying herself with the contents of a huge garbage bag, her generous mouth, I couldn't help but notice, considerably more pinched than usual.

'Are you allowed to eat yet?' The bob asked me. 'Is she allowed to eat yet?' She turned to Signora Marinello. 'Don't want that magical palate of yours to waste away to nothing now, do we?'

Food! I just about slipped back into a coma at the thought. Was it possible that eating had not crossed my mind in three whole weeks? Surely not. I usually had trouble going three minutes without planning a meal. But I supposed being unconscious must have knocked the edge off my appetite. '*Am* I allowed to eat?' I asked Signora Marinello.

'Soon, Constanzia,' she said. 'Time we got some meat on those bones. Meanwhile we feed you through naso-gastric tube.'

'Please.' The bob held a perfectly manicured hand up in front of her face to ward off this disgusting detail.

I lifted one hand to my nose and started to pull on the tube, but

Signora Marinello hissed at me to stop.

The bob looked fit to puke. 'Don't,' she chastised me. 'It's revolting.'

'Who are you?' I asked her. I really wanted to know and I had been polite long enough but she simply laughed just the sort of tinkly rich woman's laugh that I would have expected her to have and said: 'It's me, Paris!'

I opened my mouth to tell her to get her skinny little butt off my bed and out of my room but Signora Marinello beat me to it.

'I tell you before, the best thing for Connie's brain now is rest, Ms Tait. Perhaps you come back tomorrow, hm?'

Paris, since that's whom she claimed to be, stood up and straightened her skirt, which could well have been Chanel. I had never seen someone so impeccably groomed. It was vaguely terrifying. She picked up a pale pink pocketbook that matched exactly the pale pink of her suit, her shoes, her nail polish, and her lips.

'Don't worry, darling,' she breathed as she leaned in to nearly kiss me again. 'We'll get you out of here soon enough. Ciao!'

And with that, she was gone.

I opened my mouth to have a big long enthusiastic bitch about her, whoever she was, but something in the way Signora Marinello looked at me made me shut it again. She glanced furtively over her shoulder and moved in close to the bed.

'You a nice girl,' Signora Marinello said quickly. 'I can tell from when you first come in, you a nice girl.'

I nodded. I thought I even remembered her saying that.

'And you going to survive, you know, Constanzia? You going to live to be 90. That's one good brain you got there.' She took my hand. 'That brain get plenty more life in her yet. But is no going to be easy. You have to be strong. You have to be strong from now on. For yourself. You understand me?'

I wasn't sure that I did, but I squeezed her hand back nonetheless.

'I see a lot of families and friends, Constanzia, standing next to beds just like this one.' She paused and looked dolefully around the room. 'But I have to tell you, I seen none so cuckoo as yours.'

At first I thought I must have misheard her but at that moment my mother arrived struggling under the weight of a six-feet wide flower arrangement that spelled out GRANDAD.

'Twelve dollars from the undertaker down the road,' she told Signora Marinello without so much as looking at me. 'Apparently, he wasn't dead after all. And these colours! Who could resist?'

The point my nurse had just made thus perfectly illustrated, we acknowledged it with a silent glance.

And then I turned to my mother. 'Mom,' I said. 'It's me.'

'Well, of course it is,' my mother answered, irritably. 'Who else would it be?'

Seven

Other people might have suspected they were still in cloud cuckooland — a dark-eyed midget bearing someone else's funeral wreath coming in and showering their broken mind and body with pinched-lip disapproval — but for me, it was confirmation that I was in fact alive and things were returning to normal.

'I take my break now,' Signora Marinello said. 'You tell Lois next door if you need anything.' She gave me a look that I assumed referred to her 'be strong' lecture and her white shoes squeaked their way across the linoleum, out the door and into the hallway.

'So, you've decided to join us for real,' my mother said, pulling a chair closer and dragging a lurid collection of knitting yarn out of her bag. 'It's about time.'

'I'm still not 100 per cent sure what is for real,' I said, although I was definitely starting to get the picture. 'If you know what I mean.'

'I've never known what you mean,' she said, her needles clacking. 'Your father's in a terrible state. He couldn't even come back to the hospital after the first time when your face was all puffed up and those staples were sticking out of your head. He couldn't eat for a week. I made him my special coq au vin and everything. Not one single bite.'

I thanked God, just briefly, for only being able to ingest nutrition through a pipe in my nose. Mom's coq au vin was made with turkey instead of coq and grapefruit juice instead of vin. It was truly, truly vile. Still, for Pop to have been rendered unable to stomach it? Well, I had seen him dive into the hideous mess on at least half-a-dozen prior occasions so he must have been seriously out of whack to risk offending her by refusing it.

'I'm sorry, Mom,' I said and I was too. Winding up in a coma was hardly likely to prove a step forward in our troubled mother–daughter relationship.

'Oh, you're always sorry, Mary-Constance,' she replied.

She was right, I was always sorry — she demanded it of me. And half the time I didn't even know what I was sorry for. Now these may seem kind of depressing thoughts to be having, but the good news was I felt very clear about them. There was no pea-souper clouding my head as far as Mom was concerned and for that, if nothing else, I was thankful.

'As for Emmet,' she said, caressing the name of her son with a special velvety tone, 'well, if there was anything your brother could have done for you, he would have. In an instant, Mary-Constance. Without a moment's hesitation. Not a one.'

I closed my eyes. I knew what this was about too. I did know what I was supposed to be sorry for. I had been supposed to be sorry for it for quite some time — approximately a third of my life, in fact. Clearly, there was nothing wrong with my memory and I felt happy at least in that knowledge. I just couldn't believe that our first real conversation after my being in a coma was going to refer to this piece of ancient history that my mother wore around her neck like a barbed-wire garrotte.

Some years before, when I was about 21, my idiot brother Emmet, who really can be a class-A peckerhead, got it into his noodle that he was dying of kidney disease and in need of an organ transplant. Why my mother got sucked into this drama without, oh, I don't know, talking to a *doctor*, for example, I'll never understand but she took it hard. Like most only sons, he was the apple of her eye. She'd waited less than three months after giving birth to me to fall pregnant again, this time bearing a boy, a real boy, a real spoiled boy. She didn't spot his rotten core at all even though the rest of the human race could smell it a mile off.

'I'm too old,' she told me, her voice all gluey with crying, when she broke the news about his kidney over the phone. 'And your father vomits at the sight of blood. We've talked it over and decided it has to be you, Mary-Constance,' she said. 'It just has to be you.'

'It has to be me what?' I asked, not following her. Emmet had created enough storms in enough teacups throughout our childhood and early adulthood for me to know that this too would blow over and most likely be drug-related like all his other dramas. My role had always been to placate the parents and take the heat while Emmet got his shit together. It was not a role I had chosen, but it was the sisterly thing to do. It kept the peace and in our family peace was a precious commodity: you paid whatever the price.

'It has to be you that gives him a kidney of course,' my mother said impatiently. 'Your best one, too. Don't you go fobbing him off with anything shrunken or lop-sided.'

I had been stunned. She could stun me like nobody else on the planet, that woman. Did I even have a spare kidney to give, I wondered? I did a quick check of things I had learned in biology class. One heart, one liver, two lungs, one large-capacity stomach, yup, two kidneys. But did I really want to give a body part, even if it was a spare, to a lame brain who lived on cheap pharmaceuticals and McDonald's?

I had only just ever-so-fleetingly touched on this thought when I heard a sharp intake of breath from my mother on the other end of the telephone line. She is the only person I know who can inhale with venom.

'Mary-Constance,' she said, her tears dried and her voice shrivelled with whatever it was I always brought out in her, 'to think that I raised you to do unto others as you would have them do unto you. Where did I go so wrong? What did I do to deserve it? Why, Mary-Constance, just tell me, why?'

I was used to these theatrics. She had employed them my whole life and I had learned to simply sidestep her and let it play out the way she wanted it to. 'What exactly have I done, Mom?'

'You know exactly what you've done and you will have to live with it for the rest of your life, Mary-Constance. May God — and I mean this, I really do even though many others would not show such charity — may God have mercy on your soul.'

At times like that I seriously wondered if my mother's mental health was as it should be. I had tried to talk to my father about it once, about that kind of low-level hysteria she practised around the clock, but he had waved me off, telling me she was grand, that she just liked to jazz things up a bit.

'Mom,' I sighed. 'I didn't do anything. I was just thinking about Emmet's kidneys.'

'That wasn't thinking,' she said. And I could tell the clincher was waiting around the corner, idling, about to throttle off and run me down, then back up over me again, finish the job. 'That was hesitating,' she hissed. 'You *hesitated*. Over a life-and-death matter, you hesitated. My only son. Your own flesh and blood. Well, may God forgive you, Mary-Constance. May He in His infinite wisdom forgive you.' And then, dial tone.

Extraordinary. But that was not the end of it. Oh no, not by a long stretch. Even though later that same day it became clear that Emmet's life-threatening condition was no more than severe constipation brought on by Percodan abuse, my mother never forgave me. That alleged hesitation had haunted me for well over a decade and haunted me still, lying there in that hospital bed, my brain recently all swelled up and my head apparently held together by unsightly staples.

'If Emmet offers to donate me his brain,' I told my mother, 'please tell him I said thank you but no.'

111

Traditionally, flippancy had been an ill-considered weapon in the tango we tripped but the quip was out of my mouth before I had even thought to wrangle it.

Mom stopped her knitting and shot me her level-one disappointment look. 'So,' she said, 'you came back mean. They told me some came back mean and I have to tell you Mary-Constance it made my blood run cold because I knew that if mean was an option, you would take it.' She rustled in her knitting bag and pulled out a little medal on a blue ribbon, the sort of thing the nuns give you on their namesakes' feast days. 'By the way, you should be wearing this,' she said, pinning it on my gown.

I took a look. It was St Jude, the patron saint of lost causes.

I sank back on my pillows, closed my eyes and let sleep lure me out of her clutches. It was blissful.

I drifted in and out of this delightful state until the next morning, when I woke up properly and thought it might be Thursday — and I was right. Signora Marinello seemed just as pleased as I was at this minor triumph, beaming at me as though I had just solved the world's most complicated mathematical equation.

'I tell you,' she said, 'is all downhill from now. Trust me.' Her eyes narrowed. 'By the way, I take the nasty saint man off your chest and put him in the bathroom. He no good. Me, I like Honorius, patron saint of pastry-makers. You heard of him? You like pie, Constanzia? Anyway, because you do so well, I wash your hair.'

Until she said that it hadn't occurred to me to wonder what a fright I must look. My hands moved slowly up to my head. I don't know what shocked me most, the collection of bumps and ridges on either side of a fat slice above my right temple, or my hair.

'How did this happen?' I asked Signora Marinello, dazed.

'You fall and hit your head,' she said. 'Your brain is damaged but your surgeon cut open that part of your head and remove a blood clot. Is called a craniotomy. You very lucky, Constanzia, to have a good surgeon. The best.'

Actually, I hadn't been talking about the scar. I had been talking about my hair.

'No, how did *this* happen?' I asked her, pulling on what was left of my tresses. My hair had been shoulder-blade length since I was 12 years old and unless I blow-dried it for half an hour it tended to waviness. But it now felt short. And straight.

'No, we shave for your surgery over this side,' she ran her fingers gently over the bumpy scar, 'but otherwise hairstyle not included in the price!'

A sherbet of dread was fizzing in my brain like a fuse about to blow, nibbling at the corners of my mind. Something was wrong. I brought my hands back down from my head and held them out in front of me, turning them over, watching the knob of my wrists, the bones of my knuckles, the pale translucent skin of my forearms. They were attached to me, I knew they were, I was making them do things, but they did not look like my arms. They looked like someone else's. I clawed, suddenly fearful, at my throat, my fingers sliding over the ugly tracheotomy scar I was expecting and moving on to my collar bones where they moved like a piano player over sharp angles that stuck out between square unfamiliar shoulders. I ran my hands down my torso, rippling over ribs that protruded rudely beneath the skin and then fumbled under my hospital gown to feel my hipbones. My hipbones? They jutted out like the Swiss Alps. I slid my hands across the smooth skin between them as it fell from the points of the bones. From the points of the bones. My belly was concave. Positively concave.

There were no two ways about it. I was thin.

I grappled underneath myself to feel my butt. I just didn't recognise it. It had no give, no bounce, no softness; it was hard and small. I felt my thighs. They were bony. Really. Bony. Even on the inside. I mean who had bony inner thighs? No one, that's who. Certainly no one who could eat a hot-dog from a pushcart followed by a triple-scoop ice cream followed by two slices of clam pie — all within the space of an hour.

My circuitry was flipping out. I could almost hear the crackle and zzzzz of things going haywire in my head. I had been beginning to understand my predicament, get a grip on it, but now I was completely thrown. The me I knew myself to be did not have a tight butt and pointy hipbones. I had spent my whole life lamenting the absence of those very things. So, perhaps I wasn't Connie after all. Perhaps I was this mysterious Emsie who the frightening Paris had mistaken me for.

'How much do I weigh?' I asked Signora Marinello, who was washing my boyish hairdo, a plastic sheet under my head, her fingers gentle on my scalp, unaware of my panic.

I heard her scoot away in her chair so she could read something pinned up on the wall. 'You 130 pounds when you come in and 123 pounds now.'

I could hardly believe my ears. I mean, I couldn't remember the last time I weighed 123 pounds. I must have been about seven. But even worse, I couldn't remember the last time I weighed 130. All I knew was that a month ago I had been struggling to fit into my size-11 jeans and cursing the state of my soft spongy belly. It just didn't make sense.

'Are you sure I weighed 130 when I came in?' I asked.

She laughed. 'You nothing but itty-bitty skin and bone, Constanzia. And I think you are really blonde until Brazilian grow back. You know, we Brazilians are also good at football, fast cars and dancing. Such a shame we get famous for hair removal.'

Blonde? Brazilian? Was she drunk? I could hardly bear to get my legs waxed let alone my you-know-what. My hands floundered beneath the bedclothes again, scrabbling at my crotch like hungry mice. Oh my God! I was a thin blonde with a Brazilian!

At that point I thought that maybe I was still in a coma after all. That the dream-like emergence into consciousness had itself been a dream. But my eyes were open, my body was obeying instruction, my mind was following acceptable sequences of thought. I lifted my hand up to my head again and felt Signora Marinello's fingers pulsing different spots on my poor battered skull. I pressed down on them, stopping her.

'It's Thursday, isn't it?' I asked, dread gnawing a hole in my gut.

'It is,' agreed my nurse.

'It's a Thursday in,' I thought about when I had gone on vacation, 'in November?'

'Is July, Constanzia. Thursday, July 23rd,' she said softly. 'Is summer. Eighty-five degrees today. You have to know this. About the month. About the day. You have to know this three times in a row. Then we know your progress is made.'

July? What the hell? My head whirred. I had gone to Venice in October. And it was now July. How was that possible?

'I don't get it,' I said, my voice sounding frail and wobbly. 'I went on vacation in October. I've been here for nearly a month so it should be November, shouldn't it?' I wondered if my brain had muddled up how the months worked but I ran through them and they all seemed there: January, February, March, April, May, June, July, August, September, October, November, December. July definitely came before November, not after.

'I don't know about no vacation,' she said, her fingers starting to massage my scalp again, moving in tiny circles. Then she rolled her chair away from the bed again to read whatever was on the wall. 'All I know is what it say here: admitted June 29, 2004, with subdural haema —'

Jesus, there it was, the lightning flash of comprehension.

'Stop!' I cried out. 'What? Two thousand and what?'

She rolled her chair back to the bed and her hands moved down to my shoulders, which had started to shake uncontrollably.

'What is it, Constanzia? Admitted June 29, 2004. What's wrong?'

How was it possible? How could it be happening to me?

'I went,' I tried to say but my breath was coming short and fast, making it hard to speak, my chest rising and falling hysterically, 'I went to Venice in October. After 9/11. We thought about not going, well he didn't, but before that, because of 9/11, we thought about not going, Signora.' Oh, where was Tom?

'Calm down,' she said, 'is all right. You take vacation whenever you like, Constanzia. Lots of people do. 9/11 don't stop vacations.'

'*No!*' I cried. 'You don't understand. I was just there. Just before the hospital. I hurt my head in Venice. Before the coma. Where's the paper? Where's the newspaper, Signora? I need the newspaper. I need to make sure.' I was sobbing now, flailing around in the bed.

'You must stay calm, Constanzia,' Signora Marinello told me as she moved around the bed. 'You do no good like this. Ssshhhh. No good.' She fished around until she found the *New York Times* and shook it out, holding the front page up to me. 'You want this?'

I nodded and reached for it, bringing it close to my eyes. The type was blurry — through the tears or the fog in my head I couldn't tell — but the date at the top of the page was coming slowly, slowly, slowly into focus, emerging out of a shadowy nondescript inkiness to read, clear as a bell, just as Signora Marinello had told me, Thursday, July 23, 2004. I threw the newspaper on the floor, opened my mouth and howled.

My brain had eaten two years and nine months of my life.

I had left on my second honeymoon in October 2001 and now it was July 2004. There was something wrong with my memory after all: a big chunk of my life had disappeared into a black empty void, starting with my trip to Venice and ending with waking up in hospital.

'But why would that happen?' I sobbed, my head resting on the billowing cushion of Signora Marinello's breast, my tears soaking into the cotton of her shift, my heart pumping with fright. 'Why would that be?'

'Hush,' she comforted me. 'Hush. Don't be afraid. No two people is the same, Constanzia. No two people have the same injury, no two people get better the same way. I see Dr Scarpa before, maybe

I get him to come and talk to you. The brain has her own way of getting better, of protecting herself. Those years, they will come back. They are not gone forever. Hush, now. Hush.'

Signora Marinello kept trying to calm me down, to reassure me that it didn't matter, that the missing years would return — but I was beyond comforting on a rational level. I mean how rational is it to have almost three years of your life sucked into some vacuum and never spat out? It was terrifying, and I had had enough of being terrified. I needed safety. I needed rescuing, which I think Signora Marinello recognised and managed in a small way by administering extra medication. I can't specifically remember her doing so but I know that I sank back into unconsciousness. In fact, I wanted to be unconscious. I may even have hoped for another coma; one from which I could awaken and know everything there was to know about me, not just the bits some invisible foreign hand had picked out.

I'm still joining the dots a bit here, you need to understand that. My mind was still operating on its own timetable and I am very aware that I recall some large chunks of time just as fleeting moments and some fleeting moments as large chunks. It is in retrospect that I have pieced it all together to make sense. So what I remember is slipping back into blissful unconsciousness and waking up again some time later, could have been minutes, could have been hours or days, to find Mom sitting there, knitting furiously and staring at me with those beady little eyes of hers. I assumed Signora Marinello had caught her up on the latest catastrophic development. And as I looked at her I couldn't believe that I hadn't noticed how she had aged. Thirty-three months at her age made quite a difference. Her skin, of which she had always been deservedly proud, seemed puckered and uncharacteristically dry, there were wrinkled black pouches beneath her eyes and her blush was on the heavy side.

'I went to Venice,' I said, croakily, a tear slithering out from the corner of my eye and down toward my ear. We had never been the types to trade secrets or confidences, but she was the only person there and I was so full of grief and despair I had to unleash it on someone. 'But Tom never came, Mom, he let me go there all on my own. That's the last thing I remember. Being in Venice all on my own.'

My cheeks were wet, my pillow soaking up the spillage. I had rarely wept in front of my mother as she'd long since proved indifferent to tears, mine anyway. But the pace of her knitting slowed and I saw something flit across her face then, some stealthy emotion chasing itself away. 'Well,' she said, 'I will never understand you, Mary-Constance, not as long as I live.'

I wanted Tom then like I'd never wanted him before. Despite our problems, our differences — his shortcomings, my guilt — he'd always protected me from my mother, soothed me after her outbursts, buffeted me from the pain she could cause.

'I don't care why he didn't come,' I sobbed. 'I forgive him. I forgive him for everything. I just want him to come and get me and take me home. I don't know what the hell is going on. I want Tom. Why didn't he come and find me?'

My mother gave a dry little cough. 'Why didn't he come and find you, Mary-Constance? I'll tell you why. Because someone went on a second honeymoon to Venice, yes, that's true, you've got that right. You've remembered that. But it wasn't you. It was Tom Farrell. *He* was the one stranded in a foreign city he never even cared two hoots to visit in the first place, with the rest of the world going to hell in a handbag and you gallivanting around New York City with your fancy man. Lord knows I was never crazy about the man, you could have done better, I've always thought so, but he deserved better than that. A bum lying down on the street covered in old pages of the *New York Post* deserves better than that. Of course, he moved on just fine, but why shouldn't he? You certainly had no problem in that department.'

I screamed then, as loud as I could, although it didn't come out the way I wanted it to. It emerged as more of an animal moan, but a moan of such ferocity, of such depth and anguish, that Signora

118

Marinello, who must have been out in the hall, came racing in as quickly as her bulky body could carry her.

'Lois!' she called out over her shoulder as she approached. 'Lois!'

A young pink-faced nurse with messy strawberry-blonde hair appeared at the entrance to my room, her face crumpled in irritation or something like it.

'Yes?' she asked Signora Marinello. 'What is it?'

How I pitied my poor jumbled brain then. How I wished I could scoop it out of my dented skull and kiss it better. How I wanted to roll the clocks forward or backward or any which way to a time when I knew what was what and who was whom. For I knew Lois already. Only slightly, but slightly was enough. She was none other than the waitress from Bentigodi in the Cannaregio, the one who had told me she had seen my brother.

I cried out even louder from my bed and she looked at me, her face straightening into a sympathetic smile as she recognised me.

'Well, hello, stranger,' she said. 'Nice to see you with your eyes open.'

I felt a whoosh of comprehension lift me up and spin me around then, but the force of it confused me and I lost my train of thought. I had glimpsed the truth for a moment but it had been a long, long way away and I couldn't see it any more. I was speechless, wordless, thoughtless. I felt like my whole body was one big black gaping howl of rage and misery.

It's hard to explain exactly what it is like having a brain injury. I mean, it's easy enough for me to do now because the pieces of the puzzle all fit snugly into their right places again or if they don't, I can plug the gaps using common sense. Like I say, it's joining the dots. But at that time, when I was trying to recover whatever was left of me, unsure of what was real and what was not, I was jamming round pegs into square holes all the time. How could the waitress from Bentigodi be in the hospital, I hear you ask? And I was asking myself that too, but not in a 'yeah, right' sceptical way, rather in a 'how could

119

that possibly *be*' way. I just didn't get it. I just couldn't unravel it.

And I suppose that seeing and knowing Lois highlighted, at that point, the matter of Signora Marinello herself. How could she have been at Do' Mori and right there in the hospital in New York? I had gotten used to her and stopped wondering about that, such was my need to just soak up her loving attention. But if I was to believe my mother I had never been to Venice — yet I had. I was sure I had. I replayed the events of my short stay there like a movie in my head and it was picture-perfect. But what had Mom being doing there at the end, at Luca's boatyard? This unnerved me. And what had Ty Wheatley been doing there? When I tried to think how all these things could be, how these people could jump around the world and turn up in my life no matter what my state or location, my thinking could only go so far and then it stopped. I met a brick wall in my mind and banged my head against it, so to speak.

'I know you,' I said to Lois. 'You were there. We were there together.'

'Go get Dr Scarpa,' Signora Marinello told her. 'I see him before. He is upstairs. Constanzia should see him.' And off Lois went, before I could stop her, before I could demand an explanation that my exhausted grey matter could absorb.

'Is it true?' I asked Signora Marinello, even though I wasn't sure what I was referring to. 'I was in Venice, wasn't I? We had cichetti at Do' Mori. I can remember what it tasted like. The polpette!' My mouth failed to water at the prospect but I saw those luscious meatballs in my mind as clear as those round white plates.

'I don't know,' Signora Marinello answered me, shaking her head and then turning to glare at my mother. 'You know, Constanzia need rest, Mrs Conlan. Maybe you give her space now.'

I could sense my mother bristle. Prickly particles filled the air and stabbed at my skin. She didn't like being treated like an ordinary person.

'I think I know what is good for my daughter,' she replied, her voice deep and cold. 'I've known her for more than 36 years, after all, Mrs Marinello.'

More than 36 years? I turned my face into the pillow and roared again. I was 36. Only four years shy of 40. Oh, it just got stranger and stranger.

And stranger.

The squeak of a nurse's shoes and the clatter of someone with a firmer sole heralded the arrival of Lois and Dr Scarpa.

'Well, look who we have here,' a familiar voice greeted me, charm dripping from every rich rolled syllable. 'That's some fine handiwork you have going on up there if I do say so myself.'

My mouth dropped open as my eyes travelled up and down the handsome form standing beside me, gripped in expertly fitting black trousers and a T-shirt.

It was Marco, my gondolier.

Eight

Can you imagine what my poor scrambled self must have gone through then? It emerges from a coma it didn't know it was in, only to find three years of its life missing. Then it's confronted by the man who stole the heart out of its body in a whirlwind affair (that apparently never happened) in a faraway place (where it had apparently never been).

There it was, my poor muddled brain, trying its hardest to get back to a normal size and find its trusty old pathways, jump-start its nerve endings, only to be assaulted by a battery of inexplicable coincidences that just did not add up no matter how hard it tried to make sense of them all.

Now I look back and think how obvious it all was, how any idiot could have worked it out. But hindsight is a wonderful thing, right up there with insight as far as head trauma is concerned — and not everyone who has taken a knock like me gets their hindsight or their insight back. (Also, we don't really use words like idiot.) Others less fortunate can look back all they like and still never put it all together. I know this now. I know a lot now. But all I knew then was that the Venetian gondolier I had ridden like a rodeo steer in a murky hole in a backstreet canal was now holding out his hand, gold Rolex glinting, and introducing himself formally as though we had never met.

'Marc Scarpa,' he said. 'I'm your neurosurgeon.'

'Marco,' I whispered, the wind completely knocked out of my sails but traces of lust still unmistakably racing around inside me.

'Yes,' he smiled a little unconvincingly, first at me then at Signora Marinello, 'Constanzia. Still playing your little games then. Glad to see you so alert. You managed the surgery expertly. We were extremely pleased with the result.'

He paused as though waiting for someone to back this up but everyone was too busy staring at him in adoration, even someone with a recent head injury could spot that. And who wouldn't adore him? My Marco! Those lips! Those hips!

'Nurse tells me there seems to be some sort of retrograde amnesia or dissociative memory loss,' Marco said in his smooth hypnotic voice. 'This is not my field, Connie, I'm your surgeon. I'll consult with my colleagues but as your post-operative scans are clear, there's nothing to suggest that you should be at all alarmed. It is very common with — Connie? Nurse, is she listening to me?'

I was transfixed by the squareness of his jaw, the depth of his eyes, the breadth of his shoulders. He was just too drop-dead gorgeous to be a doctor, he should have been an actor playing a doctor, you know, in a daytime soap like Joey in *Friends* but taller and thinner and with better hair.

'It's just so weird to see you here,' I said.

Marco took no notice. 'It's very common with head-injury patients to have no recollection of the accident in which the injury occurred,' he told me in a clinical voice as though nothing had ever happened between us, as though I were just anyone. It was chilling. Of course, when I thought about it, I'd seen a glimpse of Marco's coldness (even if I hadn't recognised it as such) when he had talked to me about his cut-price Swiss gondolas. I'd been irked by his lack of idealism. He was a fairytale hero but seemed to lack the necessary romanticism. Mind you, at the time I had considered he had enough of everything else to make up for it. I possibly still did.

'Connie?' He barked my name with a briskness that stank of having too much of his valuable time taken up. I nodded, feebly, deeply apologetic, and willed myself to pay better attention. 'It is very common to have no recollection of your accident,' he said again but with less patience. 'The brain is an extremely complicated organ with its own way of protecting your consciousness from any undue pain or stress. It had already been through considerable trauma when you presented. You had the subdural haematoma on your right temporal lobe but were lucky to escape what's known as a contrecoup injury at the back of your head on the opposite side. This is where the brain moves vigorously around inside the static box of your skull after the impact.' He made a gesticulation representing my brain moving vigorously around inside the static box of my skull. 'Obviously, that would have complicated your recovery but I am sure Nurse has been through all this with you so if there are any questions . . .'

I could not believe he was just standing there looking at me with nothing in his eyes but a detached sort of professional interest. Was he afraid to show affection in front of my mother? Ashamed at what Signora Marinello might think of him after he left me alone in Venice? But then I remembered with a flush of embarrassment that Venice had been a long time ago, that my mother said I had never even been there; and anyway, how could Marco be both my thigh-throbbing gondolier and my brain surgeon? I groaned. What was real?

'Is there pain?' Marco asked, coming close to inspect my stapled scar. 'There shouldn't be pain. What meds do you have her on?' He checked my chart and then leaned forward to closer inspect my wound. He did not smell like the Marco I knew, the man whose salty skin sang with an intoxicating mixture of vanilla and freshly ground black pepper. This Marco had no smell at all. I sucked up another groan as he stepped back, attempting a sympathetic look.

'Tell me what you remember,' he said, employing a gentler tone.

I looked at Signora Marinello for help but she just smiled encouragingly and nodded at me. My mother was silently tsk-tsking in the background. It was a non-noise I had long ago learned to ignore.

'I remember,' I started, 'but then . . .' I fizzled out.

'Yes,' Marco prompted, those eyes drawing me in. Was it a game? Did he want me to tell them?

'I'm sure of it, you know, it's just that . . .' But I wasn't sure. Far from it. I knew what that man tasted like, for God's sake, yet he was a stranger to me. A total stranger.

As if to prove just that, Marco forced a tight smile, blew air out of his nose, and looked at his expensive watch, the sort of thing a real asshole would do. It was clear to me then that I was inconveniencing him and he gave a short throaty ahem no doubt intended to hurry me up.

'I do remember,' I said quickly, miffed but all the same not wanting him to give up on me and leave. 'I remember *you*. The gondola, the cichetti, Do' Mori. You said you were going to take care of me.'

Marco raised his eyebrows and opened his mouth, his tongue pressed against the back of his top front teeth. It was the sign of someone who had no time for this sort of crap.

'I did take care of you,' he said crisply. 'Now if you could just tell me what you remember of the accident, Connie. There are other people in this hospital, in this ward, much worse off than you who also need my help.'

My heart broke but whether it was a fresh break or it had already been broken, I couldn't tell. And hindsight still does not help me there. I had been a moron (oops, shouldn't use that one either) to think I was the only one for Marco, in the real world or the imagined one.

'I remember being in Venice, at the squero,' I answered haltingly, breathing in unshed tears and attempting to separate this cold efficient version of my gondolier from the warm magnetic one in my memory. 'And all of a sudden my mom was there and then I was here. In the hospital.'

'You don't remember running in Central Park?' Marco prompted. 'You were running in Central Park when you fell and hit your head by the restaurant on the lake, the Boat House. Isn't that the story, Nurse?'

Signora Marinello nodded in agreement but I was stunned. I didn't run. I never ran. I hated running. I didn't have the ponytail or the breasts for it. I was a walker. But those bony thighs, that tight little butt that lay underneath me — how could I explain them? If I didn't know better, which in fact I didn't, I would have to admit that I had indeed woken up with the body of a runner.

'You must remember Woody Allen,' my mom piped up from the background. 'You bled all over Woody Allen. He had caramel-coloured corduroy trousers on and you held up his film. Winona Ryder had to stay in her trailer — you know, the one that stole all the clothes. The shoplifter. It cost him $10,000.'

I closed my eyes and willed the world to go away — it was too hard to be awake in — but the world would not obey my wishes. I opened my eyes and it was still there.

'Connie?' Marco's voice was exasperated again. 'Do you remember being in Central Park?'

I felt wheels and cogs shifting slowly, rumbling loudly in my head. Of course I remembered being in Central Park. I had grown up in a grungy tenement just a few blocks to the east of it, after all, it was practically my back yard. But when I tried to conjure up my most recent memory, there was a cloudiness that I was having trouble sifting through. I saw myself walking, my coat pulled tight across my chest, my body leaning into the wind. But it was my old body, the spongy one I knew, not the tight one I had woken up with. And I wasn't in the park, I was striding past the Magnolia Bakery. My, how I loved those cupcakes.

'I'm not sure,' I said. 'I'm not sure about anything. I remember walking but not running and that was the old me not this one. You weren't in Venice?' I just couldn't believe I had dreamed it. 'At the

Rialto?' I knew details of this man's anatomy that I just didn't have the experience to conjure up unaided. I had felt him and smelled him and tasted him and a host of other heavenly morsels. I could not have made it all up. I could not have. 'It all seems so real.'

Marco turned to Signora Marinello, his luscious eyebrows raised. 'I think we need a neuro-psychological consult on this one, Nurse, it's out of my hands now. The wound is healing satisfactorily and the CT scans show that the swelling is no longer a risk to her health so I think it's appropriate that I leave her to you.'

With that he turned on his heels and left the room.

All eyes watched his delectable back as it disappeared. Even my mom had a sort of hungry look she didn't normally possess. Not for long though.

'Really, Mary-Constance, you couldn't have made more of an effort?' she admonished me before the sound of his feet had even faded away. 'He saves your life and all you can do is babble on about who knows what and ask him stupid question after stupid question. What will he think? What do they say about manners, Mrs Marinado? Do they say when you come back mean you leave your manners behind as well?'

'Time for Connie to have some rest now, Mrs Conlan,' my nurse said. 'Remember what I tell you about her brain. Needs quiet.'

I felt the dry chafe of my mother's lips on my cheek and the loneliness of my predicament suddenly overwhelmed me. 'Mom, can you get Tom to come in?' I pleaded, grasping at her arm and pulling her back to me. 'I need him here. I don't know what's happening to me. I'm scared.'

My betrayal of my husband, if indeed it existed, itched at my insides but I still needed him there with me, despite what I had or hadn't done, what he had or hadn't done, to navigate me through the awful fog in my head. My mother resisted my pull, straightening up and stepping away from me.

Paris chose that moment to stride into my room on ridiculously high heels, looking positively airbrushed and brandishing a Kate Spade paper shopping bag. 'Darling!' she cried, '*C'est ici!*'

I burst into tears. 'Please go away,' I sobbed, my chest heaving with despair. 'I want Tom. And Fleur. Where's Fleur? I need Fleur. Mom, will you tell her? Please, please, please.'

'Well, I doubt whether she —' my mother started in on me.

'Really, there's no need to —' Paris spoke over the top of her.

'QUIET!' Signora Marinello roared with admirable authority. 'Everybody out of this room right now. Leave Constanzia alone. She need REST. She need QUIET.'

'Her name is Mary-Constance,' my mother chipped in as she was herded from the room.

'Although her fans know her as Emsie,' Paris retorted.

This last comment lingered in the room after Paris had vacated it. Mary-Constance. Emsie. MC. The penny dropped. Paris was calling me MC. I felt ridiculously relieved. This skinny person with a new name quaking here inside me, unable to stop crying, a large chunk of her life disappeared into thin air, was really me. I was the right person! But I had preferred the name Connie for as long as I could remember so it was a mystery to me why I would have changed that. Only my mother called me Mary-Constance and I had never cared for it.

At that point in my recovery, by the way, I should mention that I was no longer entirely bedridden. You could be forgiven for thinking that I had been lying in bed all that time moving nothing but my tear ducts, my mouth and on a couple of occasions my hands but this is purely because, in the interests of a good story, I have chosen to leave out the details of my physical recovery. It mostly involves tubes and excretions that are frankly best not talked about.

In a nutshell, by the time I knew what was happening to me, by the stage I am telling you about now, my body had already been rehabilitated to an acceptable level. I no longer required a catheter nor round-the-clock intravenous support and monitoring. I needed assistance to get into a wheelchair and go to the bathroom but this was really a precaution, as I was pretty steady on my feet (despite the fact that my legs seemed barely big enough to hold the rest of me up). And I had suffered no injury but the one to my head, which apparently left me streets ahead of other inhabitants of Neurological Intensive Care, most of whom had been in car wrecks and were badly banged up. I was, indeed, one of the lucky ones.

Of course, I didn't feel lucky. Quite the opposite. I was terrified by the notions that time had been lost and what I thought true had been imagined. What could I trust? To whom could I turn? Marco, my lover, appeared not to know me from Adam and my husband, according to my mother, was no longer my husband — I knew it was a bad sign that he had not been there already, that his name had not been mentioned. But how I yearned for him. Truly, madly, deeply, desperately yearned for him.

I slept after Paris and my mom left. It had been a huge day. When I woke up, it was Friday. I felt calmer. Signora Marinello was still there, shuffling around the room, waiting for me to wake.

'Don't you have a home to go to?' I asked her. 'You're always here.'

She laughed. 'I work 12-hour shift,' she said, 'but you don't know how much you sleep at night when I'm at home. Maybe 15 hours!'

'I was in Venice, with Marco,' I told her, desperate to sift something sensible out of the muddle in my mind. 'I know I was. There are things I know about him, Signora. Things that I am sure I didn't dream. Private things. You know. Very private.'

Her smile was so kind, I felt better for having it pointed in my direction.

'Constanzia,' she murmured. 'You must understand . . .'

And there it was, all of a sudden: proof!

'Constanzia!' I said. 'You see! He called me Constanzia. He gave me an Italian name.'

But Signora Marinello simply nodded. 'We give all patients Italian names,' she said. 'Is a hangover from another doctor who used to work here. Was his little joke.'

'But how would *I know* he called me Constanzia?' The fog in my head had lifted enough for me to know this was important. I clung to it as if to a bright light at the end of a long dark tunnel but Signora Marinello just nodded expectantly again.

'No matter how much we know about the brain,' she said, 'is still only tiny little piece of what there is to know. And you think there is a lot to learn about her when she is awake? Well, try her when she is asleep. Even more! No one really knows what happens in a coma.' Her voice was conspiratorially low, as though she were telling me secrets she didn't want real brain experts to hear. 'But your ears? They the last thing to go to sleep, Constanzia. This we do know. I say just because your brain is asleep doesn't mean your ears aren't listening. I never tell you anything when you sleeping that I don't want you to hear if you are awake. Dr Scarpa, now, he chit and chat and call you Constanzia. Tell you he's going to take care of you. Maybe your ears take this to your brain and mix it with morphine and other sleeping drugs until you have a little cocktail of real things and dream things going on. You know those first few of days after your surgery we wake you up to see how you responding, then put you back to sleep again. No one knows what goes on in there during this time.' She put her cool hand on my forehead again. 'Not even you.'

I turned this over. She made it all sound plausible enough, she really did, yet I had tasted things in Venice that were as real as anything I had ever tasted anywhere else. I thought of the stuffed sardines at Bentigodi, sitting succulently in front of me, that heavenly stuffing of breadcrumbs, pine nuts and parsley bursting to get out.

'But how would I know what Marco looks like?' I asked her. 'And you? How would I know that?' I remembered her so clearly, leaning over the counter at Do' Mori, her smooth voice telling me that I was going to be fine, that I was going to be better than I was before.

'Constanzia, how long you been awake?' she asked quietly.

'Three days,' I said, although I thought it might have been four.

'Three *weeks*,' she corrected me. 'You been awake more than three weeks. But those first days you don't remember. You see me and Dr Scarpa plenty before you know that's what you are doing. This is a strange time for you, Constanzia, I know this. But you going to be fine. Will not always be like this. Will be better. Easier. You one of the lucky ones.'

That old chestnut. If I was that lucky, surely I would have skipped the whole blow-to-the-head coma thing and just gone on to be a supermodel. Signora Marinello sensed my scepticism.

'Besides,' she said casually, 'you not the first person to wake up thinking you seen more of Dr Scarpa than you should have.'

'I'm not?'

'No!' She was quite sure of it. 'It happen all the time. But you don't have to be in a coma to dream of that one, either. He's a nice-looking man, no?' She shook her head. 'I think half the nurses in this place are dreaming of him as well as the patients, although if you ask me he's —' she thought better of what she had been about to say. 'Never mind. Some people just like that, just made to dream about.'

'Well, I dreamed of you too, Signora. Has anyone done that before?'

'I don't think it happens so often, my love,' she answered, 'so thank you. I always say you are a nice girl.'

I slept on and off for most of the day, waking in the afternoon as the door quietly opened. There was Fleur, my real best friend; not looking perfectly put together like Paris but radiantly beautiful, just the way a best friend of mine should look. Actually, she seemed different, quite different, but I couldn't put my finger on why. Then I reminded myself that of course she would have changed — it was nearly three years since I could remember seeing her. The night before I was to fly to Italy we had gone out, just the two of us, so we could discuss my plan of action for the second honeymoon. Fleur had always had excellent advice on underwear — it was she who had gotten me into a thong — and actually, when I came to think of it, the whole second honeymoon thing had been her idea in the first place. I'd always confided my woes to Fleur. She was the best listener and despite her ingrained natural flirtation skills, at heart she could be relied on to be a girl's girl, a true friend, a best friend.

She shot me a hesitant smile from the door and I beckoned for her to come closer. I wondered if she had known that I was thin and blonde or if that was a surprise to her as well. I could not get past that, I really couldn't.

'Fleur,' I said. 'Thank God you're here.'

'Oh, Connie,' she cried and flew towards me, flinging herself on the bed and enveloping me in her arms. 'I'm so sorry. Jesus, I'm so sorry.' We wept together then, the way old friends do, loudly and gushingly, until the tears slowed and turned to embarrassed laughter and finally dried on our cheeks.

'Your mom says you're a little out to lunch,' Fleur said, sniffing.

'Out to lunch? Gee, that's the nicest thing I think she's ever said about me,' I kidded but anxiety quickly sucked the laughter out of me. 'I can't remember the right things,' I blurted out. 'And the things I can remember aren't true. It's awful, Fleur, I don't know what's happening. I don't know what's happened. Real life is all jumbled up with dream life in my head and it's horrible.'

Fleur wriggled up the bed until she was lying next to me and hugged me close. She had lost weight in the missing years or rather changed shape — that sexy butt of hers was smaller but her boobs were bigger, her waist thicker and that fabulous hair was even curlier and more lustrous than before.

'Is it true you've lost your memory?' she asked.

I nodded miserably. 'Some of it. So they tell me. I mean it's not like the guy in *The Bourne Identity* or anything, I know who I am,

132

sort of. Or who I used to be. But the past few years are gone. I mean I didn't know at first, I thought it was still back then. I thought I was okay, that everything was okay, that I was lucky to be alive but I just couldn't figure out the date. It's so weird, Fleur. I can remember going to Venice, so freakin' clearly, like it was yesterday, but Mom says I didn't go. You and I went out the night before I was supposed to fly out, remember?' I thought back to the table at the Gotham Bar and Grill where Fleur and I had split a bottle of South Australian chardonnay and a plate of Alfred Portale's Maine lobster tails with roasted fingerling potatoes while we discussed marriage-renewal tactics.

'I remember the restaurant,' I told her, 'but not much afterwards.'

'Oh, Connie,' Fleur sounded as heartbroken as I was. 'So much has happened since then. Jesus, you couldn't just break your leg like a normal person?'

'But look, I'm thin,' I said, throwing back the bedclothes and showing her my bony body.

'It's disgusting,' she agreed.

'I know, and it's not even the weirdest thing that's happened. Did you know about it?'

'The thin thing? Oh, gee, um . . .' she hesitated. 'There's a lot of catching up to do, Connie . . .'

'So, catch me up then.'

I detected a certain reluctance.

'I don't know where to start,' she said.

'Well, do you know about my accident?'

'Uh-huh.'

'Start there.'

She seemed slightly relieved and shifted in the bed to get comfortable, hoisting herself up on one elbow. 'Well, the story was that you were running by the Boat House in Central Park when you saw Woody Allen and you slipped on something, fell over and hit your head on a rock.' She stopped to have a good look at my scar, her face scrunched up in sympathy. 'He had a bagel or something, Woody Allen did. They think that's what distracted you. No, it was a pretzel, a soft pretzel. Anyway you must have been real hungry because despite being unconscious you apparently wrangled it off of him somehow. You had it in the ambulance. In fact, they had to prise it off you in the hospital.'

We were both silent for a moment. She waiting for my reaction, me hoping I had mis-heard what she said. My near-death sounded like a bad joke.

'I stole Woody Allen's pretzel?' I asked her. 'Why would I do that? Did he take it from me in the first place?' I wanted to say that I didn't even like pretzels but I was pretty sure there were photos to the contrary. Pushcart pretzels, in my opinion, while not truly a New York invention were definitely one of the reasons to live there. And I bet I knew where Woody Allen got his too because there was a grouchy woman sold them at 72nd Street and Central Park West . . . Hers were much better than the ones you could buy from the franchised carts in the park itself: hotter and she used a finer salt. I would dearly love to believe there was no truth in such a ridiculous explanation of how I jumbled my brain but sadly there was nothing unlikely about me nearly killing myself lusting after somebody else's pretzel at all. It was exactly the sort of thing that would happen.

'How do you know this stuff anyway?' I wanted to know.

'There were witnesses,' Fleur admitted. 'The guy who rows that skinny boat around the lake in the stripy shirt, he saw the whole thing.'

'The Central Park gondolier?' I asked in horror.

'Yeah, the Central Park gondolier. He was right there. He saw the whole thing with the pretzel apparently and then you fell and hit your head and he was right there talking to you when the paramedics arrived. I think maybe it was him stole Woody's pretzel and gave it to you to make a better story, but that's not what it said in the paper.'

'It was in the paper?' I was in danger of going into shock. This just kept getting more and more unbelievable.

'Well, yeah, of course it was. Front page. You're a —'

'Stop,' I whispered. 'Stop.' My head needed time to catch up with what she was telling me. I had been running in Central Park; had fallen trying to steal a famous film director's snack; then been tended to by the Central Park gondolier. Well, I didn't need to know anything about how the brain worked to figure out how Marco got into my coma as a Venetian boatman, for crissakes. The Grand Canal felt like a long, long way away then and while I felt less lonely with Fleur snuggled next to me on the bed, I still wanted Tom. He was the rock to whom I wanted to cling.

'Why isn't Tom here, Fleur? What happened?'

Fleur tensed up, I felt her body stiffen next to me. 'The thing is, Connie,' she said and she sounded slightly out of breath, nervous, 'I don't know how to put this but basically you're not married to Tom any more.'

By then, I guess I knew that but I can't say it didn't hit me like a sucker punch to hear it all the same. I had been avoiding the obvious but he would have been there, wouldn't he? Signora Marinello would have spoken of him. I think I had felt as soon as I could recognise my feelings — even before Mom told me that it was Tom who went to Venice on his own not me — that he was not in my life any more. It was like a gap inside me, bigger than any gap in my head, in my memory. And emptier than any space I could ever have imagined. But the awful inescapable fact of the matter was that at just that moment I wanted to be married to Tom more than at any other moment in my whole entire life.

'You're engaged to be married to someone else,' Fleur continued softly, compounding the agony.

'Someone else?' It seemed impossible.

'Yes,' she said. 'You would be married already but your divorce hasn't come through yet.'

The relief at hearing that flooded through me so warmly I failed to notice the catch in my best friend's voice. 'Then it's not too late,' I said, feeling a surge of determination. 'Maybe it's not too late. I feel like I might have made a big mistake, Fleur. I need him here. I thought he would be here. Can you find him? Tell him?'

At this, Fleur burst into tears again, turning and burying her face in the crunchy hospital pillows. 'Oh, Jesus, this is hard, Connie,' she said, and though her voice was muffled I could hear every word. 'I'm so sorry. I never . . . Oh, shit, fuck, I'm so fucking sorry.'

I misunderstood her anguish. 'Hey,' I said, 'it's okay. It's not your fault. It's not anybody's fault.' Strictly speaking, it was Woody Allen's fault but I wasn't going to go there. 'It's just pretty weird this whole stupid coma-then-not-remembering-stuff thing, huh?'

'Yessiree,' she answered. 'Pretty weird all right. And I think it's going to get weirder.' Her voice was all clogged up the way it gets when you're not finished crying.

'Is it true I never went to Venice?' I asked her. 'That I stood him up?'

'You didn't go, Connie. Tom went but you never turned up. You left him, sweetie. You left him all on his own.'

To what my mom told me I tended to add a grain of salt or a thousand, but Fleur I believed. She would not lie to me. Poor Tom, I thought, abandoned in a city he never wanted to go to without the wife who had made him go there. I wondered if he had availed himself of the local hospitality the way I had, in my dreams. My dreams? God, I was confused.

'It's like the shower scene from *Dallas*,' I told Fleur. 'I've woken up and none of it really happened.'

'It's happened all right, Connie. You just don't know it.' We weren't talking about the same thing but we were both right.

Fleur cleared her throat then and when she spoke her voice was shaky and scared, not a natural Fleur state at all. Like I said, she has the confidence of a European princess. 'Connie, if you really don't remember anything from the past couple of years then there are some things I have to tell you.' She was twisting a pretty old-fashioned ruby ring on her ring finger.

'You're engaged too?'

'I'm engaged too,' she said quietly, 'and I have a beautiful baby girl who is 11 months old.'

It was my turn to cry again then, I couldn't keep the tears away. How could I not know something like that? How could I not have sensed that this woman with whom I had shared every detail of my life since college had entered that next all-important stage of being a grown-up? But when I thought about it, I had noticed that there was something different about Fleur. She looked like a new mom. It was a look we had noticed (and been quite scathing of I might add) in other women in the past. It gave her a softness, an aura, a clichéd glow, that she hadn't had before. The happy glitter of motherhood. It suited her.

'What's her name?' I asked.

'Agnes,' she whispered.

'Oh, Fleur, that's beautiful. I love that name. That was Tom's grandmother's name.'

'Yes.' She said softly, sweetly, lingering over the word. A wave of nausea swept over me. 'Who's the father?' Something, it must have been fear, was pulsing violently in my stomach.

'Oh, sweetie,' Fleur said so sadly that I knew the answer before she said the words. 'It's Tom.'

Nine

I'm going to leave out the obvious histrionics that occurred after that little bombshell was dropped. For a start it's kind of a blur and for a finish I said some pretty nasty things that might give you cause to think my mother was right when she suggested I had come back mean.

This, I gather, was pretty hard for Fleur as she had already heard much of it before; you know, the first time when it had actually happened. Now when I look back I feel more sorry for her than for myself. I mean, imagine telling your best friend you've stolen her husband only to have her forget so you have to tell her all over again? I didn't see it that way right then, of course. I was incredulous, hurt beyond belief and angry. For a few seconds there I even considered grabbing Signora Marinello's surgical scissors and cutting off that thick, shiny lustrous head of hair. How could she? How could he? How could they? And a baby! If I'd been steadier on my feet I'd have stood up and decked her and then gone out and found Tom and decked him too. Of course, I was wearing a backless surgical gown and disposable underwear so riding the subway to Il Secondo would have had its problems. Still, on a better day I'd have given it a shot.

'She stole my husband,' I cried when Signora Marinello came in to see what the ruckus was about. 'Tom. She took him.'

Fleur was no longer in the bed with me but curled in the visitor's chair, her face red and blotchy with crying, her mascara smudged below her eyes. 'I did not,' she hiccupped, looking at my nurse for support, but Signora Marinello sensibly busied herself with her paperwork. 'She gave him away.'

'Why would I do that?' I beseeched her. 'Why would I? I love him, Fleur. I've loved him since I was four years old.' This was a bit of an exaggeration but I thought I had every right to feel aggrieved.

'Connie,' she argued, 'you tossed him aside like a used dishrag the moment you took up with Ty Wheatley.'

I gagged, literally gagged.

'I what?'

'You dumped —'

'I took up with Ty Wheatley?'

'You're *engaged* to Ty Wheatley.'

At that moment I felt so cut adrift from the real me that I truly wondered what had been the point in surviving my surgery. I was a foreigner to myself and a fiancée to a man in impeccable cream linen suits. Frankly, I didn't think it got much worse than that and in a week, or two weeks, or however the hell long it had been of bleak moments, that, I felt, was the bleakest.

A cavernous black hole claimed my insides, growing deeper and darker with every breath I took. I felt empty. Totally empty. It was like a hunger. A terrible, frightening hunger.

I sat up straight. Actually, it wasn't like a hunger. It was hunger. I was hungry.

The whole waking-up-out-of-a-coma thing had thrown my culinary radar for a loop, that was true, but at the moment of finding out that my husband had fathered a child with my best friend, I felt my old friend — appetite — return in spades. Maybe there was a reason for living after all. A rich fennel risotto with fresh-shaved Parmesan, perhaps. Or a fillet of grilled orata with salad greens and something tart, lemon-coriander vinaigrette perhaps, on the side.

'Can I get something to eat?' I asked, abruptly switching my attention to Signora Marinello. My mind raced with possibilities. 'Scallops maybe?' I could think of nothing but their plump sweetness, a satiny beurre blanc on the side.

Signora Marinello looked at me like I'd lost my mind (in retrospect, I got a lot of that). 'Where do you think you are, Constanzia?' she asked. '21 Club? Scrambled egg, maybe, I can do. But I think no to scallops. Still, is good that you are hungry. I tell you, is all downhill from here.'

She started out of the room but thought better of it, stopping to give us both a stern look and jabbing the air with her chubby finger. 'Now you two should behave yourself while I'm gone, okay? Remember, Constanzia, you need quiet. Quiiiiiii-eeeeeeet.'

Fleur and I both sniffed and nodded. My mind cleared of dining options, I remembered where we had been up to in our discussions. Ty Wheatley. Ty Wheatley and me.

'Wait,' I called to my nurse's retreating back. 'Did someone called Ty Wheatley ever come to see me?'

'Is he kind of English,' she asked, 'with white pants sitting up high, like this?' She pulled her waistband up in an unflattering Gomer Pyle imitation. I nodded.

'Uh-huh,' she nodded. 'But you not so happy to see him. You keep asking for Tom.'

Fleur let out something of a whimper at this and Signora Marinello shuffled off, relieved, I imagine, to escape the rather overcharged atmosphere in the room.

'Well, this is going well,' I said nastily.

'Just you tell me what is the right way to tell your former best friend that you live with her ex-husband when you've already told her two years before and that was bad enough.'

Fleur was wretched, any fool (aw, I just keep doing it!) could see that, and put like that I could see it would be kind of a bummer.

'Do we speak?' I asked her. 'Are we still friends?'

She shook her head, those beautiful curls bouncing around her face so cheerfully it was hard to believe she was unhappy. 'When you took up with Ty we kind of started moving in different circles so I guess we grew apart then,' she said, 'but when Tom and I got together . . .'

How it hurt to hear her say that. My Tom. And my Fleur. Together? What had I done to deserve that? As far as I knew, Fleur had always believed in Tom and me. Hadn't she counselled me on how to save our marriage when it foundered in the doldrums? Hadn't she told me in the car on our wedding day that if there was one thing in the world of which she was sure it was that Tom loved me and only me with all his heart and soul?

I stopped and ran that sentence through my mind again at a slightly different speed. Fleur had insisted that Tom loved me and only me and I had assumed that these were simply encouraging words in desperate times, but maybe she had reason to know for certain that Tom loved me and only me. Maybe she had suggested a bit of Fleur-loving along the way.

'Did you and Tom ever? While we were still?'

'How could you even think that, Connie? I would NEVER do that to you. Ever. Maybe I did have a little crush on Tom before but nothing ever came of it — nothing ever would have — until you dumped him so badly, and ran off with Ty. You broke Tom's heart. I just helped pick up the pieces and then, you know, it just happened.'

A smorgasbord of feeling churned inside my shrunken stomach. 'So how long since we spoke to each other?'

'Nearly two years but of course like most of Manhattan I read all your reviews — especially after that business with the place that closed down when you said you would fly to the Australian outback, in Coach, and eat live witchety grubs on the end of a stick rather than go there again.'

'I said that?'

'You sure did.'

'In the *Voice*?'

'No, Connie, in the *New York Times*!'

'THE *New York Times*?'

'Yes, THE *New York Times*.'

The look on my face must have clued her in to my ignorance. 'Oh my God,' she said limply. 'No one told you you're the *Times* restaurant critic?'

The *Times* restaurant critic? Hell-o-o! I'd spent days lying in that hospital bed listening to all kinds of doom and gloom about my swollen brain and my messed up love life and nobody had bothered to tell me I had reached the pinnacle of my career? Every food writer in New York — if not the whole country — dreamed about one day sharpening their pencil for the *New York Times*. It was the most prestigious job in the world of restaurant criticism. I thought of the critics whose words I had chewed up and swallowed in the past: Mimi Sheraton, Bryan Miller, Biff Grimes — although I was never so keen on him — and my hero Ruth Reichl, much of whose review of Le Cirque 2000 I could probably still quote verbatim.

'Fleur, you wouldn't kid around with me on something like this would you?'

'Connie,' she said and she allowed herself a smile, which made her look much more like her Mona Lisa self, 'it's true. You're the real McCoy. You wear wigs and hats and dark glasses; and restaurateurs live in terror of you. There's a picture from your high-school yearbook pinned up in half the kitchens in New York.'

'Jesus, not the one with the perm?' I'd had a weak moment back in the '80s. Not pretty.

I collapsed back on my pillows. It was all so implausible. Me? Restaurant critic for the *New York Times*? Chefs on both coasts devoured every word of those reviews; fortunes were made and lost. How would a person like me get a job like that? There must have been 10,000 other people better qualified. And I didn't know how to find the front door of the *New York Times* let alone score the prized top food job. The job Ruth Reichl had made famous with her razor-sharp reviews. Ruth Reichl! I was just not good enough. I teetered on the fence between below average and average, just like I'd been told to. The *New York Times* was a big grown-up place for clever people to work at. How the hell did I get in there without wearing an overall and pushing a broom?

Now, if you think I'm being a little over-the-top here then maybe you are not aware of the hold the *New York Times* has on the population of the city — especially the dining fraternity, which is everyone. If that paper runs a story about your restaurant opening on its front page, you will never have an empty table. Ever. If it dumps on you, the phone will instantly fall chillingly silent, rarely to ring again. Remember New York is a town where people eat out three, four, maybe five times a week — half the apartments don't even have dining tables, the city is their dining room — and trust me there's nothing a New Yorker loves better than to know more than the next guy where's the best place to get the spiciest dumplings, the juiciest soft-shelled clams, the plumpest Louisiana crayfish. That Wednesday food section is devoured by millions of eyes and discussed over millions of water coolers. It is big-time. Bigger than big-time.

'But I'm nobody,' I told Fleur, my head reeling.

'You were nobody,' she corrected me, 'until Ty Wheatley got a hold of you.'

'What did he do?'

'He took you to France, cut your hair, clued you up on wine, and got you into that job. Him and your new best friend Paris.' She did not make my new best friend's name sound like a romantic city, she made it sound like something oozing goop in the bottom of a dumpster.

'You know her?'

'Everyone knows her now, thanks to you. She was just some deeply unsexy anonymous PR hack until Ty hooked you up and clung to your coat-tails while she made you famous.'

'But am I any good?'

'Connie, you're probably one of the most talked-about women in town. In two years you've closed down a whole bunch of restaurants and made a whole bunch of millionaires. *New York Magazine* ran a cover story on you — you posed wearing nothing but a few cleverly placed bunches of fruit. You have a legion of fans that adore your every word and you get big sacks of fan mail. You were stalked for a while, too, by some waiter who lost his job after you wrote that he smelled of sour underpants and desperation.'

'I did not!' That was upsetting. I would never say anything like that about a waiter. I loved waiters. I had been one. I had probably smelled of sour underpants and desperation myself.

'Sorry, sweetie,' Fleur said. 'You did. Actually, you turned into kind of a bitch.'

'You're just saying that because I'm mad you stole my husband.'

'I didn't steal your husband, Connie. You threw him out.'

'But,' I stuttered, 'but, but, but . . .'

But what was the point in being a thin blonde restaurant critic for the *New York* freakin' *Times* if you had no husband, a creepy boyfriend, staples in your head, and were a bitch?

Miraculously, in the wake of that realisation Fleur and I managed to reach something of an understanding. She pointed out that I had already tortured her with phone calls and emails and face-to-face verbal abuse sessions; if I wanted to skip all that a second time, she said, we could just go straight to not talking to each other and that would be okay by her. This was not a bad plan but the thought of not having her in my life right then when I really desperately needed her, needed someone, seemed a trifle too much to bear. Without Tom, she was my most trustworthy anchor to the past, to me. Besides, my anger at her, at Tom, at the two of them, kind of ebbed away after its initial powerful swell and was hard to hold on to. I didn't feel as though it was permeating anything other than my stunned outer layer, which left me oddly capable of making quite a sensible suggestion.

'Could we skip forward even further and just make up with each other, then?' I offered. 'I mean I could just take your word that we've been through all the crap and we could just come out the other side.'

'Oh, could we?' Fleur's face brightened, her eyes sparkled above their panda patches of blurry mascara. 'Honestly?'

'Sure,' I said. 'Why not?'

She sprang out of her chair and jumped back onto the bed with me. 'Oh God, I've missed you so much, Connie. You wouldn't believe it.'

'There's a lot I wouldn't believe,' I told her, 'if people didn't keep insisting it's all true.' The *New York Times*? Wow.

Signora Marinello squelched back into the room then, handing me a tray bearing a sad little sandwich, a floury-looking apple, and a glass of unidentifiable juice. It did not look like something the most important restaurant critic in the world would contemplate for even a second but I was starving. Fleur went back to her chair so I could sit up and eat.

'It's good you make up,' Signora Marinello told her. 'Constanzia need her real friends.'

It had been weeks since I had eaten anything — what an unconscionable thought — and in an ideal world my first meal would have been much more of an exotic feast. In an ideal world I might have had, I looked at the clock — it was just after six — a handful of freshly roasted salty pistachio nuts (pistachio!) to get my juices flowing, followed by a little something soft and tangy to ease into the meal. Tom often made a simple tomato, avocado and buffalo mozzarella salad for me at home in the summer. It wasn't anything fancy but when the Jersey tomatoes were at their best, there was no better way to eat them. He bought the cheese fresh from Murray's and got his basil leaves extra peppery from his well-trained upstate organic farmer at Union Square. Then he drizzled his favourite olive oil, a nutty Italian one that played right into the hands of the avocado, over the top and served it with grilled ciabatta for a bit of crunch.

145

The soft subtle tastes of the understated cheese and smooth avocado mixed with the tartness of the tomatoes and topped with a sprinkling of crunchy sea salt were enough to get you seriously thinking about what you might eat next. In my ideal world, I decided, while I was on the subject, my heart hankered after sweet, rosy milk-fed lamb but it was past spring and out of the question. Perhaps a beautifully grilled fillet of Chilean sea bass? I knew the world was in danger of being fished out of the poor suckers but then God shouldn't have made them so darn good to eat. I would have it served on a risotto made with lemon zest, freshly podded English peas, fried capers, and the lightest of lobster stocks, with a simple arugula salad dressed with aged Balsamic on the side. As for dessert, well after that long it would have to be chocolate — and a lot of it. Soufflé perhaps, mousse, most likely. And then an espresso strong enough to make most grown men, Italian ones, wince. Oh, the thought of it! I would drink . . . what would I drink? Champagne. Without question. Buckets of it.

'I think is turkey,' Signora Marinello said doubtfully. 'They say no to scramble eggs.'

She and Fleur watched as I opened the sandwich to check for mustard: a fruitless search as it turned out, the whole collection was the same shade of dreary off-white but nonetheless I seasoned the limp-looking turkey with salt and pepper and hesitantly took a bite. The bread was fresh in the way that only white sliced bread can be when it's a week or more out of a commercial oven, but other than that the experience was deeply depressing. I rolled the first bite around in my mouth, chewing it down to the smallest amount so I could swallow it. It tasted of nothing — hardly surprising, I don't know what I was expecting — and I gave up halfway, washing it down with the bland juice of some completely made-up composite fruit and sinking back down into my bed, suddenly hopelessly exhausted.

'I'll go,' said Fleur, seeing this.

I smiled at her, happy that sleep, my escape from tasteless turkey and terrible truths, was close at hand.

'What about Tom?' I had to ask. 'I know it's weird, Fleur, but I really need to talk to him. I have to find a way to get my head around the whole pre-pretzel thing. Would that be okay? Would you ask him to come see me?'

'Of course,' she said. 'Whatever you want.' But her eyes were unhappy as she turned and left the room.

Ashlee, the bubbly flight attendant from my flight to Italy, came the next morning to take me to the gym for rehabilitation therapy. Actually, I had gotten used to imagined fragments from my unconsciousness turning up in my real life by then. The squat balding waiter from Alla Madonna turned out to be a wry orderly by the name of George who flirted outrageously with Signora Marinello using only monosyllables and a series of quite impressive eyebrow manoeuvres. The Pucci-clad mushroom vendor from the Rialto markets worked in the hospital kitchen and pushed the stack of meal trays from room to room. And I had seen one of the nasty grandfathers from the Giudecca pushing a toddler past my doorway, a regular visitor to a woman my age down the hall — his daughter, who had suffered a stroke and would be in the ward for a while to come.

Hunger still gnawing at me, I had attempted oatmeal for breakfast but given up after just a few spoonfuls, much to my nurse's disgust. It was grey and lumpy and approximately one million miles away from that creamy elixir poured from the silver tureen at the Hotel Gritti Palace. Plus it sure as hell was not followed by piping-hot freshly baked pastries the way I liked it to be.

Anyway, when Ashlee showed up and introduced herself as my physical therapist I was hardly surprised at all and immediately checked out her ring finger, which indeed sported a giant engagement ring. She took me down to the hospital gym and to my horror produced a big rubber ball from a collection of equipment at one end of the room.

'This is not a good idea,' I told her. 'This could end in disaster.'

'Just relax and take your time, Connie,' she said in a decidedly

147

return-your-seat-to-its-upright-position voice. 'You are in a safe environment. Nothing can happen to you but I need to assess your physical ability and see how you are doing, so we can plan your future treatment. Okay? Can you do that for me?'

The problem was that there were things about my physical ability Ashlee didn't know. Namely, I didn't have any. Throughout my entire schooling I had been plagued by a combination of excessive height and extreme uncoordination. I was always the last person chosen for any game at gym class and could not even walk onto a basketball court as a spectator without falling over my own feet and landing on my ass. I had a permanent bruise on my hip from banging into desks and doorknobs and still bore scars on both of my knees from tripping over for no apparent reason on any hard surface, preferably asphalt, something I continued to do on a regular basis well into my . . . well, my current surroundings spoke for themselves.

So when Ashlee lined me up and started throwing that big red ball at me, my life flashed in front of my eyes. It was pretty much like a scene from *One Flew Over The Cuckoo's Nest*. If they were going to judge my recovery on my sporting prowess, I was in big trouble. Predictably, I failed to catch the ball even once. I just couldn't stop closing my eyes whenever she threw it at me.

'I've always been like this,' I told her as I flailed around trying to pick the stupid thing up off the floor and throw it back. Even when it wasn't in the air I couldn't get a hold of it. 'It's nothing to do with the pretzel.'

She wrote something down on her chart.

I prayed to God to help me say something that wouldn't make me seem more incapacitated than I was. 'Look!' I said brightly and attempted a string of star jumps, the one athletic feat I'd always been able to handle as long as I got into the rhythm. Unfortunately, rhythm eluded me on this occasion. The left side of my body seemed to be working on a slightly different time frame from the right side, leaving my star jumps lop-sided to say the least. Ashlee rather predictably looked unconvinced and with a your-nearest-exit-is-over-here sign indicated that I should follow her to the opposite corner of the room where, much to my horror, she revealed a treadmill.

Now, I might have woken up with muscly thighs and been told I was a runner. But as far as I knew I had barely been able to master putting one foot in front of the other at a slow pace let alone a fast one and I baulked at trying to do so now, especially as it was on a machine and even more especially as it was some sort of a test.

'Just stand on the sides and I'll start it slowly,' Ashlee said, guiding me onto the stupid contraption and pressing the buttons with her long lacquered nails, that engagement ring picking up the fluorescent light and glowing like something out of an old *Star Trek* episode.

'When you are ready, step onto the belt and start walking.'

In the flash of an eye I was lying in a crumpled heap on the felty carpet behind the machine. It did not smell good. I was not the first person to land there and those before me had not necessarily enjoyed my level of bladder control. It did not strike me as a very rehabilitating experience.

Ashlee scribbled something else down on her clipboard before coming to help me up.

'I've always been like this,' I told her. 'You'd better put that on your chart or people will get the wrong idea.'

She smiled at me in a tolerant fashion — as though I'd just handed her a leaking bag full of vomit — and I slumped into a wheelchair. I could have walked back to my room but all that humiliation had taken it out of me.

'How was that, Constanzia?' Signora Marinello wanted to know as she helped me back into my bed.

'It's hard to say,' I told her.

'Connie has some balance and coordination issues,' Ashlee reported. 'We might want to let Dr Scarpa know about her progress. He has asked to be kept informed.'

So, Marco was taking an interest in me after all. This cheered me up significantly, as you can imagine, despite the fact that even though Ashlee was obviously engaged she got a real goofy look on her face when she said the words, 'Dr Scarpa'. An awful thought crossed my mind at that and as soon as she left the room I asked Signora Marinello to help me dispel it.

'Marco's not engaged is he?' Well everyone else was, including myself, so maybe Ashlee had every right to look goofy when she said Marco's name. She was exceptionally pretty after all, surely just the sort he would be attracted to.

'Engaged? To be married? Dr Scarpa?' Signora Marinello thought that was hilarious. 'He has too much fun being not engaged, I think.'

I felt unreasonably relieved at hearing this. I was still having trouble separating my coma feelings from my actual feelings as far as Marco was concerned. The thought of his hands on my ribs, his thighs against mine, the minty warmth of his breath on my neck, all seemed too real to leave me feeling like just another patient. I shuddered in my bed at the memory of him groaning in ecstasy as his gondola rocked vigorously in that darkened basement. But when I turned to look wistfully out the window and fantasise some more, I found my alleged fiancé, Ty Wheatley, standing there looking at me. I shuddered again. But in a different way.

Ten

'MC, darling,' my alleged fiancé drawled in his Prince Charles accent, 'at last I get a quiet moment alone with you.' He was holding an extravagant bunch of lilies, which I hate. 'For you,' he said, waving them at me with a dramatic flourish. 'Your favourites.'

Oh brother.

'I leave you to it,' Signora Marinello said quickly, making as if to leave. I no longer needed full-time care so I was sharing her with three other patients.

'No, don't go!' I didn't want to be left there with Ty. 'I might need a . . .' Of course, I couldn't for the life of me think what it was I might need. A new identity? A sawn-off shotgun?

'Yes?' Signora Marinello was not exactly helping me. In fact, I think she was trying to wean me off her. 'Might need which, Constanzia?'

'I had thought to bring some champagne,' Ty drawled, 'but I wasn't sure it would be allowed. You're looking so much better today, darling. More like your old self.'

He'd obviously forgotten that my old self looked nothing like that.

'I leave you to it,' Signora Marinello said again and this time she did.

'I do have something else for you, though,' Ty said, and he pulled a neatly wrapped blue box out of his pocket.

It was from Tiffany. Can you believe that?

'Darling,' he said, handing it over. 'I do hope you like it.'

Well, what would you do? It was from Tiffany! I stared at him, then at it, then opened it, pulling greedily on the white satin ribbon and gasping like a '50s actress when I saw what lay nestled inside the box. It was a bracelet; not that I was big on bracelets but this one was a beauty. It was a delicate circle of linked gold crosses with tiny diamonds set in between. It looked like the world's most beautiful daisy chain. I didn't know what to say. People like me just didn't get given things like that.

'It's to go with the earrings I got you for your birthday,' Ty said.

Okay, so people like me were wrong.

'It's fabulous,' I murmured weakly.

Encouraged, he slipped it onto my wrist where I have to say it looked spectacular. How strange it was, though, to be accepting such a gift from a man about whom I could remember nothing more than sharing a few monosyllables over bite-size buckwheat pancakes. And now we were getting married! I supposed I should bring up this subject but while I knew I should tread delicately, I couldn't quite remember how treading delicately went.

'So, I hear we're getting hitched,' I ventured, sounding a little more like Katharine Hepburn than I meant to.

Ty pulled his collar away from his neck somewhat nervously. 'When your divorce comes through,' he said, 'which should be any time soon, my dear. I've spoken to Thomas Keller and made a tentative date for the spring. It took quite some cajoling but I think he will do a wonderful job and the space is gorgeous. Perfect.'

'Thomas Keller?' I couldn't believe it. 'The French Laundry Thomas Keller?' His Yountville, California, restaurant was world famous. I had dreamed of going there but never had the balls to dream of getting married there. Mind you, why would I when I was already married?

'Darling, yes, of course,' Ty answered me, 'but he's here now, in

New York, at the Time Warner Center. Per Se, you loved it. Four stars, my sweet. Trust me, it's divine.'

I was getting married to a man who said 'divine'? In the spring? I was speechless. In fact, I just about gave myself another subdural haematoma trying to think of something to say that didn't express disbelief at finding myself betrothed to a well-heeled balding businessman who I had actually assumed was gay. Even if he did have superb taste in jewellery and the muscle to have our wedding reception catered for by one of America's undisputed top chefs.

'Oh, you didn't tell me,' Ty said then, breaking the silence with a quiver of excitement, 'Paris brought you the book! You must be thrilled, darling. What do you think?'

I had no idea what he was talking about but he was reaching for the Kate Spade shopping bag that Paris had left in my room after her last visit. He opened it and pulled out a paperback, a publisher's proof copy, his cheeks reddening in a way I could not believe anyone would ever find attractive, especially me.

As he turned it over, I saw on the jacket a sexy-looking woman sitting in a restaurant wearing a busty short-skirted suit, her face hidden behind a big white hat, her slender legs clad in spiky heels and crossed delicately beneath the table. *Stars something*, the title read, with *something something something* in smaller letters below it. I squinted at it, not sure that I was seeing correctly. The author's name, in big red letters, was MC Conlan. MC Conlan? Lord in heaven. That was me.

'Give,' I croaked to Ty, stretching out my arms, my fingers wiggling, diamonds twinkling, the correct words not quite on the tip of my tongue. 'Give, give, give.'

Mistaking my horror for delight, he only too quickly handed the book over.

'You know Jeffrey Steingarten thinks you could well be the next best thing,' he said smugly. 'We'll have to get him over for cocktails when you're up to it. He's promised to review you in *Vogue* and I think we might just make Hot Type in *Vanity Fair*. Fingers crossed for the *Times* bestseller list, MC. You're a shoo-in, so they say.'

Stars Struck, the title read: *In Search of the Sublime New York Dining Experience*. I felt the breath disappear from my lungs. Surely to God I had not written a food memoir? Seriously, no one but Ruth Reichl should ever have bothered. No one but her had enough to say or could say it without sounding like a tight-ass nincompoop. Especially not me. I particularly had nothing to say. It was inconceivable I would write a book. Yet, on close inspection, the woman on the front cover was definitely me. She just looked so much more sophisticated than me, so much more confident and aware of her allure, so grown-up and sort of pleased with herself. In short, so unlike how I saw myself that I had to keep checking her right hand, perfectly poised to cut into a piece of prime rib, to make sure it had the same freckle on it that mine did. What's more, according to the blurb on the inside back jacket, this woman on the cover who was apparently me lived on the Upper East Side with her publisher partner and their two cats. Cats? And there was me thinking I would rather eat a cat than own one as a pet. In fact, hadn't I been mildly famous (in the Village, or a pocket of it) for saying that somewhere?

'I don't,' I said to Ty. 'I can't. It's too . . .'

'Thrilling, yes, I know,' he agreed, even though whatever I had been going to say was not anything he was likely to agree with. 'As soon as you're on your feet we'll get together with Paris and re-schedule the book tour. I know it's a setback, MC, but with a small amount of rearranging we can get right back on track, I know we can. And of course there's that much more interest in you now that you've triumphed over, well, tragedy, I suppose. I don't think media coverage will be a problem somehow. Not at all. Paris is delighted about that much.'

My mouth was opening and closing like the last of the Chilean sea bass. 'Have I? Do I?' I was close to making some sense, I knew I was. If I could just line the words up and get them out maybe I could

154

get somewhere. 'Did I do something really bad?' I finally asked him. I just could not believe that a nice girl like myself had woken up in the middle of such a nightmare. 'I think I must have done something really bad.'

'No, no, no,' soothed Ty. 'The timing wasn't brilliant but for goodness' sake it was an accident. And I hold myself to blame to a certain extent,' he said — and get ready for this because here comes the high note on the sad-o-meter — 'over that whole Atkins business.'

Oh yes. You read it right. Atkins. More specifically, the Atkins Diet, the low-carb high-protein regime of which I had long been an enthusiastic adversary. It was the curse of the complex carbohydrate, I had firmly believed, the enemy of all serious food lovers. A swizz, a gyp, a wicked waste of eating hours. Yet it turned out that the reason I had pillaged Woody Allen for his pretzel was because, in a bid to starve off enough pounds to slither into a Vera Wang wedding gown that Ty had chosen and for which I was already being fitted, I had resorted to the Atkins Diet. The conclusion that had been drawn was that after a couple of months of low or no carbs, something inside me had snapped, making me lunge for the forbidden snack. If it hadn't been so sad it would have been funny. But it was sad. So sad that I started to cry and could not stop, despite my husband-to-be ineffectually patting me on the shoulder like I was some precious Burmese feline or something.

'Please,' I sobbed. 'I'm having a bad day. You should go.'

I think Ty was relieved at this suggestion. He stepped back and straightened his jacket, which was crumpled, of course, it being linen and everything.

'I'll be back tomorrow, my dear,' he said. 'Try to get some rest. I'm dining at Le Bernadin with Eric tonight. He was asking after you, you know. And Mario Batali sent the most exquisite bouquet to the apartment. I had them in the jardinière Jean-Georges gave us as an engagement present. You were unconscious, my darling, there didn't seem any point in bringing them in here. Oh, I'm meeting with your editor at the *Times* tomorrow — he's insistent on an update, MC, and I didn't think you'd want him to see you like this so I thought it best if I handled it myself. You don't mind, do you? Anyway, I must dash. Take care and I'll see you tomorrow.'

I found everything about him so astonishing it gave me a stomach-ache just thinking about it. He was such a name-dropper! Tom and I had always laughed at people like that. 'Oh, Emeril this and Alain that and Jeremiah yada yada yada.' Didn't he know you only showed off about people like that when they weren't your real friends? When I thought about it, though, he always was a bit of a second-hand rose, hanging around on the edges of the in-crowd. He obviously didn't know that he would never naturally be hip, some people simply weren't — me included. But the ones with money like Ty could at least get a foot in the door . . . even if it was never properly opened to them.

I was extremely tired and emotional after his visit but Signora Marinello assured me that being extremely tired and emotional was probably the best I could hope for in the next while. She said a lot of people in my position went on to be treated for depression and that I should not consider it a failing if it was felt I would benefit from anti-depressants.

'Will little white pills bring my old husband back?' I asked her.

'Nice bangle,' she said instead, checking out my wrist. 'Mister White Pants give that to you? Good taste, Constanzia. Lucky you.'

Lucky indeed. I looked at the bracelet again but the diamonds no longer sparkled quite so glitteringly. I slipped it off my wrist, pushed it under my pillow then turned over in my bed and closed my eyes.

'Well, hello you,' a gentle voice roused me out of a deep dreamless sleep sometime in the early evening. As always when I woke up these days, a row of pretzels tormented me by dancing in front of my eyes until I remembered why I was where I was and blinked hard to get rid of the little bastards. Tom, my supposedly soon-to-be ex-husband, was standing in the doorway with that same uncertain look on his face that Fleur had had in the exact same spot the day before. He was holding a bunch of red gladioli, my real favourites. Tom knew me. How he knew me.

'God, Connie,' he said and his voice, so familiar, sent shivers up my spine. 'Do you have to look so beautiful?'

Well, what can you say to something like that? Tom had never been one to say anything other than exactly what he felt: he was known for being overly frank, for want of a better word, and while at times that could be hurtful or annoying or, worse, embarrassing, it meant you were never in any doubt about how he felt. So I knew, then and there, that he really did think I was beautiful and I knew he always had thought that. So why the hell, I asked myself, sitting up in my hospital bed, was he schtupping my best friend and not me?

'You think?' I asked, then threw back the bedclothes. 'That's not the half of it. Turns out I'm a size six.' I won't say it felt entirely right exposing myself to the man who was happily ensconced with my best friend, but then it didn't feel entirely wrong either. He would always have been the first person to whom I'd crow about waking up thin. Besides, a tiny little part of me that I was actually trying very hard to ignore was quietly pointing out that no one had actually said they were happily ensconced. Fleur hadn't. And neither had Tom. Of course, he was only just getting started but I couldn't have said he looked happy. He looked . . . like Tom. My Tom. My little buddy since I was four and my husband for the past — however many, I kept getting confused — years. He didn't look like the father of Fleur's baby at all.

He seemed a little stunned at the sight of my much-diminished body but I think it actually perked him up. His face relaxed and he strode over to me, bending down to kiss me on the forehead, further checking out my slim hips and runner's legs as he did so. And why wouldn't he? I could barely keep my eyes off them myself. There was actually a gap between the tops of my thighs. A gap. Can you believe that? Just like Elle Macpherson. I thought of all the times I had promised God that if he gave me thin thighs I would go to church/give up chocolate/join a gym, never for a moment thinking that I just might one day get my wish. And I hadn't even had to go to church or give up chocolate; or if I had, I didn't remember so in some respects it didn't seem like such a high price to pay.

'Earth to Connie,' Tom said. 'Hello. Anybody there?'

I snatched up the bedclothes. I would stare at my legs again later when he was gone I told myself, turning my attention back to him. He was sitting bolt upright in his chair, his face white and panicked, the flowers splayed across his legs. 'Jesus, I'm sorry,' he said. 'I didn't mean anything by that.'

I suppose 'Anybody there?' was probably not the best question to ask someone barely out of a coma but he looked so darn wretched I decided not to take it further. Before I started an argument I wanted to find out why we were no longer together.

'A fine old mess I got myself in this time, huh?' I said, sounding far more flippant than I felt. My stomach may have been concave but there was still room in it for butterflies.

'Fleur says you have some sort of amnesia,' Tom said. He looked so worried. 'That you can't remember the past few years.'

'Yup,' I agreed, ignoring the involuntary clench in my internal organs at the sound of my best friend's name. 'Where I'm coming from I'm still happily churning out reviews for the *Voice* and married to you.'

We looked each other in the eye and it was a seriously weird, sad moment.

'Tom, I know this is —'

'Connie, you have to —'

The clumsiness was hard to handle. I mean, you've gathered I'm no stranger to the awkward moment but none of them, not even one up until that point, had ever been with Tom. When you've known each other since kindergarten, there's not much call for awkwardness. We'd been watching each other pee for more than 30 years, for heaven's sake.

'You first,' I said with forced amiability, trying to break the cycle of discomfort. 'Go on. You have all your faculties.'

Tom shook his head. 'This is all so, I don't know, bizarre, Connie. I just keep trying to put myself in your situation and I can't for the life of me even begin to imagine what you are going through but — Jesus, does that thing on your head hurt?'

'My hair?'

'No, babe, the scar.'

Hearing him call me babe made a lump rise up in my throat. I had forgotten what a sexy voice he had. How long had it been since he had called me babe?

'No, it doesn't.' Part of me wanted to jump out of bed and fall into his arms but chances were I would trip before I got that far and end up with a whole new coma and a completely different bunch of lost memories. Instead, I abandoned any attempt at a tearful reunion or polite chitchat and cut straight to the chase. 'What happened to us, Tom? I just don't get it.'

'Jesus, Connie.' At that moment Tom looked older than his 36 years. His skin was lined around eyes that were droopy with weariness: whether from being up all night with an 11-month-old or finding out his wife couldn't remember leaving him I didn't know, but either way he wore his troubles on his face for all to see.

Still, my blood pumped warmly around my body at the sight of him. Not quite as warmly as it did when a certain neurosurgeon/gondolier was in the room but it pumped all the same. Put it this way, I certainly did not feel like I wasn't married to him. Not at all.

He was reading my face as much as I was reading his, his eyes flitting from one to the other of mine. Did he think I looked older than 36? Did he like my new body, my new hair? Did he still think I was cute like I thought he was? Had I known how lucky I was to have him when I had him? It was hard to imagine how we had gotten there, to that point, staring at each other across a sterile hospital room wondering what we liked about each other and what we didn't, wondering why we weren't married any more.

'What happened?' I asked him again. 'Tell me, Tom, please. I know it must be hard for you, seriously I do, but I'm in the dark here. It's like I've woken up a whole new person and I don't know what the old person did but from what I've heard, I can't say I like the sound of her. But I still need to know what happened and you can tell me, so please, please, please do.'

He hesitated for a moment, but I knew he would do what I asked. We were old, trusted, tried and true friends, no matter what.

'Ty Wheatley,' he said flatly, 'that's what happened.'

Well, that much I knew. 'But how?' I asked. 'I hardly know the guy and suddenly we're engaged? It doesn't make sense. It doesn't sound like me, Tom. And on top of everything you know how I feel about crumpled linen. Jeez, like who can afford the dry-cleaning? How could someone like Ty Wheatley have happened to us?'

'Don't ask me,' he answered showing some signs of irritability that I suppose were not exactly unwarranted. 'It's your story. I wasn't there, you know, as events unfolded.'

'Yeah, well I'm a little hazy on the details too, what with the whole pretzel thing,' I shot back, feeling fairly irritable myself. 'So as far as I'm concerned I wasn't there either.' I checked myself, though, because Tom was still my best chance of gathering the details of how my life had gone off the rails so I couldn't afford to alienate him. 'Come on,' I pleaded again. 'Help me out here.'

He softened. 'All I know is that one minute you're walking through the Village talking to me on your cell-phone and the next you're cutting me off to take a call from someone else. Then I'm at Kennedy Airport waiting for you and finally, *arrivederci*, I'm in Venice on my own.'

I saw myself again on Bleecker Street, the beautiful brisk

morning after the lobster tails at Gotham, my coat pulled close, tears in my eyes, Ty Wheatley on the cell-phone, the smell of vanilla frosting thick in the air. I checked myself. I was confused again. Things weren't connecting. Ty Wheatley on the phone? I felt something horribly like guilt curdling inside me. But why would I feel guilt? What had I done?

'Dinner.' My Pucci-clad mushroom-seller interrupted us with a plate of something that looked like an old sneaker boiled in slimy green pond scum. Pieces of corn and carrot slid across the top in a slick of something oily and the plate was stone cold. The whole thing looked repulsive.

'No thank you.' I pushed it away, although frankly flushing it down the toilet would have been doing the poor sucker in the next room a favour, if that was where it was headed.

'Suit yourself,' Mrs Pucci said. 'Like I care.'

'You were much better as a mushroom-seller,' I told her as she left the room.

'Ain't we all,' she answered as she disappeared out of sight.

'I've got an idea,' Tom suggested and his face brightened, making him look more like the old (younger) him that I remembered. 'Why don't I ring the restaurant — they won't be busy yet. Want me to order for you? They can deliver before the rush.'

What a husband, I thought to myself. What a perfect husband.

'Bring me the *mozzarella di bufala*,' Tom instructed whoever answered the phone at work, 'and the *insalata di noci* with extra gorgonzola.'

My eyes glazed over at the thought of that sharp, creamy cheese with caramelised walnuts and pear. Something soft, something crisp, something crunchy. I could hardly wait.

'I'll have the *gnocchi di patate al tegamino* and use the primo basil from my private supply,' Tom was saying, 'and throw in the *galletto al mattone* as well, not too heavy on the mushroom sauce either, Paolo, I saw how you were plating up last night, don't drown the poor bird. Bring some spinach focaccia as well, and make it snappy, huh, I'm dealing with a very hungry woman here.'

He looked so loose and happy talking about food, my Tom. So at peace with the world and himself. So . . . unfamiliar to me when it boiled down to it. Had I not been able to make him loose and happy when we were together? Had he not been at peace with me?

'Keep going,' I said when he turned back to me. 'Tell me what you know.'

'It was the day we were going to go to Venice,' he said, 'you know, to try to start afresh. We got into a fight in the morning. About butter. God, Connie, this is such ancient history . . . are you sure we have to go over it again?'

'It's not ancient history to me,' I said. 'Please, Tom. Keep going.'

'We had a fight — you really don't remember? You stormed out, said you were going for a walk.'

I did vaguely remember us shouting at each other over the breakfast dishes although it could have been a generic memory, I couldn't pinpoint the specifics. And I had been known to walk off a head of steam in my time.

'And?'

'And so I turn up at the airport at four in the afternoon like we planned and fly off on our second honeymoon alone while you stay in New York, move out of our apartment and start your new job as the queen of dining and wining.'

This just sounded so unlike me I still could not believe it. I was just not the fail-to-turn-up-on-your-second-honeymoon type. Even in my dreams, my subconscious, I was the one who turned up, the one who did what was expected, who obeyed the rules . . . for a while, you know, in the case of Venice, until I decided to do unto someone else what was not being done unto me. And on my second honeymoon, when you really should expect things to be done unto you. Big-time.

'You're sure nothing else happened to me?' I asked Tom, determined to find an explanation for my out-of-character behaviour.

'I wasn't mugged or kidnapped or drugged or brainwashed or something? It just doesn't seem like me, Tom. You have to admit it. Maybe I was suffering from Stockholm syndrome.'

'I don't think so.' His face had hardened and I decided to steer clear of any suggestion that Ty Wheatley had kidnapped me in case there was incontrovertible proof otherwise.

'So you stayed in Venice. Without me.' All the same, I thought it might not hurt to try pointing the finger back at Tom a little.

'It was some second honeymoon, let me tell you,' he said in a surprisingly genial fashion. 'The food was crap but the markets were okay. Of course, I pretty much only left my room to buy vodka.'

Was this really happening? My life was getting more and more peculiar as the minutes ticked by.

'And Fleur?' Tom looked uncomfortable again and took off his jacket. He was wearing a cool striped shirt with floral collar and cuffs and he looked good. Very good. Delectable even. Like the Tom I had married. Better, possibly.

'Christ, Connie, the way things have turned out I feel so bad, you know, I feel like a real fucking shit but you have to remember that you left me. It wasn't the other way around. *You* left *me*.'

I did have to remember that. But it wasn't easy. 'But didn't you try to get me back? Didn't you try to talk some sense into me? Didn't you fight for me?'

'Are you kidding me? You dump me from a great height for that, that fucking *faggot* without so much as a moment's notice and I am supposed to kill myself to get you back? I don't think so, Connie. I've got my pride. I mean, fuck that.'

I had hurt him, horribly, that much was plain. He was still so angry.

'You just take up with Old Money Bags and start your new life like you never even had an old one. Shit, Connie. Forget it. Then I bump into Fleur one night and we end up having a few drinks and talking about stuff, and you know . . .'

'. . . one thing led to another. Yeah, yeah, yeah, I've read the book, I've seen the movie.'

'It wasn't like that, babe.' The anger whooshed out of him.

'What *was* it like, then?'

'It was like I didn't know you any more, Connie, that's what it was like, but I knew her. She was still the same old Fleur I had always known. And she took me under her wing and bolstered me.'

'And I didn't?'

'I don't know that you are the bolstering type, babe.'

He was right. I needed bolstering myself, more likely. But had Tom bolstered me? I wasn't sure. All I knew was that my heart was breaking all over again and there was no surgeon in the world that could put that back together.

'I'm sorry,' I said, tears I did not want to shed suddenly leaking out of me. 'I'm so sorry. I wish I could turn back the clock and try harder, Tom. I don't want to be with Ty Wheatley. I don't even know him. I'm just so scared of what's going to happen. I want to go back to the way things were.'

Poor Tom, he looked as unhappy as I felt and next thing I knew he was sitting on the edge of the bed, rocking me slowly, just like he always had when I'd been hurt or upset. I felt so safe there, wrapped up in his arms, his warmth, his concern, that it took me quite a while to notice that he didn't smell like himself. He didn't smell of anything.

'Don't tell me you're not using sage any more,' I said, pulling back from him to reach for the Kleenex.

'Too much, according to you,' he answered and there was an edge to his voice. 'Oh yeah, you've probably forgotten,' — he was rueful rather than mean, but still nowhere near as warm as he had been before — 'Pippo passed away not long after you and I broke up and he left me the restaurant. Yeah,' he said, smiling with his mouth if not his eyes at my reaction. 'Pretty cool, huh? I mean it broke my heart to lose him but to get my own restaurant, well. So, anyways, I relaunched it — man, I can't believe I am having to tell you this — as Tom's and . . .'

'And?'

'And you reviewed it and gave it one star.'

One star?

The nicest way to kill a restaurant. The kiss of death. A no-star restaurant people would go to just to see how awful it was, a two-star restaurant they would go to because they knew it would be good value for money, a three-star restaurant they would go to because they couldn't afford a four-star restaurant, and a four-star restaurant they would save up for so they could stick it to their friends who hadn't been there yet.

A one-star restaurant they would most likely ignore.

'Wow. Fleur told me I was a bitch,' I said sorrowfully, 'but I'd hoped she was exaggerating.' I waited for Tom to argue but he didn't. How it must have hurt to have the woman who had been by his side half his life deal such a horrible blow at such a crucial time. I hated me. I was a bitch. 'So what happened to Tom's?' I asked in a small voice.

'I closed it and turned it back into Il Secondo,' Tom replied. 'Then I got a guest spot on the Food Network and actually things kind of looked up from there. Don't worry, Connie, you didn't kill me. Just knocked me out cold for a while.' He looked shamefaced when he realised what he'd said but I just laughed and said: 'Hello. Anybody there?'

The truth was I was so relieved that I hadn't killed him that I nearly kissed him. And the other truth was that I had been thinking about kissing him for a while. The only thing that stopped me was that it would have meant betraying Fleur, cheating with her partner, and I didn't think I could do that, even though as far as I was concerned she had done it to me, but then I probably wasn't a good person to judge.

At that moment, a delivery boy bounced in the door bearing a steaming brown paper sack from Il Secondo.

'Thank you Lord!' I crowed, grateful that the dangerous moment had passed. 'Finally, something's going my way.'

But as Tom started to unload the food onto the tray in front of me, and I felt the warmth of the hot dishes — the spicy potato dumplings and the piping-hot Cornish game hen — on my chin, my cheeks, my eyes, as the steam rose from the food, it struck me that something was missing.

The gnocchi was made with Tom's peppery basil, I knew that, I'd heard him ask for it and the sauce was a spicy veal ragout, Pippo's secret recipe, surely Tom wouldn't have changed it, it was sensational. And the way he had always cooked game hen was to marinate it in rosemary and garlic. He loved the pungent aromas of those Italian herbs as did I. But there was not a trace of any of them in the air of my hospital room. I could feel the steam from the food on my skin, in my nostrils even, yet where I expected to find the scintillating smells of rosemary and basil there was nothing.

'Are you okay?' Tom was setting my meal up, tucking a napkin into the front of my hospital gown and organising the dishes in front of me.

'You changed Pippo's gnocchi sauce?' I asked him, my head spinning a little. 'You don't use garlic in the chicken any more?'

'What, are you crazy?' He sniffed the air. 'You can't smell it?'

I sniffed the air myself. Again, nothing. My hand shook slightly, fear nibbling at me, as I speared a dumpling, piled it high with the veal ragout and took a bite. The gnocchi was silky as I pushed it across the roof of my mouth. I felt strings of mozzarella sticking to my top teeth and rolled them away with my tongue, catching every morsel of milk-fed veal in its slow cooked tomato sauce as it swirled around inside my cheeks.

Oh, I could feel that delectable mouthful of Il Secondo's signature dish, all right. I could feel it just fine. Better than the next person even.

I just couldn't taste it.

I could not taste a thing.

Eleven

So, turns out those thin thighs hadn't come cheap after all. I had paid a far higher price than joining a gym or spending hours on my knees at Our Lady of Perpetual Suffering. I had paid the highest price imaginable: my taste. I would have given anything else, anything but that. Truly, the memory loss was nothing in comparison. I'd been getting used to it, whatever it was and whatever caused it, because while it might have been weird and surreal and deeply frustrating, it wasn't an arm or a leg. It was just two years and nine months of my life. And there were people who could help me plug that hole.

But my taste! That was a different matter. If I didn't have my taste I had nothing. I was nobody. Even the old Connie, the pre-*New York Times* version, relied on her taste for her job, her enjoyment, her reason for freakin' living. Without it I could just not see the sense in having survived the coma. I mean what was the point? It seemed cruel beyond belief. I was bereft. I screamed and howled and cried and not even the sight of the gap between my thighs could distract me. I would have had my fat squashy joined-up ones back in a heartbeat if it meant I could savour sweet and sour and salty again. I prayed to fall back into a coma and die. I pleaded for Signora Marinello to inject me with something lethal. I was wretched beyond comprehension. Wretched.

'I can see why you might be upset,' admitted Marco two days

later when he finally came to see me. I was so distressed I barely stopped to notice how hot he was. Barely. Little morsels of desire still managed to infiltrate the terror that ravaged me, but this only added to my generally anguished state.

'Loss of these senses is not entirely uncommon after a head trauma,' he told me, 'but I'm intrigued because usually it's when there is some damage to the cribriform plate, which in your situation is not the case, and even then it is rare for there to be no sense of taste at all. Are you positive about that? That there is no taste?'

Was I positive? What a question. It wasn't like taste was a small matter to me, it was a big matter. The biggest. Did Marco really think I would not fully explore the extent of my loss? He could be a real jerk sometimes that guy, morsels of desire or not. Of course I was positive, and I wasn't relying on hospital slop to test out my taste buds either. No, after finding myself unable to taste Il Secondo's finest, I had sent Tom to Gray's Papaya for a hotdog with extra mustard then to Delmonico's for take-out lobster Newburg. I'd despatched Fleur to Guss's Pickles for a selection of the house favourites, to the pushcart on 54th Street for Rolf's famous bratwurst and Berliner sausage combo and had even begged my mom to go to Two Little Red Hens for a slice of the city's best New York cheesecake — the ultimate in the battle between sweet and tart — but it was useless. All of it, useless. I could tell hot and cold, crunchy and smooth, soft and hard, fresh and stale, but I could not smell or taste a thing. I knew what the food should taste like, there was nothing wrong with that part of my memory, but it simply did not register when I sampled it.

'As I say, there has been no injury to the face, the nose,' Marco said. He put one hand on my jaw and one on my forehead, which normally would have driven me wild but I was too busy hyperventilating with fear for my future to appreciate his touch. 'However, I have seen far milder injuries even than yours where there has been some damage to the neural pathways, which has led to malfunctioning of the olfactory bulb.'

'Speak English,' I snapped. 'These are my taste buds we're talking about.'

'No, they're not actually,' he said and I saw that coldness in him again, that thread of steel that on occasion rendered him strangely inhuman. 'There is nothing wrong with your taste buds. It is a nerve issue. And in time, the damaged nerves may repair themselves and your ability to smell and taste may return.'

'May repair themselves? You mean they may not? Can't you operate? There must be something you can do. I can't go through life not tasting anything. I may as well just . . .' I tried to think of what I may as well just do. Lie around listening to Courtney Love and smoking pot all day like my brother? It was unbearable.

'There is no treatment for ageusia or dysgeusia,' Marco said, 'which are the technical names for what you are suffering, and that is surgical or otherwise. I'm afraid you'll just have to live with it.'

'You can't just leave it at that,' I cried. 'This is my taste we are talking about. It's how I make a living.' A good one too, probably, if I was working for the *New York Times*. 'It's all I have.'

'Then you'll just have to get something else,' Marco said, and he turned on his heel and left the room.

I was devastated. Totally devastated. And there was no one there to share my devastation. I was totally alone. Had never felt more alone in my old life or this torturous new one. I turned over and reached for the bag of grapes Ty had brought me from the Whole Food Market, pulling off a luscious, fat, nearly black one from the top of the bunch and popping it in my mouth.

I bit into it and felt the tight skin pop open, the soft pulp squirting inside my mouth, but there was no tartness on my tongue, no sweet after-bite. There was nothing.

Oh, the despair.

I know what you are probably thinking about now. You are thinking, boy, is this depressing, and it started out such fun. And what's more, it was about to get worse.

'Darling,' Ty Wheatley said after planting one of his dry little kisses on my eyebrow the next day. 'Wonderful news. I'm allowed to take you home.'

Home? I had been so busy panicking over my inability to taste anything that it had not occurred to me to think about going home. Home was the last thing on my mind. Signora Marinello had followed Ty into my room and was eyeing me nervously as he spoke, which in turn made me jumpy. Why would Signora Marinello be nervous about Ty taking me home?

'Holy shit,' I said. Had it occurred to me to think about going home, I might have pondered the question of where home actually was. I had assumed it would be with Tom; but Tom's home was with Fleur now, Fleur and Agnes, not me. I obviously lived somewhere else. 'You mean you're going to take me to your place?' I asked Ty.

'Our place,' he corrected me. 'Our home. And Cayenne and Jalapeno are very excited.'

'Cayenne and Jalapeno?' We had excited peppers?

'The cats, darling. Cay-Cay and Happy. They can't wait. They're scratching the armoire in excitement as we speak. They can just tell something is happening. It's hilarious.'

Oh brother.

He had a different cream linen suit on, I noticed, but it was still crinkled and he was wearing a loathsome bow tie too, blue with little red elephants on it. Worse still, when he sat down in the visitor's chair, his pants rode up and I saw he was wearing matching blue socks that also sported little red elephants. I was shocked. Beyond belief. You can see what I mean about things getting worse.

Actually, when I say I was shocked, I'm not joking. And I don't mean I was surprised, I mean I was stunned. Dazed. Confused. Such a state was I in, in fact, that almost before I knew what was happening I was being bundled up in readiness to be returned to our apartment on the Upper East Side: 63rd and Park, the home of MC Conlan, Ty Wheatley and their two adorable little Kitty McKittingtons (I kid you not), Cay-Cay and Happy.

Ty simply packed up what belongings I seemed to have, handed me a hideous greige outfit he'd brought from 'home' — the sort of thing Paris would wear but not look like a dead person in — then ordered a car (he drove everywhere in a Lincoln, just like my grand-mother) to be waiting outside in half an hour.

I remember standing in my little bathroom at the hospital, staring at myself in the unflatteringly lit mirror. Ty had brought in 'my' enormous make-up bag and it was bulging with mysterious lotions and potions that I hardly even recognised. I had been a moisturiser-only girl in my old life, a bit of lipstick and mascara and a dab of blusher if I was going out but on the whole I preferred the minimalist approach. MC, though, had a massive collection of concealers, foundations, powders, eye shadows, lip-liners, glosses and cellulite creams, for heaven's sake. I might not have had a whole brain but I still knew that even if I had cellulite no cream was going to get rid of it. Oh, what had become of me?

Anyway, there didn't seem much else for it so I clumsily applied a modest faceful of products I was able to identify. The greige shift dress and matching cropped jacket were not what I would have chosen myself but a set of cherry-red lips cheered up my visage enormously. I never would have thought to wear cherry-red lipstick in my old life. I forced a smile and to my utter amazement I had to admit that, despite the tragedy of it all, if I removed my critical eye and ignored the fact that I didn't look like me, the woman I did look like was not half bad.

Something, though, was still not quite right. Something apart from the fact that my hair was blonde on the good side of my head but dark both at the roots and on the other side. Ty already had me booked in with the new Frederic Fekkai, whoever that was. Could it be my eyebrows? They had definitely seen better days . . . I obviously plucked them a lot more than I used to and they were growing back quite oddly. I leaned in closer for further inspection and so did my mirror image, but up close she looked even less like me than before.

I was puzzled. But she was not. I was horrified but she was not. I was scared, but she was not. No matter what my inner emotion, she remained glassily smooth.

I burst out of the bathroom, my hands flapping in front of me in terror. I was going to end up in a wheelchair after all. I was paralysed!

'I can't move!' I cried. 'Look! I can't move!'

Marco was standing there, signing some forms with Signora Marinello and Ty.

'You're moving pretty well if you ask me,' he said, and despite my panic I couldn't help but notice that his eyes were running over me in a way that should have made me feel disgusted right there in front of my alleged fiancé but did not.

'Thank God you're here,' I said. 'I can't move my face, Marco. What's wrong with me? What's the matter?'

He handed Signora Marinello the paperwork, sat me on the bed then ran those long lean fingers across my cheeks, around my eyes, along my hairline.

'Very nice,' Marco said. 'I'd say it was Bill Howard up on East 73rd. He does the best work in town.'

'The best work?' I echoed.

'Botox,' Marco said. 'He's just plumped out your eyes and filled in your frown lines. Don't worry. He's done a great job.'

'I've been Botox-ed?'

'Everybody on the Upper East Side has been Botox-ed, Connie. You look good. In fact, you look great.'

His hand was still on my chin. I could barely concentrate on the shock of what he'd just told me. I'd always looked down my naturally well-proportioned nose at the nippers and tuckers and plumpers and suckers of the world, and now I was one?

'Come along MC,' Ty said, perhaps picking up on whatever danced in the air between Marco and me. 'The car is waiting.'

'I don't suppose you've discovered a last-minute cure for my taste problem then,' I said and to my astonishment my voice sounded all husky and Kathleen Turner-ish.

'No,' Marco said and he smiled at me, such a rare and blinding vision I just about jumped into his arms at the sight of it. 'But if I do you'll be the first to know. Make sure to keep in touch. I don't generally get to enjoy normal conversations with my patients.'

I stood up and our eyes lingered on each other in a decidedly non-doctor-patient fashion.

'The car, MC,' Ty reminded me edgily and I can't say I blamed him. The room hung hot and heavy with my slatternly lust.

'Good luck, Constanzia,' Marco said and he took my hand in his, then leaned in and kissed me on the cheek, his lips soft and perfectly moist on my skin. I closed my eyes and imagined the smell of him, which was quite glorious, so glorious in fact that I forgot to open my eyes again and it wasn't until Signora Marinello and Ty both coughed loudly that I remembered where I was and let Marco go.

'I'm sorry,' I said.

'Don't be,' he answered and he was gone.

Well, you can only imagine the awkward moment that blossomed after that little exchange. I blushed to the roots of my roots as I pretended to look for things that I might have forgotten while Ty burbled details of our cats I wouldn't have thought anyone but a veterinary gynaecologist would care to hear.

Finally, when there was truly nothing to do but leave, Signora Marinello was strangely subdued, shy almost, as she held me at arm's length and studied me with her earnest brown eyes.

'Don't be frightened, Constanzia,' she said. 'Will all be okay. You'll see. But remember your brain she is not better yet. You need your friends. Your real friends.' She said this last in a whisper, which I took to mean that she did not count Ty among my real friends (which was fine by me, as I didn't either). In fact, the only reason I was going with him was because nobody else had offered to take me anywhere. And because of the bracelet which Fleur had looked up on the Internet and said cost $4000.

'You know where to find me if you need me, Constanzia,' Signora Marinello whispered into my ear, pulling me into her warm doughy body. 'I will always be here. Don't forget. If you need me, just come find me.'

I hated those Park Avenue cats on sight. They were both fat and fluffy with floppy undercarriages that looked as though someone had unzipped them and taken the stuffing out. Cay-Cay — or was it Happy? I had no way of telling the snooty little creatures apart — actually arched her back and yowled at me when I stepped into the entrance hall of Ty's 12th-floor corner apartment.

The place was enormous. Frankly, I felt like arching my back and yowling a little myself. You could have fitted Tom's and my old apartment in the entry foyer. It was scarily spacious, with a hallway and bedrooms off to the left and a light-filled living room to the right. I followed Ty in that direction, trying to keep my jaw from dropping on the ground at the sight of his super-deluxe gourmet kitchen gleaming with stainless-steel bench-tops and sparkling with every appliance known to mankind — including a fully plumbed-in commercial coffee machine. It was the sort of kitchen someone like me might have dreamed of but never in a million years expect to have. I was staggered.

The rest of the apartment was just as impressive. A tastefully planted terrace ran the length of the living and dining areas . . . you could look out French doors to Park Avenue from behind the kitchen bench. The whole place was sleek and uncluttered and screamed style and good taste and huge expense. It took me a while to realise, though, that everything was beige and I mean everything: walls, parquet floors, drapes, sofas, flower arrangements, lampshades, you name it, even the books on the book shelves all seemed to have beige spines. The cats were beige. The expensive-looking art on the wall was beige. Frankly, I thought it could have done with a splash of colour but what did I know?

174

I collapsed into a stylishly upright armchair and slipped off my high heels, stretching out my legs and wriggling my toes on the Persian rug underneath the coffee table. I could barely believe that I lived there. When Ty took my bag away and disappeared back down the hall with it I sat like a stunned mullet in my chair, just wondering what the hell was going to happen next. I looked around the vast perfectly decorated space for any signs that I might have had a hand in it but there was nothing of me in the room at all. It was too tasteful for that. Then Ty bustled back, rubbing his hands together. He settled himself on the stylishly upright sofa, removed a cushion from behind his back and placed it neatly at the opposite end, then patted the seat beside him, indicating that Cay-Cay or Happy should jump up, which one of them did, curling into a ball and eyeing me beadily. Then he picked up a remote control and the room was suddenly filled with sound, which also sounded beige. I was pretty sure I still liked Madonna and Ricky Martin but clearly Ty was more of an elevator music guy.

Anyway, it was surreal. We sat there, he and I, in our $3-million-plus apartment looking for all the world just like any other well-to-do New York couple enjoying a peaceful afternoon in the home we had painstakingly perfected. If aliens had landed in our living room they would have thought us the luckiest people alive. Who wouldn't want a life like that? Park Avenue address, priceless art, beautiful jewellery. I could have woken up to a much worse scenario, put it that way, so rather than excusing myself politely and running into the street screaming, which was one of my options at around that point, I just wriggled my toes in that rug and stayed put. While it seemed strange, it didn't seem stranger than anything else. And, looking back, that whole post-hospital period had a certain dream-like quality to it. I knew I was awake and in the real world but it was almost as though I was applying the rules of a dream world: not questioning anything, letting whatever happened happen, no matter how weird. Do you know what I mean when I talk about the rules of a dream world? In a dream you never stop to question Bruce Springsteen's appearance at your lavish wedding to George Clooney in the foothills of Nepal, do you? You never rise up and wonder why 2000 one-armed unicyclists are all eating Hungarian goulash. You don't slap Johnny Depp's hand away from your breast and extract your tongue from his mouth to say, 'Stop that right now. I'm a happily married woman, Johnny. Behave yourself.' No, you just sit back and see what happens.

Also, I was tired. So tired. That first day, deposited neatly in that stylish sea of beige, I felt a weariness so deep in my bones it frightened me. My eyelids felt like lead weights that lowered themselves in slow motion to my cheeks. Lifting them was an effort almost beyond me. Sleep seemed too small a solution to that sort of exhaustion. I felt like I needed to discover a whole different method of relief. Also, I didn't know where my bed was but I did know that when I found it, I did not want to share it with Ty, no matter how high the thread count on the linen. This was a biggie. He was a nice enough man, if you liked that sort of thing. He was certainly generous and kind and under-standing — if slightly handicapped by the broom handle stuck up his ass — and I didn't mind staying at his house but I did not want his doughy flesh rubbing up and down against me. Yet when I sorted through the filing cabinet in my exhausted mind, the folder marked 'Ways To Tell The Fiancé You Didn't Know You Had That You Don't Want To Sleep With Him' was empty. The whole drawer, in fact, appeared to have been ransacked. But I was a person in need of a good long lie-down so I just had to deal with it.

'Ty, I don't like your cats,' I said, 'and I'm not going to sleep with you. Also I think you should paint at least one wall in here a pumpkin colour. Mango even.'

There was a long silence. His feelings were hurt, I could see that, but I was too tired to care. I just didn't have the energy to dress things up the way I used to.

'You don't like the cats?' He resorted to a sad sort of baby-ish voice. 'But MC, they're our little darlings.'

The one that wasn't already on the sofa walked past me, its tail held haughtily upright, its hip swinging to brush my knee with its butt. I considered reaching out to give it a good tug but didn't want to expend the energy.

'I don't know how things are going to work out,' I said. 'It's all pretty strange, you have to admit, and I'm just not sure of . . . anything. Except, you know, I might actually be more of a tropical fish person. Anyway, I just need to find a way to get through the next little while until my taste comes back. If this is weird I'm sorry, Ty. But it'll all be okay when my taste comes back.'

Ty flinched at this, his lips pursing and giving his mouth a look not unlike the asshole of one of his cats.

'Yes, well, I can't say your Dr Scarpa has been particularly helpful on that front,' he said dryly. 'It's not like we're just dealing with anybody's taste after all. You're MC Conlan of the *New York Times*, for heaven's sake. People would kill for that job.'

I must have looked alarmed because he quickly clarified that I was not one of those people.

'You got it fair and square, MC, by being the best placed person for the job. Paris put in a good word, of course she did, that's how it works, you know that, and I did my bit too. Well, Toby's an old friend. I was able to help you both out. It's just a shame that Dr Scarpa doesn't seem to take your taste as seriously as everyone else. But I've been talking to Dr Foster, MC, and she says she can clear her schedule and give you a couple of hours a day for the next two weeks at least. She thinks your memory issues may be some sort of dissociative symptom of post-traumatic stress syndrome, and, well, when you think about it half the damn country has post-traumatic stress syndrome these days so why shouldn't you? And the taste, MC, well, Dr Foster thinks that might be part of it. She thinks she can help you get it back and you're right, that's what we must work towards. You must get it back.'

I agreed with him on that one but there were still a few gaps in need of filling.

'Who is Dr Foster?' I asked him.

'Your therapist, darling. She's worked wonders with you, truly she has. Wonders.'

I was in therapy?

'And on the other matter,' he cleared his throat, 'the question of the sleeping arrangements, you have your own room, MC. You've always had your own room, the master bedroom with French doors to the terrace. I'm in the guest room past the library. I don't expect that to change at all.'

We had a library?

'We can go back to our Wednesday evening arrangement whenever you are ready, MC. Sevruga caviar, the Krug Clos du Mesnil and . . .' he blushed and gave a little cough, 'you know. As always.'

Well, this was some kind of engagement. 'We don't sleep together?' Not that I wanted to, you understand, but I was quite interested in knowing why I didn't. 'Except on a Wednesday?'

'Conflicting schedules, darling.' He was squirming. 'Your work load. My allergies. We just decided it would be better that way.'

Take away our flawless home, our gorgeous clothes and our successful careers and we really were a very odd couple.

'So, finally I get to see where you live,' my mother said as she stepped across the threshold the next day. 'Nice colour. It's so fresh.' She looking approvingly around the living room and kitchen, adding: 'So plain. Your father always wants everything so bright and cheerful. It drives me crazy.'

My father, as far as I knew, had never had an opinion on interior décor in his whole entire life. In fact, if you got him out of the apartment and asked him what colour the walls were, I doubt he would have been able to tell you.

'So, do you remember anything yet?' she asked, settling herself on the sofa (which might have looked fabulous but was actually a bitch to sit on). 'Other than your fancy Park Avenue address, of course. You don't seem to have forgotten that. You don't remember leaving your husband, breaking his heart, ruining your mother's life?'

I felt an anger surge through me then as I looked at her trying to wriggle into a comfortable position, her eyes taking in every detail, no doubt totting up a running total in her head and calculating how much I wasn't worth it. Why the hell was she so mean and why the hell did I put up with it?

'You know what,' I said. 'I don't want you here if you're going to talk to me like that.'

Her jaw dropped in amazement. 'Like what? I can't remind you what you did, how you embarrassed me and your father? I couldn't look Father Francis in the eye for a year after you left poor Tommy. It was a disgrace. And I'll talk to you any way I want. I'm your mother. Unless you've forgotten that too.'

I stopped myself from going there because had I been able to choose whom I remembered, I couldn't swear she'd make the cut. 'Mom, you never even liked poor Tommy,' I said instead. 'You used to introduce him as "the dishwasher who stole my daughter".'

'Well, that was before he was on the Food Network,' she answered, her eyes gleaming like nuggets of coal at my audacity. 'I guess I just never got to see his good side, what with you nagging at him all the time.'

This stopped me in my tracks. Did I nag at Tom? I didn't think so. I did whatever he told me to do most of the time. I was the peacekeeper, the pacifier, the good girl who would do almost anything to avoid a confrontation. Jesus, I even let him hijack my dreams, turn them into his. Chez Panisse for our honeymoon — what a crock. I couldn't make Tom do a goddamn thing. I never had been able to, had hardly bothered trying. And sitting there with my mother's sparkling eyes challenging me unblinkingly across the foreign floor of my alleged home, I realised that the well of self-doubt into which she had dipped for so long had finally dried up. And that nagging was not my problem. Being bullied was my problem.

'So nice of you to drop by,' I said, suddenly standing up and gesturing toward the hall. 'Next time we'll have cake.'

There was a moment when I thought she was maybe going to sit her ground, refuse to move, but she thought better of it, standing up and straightening her sweater.

'You've always had a mean streak, Mary-Constance,' she said. 'But who knew Woody Allen would bring it out in you? I never liked him, you know. I never knew what Mia saw in him. After Sinatra, what a choice. Those beady little eyes, that whiny little voice.'

'See you later, Mom,' I said. 'I'm going to take a nap now.'

'And for such a fancy building your doorman looks cheap,' she told me as I opened the door to the apartment for her. 'That suit! And the hair growing out his ears must be an inch long.'

'Say hi to Pop for me,' I told her and then I closed the door, resting my forehead against the cool smooth surface.

'So, that went well,' Ty said, emerging warily from his end of the apartment.

'You think?'

'Well, at least you finally gave her our address, MC. Usually you insist on meeting her someplace else. Dr Foster will have more to say on the matter, I'm sure, darling. Tea? Lapsang Souchong?'

Twelve

Actually, when it came to hot drinks I preferred coffee but it turned out Ty didn't like using his fancy Italian coffee machine. It made too much of a mess, he said. To be honest, he seemed kind of fussy on the cleaning front: snatching away my glass before I could set it on the table, obsessively removing cat hair with one of those sticky brush things, rearranging his very deliberate collection of magazines on the coffee table if you were so presumptuous as to flick through one.

Our apartment was beautiful but you wouldn't say it felt lived in. I mean the guy cleaned the kitty litter twice a day, for Pete's sake, and he'd somehow got the cats' bowels in sync. Scary. But despite our differences on the hygiene front, Ty and I got on pretty well those first couple of days. He just let me do my own thing, which was not much, and he did his, which I didn't care to know about. It didn't bother me if he wasn't there and it didn't bother me if he was. I slept, I soaked in my own beautiful big bathtub, I slept some more.

He even brought me breakfast in bed: same thing every day, orange juice in a crystal glass and a perfectly soft-boiled egg. There was a rose on the tray and a linen napkin and everything and he'd bring it in wearing a neat off-beige paisley silk dressing gown over beige pyjamas and caramel-coloured slippers (the daredevil) bearing a gold crest. It was a bit like living with an extra from

Gosford Park but it certainly had its up side.

The juice caught at the back of my throat when I drank it so I knew it was good and tart, and I could feel the little oddly shaped bits of pulp that let me know it was freshly squeezed, not made with concentrate, but there was no biting citrus flavour, no orange sensation, just the memory of what a good juice should taste like. I tended to cry a little bit every time I ate something but who wouldn't? It was like going to the bank to make a withdrawal knowing you'd paid in a check for a million dollars only to find the account had been emptied out. The thought of what I could no longer do, what I no longer had, drove me to distraction which, believe me, wasn't far.

One morning over breakfast, though, I decided to try my hardest to work with what I still had and once I stopped lamenting my lack of taste it was surprising what pleasure remained in the ritual of eating. The soft-boiled egg was really still quite pleasant. The white felt cool and fleshy and solid while the yolk was warm and creamy. I felt the yellowness of it. I fantasised about the flavour . . . racking my memory for tastes from the past, marvelling at how I had never really thought about how sweet eggs were before. I added salt and imagined the difference that would make to the egg, the sharpness it would bring. Then I remembered feeding Emmet a boiled egg when he was a baby in his high chair. I had turned my back on him for a moment to spread peanut butter on my toast and when I'd turned around again he had eaten the entire egg, shell and all. My mother had gone nuts, ranting and raging and accusing me of trying to kill him, which was way off bat as it took another 15 years for me to want to do that. I actually thought he was pretty cool when he was a kid. Anyway, throughout the rest of our childhood, any time we had eggs, my mother would pointedly say to Emmet in front of whoever else was there, 'And don't let your sister feed you the eggshells. They'll kill you. She knows this.'

Ty was hugely encouraging about any efforts to rehabilitate my culinary skills. I got the impression it was something he and Paris had already discussed. The two of them sure as hell wanted me back on track but then I wanted me there too so I could hardly complain. He agreed that it was important that we still made an effort to eat as though I could taste. We should experiment, he told me, with my damaged senses, see exactly what I still had. I think he was scared that left to my own devices I might take refuge in chocolate with low-percentage cocoa solids and great gulps of Diet Coke, which pre-Woody Allen I had never liked but which now appealed on account of the bubbles.

'So, wasabi still works,' I said, tears streaming down my face, my nostrils ablaze, after we lunched on take-out Japanese from Matsuri in Chelsea. No delivery charge too expensive, in Ty's eyes, when it came to the perfect northern Japanese lake fish. The fiery green horseradish burned the inside of my face as though nothing about me had changed yet while it throbbed inside my nose, there was no suggestion of the taste. The tempura shrimp roll turned out to be my favourite and I had previously not been a fan of tempura, finding the batter too bland. But now that I only had texture to go on, it was a pleasant surprise.

'By the way, Paris has made a reservation for the three of us at Mix tonight,' Ty said after he had talked me through the black grilled cod with sake paste — way too slimy by my account, thoroughly delicious by his. 'Time we got you out and about.'

I chomped down on a piece of crunchy lotus root. The whole troublesome matter of my alleged best friend urgently needed addressing. 'About Paris,' I found myself saying. 'You know how I feel about the cats? Same.'

I have since found out that this sort of impulsive behaviour is not uncommon among those who have hit their heads, but while it's a more honest way to behave, it was something of a contrast to the cautious manner in which I had conducted most conversations prior to the pretzel. I squirm now when I think about some of the things I said.

Ty squirmed too. 'But MC, you're such pals. You adore each other!'

'She's bossy,' I disagreed. 'Her hair is too straight. She has big pointy fingernails and she doesn't remember people's names. She makes me nervous.'

'But darling, Paris has been the key to your success. She has the contacts. A word in the right ear from Paris and you were the *New York Times* restaurant critic. The *New York Times*, MC. So long Biff Grimes! No, no, I don't mean RIP Biff Grimes, darling, I mean so long, farewell, auf wiedersehen, adieu. And hello MC Conlan. She found you an agent, MC. She got you your book deal. She took you to Paris, to London, to Venice. You love her.'

'*She* took me to Venice?'

'Yes, my sweet, you did the cooking course at the Gritti Palace, remember? Oh, I'm sorry. Of course not. My mistake. This must be so frustrating for you. I can only imagine. MC, please, don't cry, darling. Really. Should I call Dr Foster? I'll get you a handkerchief. A valium? Some brandy? Good heavens, MC, I'm not sure what to do.'

Look, if you're bored with all the crying, imagine how I felt. But how would you feel upon discovering you'd gone to Venice with Paris? She just did not look like a fun person to be on vacation with, or work with, or have dinner at Mix with. There were a lot of people I would choose to go to Venice with before I would choose her. Well, I thought I had chosen someone else . . . even if he hadn't turned up. Or I hadn't. Or whatever. Look, I was befuddled but not so befuddled that it hadn't occurred to me that I must at some stage have gone to Venice with someone: how else would I have seen it, tasted it, delighted in it in such glorious technicolour in my coma? My imagination just wasn't that good. And when I thought about it, it made perfect sense for me to have gone to the city of my dreams with my new best friend. Yet on finding out that it was she with whom I had gorged on cichetti at Do' Mori and slurped up olive oil with thick chunky wedges of warm brick-baked bread at Alla Madonna, I wept inconsolably. My face crumpled, my cheeks shone with tears, my chest heaved with sobs.

Ty was most uncomfortable with such outbursts of emotion. He seemed to think there was no problem that a nicely laundered handkerchief couldn't fix and was totally bewildered when the presence of such had little or no effect.

On that occasion, much to his relief, I took myself off to my darkened room, sobbed for a while longer, then drifted off to sleep.

When I woke up I heard voices in the living room. There was nothing wrong with my sense of hearing, that was for sure. I could hear almost every word and all I had to do was creep across the room and position my ear at the open crack of my door.

'So what did Toby have to say?' Paris was asking.

'Well, he's been very understanding so far I must say,' my fiancé answered. 'Any other editor might have cut her adrift but he seems to feel real loyalty; we've done well there, Paris. Anyway, Amanda Hesser is going to continue doing the interim reviews, which I feel okay about because we know she doesn't want the job permanently. But she could be a threat all the same. She has a following, you know, and it wouldn't do for it to build up while MC is out of the loop.'

'It might serve us well to let MC know, do you think, about Amanda Hesser? She never liked her after that ...' I couldn't quite tell what she said then, but it sounded like 'kerfuffle over the mussels' or 'kerfuffle over the truffles'. Either way, I wondered what the kerfuffle might have been. I had never been much of a kerfuffler and I had always liked Amanda Hesser, even though she was too thin and I never trusted thin food writers. I looked down at my hips. My, but there was not much to me. I had almost forgotten. I was a thin food writer myself now. Who knew?

'We've got to strike while the iron is hot though Ty,' Paris was saying. 'We've lost her regular profile while she has this taste issue and I won't pretend that's not damaging. But there is still a lot of interest being generated by her accident and recovery in general. It could even end up helping the book.'

The book! I had forgotten all about it but the Kate Spade shopping bag was sitting on a leather chair in the corner of my room. I tiptoed over to it, least I disturb the plotting going on in the living room, and pulled out the advance copy of *Stars Struck: In Search of the Sublime New York Dining Experience*. What a stupid title. It was so phoney. I climbed back onto my bed. Ty had extremely good taste in bed linen, did I mention that? Everything had a thread count of about a million and the sheets and pillowcases and bedspread and blankets and cushions were all different shades of you-know-what but still much more tasteful than anything I would ever put together. I opened up my book and started to read.

Within moments the colour had drained from my face and the full extent of how far up her own ass MC Conlan's head had burrowed hit home. Just the Foreword made me want to puke. I sounded like a stuck-up food snob who thought she knew more than anyone else in the universe and who could only just bring herself to share a tiny smidgeon of this special secret information with the little people.

Names dropped like hammers on the page: *The Alains and Jean-Georges and Daniels and Marios of the world don't head to Boise, Idaho, with dreams of making it onto the world's culinary stage, do they?*

I was sickened. Thoroughly sickened. Like a car wreck though, I couldn't quite drag my eyes away. My eyes flicked over the pages and before I could stop myself I had turned to the review of Tom's, my eyes skimming the words, my teeth biting into my bottom lip and almost drawing blood as I picked up phrases and sentences all heaving with subterfuge.

What a charming job Irish-born Tom Farrell has done with one-time no-frills neighbourhood favourite, Il Secondo, I had started off, which said it all. Imagine outing Tom as Irish in the first sentence! He would have died a thousand deaths. And he hated charming: charm was not Tom's thing. He despised any suggestion of contrivance, strived for natural authenticity; too much, according to the review. His zucchini blossoms were delicious but out of place, I wrote; the old Il Secondo regulars seemed bemused by them, asking repeatedly for meatballs that weren't on the menu. I had been a waitress at the old restaurant, I continued, and knew that aprons shouldn't be stained with red sauce and water should have ice. I revealed myself as his ex, saying it was a difficult assignment as my former husband might wish he had never met me but that would not stop him from recognising me. Still, I hoped that the fact I was the *Times* reviewer would stop him from poisoning the soup.

It wasn't a drubbing, really it wasn't. In fact, bits of it were pretty funny. But I could read between the lines and tell how much I wanted to hurt Tom with that review, and he would have too. It was awful. Fleur was right. I had turned into a bitch. A king-of-the-hill, top-of-the-heap, number-one bitch. I felt sick.

Yet, when I turned to my review of Thomas Keller's Per Se, the words rolled positively oleaginously down the page. *Like the conductor of a symphony orchestra, I wrote, Maestro Keller controls the flavours with an expert hand. 'Allegro,' he exhorts some flavours — the salt in the cauliflower panna cotta, for example — while 'pianissimo' he whispers to the heirloom radishes. 'Adagio,' he commands the rillette de lapin. Encore! Encore! Encore!*

What a piece of crap, I thought and I hurled the stupid book onto the floor where it skidded across the polished floorboards and hit the wall. Moments later, there was a knock on the door and Ty peeked in.

'Darling,' he said, 'our reservation is in an hour. Shouldn't you be getting dressed? Paris thinks the taupe. We'll be having cocktails in the library.'

I didn't quite get the chance to tell him I was running away to join the circus so he could fuck right off and take Paris with him. Instead, with a churlish huff, I dragged myself off the bed and into my walk-in closet. It was fabulous. Almost a reason to be married to someone you didn't even know. There was drawer after drawer of exquisite lingerie; rows of silk shirts; beautiful suits; gorgeous coats and jackets; and an entire section devoted to evening wear. It looked like Sharon Stone lived there. And as for shoes: they were stacked neatly on four shelves that ran around all three walls. There was a whole section of colour-coordinated running shoes, then another chunk of black plain heels, a similar collection of brown plain heels, then the same thing all over again in cream. And the evening shoes sparkled like crown jewels. There were Manolo Blahniks, Jimmy Choos. You name it and I had it: all the shoes I had ever dreamed of.

Much as I searched, though, there were no comfy slouchy clothes. Nothing for MC to mooch around in at home, no Juicy couture or spandex. There was one pair of jeans but they were hanging up with creases pressed into them. Not the sort of thing you would lie on the floor eating Doritos and watching old movies in, that's for sure. It was quite the opposite of my old wardrobe, which consisted solely of clothes you could lie on the floor and eat Doritos in. Probably MC wasn't allowed Doritos, I pondered, running my hands over the rows of beautiful clothes and ignoring anything taupe. Finally, I slipped into a simple black linen shift, found a pair of heels I could walk in, did my best with my frightening array of make-up, then took a deep breath and made for the library.

'Oh but darling,' Paris looked unnerved by the sight of me, 'the taupe is so much more suitable with a hat.'

'Why would I wear a hat?' I asked her. 'We're only going out to dinner.'

She laughed. 'Well, it's your signature, MC. You don't want people recognising you even if you're not strictly working. It won't do any harm to look as if you are, by the way; it's not as though anyone has gotten hold of the terrible truth after all. No, we've managed to keep that under wraps, thank God. Go and get the taupe hat will you, Ty?'

'Don't go anywhere,' I snapped at my fiancé who looked justifiably nervous. 'I am not wearing a hat. Can we just go eat? I'm starving.'

Predictably, I suppose, my first outing as the reborn MC Conlan was a total disaster. The restaurant was gorgeous. I hadn't realised that Alain Ducasse had stooped to a casual spin-off, and even though an entrée in a casual spin-off could still set you back $40, it wasn't an intimidating place. It was all white and glass and modern with gashes of orange, approachable staff and the magical touch, I thought, of having toast brought to the table in a funky modern toast rack with homemade peanut butter, jelly and unsalted butter. But Paris and Ty fussed about like a pair of old mother hens, not just over me, but over everything; which table we sat at, which seats we chose, what wine, the lighting, the music.

Frankly, it was embarrassing, and it made me so nervous I lost a huge glob of peanut butter and jelly down the inside of my dress and had to be escorted by Paris to the ladies' room to remove it. She and Ty then proceeded to pick the place to pieces, sucking every ounce of enjoyment out of the meal, not that there was much in it for me in the first place because it all looked so exquisite but tasted of diddly-squat. I don't know why I ordered the lobster Caesar salad because I had already discovered there is no reason to eat lobster if you can't taste it, but I chomped my way through it as Ty and Paris plotted the course of my recovery and tossed around various solutions to the problem with which I had presented them: my tastelessness.

Actually, there was a little something going on between those two. Not sexual, exactly. I think he probably was one of those non-practising anythings, and maybe so was she, but there was a frisson between them that certainly did not exist between him and me. They kind of got each other. In fact, I bet if she had been better-looking he would have been engaged to her but she didn't quite fit the bill on that front. This unfamiliar glamorous, blonde MC Conlan, on the other hand, I could see she was going to look a million dollars on the society pages! Never mind that she was marrying a man who had a thing for her new best friend and was separated from a man who preferred her old one. I was halfway through the first biteful of the most perfectly cooked piece of coconut-and-lime marinated cod when this thought struck me. The fish was piping hot and fell onto the fork in fat juicy flakes but the absence of even the slightest suggestion of what I knew must be the most wonderful flavour proved my undoing. I dropped my knife and fork onto the table with a clatter and burst into noisy, wet, undignified tears.

By the time it became clear that I was incapable of pulling myself together, my companions were so embarrassed that they agreed to put me in a car back to the apartment to 'get some rest' while they finished their meals with grace and pomposity (my words, not theirs).

I walked out of the restaurant, head bowed to hide the tears streaming down my face, my heart breaking as I wondered how in the hell I was ever going to get my life back. But when the driver turned to me and said 'Home?' I got an idea that silenced my fear.

I blew my nose and gave him my West Village address.

Home was exactly where I wanted to go.

Of course, the home I was going to was no longer mine. It was Fleur who buzzed me up when I sobbed through the crackling intercom that I'd run away from Ty. When I stepped into the hallway, the place was filled with the sound of Agnes hollering. I guess she was quite cute in an orangutan sort of way but she sure could make one heck of a racket. Cats, in comparison, seemed a very peaceful alternative; I never thought I would find myself preferring cats to anything else but every decibel issuing from Agnes's lungs seemed to push Cay-Cay and Happy a notch up my approval rating scale.

'Sweetie, what's happening?' Fleur hugged me as well as she could while jiggling the baby. 'What do you mean you've run away?'

'Park Avenue sucks,' I sniffed, looking around me. 'And I have no place else to go.'

Our apartment had been totally remodelled. The dull brick walls that we had happily lived with for so long were painted a lovely soft yellow; the scratched and damaged floor boards had been stripped and re-varnished a lighter colour; there was new modern furniture and no sign of the velvet Elvis hanging that a friend of Tom's had brought back from Vegas and that we had found hilarious. There was nothing amusing about the apartment now. It was a picture of good taste, but different from Ty's. It looked lived in and loved, not just copied out of some fancy magazine. Our old kitchen, which was bigger than most West Village kitchens but still tiny, had been totally overhauled. The old gas cook-top on which I had burned many sleeves and dish towels had been replaced by some fancy integrated thing with a grill plate and a steamer. There was a new island with an under-counter fridge and freezer that pushed out into the living room, making a breakfast bar and trending the room up hugely. In all, the apartment looked approximately one million times nicer than when I lived there and, to be honest, this did not help my frame of mind. Also, the bathroom, which in my day had been a particularly unpleasant shade of flaky and bubbling green, and had smelled strongly of rotting water, was now gleaming with white mosaic tiles from floor to ceiling. Worse, there was a built-in wardrobe in the bedroom not to mention a new king-size bed that I tried so hard not to notice I nearly broke my ankle tripping over it.

The only thing that cheered me up slightly was that baby Agnes had taken over the tiny second bedroom that Tom and I had used as an office, which he in particular had loved. He would be cranky about that I was sure — not that I wanted him to be but hey, I wouldn't be human if I didn't hope that his life without me wasn't shitty in some way. He would be unimpressed, I guessed, that his favourite room wasn't even big enough for all that baby stuff. Fluffy toys and other juvenile paraphernalia were spilling out from a trunk in the corner of the living room, taking the edges off the funky renovation.

'Nice,' I said, trying to avert my eyes from the baby vomit on

Fleur's shoulder. 'Really nice. You've done a great job.' The sofa didn't look like a fold-out but it was long enough for me to sleep on. It was red velvet with a purple mohair comforter draped across one corner and purple beaded cushions piled up along the back.

'Connie, can I get you a cup of tea or a juice or something?' Fleur suggested. 'You look whacked.'

Fleur looked pretty whacked herself. I wondered how much of the day Agnes had spent screaming.

'Actually, if I could just borrow some pyjamas,' I said. 'I really need to lie down.'

Fleur stopped in her tracks, mid-jiggle. 'Pyjamas?' she echoed. 'You want to stay the night? Connie, um. Shit. Are you sure that's a good idea? What will Ty say?'

'He won't know,' I said, sitting on the sofa. 'I guess I can sleep on this. Or maybe we could borrow your mom's fold-away bed. Didn't you sleep on it here for a while when you were waiting to move into your apartment on Mulberry Street?'

Agnes squawked then, so loudly I wondered for a while if she had pierced my eardrum. Fleur eventually got a pacifier in her mouth and then dumped her in a little chair-thing on wheels that she pushed around with her feet, hitting the walls and the furniture with a series of dull thuds that were disconcerting but at least not deafening.

'Connie,' Fleur said, sitting down on the sofa and turning me around to face her. 'I know this must be hard for you, sweetie. And if things aren't right at home with Ty then we have to try to do something about that.'

'He and Paris are so busy organising me they hardly notice I'm there,' I said. 'It's all about getting me back to work so I can promote my new book.'

'Oh honey.'

'And the book is awful, Fleur. You should see it. It has words like "cut-throat" and "fraternity" in it. If it wasn't for the freckle I wouldn't know it was me on the cover.'

'It's hard, sweetie, I know it is. And you shouldn't feel any pressure to do anything Ty and Paris tell you to. Not if you're not comfortable with it. But the thing is — AGNES! Not the lamp! Jesus!'

The little monkey was grabbing at a low-level lampshade with sticky fingers that were leaving dirty paw prints. At the sound of her mother's sharp voice, though, she turned around, her mouth curved down into an upside down 'u', and spat the dummy, literally, shrieking with such volume that I thought the new paint would flake clean off the walls.

'My God, that's horrible,' I said to Fleur, not that she could hear me. She picked Agnes up and tried to shush her but the little moppet was yowling at the top of her lungs. She did not seem very shushable.

'The thing is, Connie,' Fleur continued nonetheless, jiggling up and down and patting the raging baby on the back of her head, 'I do understand and I want to help but you can't — FUCK! Oh shit. You little — Jesus Christ. She just bit me on the ear! I can't believe it. Oh darling, I'm so sorry. Mommy's sorry. Oh shit, that hurt.' Agnes was so busy looking pleased with herself she momentarily forgot to keep up with the caterwauling. I could see two tiny tooth marks in Fleur's ear, the lobe glowing red and painful, but at least there was no blood. Agnes obviously noticed this the same time as I did and started up with the caterwauling again. Fleur looked on the verge of tears herself. She jiggled again and started up with the patting, but her face was crunched in pain. It would hurt to have your ear bitten like that, I thought. And then have a baby screech in it straight after. I had a thick fuggy feeling in my own head. It was tiredness. I needed to lie down. I slipped off my shoes and stretched out on the sofa, pulling a cushion underneath my head for a pillow and dragging the comforter onto my prone body. My eyes wanted to close and my ears were right behind them. I wondered if Fleur could perhaps do something about the screaming baby.

'Isn't it Agnes's bedtime?' I suggested. 'She must be tired after all that, um, yelling.'

'Connie,' Fleur said, and there was a sharpness to her voice that caught my attention. 'I do understand,' she continued, 'and I do want to help you and I love you and I am so grateful we are friends again but this is a pretty complicated situation. I don't know how to put this to you without hurting your feelings or upsetting you, but you can't stay here. You can't stay in my apartment.'

The rattle of a key in the lock of the apartment door stopped any further exchange and Tom came in brandishing a paper bag that sprouted a loaf of ciabatta, the leaves of a decent-sized bunch of celery and a healthy head of cilantro. I felt a flutter of excitement at the thought of his gazpacho, quelled almost straight away by the dull thud of remembering my tasting status.

Agnes screamed even louder at the sight of her father and the noise seemed to fill the room, flattening we mere mortals up against the walls.

'Connie,' Tom said, eyes wide with surprise, as he dumped the groceries in the kitchen. 'What's happening, babe? Is everything okay?'

'Connie's come to stay, Tom,' Fleur said, as Agnes continued to screech out her lungs. 'She's run away from Ty.'

'You're kidding me. What did he do to you, that piece of shit, what did he do? Jesus, Fleur, can't you do something about that crying? What's going on here? You know Connie needs quiet.'

Fleur switched the baby onto her other hip, her lips thinning and her eyes narrowed. 'Well, she's not going to get it here, which is what I was just explaining, Tom.'

Tom looked so concerned it made me feel mushy inside. I pulled myself up and made room for him to sit down next to me on the sofa. 'Babe, tell me what's happening.'

Fleur spun around at this and took Agnes into her room, no doubt to see if there was anything other than a pillow that would silence her. The room felt gloriously empty in her absence.

'Ty didn't do anything,' I said sorrowfully. 'I just don't know him. Paris is there and they're so busy managing me it just feels wrong, Tom. It creeps me out. This is the only home I know.' I looked around. 'Although of course you have done so much with the place I barely recognise it.'

Tom shrugged his shoulders and looked guilty. 'Well, it's all Fleur's work, mostly,' he said. 'You know, I was pretty happy with it the way it was. She likes all this interiors stuff.'

'Right,' I said limply. 'So, that baby sure makes a lot of noise.'

'You're telling me. I love her and all, of course I do, she's my little angel, but with the restaurant and the show, I've got quite a lot on my plate, to be honest. There's not a whole lot of sleeping going on, that's for sure.'

I'd assumed he was a guest on some other TV programme but it turned out he had one of his own, *Il Secondo*, which had tracked his progress from the relaunch after his one-star review nightmare (oops) to the impressive success he was now enjoying, with a few recipes thrown in along the way. It rated well, apparently, very well even, and meant the tables were full every night as New York hopefuls booked in to see if they could make it on to the small screen.

He'd really become something of a celebrity in my absence (as I thought of it). He too had featured in *New York Magazine*, guest starred at the Gourmet Food Institute, had appeared on the *Today* show no fewer than four times, and was talking to an agent about a cookbook.

'Wow,' was about all I could say. The celebrity had given him a certain confidence but it didn't seem to have gone to his head. He was in the same apartment, after all, when no doubt he could have afforded a fancy-pants place somewhere else; and he was there talking to me, not hobnobbing with the big boys at Bungalow 8 or wherever they hung out.

'I read the review I wrote of Tom's,' I told him sadly. 'I don't know why you are even talking to me. It was a horrible, horrible thing to do. If I found out it was you that gave Woody Allen the pretzel I would not be able to blame you.'

'I would never do that, Connie,' he said and I believed him —

and loved him so much I just wanted to curl up in his arms, order Venezuelan take-out and live happily ever after.

'So, have you worked something out?' Fleur emerged from Agnes's room looking more than a little rumpled but without the baby.

'What do you mean "worked something out"?' Tom asked.

Fleur looked embarrassed. 'Well, Connie can't stay here, Tom. There's no room. And it's too noisy. Besides, it's just not, you know, right. Oh Connie, honey, I'm sorry, I really am. I'm not really sure how to handle all this.'

'I thought you were my friend,' I said accusingly. 'You stayed here with us.'

'Sweetie, I am your friend. But I haven't been for the past two years and in the days since I stayed here with you our situation has gotten a bit messed up, don't you think?'

'Well, you can't blame me for you moving in with my husband,' I said. 'I don't remember pointing a gun at your head.' Of course, I didn't remember anything else either but she was making me feel unwanted and I didn't like it.

'Hey, come on you two,' Tom interrupted. 'Fleur, babe, we can't throw her out on the streets. This is Connie.'

'Well she should go back to Ty until we work something out. She was happy enough there before.'

I started to cry loudly and wetly and, I am ashamed to admit, purposefully. 'I don't know about before,' I wept. 'I only know about now. And then. And I don't belong with Ty. It's all beige and he talks about Eric and Jean-Georges and Jeffrey Steingarten like they're our friends and he irons the bed linen — on the beds. It's horrible.'

'Jesus, Fleur,' Tom said, wrapping his arms around me. 'Have a heart.

'Of course you can stay,' he soothed me. 'And if Agnes gets too loud, Fleur can take her to her mother's place.'

Thirteen

Having never had children — surely someone would have told me if I had left a baby sitting in a stroller somewhere — I didn't know that having your husband say you would take the kid to your mother's place if it got too loud was a crime tantamount to treason and punishable by being yelled at all night.

I slept like a baby myself. I must have had a good 11-hour stretch. But when I woke up, Fleur and Agnes had gone and Tom was sitting at the table looking grey with tiredness and sick with nerves.

'I'm going to have to take you home, babe,' he said, after making me a cup of coffee with a heart shape in the froth. He had a domestic version of the same coffee machine as Ty, only didn't mind dirtying it up. I took a sip. It was piping hot and tasted of air. I struggled for words to stave off my ejection from the only place I felt I belonged.

'This is my home, Tom. It's the only one I know. I don't belong anywhere else. You have to let me stay. Please.'

'If it was just me, you could, I swear. But there's the baby and Fleur and it's really not a great time for us right now.'

'What's the matter?'

'Oh, just the usual stuff people go through when they have a kid, I guess. You know, we argue a lot, we don't sleep, we hardly ever . . . well, you don't have to know the details, Connie, but

197

'fuck sometimes I wonder, I really do.'

'Wonder what?'

'If I did the right thing.' He sounded exhausted, ground down, unhappy. My heart ached for him. And for me. 'Maybe you're right. Maybe I should have fought for you. I was just so fucking angry when you left like that. Jesus, you always knew how to make me angry, Connie, but Ty Wheatley? That just about killed me. And once Fleur and I hooked up I kind of let it slide. It seemed the easy thing to do. But the right thing? I'm not so sure.'

'Don't you love her?' I didn't know how I wanted him to answer that question. If he did love her it would hurt me, and if he didn't it would hurt her.

'I do,' he said. Ouch. 'But not like I love you.'

Oh brother.

I could feel it myself, the old comfortable attraction between us. Sure we had fought, what couples didn't? Sure he had stifled me, but who was perfect? I certainly wasn't. I needed bolstering, remember.

It occurred to me then that with Fleur and Agnes out of the apartment there was nothing to stop Tom and I doing what we had always done in perfect harmony — when we did it. I did not know how long it had been since I'd had sex. I'd seen films where orderlies had done heinous things to people in comas but I doubted Signora Marinello would have let that happen to me. The last sex that I knew of was the canal churner that blew the top of my head off but I had imagined it. I had imagined it real well. Damn, I was horny.

But I wasn't as much of a slut in my real world as I was in my dreams. I'd lost my memory and my taste but I still knew better than to covet my best friend's boyfriend. Although God knew I was in need of a good coveting and technically he was still my husband.

'Maybe I should go home,' I said, getting up and straightening my clothes, which I had sensibly not removed. 'But I'm not going back to Ty's.'

And that only left one place.

'So, you remember where we live then?' My mom must have been waiting just inside the apartment because I had no sooner pressed my finger on the buzzer than there she was, hidden behind the open door in the cramped hallway, her lips pursed, her eyes travelling accusingly up my body and stopping at the overnight bag I had gone back to Ty's apartment and packed while he was out. 'I thought you said next time there'd be cake. My own fault, I should've known better than to listen. Oh, excuse me,' she said as I pushed silently past her. 'Is it all right for me to talk to you this way? In my house? The house you're coming to stay in?'

It was not quite the homecoming I might have hoped for but then I had not stayed a night in that apartment since I'd moved in with Tom at the end of the '80s. And on the occasion of my leaving my mom had thrown a pair of old tennis shoes and my one-eyed teddy Rueben at my retreating back.

'It's Mary-Constance,' she announced to the living room, as though they didn't already know. 'It's not working out for her over in her fancy place on Park Avenue.'

Frankie, a new one from the one I remembered, leapt off the sofa yapping in a high-pitched frenzy. He hurled himself at me, instantly attempting sexual congress with my left leg. I tried to shake him off but he was stuck like Velcro, his little sausage hips vibrating and a glazed look in his dark eyes as he humped my Anne Klein trousers.

Emmet, who was sitting at the dining table in dirty sweats, drinking instant coffee and smoking a cigarette, shot me a huge grin while my Dad abandoned the *Times* crossword to get out of his La-Z-Boy and give me a hug. Nobody seemed to see or hear Frankie, whom I was sure was in the throes of a premature ejaculation.

'Baby girl,' my dad said in his soft warm voice, 'it's good to see you up and about. Welcome home.' Actually, it gave me something of a shock to see him. He was so much smaller than I remembered. He was shorter than me. Had that always been the case? It must have been. And he'd lost hair, a lot of it, since the last time I remembered seeing him. He looked like a little old man, like someone else's father.

'Can somebody do something about this dog?' I asked, bending over to try and remove Frankie from his position around my ankle. His yapping had given way to a creepy kind of whimpering. He clung for grim death. 'Pop, could you give me a hand here?'

My dad looked down and softly clicked his fingers, at which point the dog collapsed panting in a heap on the floor. I half expected him to reach out a paw for one of Emmet's cigarettes. Pop smiled stupidly at the heinous creature and then back at me.

'Why didn't you come and see me at the hospital?' I asked him. 'I could have died.'

'Ah, darling, I did,' he answered, looking sheepish. 'Didn't your mother tell you?'

'Only Mary-Constance could be killed by a pretzel,' my mother said dismissively from the tiny adjoining kitchen, where pots and pans were being banged for no apparent reason. 'Always, you have to be different.'

'I think being killed by a pretzel would be cool,' Emmet drawled. I was pretty sure he was stoned. Well, it was 11 in the morning after all. 'Beats cancer. Or diabetes. The sort where your legs go all green and black and then get amputated.'

I don't know what it is about being back in the home where you grew up but it sure as hell brings out the childishness in me.

'Oh, shut up, you big dope,' I snapped.

'Don't you talk to your brother like that,' my mom barked. 'You're not the Queen of Sheba here, you know. You're a guest in this house.'

'Yeah, and shut up yourself anyway,' laughed Emmet flipping me the finger behind her back. '*Guest*.'

'A five-letter word that means harmony,' Pop said to himself, contemplating the *Times*.

It was like I had never left and the horror of it turned my stomach. Not even bothering to make a feeble excuse I just took my bag into the bedroom I had once shared with Emmet. It smelled of old socks and I didn't want to think what else. He had posters of women tennis players on all four walls and a collection of bongs on his dressing table. I lay on the bed, staring at the ceiling and shaking a figurative fist at the unfairness of being stuck in the middle of such a nightmare.

That night my mother served up the worst macaroni and cheese I have ever not tasted in my whole entire life. I don't know what she had put in it but it was brown, with chunks of carrot and beet sticking gluggily to the pasta. Don't think about it for too long, you'll be put off food forever. Emmet, who'd smoked so much pot his eyes were blazing red like raspberries, inhaled his like he'd never eaten anything before while my dad cheerfully ploughed his way through, congratulating my mother with every second mouthful.

I felt weak with hunger. I hadn't left the apartment all day so I knew I had to eat some of it myself. It felt every bit as bad as it looked. The pasta was overcooked and the sauce so sticky it attached itself to the roof of my mouth in a huge ball. It just about had to be scraped off with a fork. The carrots were limp and the beets raw. After half-a-dozen forkfuls, enough to make sure I could get through the night without starving to death, I gave up, pushed my plate away and asked to be excused.

'What's the matter? Not good enough for you? Not up to your usual high standards?' my mother asked.

'I can't taste anything,' I said diplomatically. 'There's not much point.'

'You've gotta eat, darling,' my father said, smiling at me.

He seemed so detached. Had he always been that way?

'I'm fine,' I said, going over and giving his freckled bald head a kiss. 'I should ring Ty.'

'Tell the Wheat Man I said hi,' Emmet instructed, his mouth full of food.

The Wheat Man was out again, much to my relief. I knew Fleur had rung him the night before to tell him where I was so I left a message saying I was now going to stay at my folks' place, that I needed a few days to myself. I asked him not to call me there and suggested he keep Paris off my back as well. Actually, I nearly caved in and asked for him to come get me. At least there was decent food at his house and my own beautiful bedroom with walk-in closet. But I remembered hearing him talk about me with Paris, and feeling the despair of not quite being the person to whom they were referring, and slunk off to bed to cry myself to sleep.

The next morning I toyed with a bowl of oatmeal for breakfast. I was so hungry but it was like eating wet cardboard. Usually I loved oatmeal but I bought mine organic and untampered with from the Whole Food Market; the stuff Mom had was radiated with strawberry and vanilla flavouring and could be made in the microwave in 15 seconds. Of course, I couldn't taste the difference but I knew it was there. It tainted the experience unforgivably, as did having Frankie trying to rut my slippers under the table.

'Guess who's got a little crush,' Emmet grinned blearily as the foul creature's yelps punctuated the air.

I was finding Frankie's affections hard to stomach. He was just another example of how out of kilter my life was. Thirty-six-year-old women weren't supposed to live at home with their parents. Restaurant critics weren't supposed to have no sense of taste. Dogs weren't supposed to have sex with human footwear.

Later, after my shower in the apartment's tiny bathroom, I stared at my naked self in the steamed-up mirror. The weight was still coming off me and I was looking more and more like a stranger. According to the bathroom scales I was now 120 pounds. And the colour of my skin had faded to a pale and uninteresting shade of grey. I looked like a person who was getting ready to disappear and that was such a scary realisation that I put my pyjamas back on and went straight back to bed, napping on and off for the rest of the day until darkness fell and I could go to sleep for real.

Emmet bought me *Gourmet* magazine the next day but the

pictures just made me cry. I pulled my knees up in my bed until I took up the least amount of space possible and willed myself back to sleep but he was bonging up and the smoke was getting caught in my lungs and giving me coughing fits. I couldn't even be bothered yelling at him to leave. Instead I stayed there, all scrunched up and choking, until I felt myself drift off. Well, I was probably inhaling enough to send me into the middle of the following week.

That night, my dad bought me a punnet of New York strawberries that he'd got from his friend Barney whose son had moved upstate to farm. At first the sight of them, so glowing with the vitality of summer, depressed me, but I'd always loved strawberries, especially New York ones, a much more rewarding prospect than their year-round California counterparts. And there's a lot you can do with a strawberry without tasting it, as it turns out. Just twisting the hull and listening for the tiny ploop as it came out kind of cheered me up. Then when I bit into each fat juicy berry, I felt the pulp explode, the juices release, and the comforting grain of the seeds against the roof of my mouth. I savoured each biteful, imagining as much as I could, then swallowing with a gulp and feeling the berry mash slide down my throat.

'Ah, don't cry there, Connie,' my dad said, sitting on my bed and looking at me sadly. I hadn't known that I was crying, actually, but I dragged the back of my hand across my cheeks and he was right. I was trying to hide the awfulness of my situation from myself but it obviously wasn't working.

'Your mother thinks it's unhealthy staying cooped up in here all day,' he said.

'What do you think, Pop?'

'I think you should do what your mother says.'

That figured. He pretty much always thought that. I loved my dad, I really did. He was there, had always been there, for a hug or a kiss or a pat on the back but anything more exacting and he faded into the wallpaper of my memory. Anything for an easy life, that was his motto. I could see it written on his gravestone. And while I was grateful that at least it meant he had shown me love and compassion in my life, I was sad that he had shown me so little of the person he really was.

Outside in the hallway, I heard Mom turn the vacuum cleaner on and start bashing it against the closed bedroom door. When I lived at home this had been her way of telling me to get up out of bed and I had always obediently done just that. I had always obediently done whatever she told me. I froze, a strawberry halfway to my lips. Anything for the easy life. Oh brother. Maybe I was my father's daughter, destined to waft through life without making a dent. I returned the strawberry to its plastic punnet, uneaten, and turned back toward the wall.

'Thanks for the strawberries, Pop,' I said. 'I'm going to take a nap now, okay?'

'Okay, Connie,' he answered me, a little sadly maybe. Did he see myself in him? Did he regret it? I doubted I would ever know as I heard him shuffle out of the room, talk in a murmur to the Queen of the Hoover, and then, thankfully, there was silence.

'Aren't you going to get up off your ass and start doing something?' Emmet said to me the next day when he came in to swap one dirty bunch of sweats for another. 'I don't feel right being the most active member of the family. Besides, I'd quite like my room back so if you could just move home with your boyfriend . . . The old man does nothing but watch the History Channel all day out there. I'm learning way too much stuff. I need to come back and spend some quality time with Anna Kournikova.'

'How long has Pop been sitting around watching TV all day?' I'd been thinking about this all night in between swirly black dreams and thrashing wakefulness.

'Hey, don't knock it,' Emmet said, sniffing a pair of socks. 'He spent 40 years repairing shoes. He should be able to put his feet up if he wants to.'

He had worked hard, our father, for Joe Rivera's shoe repair shop over on Lexington, going off to work at eight every morning and coming back at six at night. He'd hardly made a fortune but we had never wanted for anything, other than vacations, which was Mom's fault. She said she had only once left the island of Manhattan, the ocean was dangerous, and nowhere else was any better, so why the fuss? Plus, we'd had pretty good shoes considering our income. The store had a policy that any shoes repaired but not picked up within six months reverted to whichever family member fitted them. Joe had four tiny little daughters whose feet never got bigger than a size four while I was the only bigfoot who fitted a perfect size nine. As a result I was probably the only girl in junior high who wore thrift-store jeans and $300 loafers.

'But what kind of life is that, Emmet, fixing shoes and watching the History Channel?'

'I dunno.' Emmet looked in the mirror on top of the dresser and spiked up his hair. 'Looks okay to me. He's been a pretty good dad, hasn't he? Never got loaded and spent the rent money or ran off with his secretary.' He turned around to look at me and to my surprise he was nervous.

'Hey, sis, we need to talk,' he said. 'And I know now is probably not the best time to be asking you about this, but we had an arrangement after all so I need to know how soon you think I can get the 20 grand.'

'Excuse me?'

'Come on, Connie, the $20,000 you said you'd loan me. I really need it now. I've waited a whole month already, remember, while you were in the coma but the situation is getting urgent.'

My spirits were already so low that I could not even rustle up incredulity. I had known that Emmet was capable of stooping extremely low, but this was positively subterranean. My own brother exploiting my memory loss for his personal financial gain: how much did that suck?

'You know they didn't take out my brain when they operated, Emmet,' I said coldly.

'But, sis,' he whined, 'you promised me. And my guy needs the money by the end of the week otherwise, man, I'm going to miss out on the investment of a lifetime.'

'Emmet, buying drugs cannot be described as an investment. It is money down the toilet the same as it always has been. Jesus, what is the matter with you?'

'Well, thanks for the vote of confidence, Connie, but I'm not scoring. I told you, before the, you know, thing with Woody Allen. My buddy Ron needs some capital to get his hot towel dispenser business off the ground. If I don't get my share to him soon I'm out and it's going to be a winner, I know it is.'

'Well, you know what Emmet,' I'd had it with him by then, 'I don't even know if I have $20,000 but if I did I am pretty sure that the last person on earth I would give it to would be you. How much do you owe me already? I've only bailed you out like 150 times before. Well, maybe I am the one who needs bailing out this time. Did you ever think of that? And by the way, next time you try to fleece me out of my hard-earned cash, can you at least do me the honour of thinking up a better story than some phoney crap about hot towel dispensers? It's insulting.'

'I see what Mom meant,' he said, 'about the coming back mean.' He slammed the door on his way out.

I thought a lot about what he said about our dad that morning, though. He was right. He'd been a good father and there were no signs at all that he was anything other than content with his life. And that was being married to my mom. Later that day I went and watched the History Channel with him for a while. Frankie eyed me lasciviously from the sofa, his tongue hanging out, drool sliding off of it. I tried to ignore the excited pant of his breathing and concentrate on the *Mystery of Stonehenge* but it wasn't easy.

When Mom came back from the market she fed Pop and, begrudgingly, me fried bologna sandwiches. Despite the fact I could still feel the fat swilling in my stomach way after I'd finished eating, she hadn't done too badly. Nothing was rotten or walking off the plate and the whole combination was an acceptable colour and temperature.

'Nice sandwich, Mom,' I told her when I brought our plates out to the kitchen.

'Finally, I get something right,' she said, taking the plates without even looking at me. 'Saints be praised. Whatever did I do to deserve such a thing?'

Wordlessly, I slunk back into the living room where Frankie licked his lips and looked ready to pounce. Then I went back to bed.

In the night, my swirly dream woke me up again and I lay in bed in a cold sweat, my head pounding, my heart thumping. I was fighting an overwhelming dread that this was how I was going to feel for the rest of my life and it was unbearable. I just could not face a future that wretched. Something had to change, something had to shift, to improve. A person could not be expected to live with that level of despair. Panic fluttered inside me as I tossed and turned until sometime in the early hours I heard the front door open noisily, and the unsteady stagger of Emmet's feet across the living-room floor. But instead of collapsing on the sofa as I had expected him to do — it's where he'd been sleeping while I was at home — he burst into my room, flicking the light on and shrieking with surprise at the sight of me sitting upright in his bed.

'What are you doing?' I asked him.

He looked terrible. His eyes were unfocussed, his hair was plastered to his head and he was sweating profusely.

'Fuck,' he said, looking at me, then down at himself. 'Jesus.' He staggered and fell against the dressing table, knocking MC's collection of lotions and potions so that some fell over like ten pins and others rocked noisily on the surface.

I jumped out of bed and went over to help right him. 'Be quiet, Emmet, you'll wake Mom and Pop,' I hissed, but it was too late. Frankie's overgrown sausage of a body came bustling into the room and behind it, a vision in yellow quilted satin: Mom.

'Oh man, I'm going to throw up,' Emmet burbled, lurching past the both of us and into the bathroom where we heard the sound of him bringing up the contents of his stomach. It was not pretty.

'Are you happy now?' my mother said, looking at me with features so pinched they all wound up in the middle of her face. 'Is this what you wanted? Is it? You know, we were doing just fine until you came back.'

I felt a physical pain in my heart then. An actual searing pain. I didn't know how I had hardened myself against her in the past but I couldn't do it any more. The outer shell I had obviously built up to deflect her cruelty was simply not there. I couldn't turn my back and pretend she hadn't hurt me, I couldn't laugh off her words or seek refuge from them in the arms of someone else. There was no one else. I was on my own. I was at rock bottom and she was right there on top of me. But why?

'You weren't fine,' I said to her. 'You were never fine.'

The look of shock on her face almost stopped me in my tracks. I was scared of my mom the way you are always scared of the people with the most ammunition against you, the ones who can inflict the most pain. But as I stood there in my old bedroom next to a larger-than-life poster of Venus Williams, my brother retching noisily in the bathroom down the hall, my mother blaming me for I don't know what, I realised that she could not hurt me more than she already had. It was time to stop doing anything for an easy life. It was time to change, to shift, to improve.

'And of course I'm not happy,' I said to her. 'How could I be happy? There's only one person in this family who seems happy and he spends most of his time visiting the castles of England.'

'Don't you dare talk about our family like that,' my mother rasped, pulling her dressing gown closer to her body, her knuckles white as she strangled every last synthetic fibre to death. Frankie sat at her feet, ears pricked up, one eye shut, the other fixed on me. 'There's nothing wrong with our family.'

'Nothing wrong? Jesus, Mom, have you never heard of the word "dysfunctional"?'

'Don't you dare take the Lord's name in vain in my house!'

'I'm not talking about the christing jesusing Lord, Mom, I'm talking about us!' My voice was getting louder and louder, my unhappiness fighting to get out of me.

'You do that one more time and I will throw you out in the street on your head, Mary-Constance, and so help me God maybe this time you will get some sense knocked into you.'

She turned and swept out of the bedroom toward the kitchen, but instead of swallowing my emotion and going to bed with a pillow over my face I followed her. She slammed the cupboards open and closed looking for a water glass; her hands trembling with rage as she turned on the tap and filled it, then slugged it back, her tiny shoulders hunched up and quivering.

Who was this woman? I thought to myself. And why was she so angry? Why was she always so angry? We stayed there for a few moments, her radiating rage and me staring at her stiffened back as I dissected our plight, felt the heat of her fury. I hadn't done anything. I knew I hadn't. So she wasn't really angry that I'd left my husband or been half-killed by a pretzel or made my brother come home and puke his head off. She was just angry, period.

'What made you like this?' I asked, my voice soft with genuine wonder. 'Who did this to you?'

The question must have taken her by surprise. Her shoulders relaxed a little as a surprised breath escaped and I could see the muscles in her face fighting for control in the rippled reflection of the kitchen window.

'You can't be this mad at me, Mom. I'm a good person, a good daughter. I'm sorry I stole Woody's pretzel and ended up in a coma and can't remember half the stupid things I've done in the last while but . . .'

Actually, I wasn't being honest with her. In truth, I was sick to death of making apologies that were never accepted for things I had not done. 'No,' I said, changing tack so loudly I gave myself a fright. 'You know what? I am *not* sorry. It is horrible what has happened to

209

me, Mom. I nearly died, I've lost my memory, I can't taste anything, which means the only part of my life I really cared anything for is meaningless. I should not have to feel guilt just because you expect me to. For God's sake, your son is a good-for-nothing pot-smoking who-knows-what-shooting bum who has spent his lifetime sponging off of you; your husband is probably going to spend the next 20 years watching medieval sword-making documentaries; even your dog is a sex pervert. Why should I get all your disappointment?'

This thought riled me, big-time, once it was out there in the open. Why *should* I get all the disappointment?

'Has it ever occurred to you that in this family I might actually be your best bet? Have you ever considered that? Me. I may only have half a brain and no job or husband or fiancé or best friend or taste; I may have given up the biggest walk-in closet and floor-to-ceiling matching lingerie — but I am still your best bet. So why do you always dump on me, Mom? Why not dump on Emmet? Or, better still, nobody? You're always so mad with me and I never know why. I've always been too busy just trying to get on with it, get around it, get over it but I am sick of it. I am so fucking sick of it.' I was crying, of course. 'Jesus, you heard me, *Jesus*! What is the matter with you?'

Her back to me still, she turned and opened the refrigerator, pulling out the remains of her heinous mac and cheese, the sight of which only fuelled my anger.

'Put that back, it's disgusting,' I wept. 'Your cooking sucks. It's inedible. You shouldn't do it. It's a crime against produce. Are you listening to me, Mom? Are you even listening to me?'

I could hardly believe the words as they spewed out of my mouth. In fact, I wasn't entirely sure it was me saying them. Instead I felt as though I was somewhere up above us, looking down, just watching the whole scene unfold. This is quite common among those who have suffered head injuries, this looking-down-on-yourself sensation, although I didn't know it then. All part of that now-it's-a-dream-now-it's-not stuff. Anyway, while I was up there floating around I suspended my fury and noticed, first of all, how many flies had died and were buried in the light fitting in the ceiling and then how small my mother was. In my anger I had moved closer to her and I was enormous, despite the thin thighs. I loomed threateningly over her, my fists clenched at my own sides, my chin jutting out in my own anger, my face puce with fury. I didn't look one little bit like the embattled broken hard-done-by figure I imagined myself to be. But you know what I did look like? A bully.

The wind left my sails at that moment and I returned to my body, which buckled and deflated with me back in it.

'Mom,' I whispered, choked and panicked. 'I'm sorry. I didn't mean it. I'm so sorry.'

But if I had deflated, she had caved in. She had collapsed against the refrigerator, her body curved around the leftovers like a tiny comma, her rage evaporated.

'Mom?' My own fury had turned back into fear. 'Please. I said I'm sorry.'

She did not move a muscle and when she started to speak, her voice was almost unrecognisable without its trademark anger. 'You don't know how lucky you are, Mary-Constance,' she said. 'You've never known how lucky you are. I never hurt you. I never raised my hand to you. I never punished you. Not once.'

'Never punished me? Mom, you've spent my whole life punishing me.'

'Oh, you don't know the meaning of the word,' she said. She put the leftovers on the counter but didn't let go of them, didn't move away. 'The things I could tell you.'

The way she said it sent a shiver up my spine and the sounds of the city disappeared, leaving nothing in the room but what lay between the two of us.

'So tell me,' I said softly. 'I want to know.'

'Why would I tell you? Why would I tell anyone? But the

trademark sarcasm that would usually ring around my ears with such words was missing.

'Because secrets rot and fester and turn into . . . something else,' I said. And I guessed a woman who had been estranged from her own mother for nearly 40 years and never so much as spoke her name had more than a few secrets.

'Who do you think you are? Dr Phil? Some things just belong in the past. You people never seem to realise that.'

'But it might help us understand each other, Mom.'

'What's to understand?'

'You say I've never been punished, Mom, but there are other ways of hurting the people you love, you know. You always put me down. You're never happy with me. Everything I do is wrong. I don't look right. I don't sound right. I don't sit right. My hair sucks. You don't think that is punishment?'

'Estelle?' It was my dad, standing in the doorway in his pyjamas, what little hair he had bunched up on one side of his head, his face crumpled with worry as he looked at my mom. 'Is everything okay, Estelle?'

She looked at him in such a way that in a moment of extraordinary clarity I suddenly understood why we all were the way we were. And I loved him so much in that instant that I forgave him any shortcomings as a father. I had never thought of my parents as the love match of the century: mainly, I had considered my father a saint to put up with my mother and I guess at times I had wondered what she saw in him. For a woman who oozed disappointment she had always been strangely content with his little life at the shoe store, his mediocre income, his small circle of friends, his lack of ambition. But now I saw that when she needed him to, he rescued her and she was a woman in need of rescuing. She let him love her and she loved him. She really loved him. She was really capable of that sort of love and it was written all over her face.

'I'm fine,' she said. 'Go back to bed, Patrick. I'll be there in a minute.' She watched him shuffle back towards the bedroom then took the plastic wrap off the mac and cheese, straightened it out, put it back on again, and put the bowl back in the fridge.

'Your father asked me to marry him one Sunday afternoon at 3.15,' she said, without looking at me. 'We were in the elevator about to go for a walk but instead I went right back upstairs and packed my bags. By 3.55 I was sitting right here in this apartment and I never spoke to that woman again.'

That was it. My explanation. The most I was ever going to get. It occurred to me that maybe I should ring Ty and get Dr Foster's number. I suddenly felt like a person in need of a whole lot of therapy.

But there was something else. A tingly feeling had started in my toes and was travelling its way up my body, rattling my bones and giving me the shivers as it made its way to my brain where it knocked on the door, begging to be let in. A realisation was trying to dawn on me. I knew that. I just couldn't quite work out what the realisation was.

My mother gave a dry little cough. 'Anyway, you've got no business dragging up all this old dirt,' she said, the nastiness creeping back into her tone. 'It would never have happened if you hadn't come back mean. If I catch pneumonia and die from being up in the middle of the night, well, let that be a lesson to you Mary-Constance. Some things are better left unsaid. Did you ever stop to consider that?'

The bathroom door flew open and we heard Emmet go crashing down the hall and into my bedroom where the bed springs bounced as he hit the mattress. Clearly, it was me who would be spending the night on the sofa.

'No, Mom,' I said. 'I never did stop to consider that. And if you catch pneumonia and die, I promise I will learn from it.'

She narrowed her eyes, rearranged the yellow quilted satin bathrobe, summonsed Frankie who had fallen asleep post-coitally on my foot, and without another word headed back to her bedroom. The dog gave my big toe a warm disgusting parting lick and in a flash I thought of *Wild Swans*, a book I had read (most of) a few years before. I'd been outraged by how in pre-revolution China women bound their daughters' feet to stunt their growth, to keep them tiny and neat just the way men liked them. It was such a gross thing for a mother to do to her daughter, I had thought at the time, yet they did it because their mothers had done it to them too. It was just the way things were. It was history.

And in a way, that was what had happened to me. I saw that then as I wiped Frankie's slobber off my toe with some kitchen paper. It wasn't anything I had done that made my mom so mad. It was the way things were. It was history. She had bound and stunted not my feet (although I bet she'd wanted to) but me, the inner me, no doubt because that's what had been done to her.

And I could be bitter and hateful too, if I chose to be. I could follow the family tradition. But I could also stage a revolution of my own: that was the realisation battering at my brain. I could forgive my mother if I wanted to, I could take off my inner bandages, wriggle my toes, and start growing any which way I pleased. What freedom there was in that thought. What relief! I didn't have to be anything because of her; I could just be me.

What's more, I thought with a jolt, I would never have come to that liberating conclusion if I hadn't come back mean, or more accurately if I hadn't been nearly killed by that pretzel in the first place.

It was a moment of brightness in what felt like a lifetime of gloom.

Fourteen

When I woke up the next morning Frankie was lying across my chest like a moth-eaten stole and there was something slimy on my neck that was so gross I couldn't begin to contemplate its origins. Emmet was sitting at the table eating some toxic-looking pink and orange breakfast cereal. Pop was already in his chair fondling the remote control as Mom vacuumed the very sofa cushions on which I lay.

'What the hell is that?' I asked groggily, wiping at the mess on my throat.

'Well, I've been watching his head and nothing came out of there,' Emmet said with a slurp. He looked remarkably chipper for someone who had been mainlining cleaning products the night before, something we were all no doubt supposed to ignore.

'Get off me, you disgusting animal,' I said, pushing Frankie onto the floor and lifting up my legs so that my mother could Hoover beneath them. I watched her as she cleaned, her features knitted together in concentration, her eyes careful to avoid mine. Our little tête à tête in the night had obviously not changed anything for her but as I looked at my feet, still aloft in the air, a smile crept across my face. I wriggled my toes.

'I am revolting,' I told my mother as I pushed away the Hoover hose and got off the couch. 'I am a Chinese girl's feet.'

'What is it with this family and history?' Emmet grumbled. 'Haven't you guys heard of the E! Channel?'

'Do you think they fixed up all of Mary-Constance's brain?' my mom asked no one in particular. 'I hope they didn't make a mistake and leave something in there by mistake like the lady with the scissors. You know the one, Patrick. Or was it a sponge? She died, anyway. Or did she just end up in a wheelchair?'

I needed to get out of the house for a while. That much was clear. It was going to be too hard to wriggle my toes when the bandages were still so close at hand. The problem was, where could I go?

I was pondering this question in the bathroom after showering Frankie's dubious emissions from various parts of my body when I found the St Jude medal that Mom had given me in the hospital, which had caused so much eye-narrowing on the part of Signora Marinello. It was caught in the lining of my toilet bag. When I rubbed it between my fingers, all I could think of was sinking into that big fleshy bosom of hers. I needed to be held tight and comforted a little. I needed someone to help me, to guide me; hadn't she said that she would always be there, that if I needed her I just had to go find her?

'You just missed her,' the droopy-eyed fisherman from my coma told me when I arrived at St Vincent's. 'She finished her shift. She left aready.'

The neurological ward, my home for all those weeks, bustled and throbbed around me. If anyone remembered me from my weeks of lying there then they did a good job of not showing it. Unconscious I had been the centre of attention but standing on my own two feet I felt like an insignificant spinning top being knocked from one side of the stark white hallway to the other. I lost my balance avoiding a paramedic who I am pretty sure was the water-taxi driver who took me to the Hotel Gritti Palace. ('Hello. Hello. Can you hear me?' It all made perfect sense now.) Then I regained my equilibrium only to be knocked off course again by a nurse running along the corridor with an armful of IV bags. I ducked into a doorway to avoid a collision, only to ram an elderly teary-eyed couple grey with grief. I jumped backwards, panicked, and spun around, looking for the elevator, fighting back tears. Then I felt two strong hands steadying me from behind, turning me slowly around. And there was the delectable Marco.

Good grief, but that man did things to me I didn't remember any other man ever doing. If I could have pushed him into the linen closet and performed disgusting acts on him right then and there, I would have — not that I could see a linen closet and believe me, I looked. I could just tell he knew that was what I was thinking too because there was laughter, slightly mocking, in his eyes. This, as you can imagine, transformed me into a silver-tongued devil of staggering proportions.

'I am a Chinese girl's feet,' I blurted out. 'I wriggle.'

'Never been much of a poetry fan myself,' Marco said smoothly. 'So, how's life on the outside?'

'Oh, I didn't mean that about the feet,' I blathered. 'I meant the binding. The unbinding. I was just thinking about Chinese girls. You know what? It's kind of hard to explain. You're probably thinking of calling security or getting the psych team down to examine me but actually I am just here looking for Signora Marinello and I was thinking about Chinese girls' feet and I'm making it sound much worse than it is. But if you don't bind the feet they can grow. That's my point. But actually my other point is that I'm good, yes, I'm good.' He seemed slightly taken aback but I felt I was getting a handle on it. 'And you?' I inquired politely. 'How're you doing?'

'Same old same old,' he answered. 'Saving the world, bringing back the dead. I have a documentary team from Canada coming in to film me this afternoon. My 11-hour stint in surgery last Thursday was reported on CNN, I've already been asked to present a paper on it next year at a conference in San Diego. And I just got a call to say my new Porsche has arrived so you could say all is well.'

I nodded my head in what I hoped was an extremely sane and

appropriately interested way while he scanned me up and down.

'You look good, Connie,' he said. 'In fact, you look great.'

I tried desperately to think of something intelligent to say to keep him in my thrall. 'Can I colour my hair?' I settled on. 'I'm worried the chemicals might seep into my brain and mess things up.'

'I've never heard of that happening before,' he answered. 'So I think you should be okay. And it would be good to see you blonde again.'

I blushed. Oh for a gondola and a darkened basement, I thought to myself.

There was an awkward silence.

'I didn't just say that, did I?' I asked him.

'Say what?'

'The thing about the gondola?'

It was his turn to laugh. 'No, there was something about a Chinese girl's feet a while back but no mention of any gondola.'

My relief was enormous.

'Look, anyway, I should go,' he said. 'It was good to see you, Connie, it really was. Take it easy. Go blonde.'

I nodded dumbly and watched him as he strode up the corridor away from me. Those hips. Those shoulders. That neck. If I'd been a cartoon character I'm pretty sure there would have been throbbing marks emanating from my groin right then. I could near as damn it feel that man between my thighs and it was so intensely almost satisfying that I guess I may have started drooling a little.

'Hey, if it isn't missus fancy-food snob.' My Pucci mushroom-seller interrupted my lustfulness, clanking past with a multi-layered trolley full of food that I was grateful I could not smell. 'Come back for more, huh?'

I switched as quickly and politely as I could back into the real world. 'I'm looking for Signora Marinello, actually,' I answered her. 'I don't suppose you know where she lives?'

'Do I look like a telephone book?'

'No, you look like someone who would rather pee in the soup than taste it and who on occasion probably has.'

That sure stopped her short. I eyed up a plate of donkey-coloured meatballs, wondering what it would feel like to wear them.

'You're a smart ass, you know that?'

'It's the new me,' I told her unapologetically.

'I like it,' she said. 'Marinello's gone to Nick's over on 14th and Ninth for breakfast. Says she don't like my food either. No taste, the pair of you.'

Well, I could only speak for myself on that matter, I thought. Nick's it was.

I had just stepped into the elevator when I heard someone calling my name, or a variation on it. 'Costanza Conlan! Costanza Conlan!' A woman was shuffling towards me on high-heeled slides, a folded-over piece of paper in her hand and a pissed-off look on her face.

'Here,' she said, thrusting the note at me. 'I don't know what you did to get it but this is for you.' She shot me a nasty look before the elevator door closed and I opened the piece of paper. *I'm not joking about seeing you blonde*, it read. *Call me*. And there was Marco's phone number.

My feet hardly touched the ground as I glided up to 14th Street and across the avenues to Ninth. Marco, the cutest guy I had ever seen in my whole entire life, the man who caused a party in my pants, wanted me to call him. The new me was hot! And I was open to that, wasn't I? I was the new me. I could be anyone I wanted to be. Sinful thoughts infiltrated my brain and I saw myself thrashing around various unmade beds, my legs wrapped around Marco's hips, his lips on my throat, my hands on his chest.

After spotting Signora Marinello through the window, I sailed into Nick's diner with a spring in my step. She was sitting in a booth wearing a Starsky and Hutch cardigan over her uniform, even though it was sweltering outside. She looked like a big knitted mountain and my heart swelled with love as I all but skipped across the linoleum to her table.

'Signora Marinello!' I cried with excitement. 'It's me! *Buòn giorno*!'

She lifted her beautiful smooth face up at the sound of my voice and lit up at the sight of me, filling me with such hope and warmth that I didn't even notice she was sitting with someone. I launched myself into her arms.

'Oh, I've missed you,' I said into her 12-ply woollen shoulder. 'I've missed you so much.'

'Me too,' Signora Marinello said. 'Let go now, Constanzia. You squashing me.'

I stood back, still beaming. She was halfway through a mighty fine-looking grilled cheese sandwich, an ice-cream soda foaming next to it.

'Well hello,' a gravelly voice at my elbow said. 'Will you take a look at this.'

My heart skipped a beat. My loins stopped pounding. I knew that voice: that voice had spoken words to me once that had made the sort of sense I'd never heard before.

It was Luca.

He was sitting on the booth seat opposite Signora Marinello wearing a pale denim shirt that brought out the green in his eyes and the silver in his hair. He looked like just about the healthiest human being I had ever seen in my entire life and for a moment I forgot about my lack of taste, my fucked-up family, my homelessness and my giant crush on Marco, and all I felt was the excruciating warmth of his words at the squero.

'Don't just stand there,' he said, sliding over. 'Take a seat.'

I did so, zombie-like.

'Wassa matter, Connie?' There was a mischievous note in Signora Marinello's voice. 'Cat got your tongue?'

'I know you?' I asked Luca.

He raised his eyebrows, eyes twinkling. 'Well, no,' he answered. 'But I know you. Luke Scarpa.' He held out his hand and I reached for it, my fingers pressing against the dry crinkled lines of his palm. 'Pleased to finally meet you.'

'Scarpa?' I repeated dumbly, still holding his hand.

'Scarpa senior,' Signora Marinello pitched in. 'Marco's father. I wonder should I have fries. I feel like fries.'

I finally let go of Luca's hand but then didn't know what to do with my arms. They flopped uselessly on the table and I had to make a special effort to put them down in my lap. Marco's father. Of course he was Marco's father! Why hadn't I thought of that before? I knew that already. Why hadn't I asked anyone about him? Where was my head?

'So, how you doing?' Luca asked quietly.

'How do you know me?' I could actually feel him sitting next to me. And while I couldn't smell him, couldn't smell anything, my head was suddenly filled with the memory of the faint scent of lemons that had bewitched me at the boatyard in my dreams.

'Well, I don't, exactly,' he said. 'But I sat with you a few times at the hospital when I came to see Marc and Eugenia.'

'Your name is Eugenia?' I asked Signora Marinello, who nodded and stopped a grouchy waiter to order her fries. I had never thought to ask what her first name was and felt momentarily ashamed of my self-absorption. Not that I was finished with being self-absorbed, you understand. Not by a long shot.

'But why would you sit with me?' I asked as Signora Marinello munched on her sandwich, the sound of the working deep fryer underscoring a crackling Fleetwood Mac track being piped around the diner.

'I had business at the hospital,' Luca said, contemplating the cheeseburger in front of him, 'which didn't take as long as I planned so I found myself with some time on my hands, came by to see Eugenia and there you were.'

'And what better way to spend your time than with a pretty girl who don't answer back, hey Luca,' Signora Marinello teased.

'Well, you looked like someone who could do with some

company,' Luca said simply. It was just like in my dream. He had this way of making me feel I had known him forever, of dropping precious jewels into the conversation as though they were common or garden pebbles.

'You the best visitor she has all the time she's there,' Signora Marinello told him. 'You wanna meet the mother. Wheee.' She said something in Portuguese that sounded like a lot of swear words, the flow of which was halted by the arrival of a big plate of perfectly cooked fries.

'What about Tom?' I asked her. 'He came to visit me. Eventually. And Fleur. What about her?'

'Oh yeah,' Signora Marinello agreed. 'Her husband marry her best friend but she can't remember.'

'They're not married,' I pointed out. 'Officially, he is still married to me.'

'You have retrospective memory loss?' Luca seemed impressed.

I nodded sadly.

'Huh,' he chewed on his burger. 'Unusual. Doesn't seem to be much else wrong with you.'

'I've lost my sense of taste,' I said, dipping one of Signora Marinello's French fries in ketchup, something I never would have done before. I had been something of a fry snob ever since Tom told me to be. He would rather shoot himself in the head than serve fries. And as for ketchup . . . Over his dead body or yours should you attempt it, or even ask for it. 'Which is kind of a tragedy because they tell me I am the *New York Times* restaurant critic.'

Signora Marinello took a slurp out of her soda. 'MC Conlan,' she said, nodding at me.

'That so?' Luca nodded. 'And you've lost your sense of taste? Too bad. Was it injury to the cribriform plate or olfactory nerve damage?'

'What are you, a brain surgeon?'

'Nope,' he said. 'I'm a doctor. We're two different species.'

Snatches of my gondola-building dream scenario kept floating by like puffy summer clouds, changing shape as soon as I tried to latch on to them. What he was saying had some sort of relevance, I knew that, but I couldn't work out what it was.

'You don't like surgeons?'

'I wouldn't say that. My son is a surgeon. A very good one too.'

'But you don't approve.'

'I'd like him to spend a bit more time with the living,' Luca said, finishing his burger and pushing the plate away.

'But if it weren't for him there wouldn't be so many living,' I argued, patting my pocket where Marco's phone number sat although not feeling so inclined to call it as I had before. 'He saved my life,' I said. 'He saved my life.'

I heard the tremor in my voice before I felt it and to my enormous embarrassment, I exploded into tears. I hoped it wasn't a developing pattern, this crying uncontrollably in restaurants, because all the hats in the world would not be able to disguise my identity if it was going to be a regular thing.

Signora Marinello did not stop attacking her fries but used her free hand to pull a bunch of napkins out of the dispenser and thrust them at me.

'Is better out than in, Constanzia,' she said matter of factly. Then with the use of just one eye, she attracted the grouchy waiter again. 'I think we need pie.'

'I think I still love Tom even though he's had a baby with Fleur,' I sobbed. 'But I'm engaged to a man who wears pony-skin shoes. I've written a horrible book and I sound like a bitch plus I have no sense of taste but I'm supposed to be the best restaurant critic in the world.' I blew my nose wetly on a napkin and tried to regain some control. 'I hate living at home; I'm too old. My dad's glued to the TV, my brother is into his 20th year of experimenting with drugs, my mother is vacuuming the oxygen out of the air, and,' I wailed this bit, 'I have nowhere else to go.'

'Aw, come on,' Luca said soothingly. 'That doesn't sound so bad.'

'I stole Woody Allen's pretzel,' I cried. 'And everybody knows about it except me.' Strangely, though, blurting out my woes proved quite therapeutic and the tidal wave of emotion that had engulfed me started to recede until eventually I was down to just a basic snivel.

'People have done worse for a good pretzel, you know,' Luca said, and the kindness of that notion floored me.

'Cherry pie,' Signora said appreciatively as hers approached the table. 'Now there's something people do crazy things for. My cousin Cleber, he marry a woman because of her cherry pie even though he is gay. Now that's plenty more crazy than stealing Woody Allen's pretzel.'

She had me there, I had to admit, as I admired her pie: the crust was indeed crisp and golden, the brilliant red fruit spilled out onto the plate like a homemade filling would.

'Why you got nowhere else to go?' Signora Marinello asked between mouthfuls. 'What happen to the man in the white suit?'

'He has Italian decorating magazines on his coffee table and he doesn't even read Italian,' I said. 'We sleep in separate rooms. Everything is beige. I tried going home to my old apartment but unfortunately my husband lives there with his new girlfriend and their baby.'

'You're divorced?' Luca asked.

I nodded. 'Nearly.'

'Why?'

'I don't know. I can't remember. I didn't go on our second honeymoon. Tom ended up in Venice on his own and I ended up engaged to Ty Wheatley.'

'You passed on Venice? Well, that explains the divorce.' Even his gruffness was sort of nice.

'You like Venice?' I was curious about that, of course.

'My grandparents were from there,' Luca said. 'Little island called Mazzorbo out in the lagoon, famous for its duck.'

My heart was in my mouth. What did this mean? 'Your grandfather wasn't a gondola-builder, was he?' I held my breath waiting for him to answer.

'Nope, he grew tomatoes. Came to America to give his sons a better life.' He looked out the window as if to check that his grandfather had come to the right place and my eyes followed his. I got something of a shock. Last time I had looked out on the intersection of Hudson and Ninth at West 12th there was practically nothing there except jammed up traffic and empty warehouses; now it heaved with restaurants and bars and barely clad bodies.

'When the hell did all that happen?' I was aghast. Three years before, the blood of freshly slaughtered cattle beasts could still be found on the cobbled stones of the Meatpacking District. Now it was stilettos as far as the eye could see.

'I know what you mean,' agreed Luca. 'There goes the neighbourhood.'

'You live here?' I ventured.

Signora Marinello spluttered.

'Hell, no,' Luca answered. 'Shelter Island. Been there?'

I shook my head. I knew it was between the north and south forks of eastern Long Island but I'd never been there. I'd only ever been to the Hamptons once. Fleur and Roberta and I had got a holiday share with some of Roberta's friends one summer. I had missed Tom, who'd refused to join us, and was intimidated by all the other people with holiday shares so hadn't really made the most of it.

'I think you'd like it there, Connie,' Signora Marinello said, licking her spoon with great gusto. 'Sounds nice and only two hours on the bus.'

'What would you know?' Luca asked her. 'I've been trying to get you to visit for the past 10 years and you still haven't.'

'I'm from Jersey,' Signora Marinello said as though this explained anything. 'But Constanzia, she has no place to live and you have a great big empty house so sounds to me like you two should get together.' She pushed her plate away, replete.

'I'll be fine,' I said.

'She'll be fine,' Luca agreed.

Signora Marinello shrugged her shoulders. 'You need a roof over your head and some peace and quiet,' she said to me, 'and you,' she turned her attention to Luca, 'you need to stop spending so long on your own or with people in comas. You getting kind of cranky.' She then extricated herself from behind the diner table and stood up, arching her back and pulling her Starsky and Hutch cardigan around her bulging middle. 'Me, I have a date with the foot spa and the man who unplugged my cousin Nicola's drainpipes.'

She gave me a quick hug, leaned across to accept a kiss on each cheek from Luca and was gone, leaving us sitting squashed together in the booth looking at the space she had vacated.

'Technically, if I need peace and quiet and you need company, it's not such a great match,' I said to Luca, who just smiled his comfortable smile. He then pointed his finger at his empty coffee cup as a waitress came by. She was young and pretty and looked at him flirtatiously under her lashes but Luca didn't seem to notice. He was in pretty good shape for 51. And even better, he didn't seem to know it. 'You want some coffee?' he asked me but there was no point.

We sat there in companionable silence for a while, watching the ebb and flow of the diner as though that's what we always did on a Monday morning. A foursome of worn-out party boys bitched about someone called Clarence at the next table, a smart tourist couple fed toast to their baby across the aisle. I can hardly find words to explain to you the weirdness of the connection I felt with Luca because it was so low-key, so comfortable, it almost slipped below the radar.

'So you come and meet Eugenia often?' I finally asked.

'As often as I can,' he said.

'You used to work with her?'

'I did. You were lucky to have her on your side. They're not all like her, you know. Far from it.'

'They're not?' I mean I knew she was special but I'd assumed everyone with a job like hers was.

'She had a good feeling about you, Connie,' he said, 'and sometimes that's all someone in your situation needs, despite what the doctors will tell you. The right person with a good feeling. She had faith in you. Good old-fashioned faith.'

The hairs stood up on the back of my neck. 'I didn't know that,' I said to Luca. 'I don't know anything.'

He smiled that certain smile of his. 'The truth is,' he said, 'no one knows.' We looked at each other and then, like it was the most natural thing in the world, he slipped his hand across the Formica table and took mine in his. It felt so good, so at home, I just left it right there and kept my eyes on his. I didn't want anything else but for that moment to keep going forever and ever and ever. It was the weirdest thing and not at all creepy. Just natural. Unbelievably, comfortably, wonderfully natural.

'For crissakes, Dad, don't you ever get sick of this Good Samaritan shit?' The sound of Marco's voice pretty much sucked the comfort and wonder out of the scenario and I snatched my hand away again.

'Marco,' I cried with forced jollity. My, he was good-looking when he was angry but the guy seriously needed to sound an alarm on approach.

'Sit down, son,' Luca said, indicating Signora Marinello's empty side of the booth. 'Take a load off.'

Marco shook his head. 'Jesus, give it up, Dad.'

Luca shrugged. 'Just having a cup of coffee and catching up with old friends. What brings you here?'

'You can hardly call Connie an old friend, Dad. And I came to give you this. I won't be needing it.' He threw a manila envelope on the table and turned to me. 'You got my message?' I nodded. 'Good.' And he swivelled on those hips and strode out of the restaurant. Most people would have found this unsettling or embarrassing, but not Luca, he just calmly soaked it up.

'Why is he so angry with you?' I asked him.

'Oh, many reasons,' he said. 'Too many to mention and most of them perfectly legitimate. But lately,' he held up the envelope, 'it's because I want him to give up surgery and come back to Shelter Island, to help me run the medical centre. My partner's retired to Florida and I want Marc to replace him.'

I laughed. 'But he's in a different league, isn't he?'

'He certainly is,' agreed Luca. 'That's why I want him to come home. Boy needs to spend more time with the upright and talking folk.'

'If the patients at your medical centre are all upright and talking then do you need two doctors?' I pointed out, quite cleverly, I thought.

'Well, they're more upright and talking than the patients he deals with over the road there,' Luca said gruffly. 'Present company excluded.'

'Oh, he didn't really deal with me as a patient,' I said. 'He just did the operation. That whole recovery thing is not really his field.'

Luca drained his coffee. 'My point entirely,' he said, then looked at his watch. 'So, anyway, I have a train to catch.'

I forced a smile and looked out the window at the swarming crowd.

'What are you going to do?' he asked.

I was asking myself that same question but finding the options all still sadly lacking. Perhaps I would get a hotel. I had not checked my bank balance yet but surely it could cope with a hotel room for a few nights while I got my head together (ha ha). But if it took more than a few nights for that to happen?

'Connie?' Luca said. 'Do you have someplace to go?'

'Not entirely.' I answered.

He cleared his throat. 'Because, Eugenia is right. I guess I do have a big empty house. So if you're in a spot and you want to come and stay I guess it would be okay.'

'You don't think it would be weird?'

'A little, maybe. But every suggestion Eugenia Marinello has

228

ever made to me has been right on the money so if she thinks you need peace and quiet and I need company, I'm willing to agree.'

'It's still weird.'

'Well, there are a hell of a lot worse places to go, Connie. You'd have your own space, you could eat, sleep, walk on the beach, help me out with my senior citizens. They've been giving me a giant pain in the ass since Herb moved to Boca, excuse my French.'

But I don't even know you, I wanted to say, and besides people don't just take off with perfect strangers. Even if they've met those strangers before in their dreams and those perfect strangers have kept them company while they were unconscious.

'I can't,' I said.

'Why not?'

Actually, I couldn't think of a reason apart from natural caution, which I appeared to have ceased practising.

'Okay then,' I said.

And that was that.

Fifteen

'You're going where?' my mother asked me, incredulous, when I revealed my plan to recuperate at the seaside home of a perfect stranger. 'Your own home isn't good enough for you? You have to take up with a man you only met one time? Why would you do this?' She was looking at my father for back-up. 'By the ocean of all places. She doesn't know how dangerous that is? What can happen out there?'

'He's a doctor, Mom,' I said. 'I thought you'd be pleased.'

'All of a sudden you care if I'm pleased?'

Just repeat that conversation pretty much verbatim for six or eight hours and you will understand why it was with some enthusiasm that I left the house the next morning, headed for Shelter Island. Emmet, bless his heart, walked me to the Hamptons Jitney stop on 69th Street and told me to take care of myself, as though he meant it even, and suggested that perhaps once I had sussed out the scene I could call for him. He could move out there too, especially if there was a wide-screen TV, and I shouldn't worry about the 20 grand, he was okay with me letting him down.

I sat on the bus staring out the window as the dreary clutter of the city gave way to the gentle open spaces off the Long Island Expressway. Even though I loved the city with all my heart, at that moment it felt good to be getting away from it.

230

I tried not to but I liked Sag Harbor, my drop-off point. Tom had always been so scathing of the Hamptons but the shingle houses with their leafy green gardens appealed to me in a storybook sort of way. It looked like the sort of place where nothing bad could happen. Where people were nice to each other. Where the water of the harbour sparkled at the end of a neat main street with no Starbucks or T-Mobile franchises. Stepping off the bus at the firehouse, though, I grew wary. On closer inspection every second car was a Mercedes; there were too many antique stores; all the women wore white capri pants. But then the Jitney pulled away and I saw Luca across the road waiting for me, leaning against the side of an old green Chevy pick-up looking like something out of a James Dean movie. He was just the sort of guy who looked at home wherever he was and there was something infectiously comforting about that. He smiled and walked toward me, grabbing my bag and throwing it in the back of his truck, then opening the passenger-side door for me to get in.

A big fat marmalade cat with only one ear sat in a superior fashion in my seat, staring straight ahead and not even bothering to turn its big fat head to look at me.

'What is it with cats?' I asked Luca. 'Did something happen when I was gone? It's like they're setting themselves up to rule the world.'

'Meet Gertrude,' Luca said, coming over to my side and pushing the cat into the middle of the bench seat as if she were a statue. 'She's a little eccentric.'

'She's the size of a freakin' horse,' I said. 'And what's with all that staring straight ahead?' Actually, as long as she didn't try to have sex with me, I was okay with it.

'Oh, you'll get used to her,' Luca said, climbing into the driver's side and following the signs to the Shelter Island ferry. It was good to be out in the open surrounded by so much greenery. I felt slightly better straightaway. And as we crossed on the boat from North Haven to Shelter Island, I felt a further physical unclenching that seemed to

231

loosen every cell in my body. It was only a five-minute trip but I got out of the truck and stood at the back of the ferry all the same, watching the mainland get smaller and smaller as the smooth silvery sea spread itself out in front of me. I closed my eyes and breathed in the sea air, the sun beating on my face. It was the best I could remember feeling since I had been in Venice, which was a dream. But that was a good thing, I told myself. I knew now what was a dream and what wasn't; to be feeling good in real life was progress.

Gertrude had moved back into my space when I returned to the truck and for the life of me I couldn't push the darn creature over. Luca had to pull on her from his side.

'Thank you for the welcome, Gertrude,' I said sarcastically. 'It is much appreciated.' She kept staring ahead, unimpressed, in a particularly cat-like way and emitted an audible fart that made my jaw drop to my chest. The audacity of it!

'Welcome to Shelter Island,' Luca said and we both laughed as we bumped off the ferry and onto dry land. Gertrude licked a paw with a self-satisfied smirk. She had attitude, that cat. In spades.

Shelter Island was the opposite of Manhattan. A wide road stretched ahead, lush forest on either side, houses with acres in-between each other hidden by huge trees and well-kept gardens. About a mile past the ferry landing we turned off into a sleepy tree-lined street, which took us over the brow of the hill and back down toward a stunning open cove. I wondered how anyone could think that the seashore was a dangerous place; it felt like the safest place I had ever been to: the perfect antidote to the noisy high-rise city, all flat and serene and sparkly and pure. I was transfixed. Near the bottom of the hill, when we were almost at the beach, Luca turned into a leafy driveway. I found myself, and Gertrude, staring at a big rustic wooden house, bathed in sunlight and facing the sea. It had a porch that ran across the front and a big stone chimney that straddled both floors. It was the sort of place I imagined Daniel Boone would have lived in if he'd been around in the 21st century.

By the time Luca had shown me around and deposited me in my room I was in love with the house, the cove, the island; even Gertrude was starting to grow on me. She walked in front of me wherever I went, with her tail straight up in the air; and when it came to making right turns, she instead did a haughty little circle to her left.

'What the hell is that about?' I asked Luca the first time she did it and I nearly tripped over her.

'Like I said, she's eccentric.'

She certainly was. The moment I opened my bag and started to unpack she climbed into it, lay down on top of my clothes and would not get off. The great lard-ass weighed a ton and turned herself as stiff as a board. There was no way I could shift her without putting my back out so in the end I just left her there and went downstairs.

Luca had gone to work, telling me to make myself at home, which left me free to poke about his house. Turned out he had good taste as well. The interior was kind of woody with Mexican-looking rugs and big squashy chairs and lots of lamps and bookcases. The kitchen was outdated but adequate and the refrigerator was well stocked, which led me to think that Luca probably cooked rather than ate take-out. I just hoped he wasn't going to torture me with perfectly spiced culinary miracles because I had gone a whole half-hour without thinking about the state of my olfactory bulbs and the quiver in my stomach where fear lurked had, for that time, been quelled.

After wandering aimlessly around the living room, picking up books and magazines and other clues as to the nature of the man with whom I was living (boy, that was a weird thought), I pulled open the sliding glass doors out on to the porch and stepped outside.

There was nothing between Luca's house and the beach but the rest of the road we had come down, which led to a couple more houses further down the beach. It finished at an inlet, the glassy-looking water of which was interspersed with tidy wooden jetties. I'd seen movies where people lived in places like this. It was a bit like *On Golden Pond* and made me want to go fishing, which was pretty strange as up until that moment I had never before even considered such a thing. There was no sound at all but for the birds. The Shelter Island shoreline attracted a whole bunch of protected species, Luca had told me: piping plover, least tern and osprey. I certainly couldn't tell which was which — when it came to birds I knew my squab from my Cornish game hen though neither of them said much if you know what I mean — but those live birds were a musical bunch. It was such a different sound from the cacophony of the city. There were no layers of noise like I was used to. No rumbling traffic beneath clanking garbage trucks, no tooting horns atop whining sirens, no babies crying and hammers banging: just quiet and birdsong. I settled myself in one of the porch chairs and the sea twinkled out in front of me. It was the most peaceful place I had ever been in my whole life.

I sat there staring out at that beautiful sea for a while, then went for a long walk on the beach. Actually, that had been Gertrude's idea. On my way back from the bathroom I had absent-mindedly followed her until before I knew it I was across the road and walking along the warm sand of Smith Cove. I wore a short khaki skirt and a tank top I had found in my closet at Ty's place (the only concessions to the casual life I could find even though they were both Ralph Lauren); my skinny white arms and legs were dazzlingly pale against the blue of the sky, the green of the trees and the silvery shimmer of the water. I could feel my skin drinking in the sunshine, my batteries being charged. It felt good.

When I got back I made myself a late lunch of a peanut butter, celery and cottage-cheese sandwich, which satisfied as many of my senses as I could manage, then took a long, dreamless nap in my up-stairs room, which looked out over the water. When I woke up, dusk was falling, painting pinks and purples on the mill-pond seascape outside. I pulled on a sweater and went downstairs. There were signs of activity in the kitchen. The food processor was out and ready to be used. A pot of honey sat beside it and a bottle of rice wine vinegar. I picked up a knob of gnarled ginger root and scratched at the skin, missing smell like a lost limb, then went to find Luca.

After circumnavigating the house I eventually found him out front, on the slope that ran from his lawn to the road by the beach. I hadn't noticed before but the bank was terraced and vibrantly packed to the gunnels with a jaw-dropping herb and vegetable garden. There were zucchinis and summer squash, lettuce, green beans, new potatoes, basil, borage and sorrel. Halfway down the slope Luca was hidden in a patch of blossoming sage, his grey T-shirt and brown skin perfectly in tune with the tiny purple flowers. He was tilling the soil with a small hand-trowel and as I watched him stretch out at work, the sinews in his arms bulging, his ribs showing through his well-worn Yankees T-shirt, it just about took my breath away. I had seen it all before. In the squero of my dreams. What did it mean?

He spied me, finally, and sat back on his haunches, wiping the sweat from his forehead. 'Well hello you,' he said. 'Good day?'

I nodded dumbly and moved closer to him, sitting down on the grass of the terraced bank, knees pulled up to my chest. I reached out to pluck some sage blossoms, rubbing them between my fingers, holding them up to my nose even though I knew nothing would, nothing could come of it.

'And you?'

'So-so. Our receptionist is missing in action so there's more chaos than usual.'

He got back on his knees and leaned into the sage patch again. 'Long Island glacial soil,' he said, 'richest in the whole country almost. You a gardener?'

I shook my head. 'In Manhattan, are you crazy? Besides I have the Greenmarket just around the corner.'

'I suppose,' Luca said. 'Although there's nothing like eating something you grew yourself.'

'Wouldn't make a hell of a lot of difference to me right now I guess.'

'Oh, it's nothing to do with taste,' he disagreed.

'Luca, all food is to do with taste!'

235

'The flavour's only part of it,' he said without stopping what he was doing. 'It's not the be-all and end-all. I just prefer my beans to anyone else's.'

'Because you grow them?'

'Because I like growing them. Because it's nice out here and there's no bullshit. There is compost though,' he said, sitting back again and indicating the barrow full of rich garden manure next to him. 'Don't suppose you feel like giving me a hand?'

It would have been churlish not to and anyway he was right: it was nice out there. I was nursing something warm and fuzzy inside of me at just sitting there in the evening heat among the herbs and vegetables with Luca. He didn't spark that embarrassing overwhelming lustiness that Marco did but something about him struck a chord in me that felt like I had swallowed a great big fat piece of warm apple pie.

'Just take a trowel full and dig it into the soil like this,' he said, showing me how to do just that. I clumsily copied him and we worked our way along the row, me doing the front half and him stretching over to do the back. It was quiet, apart from the birds and the distant lapping of the sea and the odd yowl from Gertrude, who lay upside-down on the front lawn, fighting off an imaginary Doberman with her paws, then running around in crazy left circles.

I was trying to figure out a connection between the lost art of gondola-building and composting and it was not exactly coming to me in a rush. It was something to do with basics, I thought, but further than that and my mind turned to mush. And it was something to do with fathers and sons. 'Why do you think Marco has to spend more time with the living?' I asked him after we'd been working in silence for 10 minutes or so. 'Isn't he, like, a genius or something? He's only 29 and people are filming him and writing articles about him. Aren't you proud?'

'Course I'm proud,' Luca kept trowelling the earth.

Still, there was a 'but' hanging in the air.

'But what?' I prompted.

'But nothing.'

'But something,' I argued, dragging my trowel through the soil.

Luca laughed, loosened a little. 'I guess it worries me,' he said, 'that he goes into that hospital every day and holds all those futures in his hands, literally. Takes the brains out of those skulls, works his magic; then scrubs out and walks away like he's 10 feet tall and nothing can touch him.'

'I don't get what's wrong with that.' It was hard work, gardening: my arm was getting sore and I had a little cramp in my thigh, but Gertrude had finished playing with her imaginary enemy and had me under strict scrutiny so I didn't think I could let up.

'Well, it's not that there's something wrong with it but . . .' he pulled out a weed and threw it up onto the terrace above, where little piles of them peppered the even grass. 'You know, you are probably the first patient all year that Marc has spoken to, actually spoken to.

I felt a warm flood of happiness. There was something special between Marco and me, I had always known it.

'And that's probably thanks to Eugenia,' Luca continued, pricking my bubble a little, 'because she has a sixth sense for that sort of thing. Trust me. The woman is blessed. And Marc thinks he's saving lives and he is, of course he is, but it's just statistics.' It was just like in the boat-yard, as though we were picking up a conversation we had started at an earlier time. 'A life to him is a number. He doesn't care about the person who may or may not go on to live it. He doesn't even know about that person. A surgery goes well or it doesn't, and in his case it mostly goes well. But he does not have one clue about what happens to the folks who survive his surgery. Outcomes, as they say, are not his field. All he knows is whether he did his bit brilliantly. He doesn't know if that brain he held in his hands ever remembered anything again, ever recognised a face or a word or a memory. He doesn't know if the body that brain belonged to ever walked again, if it spent the rest of its life in a wheelchair, or dragged one foot, or lay curled up in a darkened room forever. He doesn't know how the mother of that curled-up body is going to cope with having her son in rehab for the rest of his life, how the wife of the guy who can't talk is going to stay with him, how every single person with a brain trauma has to grieve for the person they once were because they're just not that person any more and never will be again. He doesn't get that.'

I had stopped digging in the soil and was staring at him, frozen, as was Gertrude. It suddenly occurred to me she was probably the victim of a head injury herself. One ear? Eccentric behaviour? No right turns? I would put money on it. I was shocked by what Luca was saying but not only because he was saying it about his son but because he was saying it about me. I was a person with a brain trauma after all. And was I grieving for the person I once was because I was not that person any more and never would be again?

Holy shit. He'd only hit the nail on the goddamned head. I collapsed on my butt, the trowel falling into the soil.

'Hey,' Luca said, alarmed. 'Are you all right?' He was at my side, crouched beside me, one hand on my shoulder, one on my knee, looking into my face. The sound of terns or plovers or ospreys was ringing in my ears, I felt dizzy and weak.

'I never thought about grieving for the old me,' I told him. 'I didn't think she was gone, just on vacation.'

'I'm sorry, Connie,' he said.

'You think I've lost my taste forever?' The thought was like a long, deep dark well that I pictured my body lying at the bottom of.

'Connie,' said Luca, with that tenderness that never failed to stun me, 'I think there is so much more to you than taste.'

There was more to me than taste? I had no idea how he could possibly know that: it was one of those extraordinary things that he said in that ordinary fashion of his. And as his words sank in they astounded me. Before my accident I was all about taste. The me I grieved for was all about taste. What else was there?

'Come on,' he said. 'Let's go inside. It's cooling down out here.'

238

He was making pesto with herbs from his own garden; that's what the food processor was there for. I sat on the breakfast bar as he mulched up cilantro and mint with sesame seeds, ginger root, rice wine vinegar, honey, and garlic. I imagined what it would taste like and it was good. Not particularly Italian — Tom would have had a fit — but I think I would have liked it. Then he spread the pesto thickly on a sliced bun, grilled a couple of hamburgers, added fresh arugula, a slice of Amagansett cheddar and some pickle, and that was dinner. Boy, it looked great and felt just fine too. The bread was fresh with a crunchy crust and light flesh, just like the burger itself, and I could sense the chunky pesto on my tongue. It did mean something that he had grown the cilantro and garlic himself and was making it from scratch. He was right about that. In fact, it felt so darn good I ate the burger in about one second flat and Luca had to make me another one.

'Were you a neurosurgeon before you were another species of doctor?' I asked him. Like Gertrude's head injury, it suddenly seemed obvious.

'I certainly was,' Luca agreed, delivering my second helping. 'Not as good as Marc but as damn near it. And I was just like him too. Didn't stop to think about those outcomes for a lot of years, either. And when I did . . .' He stopped what he was saying and went back to the fridge for a Bud. 'You want one?'

I nodded. 'When you did what?' The pickle was really good in the burger.

'When I did I found that I could not get up out of bed and go to work any more. And in the meantime, my beautiful wife had stopped loving me and so had everyone else.'

You see what I mean about saying extraordinary things? He dropped this on me with a casualness you might expect of someone with whom you shared such confidences all the time.

'Well what made you start to think about outcomes?' I asked, chugging on my Bud. I'd never drunk beer before but now wine

239

seemed pointless. The new me liked bubbles. I didn't even mind burping.

'I met someone,' he said, compiling his second burger. 'An eight-year-old girl who'd been hit by a cab up on East 89th Street. Actually, eight is probably the best age to have a head injury like that but all the same, this little girl, Megan, was in bad shape. I did three, four maybe, even five consecutive surgeries to remove blood clots from both frontal lobes. Every time we started to wheel her out of the OR she'd start to bleed and we'd have to go straight back in again. We worked on her for 13 hours. It was written up from here to London to Sydney and everywhere in between. Hailed as a great success.'

His elbows were on the table as he took bites of his burger in between sentences. He shook some Kettle Fry chips onto my plate and then onto his own.

'What happened to her?' I asked.

'She survived the surgery, which is generally all I would know or, to tell you the truth, care about. But one day Eugenia came and sought me out, said she had someone to show me. She brought me up to NICU and took me in to see this little girl, cute as a button, wide awake and smiling like a Cheshire cat.'

'What you would call a good outcome,' I said.

'What you would call a good outcome,' he agreed. 'Except that while I was there this pretty young woman came in, carrying a box of crayons and some kids' magazines. Megan started to cry, wanted to know who that woman was. Eugenia tried to calm her down but she got pretty wound up. She wanted the woman to go away and leave her alone and she wouldn't stop crying until the woman did.'

'Well, that seems reasonable,' I said. 'What was the problem?'

'The problem was that the woman was her mother,' Luca said. 'After her accident, Megan never recognised her ever again.'

I thought ashamedly of the attraction I had felt at the thought of forgetting my own mother. But then I had beaten it. And I wasn't eight years old.

240

'That's horrible,' I said.

'It sure was,' Luca agreed. 'That's the scary thing about the brain. As much as we can fix it, we don't know how it will work once we're done. We think we know it all but we don't know a fraction of what we need to. Anyways, I didn't know who to feel more sorry for: Megan, who thought her mother had abandoned her and as far as she was concerned never saw her again; or her mother Lauren, who had to cope with a daughter who never accepted her, who screamed when she came into the room. The thing was, once I started to feel sorry for either of them, my days as a neurosurgeon were over. I was out of there in a matter of months.'

'And your wife?'

'Gone,' he said, wiping his mouth with a napkin. There was a twitch in his cheek that over-rode his gruffness and I felt sad for him. 'And who could blame her? Left me for a North Fork winemaker. They live in Napa now, making a pretty damn fine chardonnay. She's happy,' he said as he took a swig of beer. I knew he was the sort of person who would be happy that she was happy and that reassured me that bizarre as it was, I was in the right place. In good hands.

There was a silence, but it wasn't awkward, not even when Gertrude let rip one of the loudest 'p-roooots' I have ever heard emanate from a non-human.

'Is there something you need to tell me about that cat?' I asked Luca.

'You already know all there is to know about that cat,' he said, clearing the table.

I woke up the next morning to find Gertrude's head lying on the pillow next to me. She slept like a human, with her body under the covers. And when I opened my eyes and looked at her, she opened hers and looked straight back.

'Well,' I said to her, 'you're the most action I've seen in a long time, if you don't count Frankie. How depressing is that?'

She stretched her legs out straight in front of her and padded her paws, sans claws, gently on my chest. It was such a girlfriend thing to do that I found my heart swelling with affection. Who knew? Maybe I was a cat-lover after all.

We got up and both had Luca's homemade granola for breakfast, she sitting on the table and eating it out of the bowl just like me but without the spoon. She had a pretty good sense of humour for a cat.

Luca had left me a note asking me to go to the medical centre to help him out with the senior citizens' exercise class. There was a bike in the basement I could ride, the note said, adding that it might be a good idea to wear a helmet. He'd drawn a map, which was pretty simple. The medical centre was only a couple of miles down the main road.

When I got out of the shower the phone was ringing and I picked it up, expecting to take a message for Luca. But to my complete and utter horror it was Ty. My darling brother Emmet had apparently given him the number and he seemed pretty agitated.

'My dear, how could you leave Manhattan without telling me? Paris and I have been beside ourselves. You can't just up and run off to the middle of nowhere, MC. Now that you are so much better we should be thinking about your schedule. We can't afford too many more delays. There's the launch to organise, we're thinking Craft — Tom Colicchio's such a fan. Then there's the book tour: we're looking at 17 cities so far. You're hot property; Paris thinks it could all be quite explosive marketing-wise. How do you feel about that?'

I felt sick is what I felt. I felt he had the wrong person. I felt like I wanted to hang up and ride my bike to the medical centre. I didn't want to have a book or 17-city tour or a fiancé who cared more about those things than the fact that I had no interest in getting married to him which, by the way, he had so far failed to mention.

'Well, a person could just about forget that there was a wedding to be planned,' I said moodily, 'what with all this work, work, work. I'm glad you've got your priorities straight, Ty.' It was a mean thing to do because of course I had no intention of marrying him. But still.

'Oh my darling!' He at least had the good grace to be horrified. 'I'm so sorry. It's not till the spring so I didn't think it necessary to discuss it further but you are right, MC, of course, you are right. And it will be majestic: the grandest day of our lives. I didn't mean anything by not bringing it up sooner. It's just that Paris has been working so hard on the tour and you disappearing like this, well it's thrown me. It's truly thrown me. And Cay-Cay and Happy are missing you too, darling. Happy's gone potty on the hall carpet twice since you came home and left again. I don't know how Consuela will remove the stains, really I don't.'

'I have to go, Ty,' I said. 'I'll talk to you later.'

I disconnected but stayed where I was. The thought of having a majestic wedding to a man whose cats went 'potty' on the carpet had rendered me incapable of moving. I thought of the other grandest day of my life, my first wedding: the sumptuous stuffed zucchini blossoms, the dancing at Il Secondo, the feeling of having everyone I loved — and their neighbours' neighbours — watching my husband swear his undying love for me and me only . . . Snapping out of my paralysis, I picked up the phone and dialled my old home number, hoping like crazy that Tom would pick up. For once luck was on my side. He did.

'Hey babe,' he said, and I could hear Agnes gurgling into the receiver. 'So good to hear your voice. How are you doing? Emmet tells me you've moved to Shelter Island. By the ocean. Connie, are you crazy? Estelle will have a fit. What's going on?'

'Oh, I'm helping out this doctor friend of mine,' I said breezily, cursing my blabbermouth brother. 'Chez Conlan was proving unconducive to my well-being.'

'Now there's a surprise. Aw, shit. Can you hold a moment?' I heard the phone at his end clunk down as he talked to the baby. 'Do you have to keep doing that?' I heard him say. 'That's like the third time since your mommy went out. Jesus. Phwoar. Okay, maybe this time. Are you there, Connie?'

'I'm here,' I said, knowing my voice sounded sad.

'What's the matter?'

There was so much the matter I didn't know where to start.

'I miss you,' I said in barely a whisper. 'I miss our old life.' I thought at first he hadn't heard me as all I could hear was the sound of Agnes goo-ing and ga-ing.

But eventually he spoke, and his voice was sad too. 'I miss you too, babe,' he said. 'I miss our old life as well.'

'At least you've got a wife and a kid. Just what you always wanted.'

'Well, maybe it was what I always wanted, but it's not exactly who I always wanted it with.'

We both fell silent. I felt so sorry for him. And me. And the screwed-up way our lives were turning out.

'What's happening, Tom?'

He gave a chippy little laugh. 'Fleur and I are falling apart, that's what's happening. I just can't do it all, Connie. I have my show; I have the restaurant, I can't take my eye off the ball there, it would be suicide; there are only so many hours in the day yet Fleur wants me at home doing this with Agnes and that with Agnes and she's so fucking pissed off at me all the time home is the last place I want to be.'

I felt sorry for Fleur too. I was pretty sure this wasn't the way she wanted her life to turn out, either. But still, she had a loving family and a nice apartment. I had nothing. I tried to feel bitter and resentful but I have to say that to my credit, I couldn't pull it off. I just felt sad for all of us.

'I better go,' I said. 'I'm sorry. I wish you were here, Tom.'

'Me too,' he answered softly and I felt the tears well up in my eyes. We both clung on the line, neither of us saying anything, until Gertrude, the madam, padded across the kitchen bench and disconnected for me with one press of a fat ginger paw.

'Are you calling me a slut?' I asked her. 'I'll have you know that's my husband you just hung up on.' But she just turned her little left-hand circle in front of me and led me down to the basement where she stopped in front of an old-fashioned bike with a bulky black Evel Knievel helmet in the wicker basket attached to the handlebars and I put my depression on hold.

It had been quite a few years since I'd been on a bike and I take umbrage at the suggestion that it's something you never forget. I had forgotten and it was nothing to do with the pretzel. I was just rusty. The first few attempts I had at mounting the darn thing and moving forward ended up with me and it in a heap on the ground while Gertrude sat there looking straight out to sea as if the whole ugly event embarrassed her. Then, when I finally got the hang of it and coordinated my legs to push the pedals before the bike could fall over, she kept crossing in front of me so I was forced to wobble to a halt. Finally, I just stopped and asked her what she wanted. She was staring at the wicker basket and so, begrudgingly because I knew it would look stupid but really it was the sensible thing to do, I put on the helmet. At this Gertrude jumped into the basket. She manoeuvred her enormous body around so that she was pointing straight ahead like a statuesque figurehead on some ancient ocean-going vessel.

We made a pretty odd picture, I imagined, as I pedal-pushed up Luca's leafy street and made a right into South Ferry Road. Gertrude was no lightweight and I was hardly in good shape myself. Lord knew what help I would be to the senior citizens when it came to the exercise class.

Luckily, there was next to no traffic on the road so my erratic cycling was not a danger to anyone but myself and Gertrude. In fact she may even have provided a bit of ballast.

Luca's workplace didn't look like any medical centre I had ever seen before. It was a sprawling shingle building surrounded by towering oaks, a well-kept garden and a white picket fence. It looked like the sort of place someone else's grandparents might have lived in. Gertrude leaped nimbly (quite a sight) out of the basket as we neared and I followed her in the door.

'Hey there,' said Luca from behind the reception counter at the far end of the room, a pair of glasses perched on the end of his nose and a messy pile of paperwork in his hands. 'With you in a moment, Mrs Hansen,' he told a harassed-looking mom. Her scowling toddler stopped building a tower and started throwing blocks at Gertrude, who sat smugly about one inch out of his range. 'Have to introduce the new aerobics teacher to our senior citizens.'

'Aerobics *teacher*?' I repeated, horrified, as he shuffled me down the hallway and into a big empty meeting room of some sort, where a motley-looking bunch of pensioners were dressed up in a lurid collection of exercise combinations doing a series of creaky uncoordinated stretches.

'This here's Connie,' Luca bellowed, saying to me in a lower voice, 'you have to shout or they won't hear a goddamned thing.'

'Good morning Connie,' the motley-looking bunch bellowed back, excepting one old-timer in obscene orange cycle shorts who was a few seconds behind the rest and called me Bonnie instead.

'Connie is going to be taking your aerobics class today,' Luca shouted, leading me over to an ancient tape deck. 'Just press play and when it stops, turn the tape over. Most of them can't hear it anyway. Going clockwise around the room, you have Doris, Daisy, Ginger, Hank, Maryanne, Lil, Nancy, Jenny, Meg and Paddy. The guy asleep on the bench at the back is Marshall; watch out for him, he's a groper.'

'But I don't know anything about aerobics,' I protested, stunned. 'I'm a walker. Or a runner. Depending who you talk to. I've never even been in a gym. That I know of.'

'So,' said Luca with a grin, unmoved. 'Improvise.' He pressed play and released Jerry Lewis's 'Great Balls of Fire' into the room. 'I'll take you out for lunch after you're done,' he said. 'Good luck.' And he left.

Nancy, Jenny and Meg shuffled to the front and formed a straight row facing me, mirroring my every move — even though all I was doing was scratching my shoulder and looking around for Gertrude.

'She's not very good so far,' Nancy said loudly to Jenny. 'She doesn't even bob up and down.'

I started bobbing up and down in time to the music, going lower and lower each time, the three stooges in front matching me bob for bob.

'Jane Fonda uses her arms on the video tape,' Meg shouted over her shoulder to Hank in the cycling pants, who was way at the back and, if I'm not mistaken, only in it for the bird's-eye view of Daisy's not insubstantial rump.

I started punching my arms forward and backward the way I'd seen on TV ads for exercise equipment. 'Goodness gracious, great balls of fire!' I found myself shouting as I shifted from bobbing up and down to going from side to side, my arms punching the air.

'She's good!' Jenny shouted. 'She's better than Doris's daughter. The fat one with all that underarm hair.'

Doris punched the air happily behind her, deaf as a post to all but Jerry Lee Lewis's great balls. Actually, it was fun. Next came Elvis with his blue suede shoes; I had to hand it to those old-timers, their hips might not have been the originals but they could sure as hell swivel them if they had to.

We finished 40 minutes later with a rousing conga-line around the outside of the community room: Gertrude, who had joined the fray halfway through, in front; me next; and my merry band of followers, minus Marshall who was still asleep on the bench, all bringing up the rear — jumping and shimmying and sticking our legs out sideways.

At the end, there was a flurry of gnarly old high-fives and a lot of appreciation, marred only by a small altercation between Maryanne and Lil, who had apparently been deliberately pinching Doris's love handles in the conga line. Something about a boyfriend they once shared back in '45.

'I could do something, you know,' Ginger pulled me aside and told me shyly while the others shuffled their way towards the exit, 'with your hair. If you wanted me to.'

Well, I was keen to go blonde, remember, and it did look

strange, what with being all uneven and half brunette and everything. Ginger's own hair was cut in a very neat bob and was a beautiful coppery colour that matched the eyebrows she had more or less neatly drawn on above where her old ones used to be.

'You're a hairdresser?'

'First person on Shelter Island to use a blow dryer,' she said, slapping me in a conspiratorial fashion on the arm. 'Come by my place tomorrow afternoon. Luke'll tell you where. I'll bake cookies!'

At the mention of cookies, Marshall sat straight upright and started thrusting his arms forward and back as if he were on some sort of rowing machine.

'You missed it again, you old fool,' Ginger said. 'And that doesn't mean you get away without making a donation.'

'Aw, don't get your undies in a bunch,' Marshall said gruffly. 'Who's the fox?'

'Just ignore him,' Ginger advised me. 'I'll see you tomorrow. Come on you,' she pulled on one of the old man's arms, 'I'm not going to let you do to her what you did to that nice girl from Greenport. You just have to learn to keep it in your pants, Marsh.'

Afterwards Luca took me to the Shelter Island Heights Drugstore for lunch. I hadn't known that places like that still existed anywhere in the US, let alone a two-hour bus ride from Manhattan, but there it was: a corner drugstore with a coffee shop inside. We took a seat at the counter and Luca ordered a coke and a cheeseburger while I went for the toasted bagel with cream cheese and onion, which had the creamy–crunchy combination I had come to look forward to.

'Doris tells me you were pretty good,' Luca said, sipping his Coke. 'Seems like improvising suits you.'

'They could move pretty fast for old dudes,' I told him, making short work of my bagel.

'That diet of yours coming along okay?'

'If you think I'm fat now, you should have seen me before,' I told him. 'I'm the proverbial shadow of my former self.'

'Oh, I doubt that somehow,' he said, taking a bite of his cheeseburger. Clearly, he really liked cheeseburgers and I had to say this one looked mighty good for a drugstore offering: fresh sesame bun, lean beef patty, crisp lettuce, and a slice of thick buttery-coloured cheese. He had a lick of mustard at the corner of his mouth and without even thinking, I leaned across and wiped it away with my thumb.

He looked at me, those green eyes twinkling, and a hundred thousand different sensations swept through me.

'I dreamed about you, you know,' I said. 'When I was in the coma. I mean I didn't know it was a dream, it seemed real at the time. But I met you and you were building a gondola and you were kind of cranky about the world. Sort of like you are now.'

It didn't seem to surprise him at all. He just laughed.

'What did you do when you were sitting with me, Luke?'

'Held your hand, talked a little. Sometimes to Eugenia, sometimes to you.'

'What about?'

'Oh, just crap, you know. Me, Marc, life, you — although I was kind of hazy on the details as far as you were concerned.'

'But why? Why me?'

'Like I said, you looked like someone who could do with some company.'

'But there must have been other people in comas that looked the same way.'

He smiled. 'None of them had Eugenia on their side,' he said. 'She wanted me to talk to you and so I talked.'

'Hey, Luke, can I borrow you for a moment?' It was the pharmacist from the drugstore. 'Judy Watley's in here with that same skin rash.' He looked at me, 'I'm sorry, ma'am. It's hardly eating talk, I know. It's moved right up her thigh, Luke, and she wants more of the same cream but I think —'

Luca stood up off his stool and told me he wouldn't be a minute.

I picked up a cinnamon donut from the platter on the counter and took a bite. The sugar crunched between my teeth but without the taste, it was a depressing experience.

'Hey, where did Luke go?' Ursula, the waitress was holding the telephone and looking for him. 'I have a call for him.'

Seriously, it was like *Happy Days*. These people hadn't heard of cell-phones.

'He's with the pharmacist. He won't be long,' I told her.

'He's in the drugstore, he won't be long, honey,' Ursula said, quite coquettishly for someone who was 80 in the shade, into the phone. 'Do you want to leave a message with his friend?' She looked me up and down then turned away so it was harder to hear what she was saying. 'I don't know but she's tall and skinny and has funny hair. Sort of brown and white and different lengths like a punk rocker or something. Uh-huh. Uh-huh. Well, sure honey, I'll tell him. You make sure you come by and visit, won't you? It's been a long while. Bye-bye.'

Gertrude, who had clearly gotten bored sitting in the truck, scared the shit out of me then by jumping up onto Luca's stool, which also made Ursula jump sky-high and clutch at her bosom.

'That cat gives me the creeps,' she said, at which Gertrude's claws extended and gripped the vinyl of Luca's stool.

'You should watch what you say around her,' I advised. 'She's the sort who bears a grudge.'

Ursula looked at me as if I were nuts but when she turned her back, Gertrude up-ended the sugar bowl with one swift movement of her paw. She looked me straight in the eye, then jumped off the stool and strode back into the drugstore.

'I guess I had better be going,' I said to Ursula, handing over $20 for the check. Twenty dollars went a hell of a long way further on Shelter Island than it did on that other island, that was for sure.

'Be a honey and tell Luke that Marc called, will you?' she said, giving me heart palpitations at the mention of his name. 'Sounds like he might be planning on paying us a visit.'

'Oh really?' I tried to keep my voice casual. 'When?'

'He didn't say,' Ursula said. 'Sometime soon though I guess for him to be ringing here looking for his dad.'

Sometime soon? Oh brother. I had some serious hair dyeing to do. And a bit of waxing — just a bit — would not go astray either.

Sixteen

The next morning I tried going for a run to see if I really liked it or not. I got about a half mile down the beach and had to stop I was retching so hard. It was kind of galling that Gertrude seemed to be able to handle the pace yet I was wheezing like an old accordion and crippled by cramp. We returned to the house at a sprightly walk and I rang Ginger to ask if she could do my legs as well as my hair. Marco was indeed coming to visit, Luke had rung him when I'd passed on Ursula's message. Not that the waxing had anything to do with Marco, you understand. I mean, I wasn't going to sleep with him or anything just because I was staying in his Dad's house and he was coming to visit and I couldn't stop thinking about the muscles in his thighs and his exceedingly cute butt and the square breadth of his shoulders and the — well, need I say more?

Ginger's house was a cute little cottage hidden behind a statuesque stand of white oaks down by Chase Creek. A dog the size of an elephant was standing on her porch, hackles raised and barking fit to bring the place down until one look from Gertrude sitting proud in her wicker basket silenced him and he ran whimpering around the side of the house.

Ginger had a huge kitchen fresh out of the '50s with jars of preserves stacked neatly in open shelves and fresh flowers on every surface. It was mostly yellow, which was a little bit unsettling, but she'd set up her hairdressing supplies at one end of the kitchen table and without too much fuss and bother she got on with the job at hand. She apologised for not having a mirror for me to look in while she was cutting my hair but as I was still suffering from the mild delusion that it was not me looking back at myself from my own reflection — not helped by the Botox — I can't say it bothered me as much as it might another person.

She evened up my hair as well as she could, given that I didn't want it too short (punk rocker, my eye) and by the time she finished she had given me most of a cute little bob not unlike her own, except my hair was still much chunkier on the side where my scar was. But if you overlooked the asymmetrical shape and the dark roots and blonde ends, it was definitely an improvement.

While we waited for the colour to take, she filled me in on everyone in the neighbourhood and all their sons and daughters and their sons and daughters and the people who'd lived in the houses before them and their sons and daughters too. Ginger had lived on the island her whole life as had her husband, Harvey, who owned the hardware store just down from the drugstore. The place hadn't changed so much, according to her. So the summer folk who had built big houses stayed once in a while but a person could go the whole year without ever bumping into one of them and it was still, according to her, the most beautiful place on God's earth — so what did it matter?

Naturally, I was desperate to ask her about Marco but I sort of fluffed around for a while asking about other stupid things, like where you could get the best fish (Bob's Seafood), the freshest greens (Pete's Produce), the biggest milkshake (Jim's Coffee Shop).

'They sure pushed the boat out naming places, huh?'

'Well, there's no need for anything more fancy, is there? It is Bob's seafood and Pete's produce and Jim's coffee — although he's not the original Jim, but still, he's a Jim nonetheless.'

'So, what was Marco's mom like?' I finally asked her.

'You mean Marc? Marc's mom?'

I was having trouble adjusting to his real name. I nodded.

'Oh, Serena was just about the prettiest girl I'd ever seen,' Ginger said. 'What hair she had, Connie. It was jet-black and hung straight as an arrow down her back like a bolt of silk. Of course, she was probably too young when she married Luke. Hardly 20 years old and pregnant straight away. They used to come here in the summer when Luke was at college and Marc was a baby. Luke Junior'd work pumping gas down at Piccozzi's but I don't know that he had to, Luke Senior was putting him through med school and all, but he's never been one to sit around wasting time, has Luke. Then it got that he was so busy at the hospital that just Serena and Marc would come here for the summer. I can still see her now, pushing that stroller up the hill in a flowery sundress and a big straw hat.'

She sounded beautiful, like someone F Scott Fitzgerald would sit on the porch and moon over for decades. I bet Marco would want to marry someone just like her.

'Then they divorced and it was just Luke here on his own, poor soul. Everyone on the island has tried to marry him off at some stage but he just says he's not going to make the same mistake twice. He'll know the right one when she comes along, so he says. But he hasn't known her yet! Now this hair of yours is resisting my dye, Connie. Should be done by now but I think it needs a few more minutes.'

We decided she should wax my legs while we waited but what I hadn't realised was that she had never waxed a leg before in her life. She'd just been to the drugstore and bought a Veet home waxing kit. Well, how hard could it be, she asked?

Quite hard as it turned out. She got the wax strip on my calf all right but when it came to pulling it off she told me she was too scared.

'Just do it,' I soothed. 'I don't mind. It won't hurt.'

I was wrong. It hurt so much I just about hit the roof. She was doing it too slowly or too quickly or something and the second strip was just as bad. By the third, she was crying, Gertrude was howling, I was near back in a coma, and we had only done one stripe on the front of a single leg. I had to wax a matching stripe on the other leg myself. It was quite traumatic for a beauty salon experience. And once Ginger dried her eyes and stopped shaking, we decided that the backs of my legs and my bikini line would just have to wait another day.

Of course, all this took somewhat longer than anticipated and it was only when my scalp started tingling in a mildly painful way that had up until then been disguised by the far worse pain in my shins that we remembered my hair dye.

'Oh, my,' was all Ginger said when she washed out the chemicals in the kitchen sink. And when she finally brought me a mirror I could see why. The woman in the looking glass now had purple hair.

'Well, it's not completely purple,' said Ginger, and she was right. Only the bits that had once been blonde were purple, the roots were actually quite a nice rich chocolate shade, which I think might even have been my natural hair colour. Of course, no one was going to notice the nice rich chocolate with all that purple on the go. And what the heck would Marco think?

'Isn't this the same colour that Jenny and Nancy and Meg have in their hair?'

'Well, yes,' admitted Ginger. 'But I thought on you it would look different.'

Turned out, it was the only colour she had. Also turned out she had only worked as a hairdresser for three weeks back in the '60s when the place that was now an empty lot had been a hair salon. That was before it burned to the ground after someone, it had never been established who (although I now had my suspicions), left the heated rollers turned on too close to the hairspray over Thanksgiving.

It was too late to go to the drugstore for more dye and Ginger did not think my hair could take it anyway. I just had to believe that surely Marco would rather see me purple than bald. It was only hair, wasn't it? I put on my Evel Knievel helmet and cycled home.

When Luca saw me, his jaw dropped down to his chest and he looked at me in a very peculiar way, like he'd never really seen me before or something.

'It's only hair,' I snapped grumpily and he recovered himself immediately.

'Actually I like it,' he said. 'Very pretty.'

I thought about Serena with her bolt of black silk running down her back and then showed him the two red spotty landing strips up the middle of my shins.

'You want to borrow my razor and do the sides and the backs?' Luca said as he started to unpack a sack of groceries. I didn't but I felt a little tug on my heart at the offer.

I went upstairs and pretended not to ready myself for Marco's arrival, but just before seven I heard a car on the gravel outside and dabbed extra lip gloss on my lips. Then when the doorbell rang I lost my nerve, picked up a silk scarf and wrapped it around my head the way I'd seen David Bowie's Somalian supermodel wife do. The effect on me was much more British charlady than Somalian supermodel but it did hide the purple. The doorbell rang again. Maybe Luca was in the garden and couldn't hear it. My heart hammering in my chest, my loins aching with longing, my teeth clenched in anticipation, I followed Gertrude down the stairs and, as the doorbell rang for the third time, I pulled open the door.

Ty was standing there with a huge bunch of lilies and a funny little man in a white chef's outfit. 'MC, what's that on your head?' he asked, aghast.

'What are you doing here?' I demanded. I couldn't remember being less pleased to see someone. If Marco was a 10 on my lust scale, my fiancé was a zero. Below zero.

'Darling, I've brought Monsieur DuCroix from Le Petit Cochon to cook for you,' said Ty, looking fondly at Monsieur DuCroix, who in turn motioned to three state-of-the-art coolers a driver was unloading from a town car.

'May we come in?' Ty asked nervously.

Frankly, I didn't want him to but what could I do? I opened the door wider and Gertrude pushed past me. She headed straight for the Frenchman: but the moment she rubbed her great ginger carcass against him he went quite red and started sniffing and sneezing and babbling hysterically in French.

'Could you, please, MC?' Ty pleaded.

'Could I please what?'

'Do as Monsieur DuCroix says,' he cried across the din of the yowling cat and the burbling chef.

'I don't know what Monsieur says, Ty, I don't speak French.'

'Oh, but you do,' he cried. 'We taught you. Madame Solange at the Institute taught you. Surely you haven't forgotten that!'

Monsieur was hopping around now, with Gertrude clinging to his trouser leg. Actually, it was pretty funny. 'Fa fa fa fafa,' it sounded to me like the Frenchman was saying. 'Achoo. Fa fa fa fa.'

'Get rid of the cat, MC,' cried Ty. 'Monsieur is allergic. And what happened to its ear? What sort of cat is it anyway?'

Alerted no doubt by the various screams and shrieks, Luca appeared from the garden with an armload of vegetables, which he quickly dumped in order to separate Gertrude from the little Frenchman. She could tell when people were allergic, he said, and stuck to them like glue just to be curmudgeonly.

'This is Ty, my, erm —'

'Fiancé,' Ty interrupted, stepping forward and taking Luca's hand. 'You must be Dr Scarpa Senior. I can't tell you how much I appreciate you taking such good care of MC. Of course, I'm hoping to lure her back to the city and I've brought along Monsieur DuCroix to help me in this endeavour. Could we possibly trouble you for the use of your kitchen, Dr Scarpa? I know it's short notice but I really wanted it to be a surprise. Please forgive the intrusion. Driver, if you could be back here at 11 that would be superb.'

'It's Luke,' said Luca. 'And you can trouble me all you want.

Knock yourself out, Mr DuCroix. Does your driver want a drink before he goes? Anything I can get you, buddy? No? Try Jim's up on the main road. Good cheeseburgers.' He turned then to the shaky little chef, picking up one of the crates of provisions, and guided him to the kitchen, leaving me alone with Ty.

'You should have called and told me you were coming,' I said, heading out onto the porch, knowing he would follow me. 'And I would have told you not to.'

'MC, I feel terribly bad about our conversation yesterday. I realise that I may have sounded overly concerned with your book tour and that's not how I meant it to be. I'm concerned about a lot of things, of course I am, we all are, not the least of them being your health and welfare and our wedding, my darling, I should have mentioned the wedding and our life together, the one we planned. I'm trying to make it up to you, MC, that's why I'm here. I'd like you to come home.'

Listen, I'm not a hard-hearted person. I hadn't been before the pretzel and I wasn't one after. I felt sorry for Ty; I could see he didn't quite know how to handle the situation he found himself in but then neither did I. And I couldn't figure out for the life of me how I'd got into the situation in the first place. He was a nice enough man, if you liked that sort of thing, which I seriously could not believe I did. And neither could I imagine what he saw in me. If you took away the fact that I was the *New York Times* restaurant critic, I was just not his type. And something had taken away the fact that I was the *New York Times* restaurant critic, so where did that leave us? It left us as a well-to-do wannabe with a pretentious palate and a lot of allergies engaged to a woman whose job he probably wanted but could never ever have and who now no longer had it herself.

'Why in the world do you want to marry me?' I just out and asked him as he shuffled around on the porch trying to avoid the last watery rays of sumptuous evening sun.

'My darling, we are perfect for each other,' he said, getting a spotty handkerchief out of his pocket and wiping his brow. 'We belong together, you know that. We like all the same things, we like all the same people, we share all the same dreams and goals.' He was sweating on his upper lip and looked supremely uncomfortable. 'I just want things to be the way they were, MC. As before. When I knew what you wanted.' He started as a bug flew past and flapped his hand wildly around in front of his face. 'We talked about growing old together and having our "own" table at Daniel and vacationing in Paris, eating at l'Arpège and going to Le Louis XV in Monte Carlo.'

'We did?' I was genuinely surprised. He couldn't eat wheat, shellfish, dairy products or nuts.

'We did, my darling. We talked about the books you were going to write about cheese and French bread and champagne. About the *Times*, about publishing tie-ins, about our future together in New York.'

'I just don't remember,' I said, more to myself than him as the doorbell rang again. My head was itchy underneath my turban so I pulled it off, revealing my purple ends to the world and to Ty, whose eyes nearly popped out of his head. He staggered to the porch chair and sat down, fanning himself. It didn't matter now if Marco saw my purple hair, I supposed, because I was hardly going to be able to sneak off and make mad passionate love to him when my pesky betrothed was right there in the house.

Through the glass slider I could see Luca open the door and act kind of stand-offish with his son, which surprised me a little, stand-offish not being a trait I associated with him. But it turned out it wasn't Marco at the door at all.

It was my husband.

'Tom!' He was holding a big wicker hamper, which Luca, with something of a wry smile, took off his hands. I thought seriously for a moment of pushing Ty over the porch railing onto the lawn below but instead leaped through the doorway into the living room and threw myself into my former loved one's arms, swinging him around so he was facing the other way.

'Babe, what happened to your hair? It's . . . well, it's just not you.' He took me in his arms nonetheless and pulled me so close to him I could feel how pleased he was to see me, if you know what I mean. 'God, you smell good.'

'What are you doing here?' I asked him. 'Where's Fleur?'

'At home. Listen, babe, there's something I need to talk to you about. Is there somewhere private we can go?'

I was flummoxed, to say the least, but Luca came to the rescue.

'I'll take care of it,' he said referring, I hoped, to the small matter of my fiancé on the porch and his accomplice in the kitchen. 'You might like to show Tom upstairs.'

I grabbed my husband by the hand and pulled him up toward my room. 'Back in a minute,' I said gratefully to Luca. It was terrible what I was doing to his house, turning it into a receptacle for men I was no longer interested in but engaged to, or interested in but no longer married to, or interested in and just plain hoping I might get to sleep with. I trusted he would understand.

Still, I was having a hard time maintaining my composure. 'Tom, what's going on?' I asked flopping onto my bed. He sat down awkwardly beside me.

'You said you missed me. You said you wished I was here.'

It was true, I had said those things and I'd meant them at the time because I was sad about being engaged to Ty. But that was yesterday.

'I've left Fleur,' Tom said. 'My life's a mess without you, Connie. I want you back.'

My mind turned to gumbo.

'You've left Fleur?' I was appalled. 'And Agnes?' Even more appalled. 'For me?' A flutter of hope. A wave of pity. Some nausea just for good measure. 'Tom, that's crazy!'

'No, Connie, it's not. Can't you see?' He turned to me on the bed and his dear handsome face was twisted in anguish. 'I don't belong with them, I belong with you. We never should have split up. I never

260

should have stayed in Venice without you. I should have turned right around and come straight back to New York and fought for you with everything I had. We know each other so well, babe, we're soul mates, we belong together. I can't think of anything but you. It's driving me crazy. I want things to be the way they were, Connie. Just me and you, the brunette you. I don't care if you can't taste anything. I don't care that you don't work at the *New York Times* any more. I can take care of you properly now. We belong together, babe, you know we do.'

He was the second person to tell me we belonged together in less than half an hour. Yet had he ever said it to me before? Had Ty? I struggled to understand what belonging together really meant; what would make me belong to someone and not someone else, but I couldn't make sense of it.

'Tom, what about Fleur and the baby?'

'Two wrongs don't make a right, Connie. I've been thinking about nothing else since you were in the hospital. I was wrong to let you go and I was wrong to start seeing Fleur but I can fix it all now. Fleur will be fine, she's strong, babe, stronger than you or me, for that matter. It'll be tough to begin with but I'll look after her and Agnes, you know, financially. The important thing is to set things right.'

Ty showing up had thrown me for a loop but having Tom sitting on my bed declaring undying love for me was proving almost too much to process. I thought of the way I hankered for him when I came out of my coma, but I hadn't known then about Fleur and the baby. Could I break up a family, my best friend's family, to get back the man I once loved and still possibly did? Did I want a man who would do that?

It didn't feel right but I didn't know what to do about it. 'Well, what was in the hamper?' I asked him, by way of a diversion.

'I'm going to make you your favourite meal,' he said with that loose smile that brought back so many happy memories. 'Stuffed zucchini blossoms, melanzane parmigiana, sugar-snap risotto, baked orata, chocolate zabaglioni. What, you don't like that any more?'

261

'Well, you're not going to believe this,' I said and a nasty little rumble reverberated in my stomach, 'but it's maybe going to get a little crowded in the kitchen here tonight.' I tried to make light of the situation. 'You're not the only one who has turned up with cooking knives, Tom. This is kind of awkward but . . .'

He looked perplexed.

'Ty is here,' I said brightly. 'He arrived just before you did.'

Tom started nodding and saying, 'yip, yip, yip,' under his breath like he was agreeing with a whole bunch of stuff although under the circumstances I thought that was probably unlikely and besides, I wasn't actually saying anything.

'So, so, so,' he said, and his lips were white as he chewed at them with his teeth. 'What's he here for? Ty. What's he here for?' He was angry, a sort of suppressed anger that added a certain resonance to the nasty feeling in my gut.

'Well, whether I like it or not I am still engaged to the guy, Tom,' I said gently, 'and he came to surprise me with a romantic dinner. Although of course he doesn't cook for himself so he brought Monsieur DuCroix to do it for him.'

'DuCroix? From Le Petit Cochon? That cocksucker. To cook for you? That little French faggot, what the fuck would he know?'

Actually, now he was annoying me. Sure, it wasn't an ideal situation, him leaving his wife, my best friend, and their baby for me, who was engaged to a man who had turned up with one of the city's best French chefs to talk about our wedding. But it wasn't ideal for me either, and you didn't see me tearing my hair out over it and Lord knew I had more of an excuse to be doing that than he did.

'What's Monsieur DuCroix ever done to you?' I asked Tom, who was pacing around the attic room rubbing at his chin.

'Just fuelled the city's obsession with the fucking French. Jesus, how many French people are there living in New York, anyway? Hardly more than a handful and yet it's foie gras this and Ducasse that and Bouley blah blah blah. It makes me fucking sick.'

It was a song he'd been singing since way back when and I'd thought it was pretty stupid then too. What did it matter if New Yorkers liked French food? Who cared?

'You know, it doesn't mean nobody likes Italian, Tom,' I said to placate him. 'But maybe we could talk about this another time.'

'Fucking A,' Tom agreed. 'How about now we talk about you not marrying Ty. The guy's a fucking dumb-ass, you know that, I know that, everyone knows that.'

'I'm not going to marry him,' I said. 'And I probably would have told him that by now if you hadn't appeared out of nowhere and gate-crashed my romantic surprise.'

'So, give him his fucking marching orders,' Tom demanded. 'Tell him to take his puffed up little frog and get lost.' Talk about irritating! He was so freakin' overbearing. If I was going to call off my wedding I would do it for my reasons, not just because my estranged husband told me to.

'Don't tell me what to do,' I said and I felt prickly in a way that was horribly familiar. Then the doorbell rang again. This time I knew it must be Marco — I wasn't engaged to or estranged from anyone else — and my stomach gave a little flip. 'I'll just go and get that,' I said, relieved to escape the tension. I slipped out of the room and down the stairs where Luca had opened the door and was welcoming his son.

'So, I guessed it must be you,' Marco said when he saw me standing goofily at the foot of the stairs, suddenly shy in his presence. 'Though I was expecting a blonde.'

He was wearing a white T-shirt, dark blue jeans and boat shoes, and had a caramel-coloured jacket slung over one shoulder.

'Guessed it must be her what?' Luca wanted to know.

'Staying with you,' Marco said, coming over and giving me a kiss on the cheek, a squeeze on my upper arm lasting just a few seconds longer than was strictly necessary.

'Who the fuck is this?' Tom demanded, clomping down the

stairs just at the moment I was looking longingly into Marco's eyes.

'This is my son Marc,' Luca said politely. 'He's just joined the queue.'

'The queue?' Marco looked around and took in M. DuCroix in the kitchen, Ty sweating nervously on the porch and Tom looming above me on the staircase. 'What's going on?'

'This is my ex-husband Tom,' I said by way of introduction. 'And that's my fiancé, Ty. And this is his chef, M. DuCroix, who's going to be cooking for us tonight.'

'Not if I can help it,' Tom said, pushing me out of the way and marching into the kitchen where he picked disdainfully at the Frenchman's mise-en-place: poking at the truffles, mocking the frogs' legs, turning his nose up at the bottles of Bordeaux. M. DuCroix called something vaguely hysterical in French to Ty, who came in from the porch, shook hands with Marco, saw Tom in the kitchen, and went right back out to the porch again.

I half expected Buster Keaton to start opening and closing doors. It was farcical, to say the least. I looked pleadingly at Luca, who was really my only ally, but he merely shot me a wicked grin, shrugged his shoulders and offered his son a beer.

'No thanks,' Marco said coldly. And then he turned to me. 'It's you I came to see.'

Naturally, I blushed like an idiot and became transfixed with his belt buckle.

'Suit yourself,' Luca said evenly and melted away, leaving just Marco and me in the living room with only the sounds of M. DuCroix and Tom arguing in the kitchen and Ty babbling into his cell-phone on the porch.

'Let's go for a walk,' Marco said. Like a lamb to the slaughter I followed him blindly out the door, down the driveway, across the road, and onto the smooth pebbles of the beach.

'You came here for me and you weren't even sure it was me?' I asked him as we walked along the shoreline.

264

He nodded, smiling at me. Those teeth. Those lips. That dimple.

'You've made quite an impact on me, Connie,' he said. 'And I'd like to get to know you better.'

'Ha ha,' I laughed, mirthlessly. This was like a dream. My dream. The handsome gondolier turning his attentions on the unlikely damsel with the purple hair.

'In fact, I have dinner reservations tonight at the Frisky Oyster in Greenport,' he said. 'For the two of us. They don't usually take late reservations — you have to book a month in advance — but I managed to talk the maître d' around. It's the hottest ticket on the North Fork: you know, it's like Babbo in the country.'

'You booked a table for the two of us?' I asked him, trying to keep the incredulity out of my voice. 'Like, on a date?'

'Yeah,' he laughed. 'Like that.'

I wanted to stop right there and have sex with him on the beach, I really did. Never mind going to the Frisky Oyster, I was the frisky oyster. And he didn't need to feed me, to spend money on me, to impress me with his power over a hot-ticket maître d'. He'd already done enough just by coming all that way to see me. I just felt so pathetically grateful that someone like Marco, someone drop-dead gorgeous, someone even Fleur, my former, current, and soon to be former again if Tom had anything to do with it, best friend would consider too good for a mere mortal, had shone his light in my direction. Things like that didn't just happen to me.

'You don't mind my hair?' I asked Marco, flicking at the ends of my purple bob.

'Well, you must have a hat,' he said. 'Come on, let's go.'

'As long as it's okay with your dad.'

'It's got nothing to do with my dad,' Marco said, impatiently kicking at the pebble.

'You don't want to see him, to visit with him a while?'

'Constanzia,' he said in a dark oily voice full of the promise of sweat and aching thighs, 'I told you, it's you I came to see.'

He pulled me to him then, right up close, and I could feel how pleased he was to see me as well. But instead of politely moving my hips away as I had done with Tom, I pressed myself right into Marco and wriggled. I felt a hot rush scream through me from my toes to the top of my head and an embarrassing groan escaped my lips. A groan that made it clear I had not been in such close proximity to a hot-blooded male in quite some time.

But the groan did not last long. Marco silenced me by holding one of his glorious fingers up against my lips while his other hand, firm against the small of my back, pulled me closer still. He stroked my cheek, pushed a purple tendril behind my ear. He was just so goddamn gorgeous to look at I almost had to turn my head. But his eyes, so full of darkness and desire were mesmerising, drawing me in.

'Please,' I begged him. 'Please.' But I didn't know what I was begging for. I just knew that whatever I had right at that moment wasn't enough. He was overwhelming me, I didn't know how to handle it. He shimmied me up the beach, thigh against thigh, away from the water, and slowly, gently, lowered me to the ground, between two dinghies upturned beneath a willow tree. Eyes still on mine, he slid one of his knees between my legs where I was sure he could feel the throbbing, then came down to join me. I barely had a chance to remember I was seven years older than him.

'You're so beautiful,' he said to me, just a whisper away from my mouth, before moving his lips down to my neck, murmuring into my skin and taking me places I hadn't been in quite a while. 'You're so beautiful, Connie,' he crooned, 'I want to take you right here on the beach. I want you so badly. I want all of it, baby.'

I felt a little squeamish at the talk, I admit, I was never much of a one for the running commentary, but I wasn't in it for what Marco was saying to me. I was in it for what he was doing to me. My brain could turn off, poor beleaguered thing, and let my body do all the work.

'You are just incredible.' My eyes were closed as he whispered in my ear, every breath lighting torches throughout my nervous system. 'Amazing. You are — Jesus fucking Christ!' The change in tempo was frightening. Marco was suddenly bucking on top of me like a wounded steer. 'What the fuck is that?' he shrieked, writhing around, bruising me significantly in the process. 'Get it off! For fuck's sake, get it off!'

He flipped off of me and jumped to his feet, leaving me spreadeagled on the sand — but at least I could see what the problem was.

Gertrude.

The little she-devil had jumped on Marco's back and was clinging there like a rucksack, her claws attached to his skin through the cotton of his expensive T-shirt.

Flustered, I scrambled to my feet and tried to pluck the wretched cat off but she just dug her claws in, leaving Marco screaming in pain.

'That old bastard,' he roared. 'That fucking old bastard.'

'It's Gertrude,' I told him, leaping around and trying uselessly to relieve him of her. 'The cat.'

He finally reached one long arm over the opposite shoulder, grabbed the cat around the neck, sustaining several bites in the process I might add, and with one mighty wrench pulled her off his back and flung her across the pebbles into the long grass where she hit the ground with a bloodcurdling yowl.

I know it must have hurt, having her cling to his skin and all, but frankly I thought it was a little uncalled for. I scurried over to where she was lying, relieved to see her shaking her head as if she couldn't believe what had just happened.

'It's okay, girl,' I said soothingly, giving her a pat.

'That fucking cat,' Marco spat. 'I bet he taught her to do that.'

The mood, you could say, was gone.

'Luca? I think he has better things to do than train a brain-damaged cat to attack you.'

'It's not Luca, Connie, it's Luke,' Marco said. 'And I'm not

Marco, I'm Marc. That Italian crap is just something Marinello and he cooked up when they worked together to help the hours pass quicker. Jesus, what has that fucking thing done to my back?'

He took off his shirt, and although I was smarting from him being so terse with me, I am embarrassed to say that the mood came right back. He truly was a perfect specimen (well apart from the claw marks with their little beads of blood that Gertrude had gouged out of his flawless brown skin, that is).

'Eeergghh,' I said, abandoning Gertrude and approaching Marco for a closer inspection. What can I say? The man appealed to me on levels that only my hormones can explain.

'Well?' he asked again. 'How bad is it?'

'I think we should go over to the house and put some antiseptic lotion on it,' I suggested. 'And you might want to borrow a shirt from your dad.'

'And then we're getting out of this shit-hole, okay? I'm taking you to the Frisky Oyster and then we're driving back to Manhattan. I fucking hate this place.' He stomped across the road, shirtless, and I followed meekly behind him.

What was I going to do in Manhattan, I wondered? Did Marco realise I didn't actually have anywhere to live but there in Shelter Island? Was he going to take care of me the way Luca had? Make sure I ate even though I wasn't hungry? Put fresh flowers in my room? I watched the muscles under his bloodied back move beneath that beautiful skin as he strode across the road in front of me and I wished then that he did not have such an overwhelming physical effect on me, because it occurred to me that I didn't actually like him very much.

Just as I thought that, Gertrude made one of her cute little circles in front of him and he kicked her so swiftly up the rear she didn't see it coming. Of course, she weighed 20 pounds so she didn't exactly go flying through the air and I bet it hurt Marco almost as much as it hurt her, but she howled in pain and humiliation anyway and my cheeks burned for her.

'Hey, buster, just you leave her alone,' I cried. 'Jeez, that was mean, Marco.'

'I told you, my name's Marc,' he said acidly, shaking his foot. 'And who gives a shit about some stupid cat?'

'I do,' I said. 'And so does Luca. You can't just turn up here and start beating up on his animals. That sucks.'

'Well, he's really pulled a fast one on you, hasn't he? Don't let that old bastard get to you, Connie. You're not his type. Trust me.'

He was mad at his dad. So mad. And I could see it as clear as I could see the enormous Gertrude sitting gingerly on her aching tush. He was a grown-up, clever, successful 29-year-old just trying to get back at his father for whatever crimes had been committed in the past. So Luca had worked too hard and abandoned his family. He knew it, didn't he? He was sorry, wasn't he? Marc was behaving like a spoilt little brat and I knew from experience that if you hung on to blame it turned rancid and bitter inside you. All the good looks in the world could not hide that sort of ugliness.

'Why would I trust you?' I asked him, my hands on my hips, my loins no longer throbbing. 'I don't even know you. You turn up here with some dinner reservation after hardly giving me the time of day for I don't know how long and I'm supposed to trust you? Well, I don't. I think you're a tight-ass namby-pamby big old brain surgeon who's still pissed off his parents got divorced, Well, get over it *Marc*. You're a grown-up now. You should stop torturing your dad and get a life.'

I pushed past him, picked up that big heap of a cat and charged into the house — where I found Tom, flaming red in the face and about to punch out the lights of M. DuCroix whose white chef's jacket was spattered with tomato sauce.

'Just go back to your own country and stop poisoning ours with your disgusting offal and your stupid fucking roux,' Tom was yelling.

I looked at him, looming in a vile fashion over poor M. DuCroix, and I knew then that we did not belong together. Tom did not want me the way I was, the way I wanted to be and I did not want to be the person he desired. I'd tried being her: it had made him angry and ended up with me walking out on the day we were due to fly off on our second honeymoon together. I didn't need my memory to know we were a gone-burger. And Tom could pretend to be Italian all he liked but I was through with make-believe.

'Where's Ty?' I asked, which stopped him mid-rant.

'Your boyfriend has a migraine,' Tom said in a simpering voice. 'He's taking a nap upstairs. Where the fuck have you been?'

'For crissakes, you think the old bastard would have a decent first-aid kit,' Marc roared from the downstairs bathroom. 'Connie, could you at least give me a hand here?'

My heart was sinking, and so was the cat in my arms. She was too darn heavy. I placed her gently on the floor, apologising for any part I may have unwittingly played in her maltreatment. She gave me quite a nice look as she headed out the door again, turning to make sure I followed. Which I did. There was no one left in that house for me.

Out front in his garden Luca was crouched over a row of baby carrots. He looked up as we approached.

'Hey you,' he said softly. 'Why the tears?'

I was crying, of course I was, copiously. The tears just swept down my cheeks, I could feel them dripping on my collarbone. When I went to speak I realised that I couldn't. There was a ball of despair in my throat that was choking me. I panicked, waving my hands around like Ty with a thousand flies.

'Breathe,' Luca said, getting to his feet. 'Breathe, Connie. It's okay. Just breathe.' And he guided me down the grassy terrace to a bench, half-hidden in the leaves of a vine that grew over a rickety wooden fence between his place and the overgrown garden of his neighbour.

I tried to breathe but it seemed a foreign thing to do and I was so busy crying I didn't know if I could fit it into my schedule.

'Take it easy,' Luca said in his gentle gravelly way, and he started rubbing my back in a slow easy rhythm. 'You're doing fine,' he said. 'Just fine. Too many cooks spoiling the broth, huh?'

'Marco's just —' I started. 'And Ty's got — and Tom—' His name exploded out of me and I felt a pain so sharp I wondered how I would survive it. 'He doesn't want me,' I sobbed. 'And it's not even me anyway.' But the words wouldn't come out properly.

'Let it all go,' Luca said. 'Start again, Connie.'

'Why did this happen to me?' I wept. 'My life is such a mess. I don't know who to be with or what to do and without my taste I just feel like a big old waste of space, an empty slate. I don't know who I am without my taste, Luca. It would be like if Marco lost his hands and couldn't operate any more. Or if you lost your . . .' I tried to think what Luca couldn't do without. 'If you lost your hands and your voice . . . and your legs,' I added. But I didn't have the same conviction I had about myself without my taste or Marco without his hands. Maybe that was why Luca wanted Marco to come back down to earth with the real people. Maybe he was a little one-dimensional. Maybe it was good to use more than one bit of your body in case you lost one vital piece in a nasty pretzel accident.

Luca kept gently rubbing my back, didn't say anything, and I hiccupped loudly and gave an unladylike belch, which ended my crying jag.

'You think there's more to me than my taste, huh?' I asked him and he nodded. 'You think I can have an okay life without it?' He nodded again.

I contemplated this seriously, for the first time; actually, when I thought about it, it wasn't so scary. I would still be able to walk in the sun, take aerobics classes with octagenarians, drink beer on the porch, feel Gertrude warm and furry beneath my fingers. I could shop and talk and go to the movies and get my hair done (sooner rather than later) and even travel to Italy or Spain. I could write still, I hadn't really thought about that. Maybe I could write a whole book about not being able to taste. Maybe that would sell better than that other dreadful tome Ty and Paris were trying to hock. Maybe it would be made into a movie and Charlize Theron would play me. I laughed.

'How cool would that be?' I asked Luca. 'Charlize Theron.'

He just raised an eyebrow and nodded.

Maybe I should take his advice, let it all go and start again. It wasn't as though my life had been perfect before. Why was I clinging to it? So, I had been the *New York Times* restaurant critic, the most powerful arbiter of taste in the entire country, and that had been snatched away from me. But it was only a job! There were other jobs. I could still see and hear and feel, couldn't I? A wave of optimism spread through me and tickled my insides. I looked around at Luca to see he had been watching me, reading my thoughts, and he looked proud, almost smug, like he had been waiting for me to reach this conclusion.

'How do you know all this?' I asked him.

'I don't know shit,' he said, 'but what I see. And there's a hell of a lot worse things you can be than an empty slate.'

I was suddenly very aware of the warmth of his thigh against mine on the garden bench.

'I dreamed about you,' I told him. 'When I was in the coma. I told you that.'

'You did,' Luca said.

'Marco was there too,' I said carefully, 'and Signora Marinello. We went all over Venice eating the most exquisite food.'

'Venice, huh,' Luca reached beneath the bench and pulled a couple of beers out of a cooler, flipping the tops off of them. I don't know how long they'd been there, they weren't icy cold, but they were perfectly drinkable and the bubbles went well with my optimism.

'We started out at this place called Do' Mori eating cichetti,' I told him. 'You know, it's like tapas, but Venetian.'

'I know about cichetti,' Luca said. 'You have the polpette? The meat balls?'

I nodded. It was like being back at the squero again. 'And the tuna,' I said. 'And Signora Marinello's fresh-baked bread with fried shrimp and zucchini. Then we went some place else and I had pregnant sardines stuffed with pine nuts and breadcrumbs and we had fondi, the artichoke hearts. God, it was all just so delectable. But turns out I wasn't even there.'

'Oh, you were there all right,' said Luca, taking a chug from his Bud. 'Just not in the usual way.'

'Luca, I was in the hospital in a coma.'

'Cenando con gli angeli,' he said matter of factly. 'Eating with the angels. That's what my grandmother said when it happened to her: "I've been eating with the angels." Sounded kinda nice, I always thought.'

A lump rose in my throat; my heartbeat quickened.

'Nonnina, now there was a woman who loved food,' Luca continued. 'And whatever she cooked she had grown herself or if she hadn't she could throw a stone and hit the guy who had. Well, so she said.'

'She was in a coma?'

'She had a stroke, pretty severe. I got to sit with her a couple of nights, held her hand, talked to her. She wasn't lucid, not most of the time anyway, but one morning she woke up and turned to me and she was all there. "I've been eating with the angels," she said and she told me she'd been having bean stew with grilled veal and stuffed crabs with fennel risotto and *pollastro in squaquaciò* — that was chicken done her favourite way.'

'What were the angels doing?'

'Feeding her, in her dream, that's what she told me. Her own grandmother was there, she said. And some little kid she'd been to school with who'd drowned. My grandfather was there. And so was I, she told me. And it made her happy to be going where she was going. She wasn't scared any more.'

I started to cry again. 'That's so sad,' I said. 'Did she . . . ?'

Luca nodded. 'Not even an hour later but you're missing the

273

point, it wasn't sad. She was happy. She was going to be eating with the angels for ever. That's what she said. There are worse fates, believe me.'

'You think that's what I was doing? Eating with the angels?'

'Uh-huh. Yes, I do. But your angels weren't taking you away, Connie, they were bringing you back. You could have died, but you didn't. First, Marc saved you with his surgery; then Eugenia saved you by looking after you; and now . . .'

Luca had been in my dream. What did that mean?

'Now, what?' I asked him.

'Now you don't need angels. You don't need anyone. You can do it yourself, girl. You are doing it yourself.'

He was right and I felt it so deep in my bones it was like a transfusion of hope from some higher being. I closed my eyes and took a deep breath . . . I was an empty slate but I could fill myself the way I wanted to. I was not going to veer in one direction because of the way my mother was, or in another one because my husband wanted me to, or in a different one because of the things one very sexy asshole I hardly knew made me feel. I was me, Connie Farrell. Yes, I liked that name and I was sticking with it.

I opened my eyes and smiled at Luca.

'Come with me,' he said. 'I want to show you something.'

We followed the slope downhill close to where the section flattened off and there, clinging leafily to the rickety wooden fence, was a tomato vine extraordinary in that despite its virulent greenery, there was only one ripe red tomato hanging from it.

'I've been thinking about Nonnina all day,' Luca said, kneeling down and cupping the single fat fruit gently in one hand. 'She brought the seeds for this vine over from Mazzorbo. They don't come much more heirloom than that. Every year she harvested more seeds and replanted. Then my mom did the same thing. Never tasted tomatoes like it. Luckily for me she froze seeds as well because darned if I've been able to get any fruit these past few years.

Sometimes the seedlings just withered up and died on me. Sometimes the vine grew, but the tomatoes never ripened. No matter what I did, nothing. Then this morning I see this sitting here. Just showed up when it was good and ready.' With one deft movement of his hand he plucked the plump tomato off the vine.

'Luca!' I gasped. 'You should save it for something special!'

'This is something special,' he said and pulling a pocket knife out of his jeans, he sliced the fat red fruit deftly in two and handed me the bottom half.

It was the perfect temperature and as smooth as a stone. Its juice ran gently down its sides and into the palm of my hand. Luca, his green eyes shining at me, bit into his half and my mouth watered just looking at him. I took a bite myself, the juice running down my chin, my hand, my arm. At first I thought there'd been an explosion, that my head had been knocked clear off my shoulders. The sourness of the first bite hit the roof of my mouth like a high-pressure hose and then at the back behind my teeth there was a tingle as the acidity hit home. Finally I felt the sweetness echo in my throat as I sucked on the seeds and chewed the flesh. The *sweetness*.

I could taste it.

'Oh my God,' I whispered. 'Luca. Oh my God.'

'So,' his smile was tender, his green eyes far from curious, 'you think it needs salt?'

I shook my head, licked tomato tang from my lips. It needed nothing. And neither did I. I had it all right there and it was so simple, so beautiful, so perfect. Everything was all right.

And it was delicious.

Epilogue

Come on, you must have known there would be a happy ending. Maybe not there in the middle when it was all such a hopeless mess but towards the end when I was juggling all that man flesh out at Shelter Island? Now that had potential. Hey, for a while there it looked as though I could actually have had my pick of happy endings: with Marco (yeah, right) or Tom (not likely) or even, if I decided to care a whole lot more about antibacterial detergents, Ty.

But Luca?

Well, I was dumb (pardon me) not to have seen it sooner. He told me in my dream that he had everything I needed, and that I should trust him and everything would be all right. If I hadn't been sexually obsessed with his son or blindsided by my ex or hounded by my fiancé, I might have seen it sooner. I just needed to stand back and look at the thing from a distance.

And when I did, boy, was he my cup of tea.

It's taken a while for us to settle down, I guess. There's a 15-year age gap, after all; we think about some things differently. Kids, for example. Luca wouldn't mind a couple more but I just need to make sure that's what I want. They'd be cute, though, those bambinos. I mean look at Marco. Anyway, number-one priority is to make sure I'm not stepping back into another relationship where I'm being shaped by someone else. We don't live together, for example. Luca's out on the island and I have a really badly decorated apartment on West 17th Street. We spend weekends together and one or two nights during the week, which we spend curled up in bed surrounded by empty Chinese take-out boxes. We drink beer and eat cereal out of the box and I know I told you my Sailor's Delight washed-rind cheese was only hours away from reaching its prime, but I ate it before it got there. What's more I had it on bread slightly lacking in salt with quince paste I had to scrape mould off of. I haven't darkened the door of a four-star restaurant since I got my taste back and nor probably will I. I'm a regular at The Red Cat, my favourite bistro just around the corner, and I like eating cheeseburgers on the beach with Luca or fries and pies at Nick's with Eugenia.

My taste has come back, but it has changed. Boy, has it changed. I no longer care if my turbot comes with a béarnaise mousseline or my pig's trotter with 65-year-old red wine vinegar or your choice of pens to sign the check, madam. I like to eat my food, not describe it, which is what I told Toby, my editor at the *New York Times*, when I met up with him. He seemed quite relieved; to be honest, I think he might have found me a bitch to work with. In fact, he told me he found me a bitch to work with. So restaurant reviewing is now a thing of the past. My publishers dropped me like a hot potato when they found that out, thank God. My book never hit the streets. I still write for the *Times* dining section though only now I write about the people who produce our food, about where it comes from and how it gets to us. I'm freelancing too for the annual produce issue of *Gourmet* and I'm loving it. I get to meet eccentric chicken farmers, organic beet growers, nutty bakers, and lovable confectioners. Plus I have time to do the things I want to do, like walk in the park, tend the garden I have growing up on my roof terrace, and avoid chunks of stewed apple that Agnes flings at me from her high chair when I look after her every Thursday.

Fleur and Tom are still together, by the way, and actually I think they are a pretty amazing pair. She stands up to him in a way I never could because she knows so much about herself in the first place, who she is and what she will or won't put up with, whereas I was too reliant on him for my identity to fight for it. They're well matched. He's full of bullshit and she won't take any. Of course, I've never told her about Tom coming to Shelter Island that night, and I won't. I don't talk about it with him, either, and I know it makes him mad that I'm with Luca now but not as mad as it made him when I was with Ty, the dandy who incredibly lured me away to a well-heeled life sautéed in nonsense and peppered with pretension. But on that subject, rather unbelievably Ty and I have become good friends. I told you he was pleasant enough, I just never wanted to marry him and frankly, post-pretzel, I don't think he wanted to marry me either. I suspect one day he will get over himself and fly off to far-flung parts with Paris or an off-Broadway chorus boy but in the meantime we meet quite regularly at the Fairway Café for brioche — sometimes, speaking of unbelievable, with Emmet.

Turns out the heated hand-towel investment was not a euphemism for a crack deal. Emmet indeed swindled the $20,000 out of Ty but then went on to make a small fortune, has paid him back with interest and is pretty much on the pig's back himself. He still lives at home, of course, why wouldn't he? But his drug use is positively recreational and in fact, he spends a bit of time with us at Shelter Island where we eat burgers and play gin rummy and drink beer and laugh at each other and ourselves. In fact, he's coming to Venice with us next fall. Luca is taking us to Mazzorbo in the duck-shooting season so we can have wild duck soup followed by wild duck tagliatelle followed by roasted wild duck at Trattoria Maddalena, his favourite.

I'd like to tell you that Marco, sorry, Marc was coming too and that we were all one big happy family. But for a start that would be creepy and for a finish, he's still a giant pain in the ass. He's scandalised by his father's relationship with a much younger woman whose brain he patched up but frankly he should walk a mile in my shoes. I'm the one dating the guy whose son I once imagined I had done many disgusting things with, after all. Actually, that has been the subject of quite some angst on my part but I am getting over it with the aid of a neuropsychologist called Harvey who has helped me stand back from the close-up and see the big picture. He's not only helping me pick my way through the minefield of head trauma recovery, but we're doing time on Estelle recovery too. I suppose you could say I am a work in progress.

I haven't reclaimed those two years and nine months, and I may never, but their importance is fading anyway. I'm concentrating more now on who I want to be rather than who I was and it's weird how little the missing time matters. I wonder about that day I keep remembering, the one where I'm walking by the Magnolia Bakery after the butter fight, talking on the phone, deciding not to go to Venice. I wonder about that a lot. Harvey says it is probably significant in some way, it's the major punctuation mark in my memory loss, after all. But he says there may not be one single magic key that unlocks the mystery, that there often isn't, that it could be something as simple as the moment I realised that I'd had enough of Tom's temper, that my life with him was over, that Ty could help me start another one. Actually, we had high hopes on the pretzel front for a while there, Harvey and I. He said it was possible that if I did suffer from post-traumatic stress syndrome then pretzels could possibly trigger some sort of reaction that might fill a few gaps in my recent past. But after visiting the 20th pushcart where nothing was triggered except fleeting thoughts of Woody and my old friend hunger, we gave up on that. In fact, Harvey said he was developing a mild aversion to pretzels and couldn't believe that I never got sick of them (which was not a psychological issue but interested him nonetheless).

Oh, and by the way, I'm not thin and blonde any more. I guess that had to happen. The real me is truly neither of those things. I'm back at just under 140 pounds with a traditional bikini wax, a wrinkly forehead and brunette hair that is heading towards being shoulder length once again and is the subject of much gentle mirth between Luca and I, and you'll laugh when I tell you why.

Luca's certainty was something I admired in him from the start, before I even knew I had met him. But when I bit into that tomato and saw him smiling at me, I realised that it was not a generic certainty, that he was absolutely sure of me, of the future, of us. But how could that be?

'How did you know?' I asked him, later that night. 'About me.'

'*Cenando con gli angeli*,' he answered slowly. 'Nonnina. I was one of her angels, I told you that.'

I nodded.

'She said I had an angel too, in her dream.' He laughed then, a shy almost embarrassed laugh. '*La ragazza dei capelli viola* — the girl with the purple hair. Never gave it much thought, never made much sense until you came back from Ginger's with that head full of lilac.'

I remembered the look on his face when he'd seen me with my horrible dye job, the feeling I'd had that he was seeing me for the first time.

'You weren't sure before then?' I asked, my heart fluttering.

'I had my suspicions from the moment I first laid eyes on you,' he answered, 'but show me a guy who doesn't need a little help from the angels every now and then.'

Can you see now why I thank heaven. Soon-Yi didn't bake cookies that day? The truth is, that pretzel didn't ruin my life, it saved my life. Without it, I don't know who I'd be but it wouldn't be me. And I'd be minus a man who not only believes in angels and gives great peppermint foot rubs, but whose idea of a perfect meal is anything as long as I'm eating it with him.

It's a matter of taste.

Acknowledgements

Without wanting to sound like Halle Berry at the Oscars, this book would never have happened without the enormous warmth and extraordinary generosity of a whole host of wonderful people. I'm lucky to have the friends and family I have and to meet the people I do along the way, I know that. Seriously, it makes all the difference! And as usual I want first and foremost to thank my husband Mark Robins, who not only cooks and cleans from daylight till dusk but also has enough faith in me for the both of us.

Sally Spector's book *Venice And Food* (Arsenale) led me first to her door in the Cannaregio and then to the doors of many a fine Venetian eating establishment that I would otherwise never have discovered. Without them, the first few chapters of this book would be nowhere near as delicious. And the memory of lunch on her friend Luisa de Perini's sun-drenched terrace near the Rialto is something that can still cheer me up on a wet grey day.

Big huge sloppy kisses and all my love always to my Rome-based cousin Frances Kennedy, who came to Venice to translate for me and without whom I would never have found real-life gondolier Davide Scarpa and gondola-maker Gianfranco Vianello nor would I have had so many laughs. (We'll always have 'half a date', missus!)

In, New York, well, where do I start? By thanking Bridget Freer who not only entertains me year after year when I descend upon her adopted city but who personally put in loads of spadework on the research front, including clinching a meeting with Ruth Reichl and getting my foot in the door of the James Beard Foundation. What a hero! And thanks too to her husband Ed, who lets me drag Bridget away and keep her out at night and then lets me come to their apartment and drink all their champagne. And welcome to the world Stella Needham!

Thanks to foodies John Mariani, Ed Levine, Adam Rappaport, Arthur Schwartz, Gael Greene, Marian Burros, and Erica Marcus, to name but a few — I still can't believe they took time out to talk to me. And without the help of the book *Dining Out* by Andrew Dornenburg and Karen Page (John Wiley & Sons, Inc) and the encouragement of Caroline Stuart and Arlyn Blake at the James Beard Foundation, they might not have.

Thanks, too, to chef/owners David Waltuck at Chanterelle and the lovely John Villa at Dominic, for giving me their side of the story; and to Daniel Boulud, not for the crappy table but for coming to talk to me when he saw me taking notes. Good result.

As for former *New York Times* reviewer and *Gourmet* magazine editor-in-chief Ruth Reichl, well, what can I say? She not only put on the Gourmet Institute — what a happy coincidence — at which I did a year's research in the space of one weekend, but she took time out of her hectic schedule to meet with me. She probably is the only person who should ever have written her food memoirs (*Tender At The Bone*, Broadway Books, and *Comfort Me With Apples*, Random House). More importantly, she truly believes that inviting people into your house for dinner beats the heck out of a restaurant — and ain't that the way it should be?

To Amy Rosmarin, thanks for the insight into tastelessness, so to speak. Joan Baren, you saved me that day on Shelter Island and I treasure the memory. And Richard Ruben: for the Greenmarket, the Red Cat, that African place in Brooklyn, every minute of your company and for reading my manuscript, thank you from the bottom of my heart.

On the medical front, much appreciation to Gill Hood at Auckland ICU for her time and patience and emails, and to clinical neuropsychologist James Cunningham for his insight and humour and introducing me to raisin toast at Savour and Devour.

To all the usual suspects at Random House New Zealand, my deepest gratitude, as always. And I count myself very lucky to have Ann Clifford on my side come editing time. Missus, it's always a pleasure.

As for Gwenny, you and Helen are going to read all my books before I let go of them now and same-same Rachy-rach, but differently, okay?

To my friends whose mothers can't cook, thanks for sharing your disgusting stories and sorry if it gets you in trouble come the next family roast (charred with lumpy gravy). It seems many an ace cook has a mother of the 'Estelle's Surprise' variety. My own was not one of them, by the way, let's make that clear: our family roasts are not ones you want to miss out on!

Finally, to Anna, Ken, Angus, and Hugo, here's to the future.

And to Kaywyn McKenzie, a real-life angel: you're for ever remembered with wings and a halo.

All my love.

SK

Eating Out Guide

It seems silly for me to have done all the vital 'research' and keep it to myself so here are my picks of the best places to eat in two of my favourite cities, Venice and New York.

Venice

Al Covo

Campiello della Pescaria 3968

Vaporetto Arsenale

Ph 522 3812

Definitely on the tourist route and expensive for what it is but good all the same and in quaint surroundings.

Alla Madonna

Calle della Madonna 594

Vaporetto Rialto

Ph 522 3824

The Grand Canal's just a stone's throw away but it's mostly locals feasting on fresh seafood in here. Busy, no frills, no bookings.

Bentigodi

Calleselle 1423

Vaporetto San Marcuola

Ph 716 269

Venetian food with a modern twist: the 'pregnant sardines' in this white-walled osteria are to die for.

Do' Mori

Calle do Mori 429

Vaporetto Rialto

Ph 522 5401

The most wonderful no-frills wine bar — when you eventually find it — with delicious snacks and more atmosphere than you can poke a stick at. Perfect for elevenses after trawling the Rialto markets.

La Caravella
Calle Larga XXII, Marzo 2398
Vaporetto San Marco
Ph 520 8901
We stumbled on this place our first night in Venice and although it was pricey and a bit grown-up, the service was wonderful and I still dream about my fennel and lobster risotto.

Paolin
Campo San Stefano 2962A
Vaporetto Santa Maria del Giglio
There's much debate about where to get the best gelato in Venice. This is apparently the oldest gelateria, a good spot for people watching, and I can vouch for the chocolate and liquorice flavours!

Trattoria Ca' d'Oro (aka Alla Vedova)
Ramo Ca' d'Oro 3912
Vaporetto Ca' d'Oro
Ph 528 5324
Almost impossible to find but when you do, SO worth it. Try the cichetti at the bar or even better, ring and book a table and dine with the locals. Our favourite Venice find.

Trattoria Maddalena
Mazzorbo 7C
LN Vaporetto from Fondamenta Nuova
Ph 041 730 151
Wild duck is a specialty during the lagoon duck-shooting season at this untouched mom-and-pop backroom restaurant on an island 45 minutes

from Venice. Have the duck tagliatelle followed by the roast duck.

New York

Artisanal

2 Park Ave at 32nd St

Subway: 6 to 33rd St

Ph 212 725 8585

I discovered this place researching my cheese-making story *Blessed Are*: most dishes on the menu include cheese and there is even a fromagerie in the restaurant. Exquisite. For the non-cheese version, try Picholine further uptown.

Caserta Vecchia

221 Smith St, between Baltic and Butler Sts,

Carroll Gardens, Brooklyn

Subway: F, G to Bergen St

Ph 718 624 7549

Delicious home-style pizzas and pastas on this up and coming boulevard of food.

Craft

43 East 19th St between Broadway and Park Ave South

Subway: N, R, W, 6 to 23rd St

Ph 212 780 0880

Leather walls and dim lighting make this the perfect spot for a woman of a certain vintage. Choose how you want your food cooked and share the sides. Delicious.

Daniel

60 East 65th St between Madison and Park Aves

Subway: F to Lexington Ave-63rd St; 6 to 68th St–Hunter College

Ph 212 288 0033

Very grown-up four-star restaurant with sublime food and fellow diners providing a feast for the eyes. Watch out for the one dud table! We rejected it but were made to wait nearly an hour for another one. Luckily, it was worth it.

Fanelli's Café
94 Prince St at Mercer St
Subway: N, R, W to Prince St
Ph 212 226 9412
Great bar, excellent shoestring fries, club sandwiches, and blackboard specials. Corner bistro meets local pub.

Jean Georges
Trump International Hotel & Tower, 1 Central Park West at
    Columbus Circle and West 60th Street
Subway: A, C, B, D, 1, 9 to 59th St-Columbus Circle
Ph 212 299 3900
Another four-star job and a truly memorable lunch. Worth it just for the theatre of watching a pineapple being undressed and having differently flavoured marshmallows chopped up in front of you.

Joe's Pizza
7 Carmine St at Bleecker St
Subway: A, C, E; B, D, F, V at West 4th St
You'll recognise it from many a movie . . . great for pizza by the slice, which is hard to come by these days. For the whole pie, apparently John's Pizzeria down at 278 Bleecker St is pretty good.

Katz's Delicatessen
205 E Houston St at Ludlow St
Subway: F, V to Lower East Side-Second Ave
Ph 212 254 2246
An institution and apparently the only deli where pastrami is still hand

sliced. Can be a bunfight but if you don't fancy joining the throng at the meat counter, there is table service along the left hand wall, which means you can have fries with your sandwich and hot dog.

Lupa
170 Thomson St between Bleecker and Houston Sts
Subway: A, C, E, F, V, Grand St S to W 4th St
Ph 212 982 5089
I've never been to its swanky big-brother restaurant Babbo but celebrity chef Mario Batali's osteria Lupa suited me down to the ground, especially when it came to paying the bill. If you can't get a booking, try just walking up and waiting for a table. Great service.

Magnolia Bakery
401 Bleecker St at 11th St
Subway: A, C, E; L at 14th St-Eighth Ave
Ph 212 462 2572
Step back in time at this tiny bakery famous for its cupcakes.

Matsuri
363 W 16th St (Maritime Hotel) at Ninth Ave
Subway: A, C, E to 14th St
Ph 212 243 6400
Modern Japanese food in an enormous stylish cavern beneath a funky hotel.

Mix in New York
68 W 58th between Fifth and Sixth Aves
Subway: F to 57th St; N, R, W to Fifth Ave-59th St
Ph 212 583 0300
The toast alone makes it worth a visit — and the loos are pretty good as well. My cod 'à la vapeur' was the best-cooked piece of fish I have ever had.

New York Noodle Town

28 1/2 Bowery at Bayard St

Subway: J, M, Z, N, Q, R, W, 6 to Canal St

Ph 212 349 0923

I can't remember how I found out about this place but I'm glad I did. On a rainy day with ducks hanging in the steamed-up windows and hardly a word of English being spoken, you could be in Hong Kong. Good for more than just noodles.

Palma

28 Cornelia St between Bleecker and W 4th Sts

Subway: A, C, E, F, V, Grand St S to W 4th St

Ph 212 691 2223

Family-run Italian restaurant in this very foodie street in the West Village with good, simple food and a lovely courtyard out the back in warmer weather.

Pastis

9 Ninth Ave at Little West 12th St

Subway: A, C, E to 14th St; L to Eighth Ave

Ph 212 929 4844

I was addicted to this Parisian bistro lookalike until I noticed that the coffee was cold and watery and the staff rude and inattentive. Took a while though.

Pearl Oyster Bar

18 Cornelia St between Bleecker and W 4th Sts

Subway: A, C, E, F, V, Grand St S to W 4th St

Small café-style restaurant famous for its lobster rolls, which I actually haven't tried but I can vouch for the fries.

Peasant

194 Elizabeth St between Prince and Spring Streets

Subway: N, R, W to Prince St; 6 to Spring St

Ph 212 965 9511

Lovely Italian food, much of it cooked in a wood-fired oven. Try the sardines.

Per Se

4th Floor, Time Warner Center

Ten Columbus Circle

Subway: A, C, B, D, 1, 9 to 59th St-Columbus Circle

Ph 212 823 9335

Probably the most amazing meal of my life. Thomas Keller's West Coast restaurant The French Laundry is already a legend and I'm sure this East Coast one will be too.* The nine-course chef's tasting menu did not hit a single sour note and the service was impeccable and friendly to boot. Simply wonderful. Worth the arm and the leg it costs.

* Per Se has since been awarded four *New York Times* stars.

Peter Luger

178 Broadway at Driggs Ave, Williamsburg, Brooklyn

Subway: J, M, Z to Marcy Ave

Ph 718 387 7400

Porterhouse steak served by crusty old waiters in a rustic setting. A must. And I'm usually a vegetarian.

Sueños

311 W 17th St at Eight Ave

Subway: A, C, E to 14th St; L to Eighth Ave

Ph 212 243 1333

Gorgeous Mexican with a modern twist and as many Margaritas as you can handle.

The Red Cat

227 Tenth Ave between 23rd and 24th Sts

Subway: C, E, to 23rd St

Ph 212 242 1122

Very yummy food in relaxed surroundings: this would be my local if I lived in Chelsea. Its sister restaurant on the lower East Side, The Mermaid Inn, is also worth a visit especially if you love fish.

Union Square Greenmarket

Union Square

Four days a week this busy downtown square is transformed into a bustling market with local growers selling their wares — and it is a must-see in my book. Wander around on your own or even better take award-winning cooking teacher Richard Ruben's market tour, then follow him a few blocks north to the Institute of Culinary Education and make lunch with your purchases. One of the best things I've ever done in New York City. Check out the institute's website at www.iceculinary.com.

*The *Time Out New York Eating & Drinking* guide (available everywhere in Manhattan or go to www.eatdrink.timeoutny.com) is an invaluable companion, nicknamed TONY, if you're serious about eating out in New York. And for places to go in Venice, I can heartily recommend the expensive (for something so small) but nonetheless excellent *Time For Food*, *Venice*.

'Do I miss going out for dinner? Nah. Cooking is a great joy: I go home, pour myself a glass of wine and go into the kitchen, the guys come in and peel the cucumbers or whatever and then we have dinner. It's the best part of the day, that part where you put on your blue jeans and a T-shirt and start cooking. It's just everybody there being themselves, and it's much more satisfying.'

Ruth Reichl
Editor-in-Chief, *Gourmet Magazine*, New York City
New York Times Restaurant Critic 1993–1999

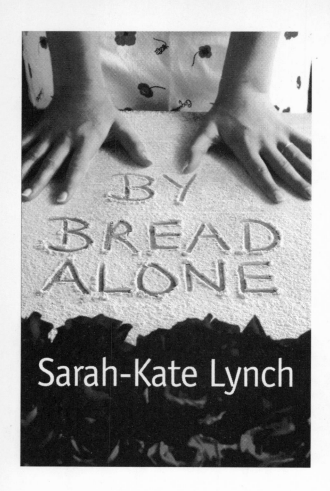

BY
BREAD
ALONE

Sarah-Kate Lynch

Esme has an adoring husband, a wonderful son, an evil goat, some angry bees and a suspicion that she will never be happy again. Even baking her precious sourdough no longer works its usual magic. All it does is transport her back to the salty little French bakery where she found and lost her first true love, Louis, the village boulanger. When a chance meeting with this bewitching morsel from her past breathes fresh hope into Esme's life, the grass starts to look greener on his side of the fence. But is Louis really the secret ingredient she needs for a blissful future? Or is the recipe for happiness closer to home?

'Witty, charming, faithfully passionate to its subject and emotionally adept. If only this book was a man.'
Sunday Star Times

'Truly, madly, deeply humorous novel.'
Next

'Clever, moreish, light yet strangely satisfying.'
Canvas, New Zealand Herald

Blessed Are

Sarah-Kate Lynch

Blessed are Corrie and Fee, for theirs is the kingdom of the world's tastiest farmhouse cheese. Tucked away in a corner of Ireland, the lifelong friends turn out batch after batch of perfect Coolarney Blues and Golds, thanks to co-operative cows, pregnant milkmaids and the wind blowing just so in the right direction. Add to this mixture Corrie's long-lost granddaughter Abbey, fresh from a remote but by no means backward island where her husband has been on a mission — just not the religious kind — stir in New Yorker Kit Stephens, heart-broken, burned-out, hung-over and hung-up, and what you have is a lot of spilt milk.

Corrie and Fee don't have time for crying over it, though, they must use their charm to turn bitterness and betrayal into happiness and love — or the secret ingredient of Coolarney cheese will be lost to the world for ever.

'Funnier than anything I've read in recent years.'
The Press

'Seductive, feelgood but not pulpy. It fills you up, like cheese itself. But it bubbles, too, like champagne.'
Weekend Herald

'For anyone who loves to laugh when they read, *Blessed Are* is an essential buy.'
The Gisborne Herald

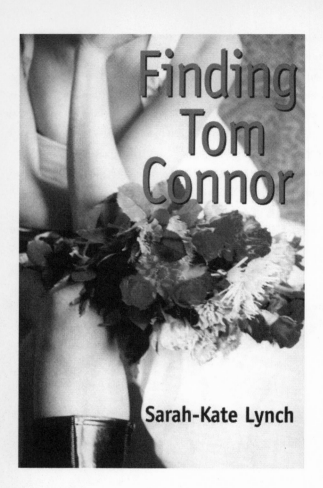

Finding
Tom
Connor

Sarah-Kate Lynch

When jilted bride-to-be Molly Brown arrives in the seemingly sleepy Irish seaside town of Ballymahoe, she has greasy hair, a fractured arm, a broken heart, three extra kilos and no time at all for the charm of the locals.

It's been a crappy few days and her wedding dress is starting to smell, so if she could just lose her terrifying aunt and find Tom Connor perhaps everything, herself included, could return to normal. Unless, of course, there's no such thing . . .

'The most hilarious and irreverent New Zealand novel in many years. A wickedly funny debut.'
Sunday Star Times

'I loved it!'
Dunedin Star

'Fast-paced and funny.'
Waikato Times